The Miracle Mile
A Novel by Mark A. Goldstein

This is a work of fiction. Similarities to real people, places, or events are entirely coincidental.

THE MIRACLE MILE

First edition. June 25, 2024.

Copyright © 2024 Mark A. Goldstein.

ISBN: 979-8227025012

Written by Mark A. Goldstein.

Table of Contents

Part I – City Centre

To me, every hour of the day and night is an unspeakably perfect miracle.

    -Walt Whitman

Suddenly, I'm startled awake by a loud banging outside my apartment. Living on a busy street in City Centre, I'm used to the near-constant noise of cars, buses, and other vehicles rumbling down the street to their intended destinations.

As I sit up, still somewhat dazed from being woken up so abruptly, I glanced around and noticed that it was nearly 7:00 a.m. The alarm was set to go off in just a few minutes anyway, but it would have been nice to sleep a bit longer and wake up to soft music filling the apartment, rather than the sound of boxes slamming, signaling to me, hey, Parker, time to wake up and get ready for work.

I rub my eyes while looking out of the front window, where I notice a large truck being carelessly unloaded, from my perspective on the fourth floor anyway. I'm not sure what the driver was thinking, not that I would have ever considered asking why he couldn't unload his boxes more quietly, given the early morning hour.

The crates were no doubt filled with produce to be delivered to the grocery directly across the street, where the assortment of papayas, grapefruits, mangoes, and various other items awaited the customers who would be eagerly anticipating their arrival.

I wish he could be a little bit quieter, I said to nobody in particular. My apartment is small, tiny to be more truthful, and I have no roommate to hear what I might have to say at this time of the day, or even a cat or a dog whose ears might have perked up when I spoke, because I don't have one of them either.

I'd better get my ass moving, I thought, or I'll be late for work. I set up the coffee maker, but as the water dripped into its four-cup carafe, I managed to carelessly drip water all over the bathroom floor while hurrying through the tedious but necessary morning tasks before leaving the apartment.

I stepped out of the shower and into the aroma of the South American blend that filled the apartment. I sat for a few minutes with my coffee at the small table in front of the window facing the street. The driver of the delivery van must have noticed the movement from above, and he looked up and gave me a little wave.

I'm tempted to give him the finger, but hell, I'm not like that at all. He has a hard enough job I'm sure, maneuvering through city traffic, moving heavy boxes around, and listening to customers complain. *Why is this lettuce wilted again?*

Well, most of us have jobs we don't like all that much. I better be heading over to mine before I'm late again. The last time, Ms. Millerton was pretty vocal and made a big deal out of my tardiness.

There was a large crowd waiting for bus 9 at the corner, including me. Then some considerable pushing and crowding to get on board before the driver, who at his discretion, might at any moment pull the lever that closed both the front and rear doors. This would be the signal for those still on the sidewalk that they would have to back off a bit and wait approximately three and a half minutes for the next bus to arrive. Somehow managing to find a window seat, I looked out into the hazy morning.

I enjoy the fifteen-minute bus ride to my office. City Centre is always bustling and full of energy at this time of day, with cars, trolleys, cyclists, and pedestrians all hurrying to get somewhere. Who knows where they are all heading? To work for an early shift maybe, back home from a late shift possibly, or simply to school, the market, or even to Grandma's house. Well, most likely not to her place at this hour, unless she is an early riser and is up and about making breakfast for them.

Other than the coffee, I had not taken any breakfast, though I would have loved to linger at home in front of my kitchen window enjoying eggs and sausage, or maybe even just a bowl of cereal while looking at the people in the street below instead of through the slightly grimy window of the crowded city bus.

We come to a stop precisely at 8:09 a.m. as scheduled, in front of the large Government office building where I work. The transportation system in the city is very efficient. The buses and trains are almost always on time unless preempted by something quite unforeseeable, like an earthquake or heavy snowfall.

But snow is uncommon in the Western District where City Centre is located, although much more frequent in the mountainous regions in the Districts to the north or east of where I live. Since the last major earthquake occurred nearly two decades ago, people have become accustomed to the timeliness of the buses, trains, and trolleys that pass through town.

I'd hear people complain quite vocally when on the rare occasion they had to wait for even a few extra minutes, particularly if they forgot to bring their umbrellas, or if the weather prognosticators misread their radars and had called for clear skies.

The Office of Accounting Payables and Receivables was just beginning to awaken when I sat down at my desk. As usual, I was one of the first to arrive. The Timekeeper noted my arrival time as 8:13 in the log he keeps, which meant that I would be able to leave at 3:58, exactly seven hours and forty-five minutes later, provided that I limited my lunch break to just thirty minutes.

Everyone is required to initial the Timekeeper's log before work, and again when leaving for the evening. Sign in here, Parker, if you don't mind. Thank you, sir.

The Timekeeper's job is a coveted one, though I can't imagine why. It seems by all appearances to be worse than monotonous and I have a hard time understanding how anyone could be expected to sit in front of a clock for eight long hours every day logging in and later logging out each of the sixty-two employees in my invoicing division alone. When the entire office is counted, there are more than 250 employees to account for.

That's a lot of hours, schedules, absences, illnesses, and holidays to keep track of. For that reason, the task of managing all this, every day, 260 days each year is not taken lightly. Other than the Superintendent, the Timekeeper had what many of us considered to be the most prestigious job in the office.

I had no interest in pursuing it, and would much rather have moved to the floor above, to the Office of Sanitation and Debris Removal, where my best friend Carleton worked as a computer technician. I know next to nothing about fixing computers, and even less about sanitation, which probably explains why I work on the floor that I do, rather than upstairs on Carleton's floor.

In addition to fixing computers, Carleton could fix just about anything else. If my computer at home came down with a virus, or even if my TV felt a bit under the weather and couldn't pick up a signal, Carleton would come to the rescue and make a house call.

My expertise is in processing invoices and cataloging receipts and pending transactions. I know you're thinking that this sounds like tedious and meaningless busy work. Lots of people think that, including my partner Francis, who likes to make disparaging comments about my job.

What does he know? He works in the private sector and doesn't understand how Government bureaucracies function. He's a bright guy with a good job, but he can be overly critical of others. He has a master's degree in something, I forget exactly what. Public Policy, or economics, something along those lines.

Carleton never makes negative comments about my low-level clerical job and he knows that I am planning to work my way up in the Government. He and I have been best friends for years now. I am tempted to ring his number right then to ask him how his date with

Clinton had gone last night, but realize what a bad idea this is before I can even reach for the phone.

I noticed that my boss, Ms. Millerton, had already logged in with the Timekeeper. Even the boss is required to sign in, and she is now arranging things on her desk, which sits on an elevated platform that faces directly in my direction. Positioned in this way, she can observe everything that goes on. And everything that I probably shouldn't be doing.

She has a particular distaste for making personal phone calls while on the clock. The last time she caught me red-handed, she threatened to put something in my Permanent Record.

There are twelve of us Processors, all facing forward in this fashion, so that Ms. Millerton, who sat a meter or more higher than we did, can quite easily look out onto the neatly arranged rows of those she supervises.

It is her responsibility to make sure that everything runs smoothly and on schedule, with no unnecessary disruptions or interruptions to the expected workflow. Productivity is her primary objective and she performs that function with great authority.

Ms. Millerton maintains files for each of her employees, where she catalogs things like reprimands, performance issues, attendance problems, and complaints. Also, items like promotions, bonuses, and awards are documented there. All of this information collectively is commonly known as your Permanent Record.

Now that she is situated at her desk, I better get to work. I check my inbox and notice that there are close to 100 receipts to be logged and filed. How all of that work managed to migrate to my desk overnight is quite a mystery. It will require the somewhat tedious process of matching the receipts with the invoice entries listed in the master log. This confirms that the amounts credited are accurate, after which the entries in the log book need to be appropriately initialed by me, and then stamped by Ms. Millerton as well.

After that, each receipt has to be filed in its proper place, in alphabetical order in the row of file cabinets that stand behind where the twelve Processors sit. These file cabinets are kept locked at all times and only Ms. Millerton and her boss, Mr. Sanderson, have the keys to them. Our filing can be finished only after either of them has agreed to open the cabinets, and then lock them back up again after all of this is completed.

She keeps quite busy with the numerous demands that each of us Processors place on her, reviewing, stamping, locking, unlocking, not to mention numerous other responsibilities that I have no knowledge of, or even want to. She is constantly going in and out of Mr. Sanderson's office throughout the day for meetings concerning supposedly important matters, but his office door is always closed when she is there. The other Processors gossip constantly about what goes on behind closed doors, but I usually ignore them.

I've got enough to do without letting them distract me. I counted ninety-three new receipts that seemed to be waiting impatiently for me to arrive and I want to finish reviewing and then logging them in before lunchtime. I'm going to meet Carleton out front where we like to eat the sandwiches we get from the deli shop across the plaza.

A problem sometimes arises when Ms. Millerton is absent for any reason, whether a holiday, an illness, or any sort of unforeseen event that causes her to not show up for work. The keys to the file cabinets are kept locked in a separate storage closet in another part of the office, which she also has a key to. Only she and Mr. Sanderson have a set of both keys and the authority to open both the closet and the file cabinets.

One other person has the authority to open the closet, but not the cabinets, and a fourth person the cabinets, but not the closet. That way, in the unusual event that Ms. Millerton and Mr. Sanderson are both absent at the same time, the processing can still go on unabated. I avoid thinking about the calamity that ensues if anybody else with a key decides to call out.

I tried to explain these security procedures to Francis one time, while we were out at a bar getting slightly shitfaced with our friends. How stupid is that, Parker? All that nonsense over some cabinets filled with useless receipts that nobody in their right mind would want to steal.

He didn't seem to understand. So I said, the preservation and safeguarding of Government documents is a critical part of the work I do. I'm sure your office has similar procedures to protect the integrity of its work product. Our work product is worth protecting, he answered. Yours isn't worth the cost of the ink it takes to produce.

We argue a lot about my job. He thinks it's pointless and that my bosses are corrupt. We argue about a lot of things, but we agree on one of them; let's order another round.

• • • •

One day, Ms. Millerton called out with a bad viral infection. She must have felt pretty sick because she hated missing work. I don't know much about her personal life, but I don't think she has much going on outside of her job. She doesn't talk about her hobbies or friends or anything like that. I know she likes to visit with the relatives now and again, but I think they all live in the Northern District, which is a couple of hours by car.

This day is not looking like it will turn out to be a particularly good one. I was in the unfortunate position of having a shitload of invoices and receipts that needed filing. As we've seen, The Office of Accounting Payables and Receivables has strict rules regarding its official documents. Once logged in by a Processor, each document had to be stamped by either the Senior Supervisor or Superintendent, and then filed as soon as reasonably practicable, but in no case more than three hours after the time showing on the stamp.

This was somehow linked electronically to the Timekeeper's clock that he kept on his desk. The Timekeeper and Ms. Millerton were somehow able to communicate this way and keep track of how that three-hour time limit was, or maybe was not, being complied with. Why anyone would give two shits about any of this is beyond me. I know the Timekeeper doesn't; I think he hates Ms. Millerton.

Since she is out sick, I'm left with no other choice now and have to ask Mr. Sanderson to stamp all of those invoices and receipts. He seemed very busy attending meetings and consulting on various important matters, but nobody knew what those were.

Not only would he need to unlock the file cabinets, but he would also have to wait, and presumably watch while I made sure that all of the invoices and receipts were placed in their proper file folders. When I knocked on Mr. Sanderson's office door, he was on the phone dealing with what he was at least making sound like an important matter.

I will bring the keys later, Mr. Parker, when I am not so busy.

When more than two hours had passed and Mr. Sanderson was still locked in his office, I started to get nervous. On a recent occasion, I had failed to complete my filing within the required three-hour limit and had been reprimanded for a breach of Government Policy. I knew if I got hit with another warning, that I would be in hot water with Ms. Millerton and she would probably put something in my Permanent Record. It was late in the day too, and people were starting to head for home.

Excuse me, Mr. Sanderson, but do you think you might be able to open the file cabinets for me now? I've got at least twenty minutes' worth of documents that need to be filed soon.

Can't you see I'm busy, Mr. Parker? The Government is not overly concerned with your filing at just this moment, I'm afraid.

There are more pressing matters that I am attending to right now that should be obvious to you. Even as a Processor, you should be able to appreciate that there are priorities to be weighed, deadlines to be met, and greater compliance issues to be considered.

By the time Mr. Sanderson was finished with his more pressing matters and brought the keys to open the cabinets, everyone else had gone home.

While waiting for him to finally get his fat ass over here with the keys, I sat at my desk with Carleton discussing our options for Saturday night at the gay clubs we liked to go to in City Centre.

Now, here comes my boss with the keys, finally. Mr. Carleton, do you have access to this section of the Office of Accounting Payables and Receivables? Correct me if I am wrong, but aren't you employed in the Office of Sanitation and Debris Removal upstairs? It is highly inappropriate for you to be here disturbing Mr. Parker, who despite the late hour, has not completed his required work assignments.

It was after 6:30 p.m. by the time I finished and I finally stopped at the Timekeeper's desk on my way out. He didn't make any effort to hide his displeasure at having to wait so long for me to get done. He is not allowed to leave until everyone has signed out.

What's the matter, Parker; falling behind at work again? You need to manage your time better and hope that Ms. Millerton doesn't notice that you missed your deadline again. And she's probably going to find out from somebody that you were just sitting around with your friend, Carleton, and not actually doing any work. I wouldn't expect to see any overtime pay in your next paycheck.

I'm sorry you are going to be late for dinner, I told him. But I had to wait for Mr. Sanderson to bring the keys over.

He already knew that; he sees everything that goes on in the office. He didn't have to be such a prick about it. What did he think I was doing for the last hour and a half, scratching my balls?

Good night to you then, Parker; sign out here if you don't mind. Good night, sir.

• • • •

I had to climb the four flights of stairs to my flat while carrying two bags of groceries and four pints of ale. It is an old apartment building and doesn't have an elevator. I barely managed to avoid dropping the packages, which would have likely meant a shortened lifespan for the ale that I brought to share with Francis. We had previously arranged to meet for dinner at my place after work.

Where have you been all this time? I've been sitting around doing nothing for over an hour. I was pretty drained from the long day and the walk up the stairs. I'm sorry I'm late, I said, but Ms. Millerton was out sick today and I had to wait on Mr. Sanderson to finish.

Why don't you quit that stupid job and apply for something better in another department? I said, I'm well-liked there; you know that. Besides, I might be up for a promotion before too much longer. I heard from the Timekeeper that there is going to be an opening for an Assistant Secretary in charge of receivables. I've already got my resume updated so I can apply for it once it is posted.

Wouldn't that be a cause for celebration; why can't Carleton get you in where he works? He knows everyone there and fixes their computers. Let him pull some strings so you can quit working for that bitch Ms. Millerton.

She's not so bad to work for, Francis. And I don't know a thing about either sanitation or debris removal; what kind of job could I get there? My God, Parker, how smart do you have to be to manage people who pick up the garbage and clean the latrines?

I was too tired to argue about it anymore, so I just ignored his sarcastic comments and opened two of the pints that had luckily survived the trek up the stairs. Here, Francis, have a beer. And can you shut up and quit bugging me about my job for once?

For nearly seven years, Francis and I have been in what most of the outside world would consider an exclusive relationship. I'm not completely sure about this though. I hadn't been with anyone else over that time, but I was tempted to. I can't say this with any certainty, but I'm not sure I believe in his complete and unquestioned fidelity.

This relationship of ours presents a dilemma for me for different reasons. Whenever I seriously consider them, in my view anyway, our problems can be reduced to just two primary ones. They are probably not mutually exclusive, which I guess is the nature of dilemmas and the reason I am often frustrated with him.

The first is that he is selfish. Okay, I said it, and I'm not the only one who does. Even his friends are sensitive to his egotistical nature. The second is that I love him. When I imagine myself without Francis, it seems as if my world would be incomplete, as if parts of us are inseparable, like your foot to your leg. Would I have to limp and stumble around forever without him?

Other people don't always seem quite able to understand this. They might ask something like; why can't you learn to walk on your own? I might answer something like; why can't you learn to mind your own business? I might, but I never have. My answer is inevitably the same as the second problem; I love him.

II

This flat I live in is so small and very cramped even for one person, but when Francis is there, I am even more aware of its nearly suffocating dimensions. We can hardly move without bumping into something, or else each other. Whatever one of us does, there is an almost certain probability that the other one will see, hear, or worst case, smell it.

I have been seriously considering the idea of moving to a bigger apartment for some time, but rents in City Centre are obscenely high and I haven't found anything that I can afford that would not be an embarrassment to anyone who decides to visit. If only I could land that promotion to Assistant Secretary, the additional income and benefits might compensate for the added expense of a decent-size apartment. Maybe I could use some help searching.

Everyone knows that the Government is a bureaucratic quagmire, but working for it confers certain benefits. For starters, I qualify for assistance in finding housing through the Office of Housing and Rental Subsidies. To be considered for a rental subsidy, I had to appear in person for an interview and fill out the various forms that were required.

Everything that involves the Government also involves a ridiculous number of forms, as if such things are written into the law. There is no online application either; if you want to take advantage of the benefit, you better show up and let them eyeball you.

I arrived at the Office at my scheduled time and stopped at the Registrar's desk. Sign in here, Mr. Parker, and take a number and be seated until a Housing Officer becomes available to meet with you personally. Sir, do you have any idea how long the wait might be? I did make an appointment yesterday.

Well now, that is hard to say; it is Saturday after all and we are quite busy as you can see. I looked around, and he was right.

The waiting area was full of people sitting on what looked like uncomfortable plastic chairs, fidgeting and squirming around impatiently.

He continued, now if you came on a Friday, the wait would hardly be worth mentioning, but today is not Friday, it is Saturday, unfortunately. Here Mr. Parker, take a number and these application and credit forms to be filled out while you wait. Please print all the information clearly and use black ink only; we cannot accept any applications with cursive writing or any done in blue or red ink.

I found a chair, then fumbled around looking for the pen I previously stashed somewhere in my backpack. Shit, it was blue; wouldn't you know it. I'm sorry Mr. Parker, but all of our pens are in use at the moment. I will have one available for your use when the next person completes their forms, assuming that their pen does not run out of ink by the time they are finished.

It took a good ten minutes to get a black ink pen and another fifteen to complete the nearly endless forms. Every question you can think up was included; references, deposits, pets, past addresses, reasons for moving, evictions, relevant crimes, you name it. When I finally got everything filled out, I had cramps in my right hand. But not wanting to have to redo them, I was careful to print everything as legibly as I could.

Finally, the Registrar called out my name and number; Mr. Parker, come this way, please.

The Housing Officer shook my hand and took the paperwork. What is wrong with your current flat, may I ask? Well, I said, it is quite small, just a studio, and very cramped. It says here that you are not married and have no dependents residing with you; is that correct? Yes, but I do have a partner and we share the apartment often. I see; well I'm not supposed to consider such issues, just how many family members live in the dwelling, not the nature of your personal relationships or how many visitors you may or may not be entertaining on any given day.

The appropriate size of the home is determined by the size of the family actually living there; that makes sense wouldn't you agree? I didn't agree but resisted making any smart-ass comments that would piss off the Housing Officer. I looked him over more carefully while trying to think of a good come-back.

He wasn't a bad-looking guy and I noticed that he wasn't wearing any type of ring. Could be gay, I'm thinking. Maybe if I flirt with him a little, he might bend the rules some and actually decide to help me. I gave him a little smile, subtle I thought, but slightly suggestive. He gave me nothing in return except a funny look.

Would your partner be moving into the new flat, assuming that you were to qualify for one? No, it would just be me. I see, and what sort of place might be of interest to you? I told him, in City Centre, preferably at least seventy or eighty square meters, with a spare bedroom maybe, or at least a small study.

I kept getting the sense that I might have to come up with something better. My good looks and my shrewd inference that there might be something extra in it for him were not going to make it on their own merits.

I just thought of something. I said, my parents visit from the Northern District and I can't even cram a second bed in my flat. I wind up either sleeping on the floor or renting a room for them in a hotel somewhere. If they stay for an extended holiday, they wind up in a dump because they don't have a lot of money. My father is on disability, which pays like you know what.

I'm sorry for your personal situation, but as I have already explained to you, a place that size for just one person would be quite difficult for me to arrange. Are there any special circumstances? I thought about that question for a moment, hmm, special circumstances, what bureaucratic loophole might he be referring to?

Yes, it is difficult for me to climb the four flights to get to my current flat, since there is no elevator. And as for my parents, well you can imagine how that goes. My mother nearly fell on them the last time they were here. Good one, I thought; this guy probably has a nice old lady for a mother and can relate to my problem.

I understand completely, Mr. Parker, but as we have already discussed, your mother does not live in the dwelling. As for you, do you have any certifiable disabilities, perhaps an old injury or medical authorization for special housing accommodations? No, nothing like that, I tell him. No unusual dispensation, no qualifying exceptions, no extraordinary hardships? I wondered how much time I might get to think something up. No, I guess not.

He said, that's too bad; if there was some sort of exception or medical qualification, we might be able to help you. The Government takes great steps in providing housing assistance to those with special needs; but you, Mr. Parker, fortunately I might add, do not appear to have any such needs and therefore would not qualify for assistance. Shit, this isn't going well at all, I realize.

My head was throbbing from all of this, but I seriously doubted that a headache would qualify for special dispensation. Maybe he had a couple of Tylenols he could lay on me at least.

I would be happy to refer you to our Office of Real Estate Placement; I know that they have some larger apartments available. But rents in City Centre may be high based on your salary as a Government Processor. Perhaps if you were to be promoted at some point, say to an Assistant Secretary, you might be in a better position to afford one of them. Gee, thanks a lot, I say to myself.

· · · ·

I guess it might be worth a try at least. But the Office of Real Estate Placement would already be closed by the time I could make it over there after work. I'll have to see if I can get another Saturday appointment instead.

I can't believe you are going there again, Francis complained. I'm not going again; I went to the Office of Housing and Rental Subsidies last time and they couldn't help me. Too bad I didn't think this through ahead of time. I might have come up with an elaborate plan that included some sort of special dispensation and I could be packing my bags by now.

Why bother, Parker? They are both Government offices run by bad-mannered public servants. I can't understand why you are so determined to waste your time and screw up another weekend. I told you, Francis, I need to find a bigger apartment; you know how crowded this one is.

I'm like an angelfish in a fish bowl, I said. What the hell are you talking about, Parker? You may not know this, I said, but if you put an angelfish in a small tank, it won't grow near its full potential. But move that same fish to a large aquarium and it will thrive quickly and develop into a colorful and graceful angelfish. It can live a much longer life there too, up to fifteen years.

How do you expect me to grow in this tiny place? He answers with his frequent sarcasm. He says, maybe try changing the water more often? Are you angelfish, Parker? No, but I am an angel, don't you think? He gave me a funny look, I guess somewhat unconvinced by my analogy.

Do you want to come along with me tomorrow, Francis? No, I don't feel like spending my day off in a Government office; you might be there for hours. In that case, I will go early when they first open and then we can do something in the afternoon after I get done. Let's meet up and go out for an early dinner, how does that sound?

Why don't you be an angel and make us dinner in your flat instead? Even if it is a little bit cramped in there. But do me a favor, no fish.

• • • •

I hate it when Francis is right. By the time I managed to get over to the Office of Real Estate Placement, the waiting area was already crowded with people who also must have needed a larger apartment. I could wind up killing half a day here, easily.

After completing the required registration and application forms using the black ink pen I remembered to bring this time, I had to wait for nearly an hour before a Housing Administrator was finally available to meet with me.

Glad to meet you, Mr. Parker; sorry for the delay. Let's see what we might have available for rent with at least three rooms, shall we?

He showed me various listings that appeared on a large computer screen, with detailed descriptions of included amenities and five or six photographs of each unit. They look very nice; thank you for showing them to me. But is there anything available that might be a bit more affordable? I'm not sure I would be able to manage any of the ones we have seen so far; I mean these prices, my God.

Ah, yes, the rents in City Centre are quite high. I can barely afford to live here even on my salary as a Housing Administrator. I can appreciate the position you are in, Mr. Parker, since I see here that you are a Government Processor, not an Administrator, or even an Assistant Secretary. We do become aware of less expensive units from time to time, but they tend to be in the not-so-desirable neighborhoods in the inferior districts, I'm afraid. I'm not sure that I would recommend them to someone like you.

I'm starting to get a little pissed off by this time. It's bad enough sitting around wasting another Saturday, but why do I need to be reminded by this overpaid civil servant how much more money he makes than I do?

May I ask what you meant by that last comment, someone like me? He said, well, you seem to be quite neat and well-groomed, not impoverished or desperate for a place by any means. I meant no offense; it's just that the flats in the lower-class neighborhoods might not be a good fit for someone of your persuasion, if you get my meaning. You and your friends may feel uncomfortable around some of your neighbors; they may not seem very pleasant and possibly not always civil to someone of your affiliation, if you get my drift.

I think I got it. Low-life neighbors who can't keep their homophobic mouths shut or their bigoted egos in check. I'd still like to have a look at them, sir, if you don't mind.

Of course, Mr. Parker, I would have no problem showing them to you, but at the present time, there seem to be none available that fit your requirements. The housing in City Centre is not only expensive but in short supply as well. Those two things go together for the most part I imagine, like ham and eggs, or wine and cheese.

I'm sorry, I said, what is that again? Is there a short supply of either ham or wine in City Centre? Ha-ha, you seem to have quite a sense of humor, Mr. Parker; no, as far as I can recall, there are plenty of each at the Whole Foods grocery just down the street.

I was glad to hear that at least. I'd need to stop and pick up some groceries on my way home, that is if I was still up for cooking dinner by the time I finished talking to this knucklehead. That's good to know, sir. I am planning to make dinner for my boyfriend later this evening. Do you suppose someone of his persuasion might enjoy Prosciutto with capers, and maybe a decent bottle of Tempranillo?

Yes, I would imagine so, in fact, that sounds quite appetizing to me at the moment, since I haven't yet had my lunch. But let me ask you a question, Mr. Parker; have you considered moving out of City Centre and into the Province? The rents are considerably cheaper and the demand for apartments is far less. Many people who live in the Province buy real estate as opposed to renting. In fact, there are any number of places for sale that you might like and could reasonably afford.

The houses he showed me were mainly single-family dwellings, quite spacious, with gardens out front and white-painted fences. Here, take some of these brochures with you and let me know if you are interested. We can arrange for the required loan applications, insurance binders, real estate covenants, titles, deeds, recording documents, and the rest of the paperwork that will of course be required if you decide to buy a place, rather than rent one. This office provides a great resource to help guide potential buyers such as yourself through the intricacies of home ownership.

My head was spinning from all of this now, so I just thanked the Housing Administrator for his time and tucked the brochures under my arm.

I'll show the pictures to Francis later when he comes for dinner. I think he will be open to the idea of me living in the suburbs. It's not all that far away, less than thirty minutes on the train, probably.

Before today, I hadn't given a moment's thought to leaving the city. It might work out well for the two of us, now that I think about it more. It would give us more space in a lot of ways. It might be good for our relationship to not be quite so on top of each other, literally.

Now, I have to hurry to the grocery to pick up some wine and the ham I am going to use for the appetizer that hadn't even crossed my mind until the subject came up while we were discussing affordable apartments in the inferior districts. I cringe when I think about what the Housing Administrator had to say about my neighbors there, who might not be so friendly, and who I'm pretty sure never ate Prosciutto with capers either.

While walking to the store, I printed an entire dinner menu in my mind. I decided to surprise Francis by making him a special dinner. He's going to love what I come up with.

In City Centre, we usually eat in restaurants, but I am a pretty decent cook when I get motivated. Francis is a god-awful cook, and the kitchen is like a foreign country to him. If I asked him to grab the juice squeezer, he'd probably run to the bedroom and get something out of the nightstand that he ordered from an online porn site.

My mother spent many patient hours with me in the kitchen when I was growing up. She explained the differences between searing and sauteing, and the subtleties between coriander and cumin. She cooked every night because we never had money to spend on restaurants.

My kitchen is ridiculously small and not exactly conducive to any serious culinary purpose. The stove has just two burners and the fridge barely holds the ale that Francis and I like to drink when he comes to visit. The kitchens in the brochures seem cavernous by comparison, boasting modern refrigerators with ice and water dispensers, separate built-in ovens, and ample counter space on which to work.

Mine will have to do for tonight. I've decided to make stuffed chicken Marsala, twice-baked potatoes, and roasted asparagus with herbs de province. Along with the Prosciutto hors d'oeuvre of course. Francis is going to be pleasantly surprised when he walks in.

. . . .

Before heading back home, I decide to stop for a visit at the square where Carleton lives, since it's within walking distance from Whole Foods. I've got at least an hour to kill before I need to take the bus back home.

It's a warm, clear day, so we grab lattes and scones from the cafe across from Carleton's apartment. Hey, Parker, what is all that stuff you got there? I show him the brochures that the Housing Administrator gave me. What do you think of the idea of me buying a house in the Province and moving away from City Centre?

You? Moving to the suburbs? I'm giving it some serious consideration, I tell him. Carleton knows I am not happy with my living situation. I've complained to him about the noise ever since I moved there.

It's an interesting idea, Parker, but are you sure it wouldn't be too far away? No, I don't think so. I could take the train and commute to work, it's only about half an hour and the trains are almost always on time. He said, living in the suburbs, wow, I never imagined it.

Your apartment is so small, and to tell you the truth, I'm not crazy about going up and down all those stairs when I come over to your place. Sure, the lifestyle would be a lot different, but the idea seems like a good one maybe.

Yeah, Carleton, four flights with no elevator can be a pain in the ass. Remember when I moved in and you helped me to somehow get my bed up there? Yes, I remember. And I remember Francis wouldn't stop bitching about it. Tell me, what does he think of the idea?

I haven't told him yet; I'm planning to talk to him tonight when he comes for dinner. I've got everything I need here; there weren't any shortages of anything at the store.

Carleton got quiet for a little bit and I think was contemplating everything we talked about. I hope Francis doesn't overreact when you tell him. Let me look at those brochures. We flipped through all the listings for the houses and compared the pictures and the descriptions. That's a nice one with the white fence around it and the little garden out front. I agree, that's the one I like too, I told him.

The house was in the Miracle Estates East subdivision, at the very end of a long block in what appeared to be a quiet cul-de-sac. I wonder if Francis will like it. I think he might actually, Carleton said. Look, it even has a carport where he can park when he visits. What about the location though; I mean you don't have a car or anything. Is there much around there?

That's another reason I chose this house; it's really close to a train station and only a few blocks to the east entrance of The Miracle Mile. Yeah, I've heard about that place, Carleton said. That's where all the shops and pubs and stuff are, right? I think so, but I've never been there. Me either. The Miracle Mile, huh?

• • • •

By the time I arrived home, it was almost 5:00. Francis would not be here before 6:30, so there would be enough time to shower and start getting things ready.

I was looking forward to spending time alone with Francis and what I knew might turn out to be a romantic evening. Going without him to the Office of Real Estate Placement had been the right decision, even if I was a little bit pissed off earlier because Francis seemed disinterested in going. It gave him the chance to do whatever he wanted to during the day and gave me the chance to cook up this little dinner party. I'm going to do this just right, and after dinner, bang, the fireworks might go off. I have it all planned out.

It had been a few weeks since Francis and I screwed around, and by now I was just about ready to blow someone's brains out. I turned the music player up a bit; the walls are pretty thin in such an old apartment building, and I can do without the funny looks I might get from the neighbors tomorrow morning when I walk to the corner newsstand to pick up the Sunday paper. I can hear it now; must have been quite a time last night, huh Parker?

I hope it is. I set the table and arranged the calla lilies that I bought, and then brought out the expensive Bordeaux wine glasses that my sister sent me for a housewarming gift when I moved in. I lit the candles and uncorked the wine so it would have time to breathe, while I sauteed the chicken in white wine and garlic. Then I scooped the roasted potatoes carefully from their skins before returning them for a second time, their reincarnation now having been pureed with some whipping cream and Hungarian paprika.

While the marsala simmered, I rinsed the capers and carefully arranged them on a platter, along with the Prosciutto and aged Asiago cheese that I remembered was still in the refrigerator.

I was happy with myself now, having accomplished quite a lot in a single day, with still some time left to relax before Francis came over. I took a shower and splashed on some Armani eau de parfum, before settling on the sofa and sampling the Tempranillo that was ready for anything now.

Francis is sure going to be surprised. He's probably expecting to just order a pizza or maybe pick up something from the KFC down the street. I hadn't cooked for him in weeks. I had another thought then; let me clear away the everyday dishes and use the porcelain china with the delicate rose-color etching instead. They hadn't escaped their confinement from the buffet cabinet in the past year, but this seemed like a good enough reason for them to get out for a change.

I hope he is careful and doesn't break the handle off one of the teacups. They have been in the family since my great-grandmother found them at an estate auction where she grew up in Transylvania.

While waiting, my mind drifted back to the conversation I had with Carleton earlier while we were having coffee and looking at the brochures. How have you two been getting along? Are things going any better lately?

I don't know, Carleton, about the same I guess. I had to admit to my friend that I wasn't all that pleased with Francis right now.

You understand this, Parker; I don't want to pry into your business or be over-critical. But you are my best friend and your happiness is important to me. Important enough to justify the possibility that I may be overstepping my bounds here, and risk having you respond by telling me to piss off. In that case, I'll shut the hell up.

I do love him; you know that, Carleton. I try to do what is right when it comes to Francis, but I'm not sure that he is even aware of it much of the time. I don't think he pays enough attention to me. I may never know for sure if he is the right one; do you know what I mean?

Of course I do, Parker. And I also know that the heart may sometimes go one step too far. It may take you too close to a cliff or some other dangerous place that you might be better off staying away from. I see the good in Francis too; I've known him most of my life. I'm sorry for prying; enjoy your dinner date. I'll see you at work on Monday.

• • • •

Hey, it smells pretty good in here! Francis came into the kitchen and put his arm around my waist and gave me a bit of a hug. Is there any ale left? Yes, I told him, and there is wine on the table as well. Let me pour some for you.

Now, the chicken was done simmering and everything was nearly ready. I brought out the appetizer; sit down, Francis, and have some Prosciutto with your ale if you'd like. I noticed that he hadn't touched the wine and was just standing, looking at the table setting with a bit of a confused look on his face.

It looks like you made a big deal out of this dinner; I thought we would just eat something quick and hang out for a while. You didn't tell me you planned for anything like this. I wanted to surprise you, Francis. I haven't cooked for you for so long.

And why the fancy dishes; aren't you afraid I'll break one? We have to eat pretty soon; I can't stay too long tonight. What? I thought we were going to spend the evening together. What's so important that you can't be with me tonight? I'm sorry, Parker, but I told Winston that I would go out with him and his friends to a club tonight.

Seriously, a club? The same ones we can go to any night we feel like it? The same ones you hang out in nearly every weekend? I spent hours planning this dinner. Are you telling me you would rather spend your Saturday night with Winston?

I tried hard not to show my disappointment, but I knew that I wasn't even marginally successful. I couldn't possibly hide how I was feeling now. I'm sorry, Parker; I didn't realize. We can do something by ourselves next weekend, okay?

I became very quiet then. It wasn't one bit okay, but I didn't feel like creating a scene or getting into a big argument. He barely noticed the effort I made tonight, the beautiful table, the flowers, or the hors d'oeuvres that never would have even materialized but for my prickly conversation with the Housing Administrator. I just gazed at the table, despondent. Afraid of breaking a dish, really? What about breaking my heart?

During dinner, it was quiet and without much conversation. I'm normally kind of chatty and my discomfort had to have seemed palpable. I shut off the music that was playing and turned on CNN instead, so at least there would be something to fill the awkward space.

My chicken Marsala didn't taste right to me and it seemed dry. Had I left out some of the ingredients in my excitement and anticipation of our evening together? Or was my mouth so dry that I couldn't taste much of anything? The Tempranillo did not seem as fragrant as I remembered and tasted flat somehow, like my mood.

He got up to leave after he helped clear away the dishes. Then he saw the brochures that I planned to show him later, while in my mind at least, we snuggled on the sofa enjoying the cappuccino that we were not going to have after all.

What are these, Parker? Nothing, just pictures of some houses they gave me at the Office of Real Estate Placement. I don't know why you would bother with the Government; do you think they are going to find you a house like one of those in City Centre? This flat is about the best you can expect from them. These places must cost a fortune. They are not in City Centre, I told him, they are in the Province.

I perked up just a little bit then. Francis seemed pretty focused on the pictures and descriptions in the brochures. The Housing Administrator thinks I can afford to buy one of them, and I've been thinking I might just do that. What do you think, Francis, don't the houses look nice? Look at this one; Carleton and I both like it. It has two bedrooms, a garden out front, and even a small carport.

Are you serious, Parker; do you know who lives in the Province? No, not really, who? Straight people, that's who. People with children and old people they put away there; that's who. What were you thinking, Parker? You can't live there with nothing but straight people for neighbors; my God, what in the hell were you thinking?

Why did his reaction have to be so negative? We hadn't even had the chance to discuss moving to the Province. Carleton was afraid that Francis might react this way.

Can't we even talk about it? Aren't you interested in at least going along with me to have a look at some of the houses? I don't know, Parker; this seems crazy to me. I'm late now. I'm sorry babe, but I have to leave. You can show me the rest of the pictures later.

After he was gone, I poured my third glass of wine and sat on the sofa looking over the brochures again. I thought more about what Francis had said. It makes no sense to me. My neighbors wouldn't even know I was gay, and why would they care? I'm a quiet person and polite to my neighbors. I'm not going to have loud parties, and of course, I would keep the garden neat and looking nice, planting some hydrangeas and maybe a few azaleas.

I might even get a dog, take walks in the park while waving to the neighbors; good morning, isn't a beautiful day? That would probably be the extent of our relationships. How did Francis become such an expert on people in the Province? It made no sense to me.

I had an unsettled night and a hard time finding any peaceful sleep. There was a lot of noise on the street in front of the apartment, and I could not push aside recurring thoughts of my disappointing evening with Francis. By 7:00 a.m. the produce truck was making another delivery right under my window and woke me up again.

Conceding defeat, I get out of bed and flip on the coffee pot, which I set up before going to sleep. I have to admit that I am somewhat of a coffee snob, and a bit obsessive-compulsive when it comes to how I make it. I carefully measure and grind the Brazilian beans into their filtered basket, then pour fresh distilled water into my trusted Mr. Coffee machine.

I never use the municipal water out of the kitchen faucet, preferring bottled water instead. It does not have the unpleasant metallic tinge to it that might give the coffee a slightly harsh and unpleasant character. I imagine the water in the Province might taste better and not be polluted like the water in City Centre.

It was too early to call Carleton, so I sent an email instead asking him if he wanted to go with me this afternoon to look at some of the places for sale in the Province. I did not have a car or even know how to drive one. But if Carleton is busy or doesn't feel like driving me around, I can take the train to the Province and then a local bus to get to the realtor's office. It isn't so far away, not bad really. Less than thirty minutes on the train.

Carleton wrote back and said he would go with me. That afternoon we toured several flats and houses that were featured in the brochures. After looking them over carefully, we still both liked the same one I showed Frances in the Miracle Estates East subdivision, with the white-painted fence and carport out front. It was at the very end of the block, and directly across another house nearly identical to it, separated only by a short footpath. All the other houses on the street were set further back, so there would be quite a bit of privacy.

What a difference from my tiny flat that is so noisy on the weekends and where my sleep is usually disrupted. I think I'm going to do this Carleton; I like this house the best by far. I do too, he said. And it sure will be quiet at the end of the cul-de-sac with no traffic directly in front. And just that one house across the footpath; you probably won't hear anything.

We say goodbye to the realtor and drive back to City Centre, where we head to one of our favorite bistros for a late lunch. What about Francis, though? I thought you said he wasn't overly enthusiastic about your plan to move to the Province. It seems otherwise to be an excellent living arrangement, but how strenuously do you think he might resist?

He's going to just have to get used to it, Carleton. After that disaster of a dinner date last night, I decided that I need to make decisions that are in my best interests. If they happen to conflict with what Francis thinks, so what? It's not like I am asking him to move to the Province. He can live wherever he likes.

His flat is much larger than mine and doesn't face a noisy street either. It is plenty big enough for the both of us, but I didn't hear him come up with any type of counter-proposal, like me moving in together there. It's been almost seven years; that would not have been such a crazy idea.

He can do whatever he likes, but I'm not planning to cook any more special meals for him now, even after I move. I spent nearly two hours making dinner for him, and he just left after about half of one. Sure, the kitchen is much larger in the cottage than in my apartment, but I may just use it to cook for you or my parents when they visit.

I won't have to sleep on the floor anymore when they do come, and I won't have to worry about my mother falling on those damn stairs either. They are older now and shouldn't have to do that anymore. Why can't Francis understand something that logical? His apartment building has an elevator and his parents are both dead, so they wouldn't be climbing up and down all those stairs anyway.

That's true, Parker, but his parents never visited Francis even when they were still living. Carleton had known Francis since their primary school days and they grew up in the same neighborhood. I was always fascinated to hear stories about their childhood. I learned quite a lot about Francis through Carleton's recollections of their early years. I never met either of his parents before they died and Francis didn't have any brothers or sisters. What was his family like, Carlton?

I think Francis disliked his father and never had a close relationship with the guy. I'm sure he never wanted him to visit. He missed his mother though; she was a nice woman and was good to us. She never went anywhere without her husband though. He controlled her pretty much and he had a bit of a mean streak too. He wasn't exactly what you would call pleasant around gay people, especially his only son.

He thought other people were constantly judging him because of it. The snide homophobic comments and funny looks from the neighbors were mainly in his imagination. I don't think anyone cared that much about us being gay except for him.

My recollection of things growing up was different. If people didn't care that much about us being gay, nobody bothered to clue me in. In many ways, my adolescence was stolen away from me, like it never could have existed. If an angelfish cannot flourish in a fish bowl, imagine how hard it must be for a child to thrive in a closet. Growing up, we made sure to build our closets carefully, with solid walls and double-bolted locks. They were the only really safe place to hide, at least until graduation came and nearly all of us either went away to college or moved to the paradise better known as City Centre.

My first boyfriend, Duncan, had a particularly hard time. We met when we were both sixteen. His parents refused to even acknowledge the concept of homosexuality, let alone the reality that their own son was gay. You can bet my presence in their home with Duncan smiling and blushing around me did little to endear them to me.

They were religious nut-cases and never seemed to get tired of trying to drag him to one of their insidious prayer retreats, or some other fucking place where he didn't belong. It was bad for him, and it still saddens me when I think back to those days we shared. Shit, we were still teenagers, but we had something really good together. I was crazy about him.

His parents wanted no part of that. They hated me, I'm sure, and had no problem making me feel bad about doing the unthinkable; loving Duncan.

Their wariness of me did nothing to discourage him though. He had a single-minded resolve to keep me around as his boyfriend, despite their circumspection. Come for a sleepover Saturday night, Parker. No, your parents don't want me there, I told him. It's my house too, they can't control everything I do. We'll go with them to church on Sunday morning and make a good showing. One hour of bullshit and you and I can spend the whole weekend together. It will be fun, I promise.

I'm not too sure about this, Duncan. You can sleep in my room, he said. I can, really? Sure you can, and I'll give you the best blow job you've ever had.

The gay subject was off-limits with my parents for the most part. The whole concept was so alien to them; the word gay simply did not exist in their language or in their experience. And yet I had no recollection of either of them being openly hostile to anyone. Blissfully unaware possibly, but not homophobic. It was just some problem out there they had zero familiarity with. Maybe they thought by eliminating the word from their vocabulary, they might get rid of the problem along with it. They had to have sensed the closet walls, but they either pretended not to, or else they were blinded somehow by their presence.

The underlying shame and guilt of my homosexual nature were always present in some form, by implication at a minimum, or occasionally by something more overt. I knew other gay boys in school, but it was our own little secret; a dark and unseemly secret that we sure as hell didn't want to get out. We knew that we were different, but we were made to believe that we were somehow bad people as well.

The truth is that I was a good kid. I was also lucky to have loving parents who did what they were supposed to with respect to my sister and me. Their love was given to us with no conditions, even if they didn't know to ask the right questions. And I returned the favor by trying hard in school and on most occasions, avoiding trouble. It's a shame that they did not really know me until after I flew from the not-always-so-cozy nest they tried so hard to build.

So through no particular fault of my parents necessarily, my adolescence was stolen anyway. This critical developmental period became obscured nearly beyond recognition for us gay kids. The rites of passage were largely missed out on. We were painfully aware of them, but they just skipped right on past because we were not allowed to take part in them. Adolescence should be the time when sexual identity and self-esteem are shaped. It's where we should be learning to form meaningful relationships. What a difficult puzzle for any kid to crack. How could we be expected to solve it when we were missing some of the most important pieces?

It becomes even more complicated once we find ourselves in these relationships because everyone's expectations are so screwed up. Including our own, unfortunately. Suddenly we go from being told that we are perverts, to being told that we are equal. You've got all your rights now, so quit complaining and get off that silly throne. Oh, by the way, the Constitution has been amended so now you can get married. Great, right? Well...not totally.

During the years that we should have been honing our relationship skills, we were not allowed to touch the tools that were needed. It was too dangerous for us to do that; we might get the shit beaten out of us. Our parents might abandon us and our friends would scorn us and never want to hear from us again.

Instead, we just hop in the car and immediately start speeding off down the highway of love and romance, without the benefit of getting to practice on the side streets first. Of course, we crash head-on much of the time; what else would anyone expect?

The steering is a problem for Francis and me. We both understand that, but stay along for the ride anyway, anxious sometimes about the awful ditch we might wind up in. But we keep driving, trying to move forward. Will the two of us ever figure out how to smooth out the ride, or learn to steer around some of the ruts?

III

The white cottage sat at the end of a long row of similar houses, each with a mature dogwood or crepe myrtle in front, surrounded by a small garden, and with a carport off to the side. I would have little use for that, but Carleton or Francis would be able to park in the carport when they visited, their cars shaded from the hot sun in the summertime and from anything that might fall from the tree.

Are you sure he will come to visit here, Parker? This move to the Province could be the end of Francis as we know him, don't you think? That thought worried me if I let it. Deep down, I felt sure that he and I would work it out, that what we shared would be plenty strong enough to survive something like moving half an hour away to the Province. But either way, I need to make my own decisions now, even if that means Francis and I might drift apart. I would be very sad if it were to happen, but I don't think that it will.

I sure hope not, I said. I know he can be difficult sometimes, but I still want to be with him. Maybe before long, he will come to appreciate the advantages and learn to enjoy the peace and quiet of the Province; who knows?

I called Francis later that evening with what I thought was the exciting news. Parker, it's a bad idea, don't do it, stay where you are. Carleton saw the house and he didn't think it was a bad idea at all. Come on Parker, Carleton has the IQ of a cantaloupe; he works for the Department of Trash and Garbage Collection, remember? It's Sanitation and Debris Removal, I said. You haven't even seen the house; why can't you at least go with me to look at it before you rule it out? And why do you need to insult Carleton that way?

I don't have to see it; I know what it's like. You don't know everything, Francis, even if you think you do. I know this much; you won't fit in and they don't like gay people there. They won't even know I am gay, and so what if they do? We have laws in this country protecting us, remember?

That part was true anyway; anti-discrimination laws were in force in every district and there were no restrictions at all with respect to gay people. We could live wherever we wanted, or even adopt children or teach in grade-schools now. Why would they possibly care about me? I'll have my own house with my own garden and my own carport; nobody will even notice me there.

Arguing with him is pretty pointless and I am tired of doing it. He is being selfish again and isn't even listening to what I am saying.

This is crazy; you are making a huge mistake. They won't take kindly to you as their neighbor. I said, they won't even know I'm gay; are you going to tell them? What are you going to do, put up a sign on the lawn?

They'll know; you think it will be hard for some bigot in the Province to figure you and Carleton out? They are not that stupid, and when they do, they will not like it one bit. Stay in City Centre where you belong, Parker. I can't get a good night's sleep in City Centre, I said. Stay here where you belong, not in the Province with nothing but straight people.

• • • •

I had my fair share of problems with straight people, but that was years ago when we were in secondary school. Back then, I had been shoved around by them on numerous occasions, the teachers obliviously content to look the other way.

Duncan was my protector then. To the average onlooker, he seemed ill-equipped in his role as my bodyguard, smaller than many of our schoolmate tormentors. But he wasn't afraid of them, or much of anything else as far as I knew. He was ready to go toe-to-toe with anyone who might threaten me.

We met on my 16th birthday and he was the first boy that I was seriously into. I had a few other sexual encounters before him, but they were nothing more than guilt-ridden pleasure trips with guys I hardly knew and who didn't give a shit about me.

The first time I saw Duncan smile, I felt a jolt strong enough to snap the lock right off the fucking closet door. Later on, the entire room crumbled under the weight of my feelings for him.

I still think about him and his gentle nature sometimes. It is strange though, it is nearly impossible for me to picture him. We never took any photographs together and so much time has passed. If he walked right up to me today, I don't know if I would even realize it was him.

Things had to be much better for gay kids in the Province nowadays. How could they not be? Homophobia, like racism, still exists, but it is not considered very fashionable. The laws are liberal and unequivocal when it comes to equal rights for everyone. The public schools in the Province are known for their policies regarding inclusion and tolerance. So why is Francis so adamant when it comes to gay people living there?

I don't think he considered the advantages that living in the Province might bring. In the summertime, for instance, we love to take long weekend trips to the Western Shore, where the climate is more temperate than in the sweltering heat of the city. It would be a relatively easy two-hour drive to the gay beach from the Province; whereas from City Centre, it could easily take three hours or more after contending with the traffic congestion from all the people hurrying to get to the beach.

I love the Western Shore and want to live there someday. The small town where we always hang out has a kilometer-long wooden boardwalk, with ice cream stands that sell saltwater taffy and caramel-popped corn. The quaint streets are filled with little shops that have everything from souvenir trinkets to Continental art.

After drinks with our friends, we would stroll down to the boardwalk and feel the cool late evening breezes, while listening to the sound of the sea at peace with itself. The promenade is lit up with excitement at night; there are carnival games, carousels, and shops that sell nothing but cotton candy and licorice. The boutique hotels with their trendy cafes and bars open right in front of the wide sand beach. Francis and I enjoy sitting on one of the white-painted benches that line the wooden walkway, holding hands and enjoying the smell of the surf and the French-fried potatoes.

The straight people there did not seem bothered by us at all. Why should they be any different in the Province?

• • • •

I overslept on Monday morning and missed the bus I normally take. The Timekeeper raised an eyebrow before logging me in at 9:04. Having trouble sleeping at your place, Parker? He seemed to like sticking his nose in other people's affairs for some reason. I resisted any temptation to suggest that he pay attention to his clock and his log, and mind his own damn business.

Yes sir, it gets pretty noisy on my street. It wakes me up during the night. I imagine so, he said then. Lots of loud trucks making their early deliveries too, I bet. I used to live on your same block, right next to that stinking grocer you got there. That was before they promoted me to Timekeeper and we moved to our brownstone where it is quieter. Sign here, Parker, if you don't mind.

I wondered how he knew where I lived. I don't remember ever mentioning my building to him, or the grocery store across the street either.

Everyone else was already busy working away by the time I got settled at my desk. I could sense Ms. Millerton glaring at me with eyes just above the top edge of the reading glasses that she kept just below the bridge of her nose. This way, she could look out over them and observe what the Processors were up to when she was not absorbed in reading her reports or doing paperwork.

She must have been rather far-sighted, which was probably not a bad thing for someone in a position like hers, where being able to keep a good lookout was an important aspect of her job description. She was like a hawk perched on a tree limb watching for prey.

Mr. Parker, may I see you, please? I walked toward the front of the office and up the three steps to the raised platform and the huge desk where Ms. Millerton sat.

I hope that you are feeling better and have recovered from your illness last week. Thank you, Mr. Parker, but I did not call you up here to discuss my health, which is quite immaterial to the work we are required to do. It is my understanding that you kept the Timekeeper until past 6:30 one evening while I was away, and because of that fact, we are required to pay him overtime. Before I record this in your Permanent Record, I should point out to you that this is the second such occurrence in the past ninety days, and that I am now required to give you a verbal warning. But first, I must inquire if you controvert these facts in any way, or if you intend to challenge the validity of what we have discussed.

No, Ms. Millerton, I was working late that night, but there were extenuating circumstances.

Mr. Parker, we record only the time worked and not every conceivable circumstance, but since you have raised the issue, I see that in this particular case, you also exceeded the mandatory three-hour filing deadline by fourteen minutes, according to the time stamp on the last of the invoices filed.

Yes, I did go over time, but as I was about to explain, Mr. Sanderson was not available. Mr. Parker, I believe it would behoove you and be in everyone's best interest if you would not attempt to justify your mistakes by blaming others. Mr. Sanderson is a very busy man as you well know, and it is your responsibility to see that the filing is completed on time, so that the Timekeeper can go home to his wife and supper, and so the Government is not burdened with the costs of needless overtime pay.

Yes, Ms. Millerton, but I wanted you to understand that I had no control over the delay. I had to wait nearly an hour and a half for Mr. Sanderson to bring the keys.

Since you keep bringing up Mr. Sanderson's name, for what reason I can't fathom, he also mentioned that your friend Mr. Carleton was wasting your time and distracting you from your job, and since he works upstairs in the Office of Sanitation and Debris Removal, he has no business being in this office in the first place. Now, please sit down while I note these infractions in your Permanent Record.

I met Carleton at the deli across the plaza, where we had to hurry and eat our lunch within the thirty minutes allotted. Can you believe this Carleton? More crap put in my Permanent Record; how the hell am I going to get that promotion I've been waiting for? Mr. Sanderson had no right to complain to Ms. Millerton, what a shithead. He knew it wasn't my fault that I had to sit around for so long waiting on him to finish my filing. I wonder if the Timekeeper gave her an earful too. He's into everyone's business and knows too much about me. I don't know if I should trust him.

It's the same thing where I work, Parker. One time our entire network was down because a server I had requisitioned from the Department of Technology and Information Services was shipped to the wrong office, where it just sat in their mailroom for three hours before someone bothered to call me to come and get it. They had the nerve to issue me a verbal warning for that, can you believe it?

I said, I believe it, but what are my chances now for that promotion to Assistant Secretary? I'll put in a good word for you with my boss, Parker. He's good friends with Mr. Sanderson. Hey thanks, Carleton. Let's hurry back to work; I don't want to piss off Ms. Millerton again.

. . . .

The Housing Administer shook my hand when I returned to the Office of Real Estate Placement the following weekend. I see from the notes my secretary left here that you inquired about several properties and went on a tour of them. Yes, I saw a house in the Miracle Estates East subdivision that I am very interested in. When do you think I might be able to move in?

Well now, you seem to be moving very quickly in that regard, but as I believe we discussed during your last visit here, there is a good amount of paperwork that has to be completed first. Licenses, permits, deeds, mortgage insurance, and such other items that may be necessary. But I will make every effort to expedite these sometimes nettlesome details and move things along, and if we don't encounter any unusual circumstances, hopefully, be able to complete all of the necessary transactions and have you moved in within the next sixty days or so.

Unusual Circumstances; may I ask what you meant by that? Well, how should I say this; each applicant is an individual and carries a unique set of circumstances and associated risks. In addition to the financial requirements requisite to obtaining a note, there are real estate compliance issues, not to mention borrower's covenants, title certifications, inspection of the premises, and so forth.

Your job Mr. Parker, is to carefully complete all the required applications as soon as you can. Our job is to do everything else. We will file all the forms that are needed with the appropriate bureaus and departments; the Office of Real Estate Compliance, the Office of Title and Deed Recording, the Office of Real Estate Lending, the Office of Insurance and Risk Control, and so on and so forth. Oh yes, then a background check will need to be completed as well.

Can you tell me the nature of the background check, sir? Of course; we have to check for a criminal history, confirm your moral character and good name, do an assessment of the applicant both from a financial perspective as well and take into consideration the ethical and moral attributes of the person who is seeking our services.

You can understand, Mr. Parker, our reputation demands that we do our due diligence; you would want to feel comfortable with the type of person who might wind up living next door to your own family, am I correct? I said, I don't have a family, sir. I see, well we're not supposed to ask those types of questions, or at any time consider familial relationships as being determinant or qualifying for owning real estate. Now if you would just like to sign on the bottom of this form next to where your name is typewritten, we can get on with the process of completing all of the paperwork and you can get on with the process of buying furniture for your new home or whatever it is that you need to do while we do what we need to do.

Geez, this guy is exhausting; I wonder if he'll ever shut up.

No wonder I was so tired by the time I returned home and made it up the four flights of stairs to my flat. Damn, I wish there was an elevator in this place. Well, no matter, I won't need one at my new home.

I sat on the sofa with a bottle of ale left over from my romantic dinner date that turned out to be anything but. I needed to quench my thirst from the long walk back and the warm, humid evening. I was at home by myself again on a Saturday night, with Francis out at the clubs with his friend Winston. I sat there alone with nothing to keep me company but my cool drink and my troublesome thoughts.

Our seven-year anniversary would be here in just a few more weeks, but not for the first time I had reason to wonder whether or not we would make it to the milestone together. I was troubled by the direction in which things seemed to be heading and now I seriously questioned if this move to the Province might signal an end for the two of us.

Seven years is a long time, I said out loud to no one in particular, as I opened a second bottle of ale. Maybe I will get a dog when I am settled in the cottage, to keep me company and to at least have someone around to hear what I have to say. And if one of the neighbors should happen to overhear me, they won't think I'm some nut case talking to myself.

I'm not quite ready to just give up on Francis, but I know this will take a lot of work. I can't come up with any easy explanation for why things have changed between the two of us. My feelings for him are still strong, even if some of the exhilaration from the early days of our relationship has diminished. This seems normal enough, doesn't it? After all, we're not the first couple in the world to experience a waning of the magic in their romance.

Whenever I try to bring up the subject, Francis gets defensive and doesn't want to talk about it. He doesn't like to share his feelings the way I do, and I find that frustrating. We're going to have to talk it out at some point if we expect to make any significant progress. I would bring up the idea of couples therapy, but I'm thinking Francis might just laugh at that suggestion.

We could learn to become better communicators. I don't know if he simply believes that things are okay as they are, or just refuses to consider any alternatives or listen to my point of view. That's because he won't talk about it. I've known from day one that Francis finds it hard to express his feelings openly, even with me. I think he uses his friend Winston as a source of advice, or empathy even. He probably shares too much information with him in the process.

I'm fine with that actually; hell, I probably share too much personal information with Carleton as well. If Francis relies on his friends for support or counseling, so be it. I don't mind that he goes out and spends time with just his friends some of the time. But he hasn't been spending enough quality time with me lately, and that's a problem we better start fixing.

I feel a familiar wave of misgiving beginning to settle over me as I sit at home alone. What is he doing right now without me; is he screwing around? Instead of just sitting here, should I be downloading Grindr and see if anyone is checking me out? Maybe it is about time for me to start looking for someone else, someone more accepting and more committed than Francis. Doubt continually drifts in and out of my consciousness, unsettling my thoughts and leaving me more uncertain about our future together.

Pushing my apprehension and depression temporarily off to the side, I picked up my mobile to call Carleton, who also did not have a date on a Saturday night. He'd become quite infatuated over the last couple of months with this guy named Clinton. I'd met him just one time and had not formed any opinions, but Carleton was captivated by him, that was clear.

Quite unexpectedly, at least from Carleton's perspective, I'm sure, Clinton decided unilaterally and totally out of the blue, that the two of them should now view their relationship in purely a historical context. In other words, without any warning, Carleton had been unceremoniously dumped.

He tried to hide his disappointment and sadness over the recent events, but I knew Carleton much too well for that. I could feel the pain I saw on his face as if it were my own. Even Francis felt it. He needs your friendship and support now, Parker.

Let me be clear; I am not impartial when it comes to how I view Carleton. Forget about Clinton; what a dumb-fuck he is. Still, it is hard for me to believe that someone like Carleton has managed to remain single. Even considering the lack of objectivity implicit in my close friendship with him, Carleton is an excellent catch.

I had been under the mistaken impression that he and Clinton were moving along really well, pretty hot and heavy too from what steamy details I was able to squeeze out of Carleton. But then Clinton rudely dumped a bucket of water on things, extinguishing both the fire and Carleton's dreams.

He answered quickly on the first ring. Had he been waiting expectantly by the phone for the unlikely possibility that it might be Clinton calling with a change of heart, or to try to explain the mistake he had made?

How are you feeling, Carleton? I'm good, well better than yesterday anyway, not too bad, I guess. Want to talk about it? It's okay, Parker. We all have to endure suffering; what else is life for? It's over now; I know he won't be coming back. He hasn't even bothered to check on me or come up with any sort of explanation for what happened.

I sensed his voice quivering a bit; fighting back tears during brief gaps in our conversation. Suddenly, I was pissed at myself for not being there for him. Want me to come over to your place? I can be there in about fifteen minutes. No, he said, it will be okay; I'm ready to move on without him. Tell me what's up with you instead. And don't worry about me, Parker; if I get the urge to jump out the window, I'll call you first.

I said then, you Promise me? Of course; I sure as hell wouldn't want to call Clinton. By the time he'd show up, they would have already zipped the body bag closed and tossed me into the ice box.

The subject shifted over to Francis then, an easy enough transition since we were already on the subject of problematic boyfriends. I valued Carleton's opinion and he spoke openly without being critical. Maybe my timing is bad, he said, with Clinton just leaving and all that. I don't want to burden you with my own problems or make it seem like I am judging Francis. No, please tell me what you are thinking, I said.

Carleton has good insights when it comes to matters of love and romance. He is very perceptive too, and has known Francis from their early school days, long before I came into the picture. Here's the way I see it, Parker. Francis has a big heart, but he doesn't like to show it. His comfort zone is in a place where he doesn't have to share too much. It comes across as being selfish, but it's more complicated than that.

He is a private person in many ways and has a hard time expressing himself when it comes to personal stuff. I think his father may have beat on him when he was small, and was probably still shoving him around when Francis came out to his parents even before he finished secondary school. This couldn't have done much to boost his self-esteem.

You may represent something to him that he thought he might never have, or deep down, someone he does not deserve. Keeping a cool distance might be his way of compensating for the fear that he may not be worthy of having a guy like you. I think he is afraid of showing how important you are to him and leaving himself vulnerable should you decide to call it quits. I could be wrong about this, Parker, so feel free to tell me to shut up if it sounds ludicrous to you. My gut tells me that the thought of you breaking up frightens him terribly.

I pause to consider what Carleton has just revealed, suddenly remembering Francis' earlier crack about the cantaloupe and his reference to Carleton's supposedly low IQ. I had to laugh a bit. What's so funny, Parker? Oh, nothing at all; just thinking of something he said the other day.

One more thing, Parker; the reason Francis is making such a fuss about you moving to the Province is because he doesn't want to be far from you. But wait, Carleton, he's out with Winston again tonight and hardly noticed the romantic evening I planned last weekend. He said, he is preparing for when you move away and the possibility that you might meet someone new in the Province. But he says there are only straight people in the Province. Carleton said, he doesn't know who lives or doesn't live there; only that he doesn't want you to.

• • • •

The next time I had to appear at the Office of Real Estate Placement, the Housing Administrator met me as soon as I finished signing in at the Registrar's window. This surprised me, as it was another Saturday and quite a few people had already taken a number and were sitting, not all that patiently, on plastic chairs in the waiting area. I sensed some of them shifting uncomfortably and mumbling something unintelligible when my name and number were called ahead of theirs.

Come in straight away, Mr. Parker; please sit down. I noted an unusual circumstance with your application that we must address without delay. It seems that in the marital status section, the form requires that one of four boxes be checked; married, single, divorced, or separated.

I see here that you have failed to check any of the four boxes, but instead drew an additional box in pencil, labeled it as "other", then checked this new box instead. So what I need to know is this; are you married, single, divorced, or separated?

Well, sir, I am none of those things.

You must be one of them, otherwise there would be additional boxes available for you to select from. I am partnered, sir. I see, Mr. Parker, but there is no box for partnered. Yes, sir, I noticed that, which is why I wrote it in.

Are you planning to be married anytime soon? We haven't decided on that, sir. Of course, it is none of my business, and personally, I don't even like having to ask so many intimate questions, but it strikes me that you could get married if you so choose since it is legal now, and that since you have not done so, then you must be single.

No, as I've said, I am certainly not single. I am in a committed relationship with my partner. I see, so the divorced or separated boxes would also not be appropriate? No, I'm afraid not, I said.

Well, this is indeed a problem; that is to say one of the boxes needs to be checked for us to proceed with your application. I said, one is checked, sir. The other box is checked.

I see that, but unfortunately, we are not allowed to alter the forms in any way. These forms are drafted by the Executive Director of the Office of Real Estate Compliance, which this office reports to. We are under strict orders not only to have them filled out completely in triplicate, but also to not make changes to them under any circumstances. Therefore, since you have already stated that you are neither divorced nor separated, that leaves us with just two choices, married or single. And since you have also indicated that you and your partner have not decided whether you wish to get married, that leaves us with only single. So, I will simply check that box and ask that you initial the changes here.

But I am not single, sir. Yes, I understand that, but according to the Executive Director you are; initial the form here if you would please.

Miracles, in the sense of phenomena we cannot explain, surround us on every hand; life itself is the miracle of miracles.
        -George Bernard Shaw

IV

Six weeks later, I received official notification in the mail that my application had been approved and that all the regulatory requirements were now satisfied. The statutory details of all of this paperwork were a blur to me, but as the Housing Administrator had promised, they did most of the work. On the first day of the next month, I would be able to move into the house that Carleton and I agreed was the best one for me. The one at the end of the block in the Miracle Estates East subdivision, with just a short footpath out front between my house and the one across the way.

We rented a small van, and Francis and Carleton helped load the back of it with the few pieces of furniture that I was able to cram into my tiny flat, along with my clothes, books, music player, and the rest of my personal items.

The hardest part was when the three of us struggled to get the bed down the four flights of stairs. I still can't believe this damn building doesn't have an elevator. It's all I can afford in City Centre, Francis.

After we finished unloading everything into the cottage, the three of us sat on the sofa, drinking sodas and resting from what had been a strenuous day. I felt quite tired and a little overwhelmed. I was nervous too, like a kid about to head off to college, far away from everyone he knew.

After the two of them leave, will I be homesick and wish that I was back at my place in City Centre? I considered asking Francis to stay here in the Province with me tonight, but we both had to get up early in the morning for work and I decided not to.

Francis got up first; we better get going, Carleton. We need to return the van once we get back to the city, and they charge by the hour. I was a bit anxious about being alone. I think they both sensed that as we stood together out front by the van parked in the carport.

The place is very nice, Parker. It will be quiet at night, that's for sure. We'll figure out how to make it work. Thanks, Francis; I appreciate that. See you at work tomorrow, Parker. Thanks for all of your help, Carleton.

Once they were gone, I felt more at ease. I unpacked my clothes and hung a couple of pictures in the living room. I walked around the cottage and checked on the garden out front. The flower beds were nicely mulched and maintained. Two or three azaleas, and maybe a small Japanese Maple would fill it in nicely.

My neighbors will be happy to see how I take care of the cottage. I wonder who lives in the house across the footpath. The shades were drawn and there wasn't a car in their carport. We had not seen anyone around while we were moving in. They may be away for the weekend; the Western Shore probably. The weather this weekend is warm and pleasant; that's probably where they are.

Now that I live in the suburbs, I have to wake up about forty-five minutes earlier on weekday mornings to catch the commuter train that goes into City Centre. It drops me off just three blocks from the Office of Accounting Payables and Receivables. Because the street is so quiet and there is no traffic noise, I am not going to be disturbed at all during the night. I will probably manage to get as much sleep or even more than I did before the move.

On Saturday night, Francis stayed over at the cottage for the first time. Work was often stressful for him and he needed to get away from the city for a couple of days and just relax. He has a good job that pays a lot of money, but the hours are long.

Tell me, Parker, have you had the opportunity to meet any of your neighbors yet? When I pulled up the driveway, I saw the guy who lives in the house with the double-wide carport across the footpath. What's up with him, anyway? He gave me some weird look when I got out of the car. Do you know him? Yeah, that's Thomas; he's okay I think. Francis asked, what the hell is his story?

He's a few years older than us and lives there with his wife and a couple of teenage boys. The older one is nineteen years old, I think he said, but I haven't seen him yet. Ms. Thomas brought over that potted philodendron by the window to welcome me to the neighborhood, and when she realized I was here alone, she came back later with a pot of beef stew. There is still some left if you would like a bowl; it's pretty good.

I don't think I'll get too close to the new neighbors. She seems very nice, but I'm not so sure about Thomas. He strikes me as a bit of a know-it-all and is a little too friendly for my liking. He gets right up in your face when he talks to you, and I find him intimidating. Doesn't matter, it's not like I'm going to be hanging out with him ever. I'll try to ignore him.

Since it was Saturday night, Francis and I decided to check out the Cinema in The Miracle Mile. The Miracle Mile is an area of about two square kilometers right in the center of the Province and surrounded by four distinct residential areas where nearly everyone lives. These are arranged in a checkerboard-like pattern and consist almost entirely of houses and condominiums.

Practically everything you might want to do for work or leisure is located within the confines of The Miracle Mile; offices, restaurants, museums, and theaters are all within its gated entrances. It is to the Province what the Municipal District is to City Centre, a bustling hub of activity, especially on the weekends.

In addition to the smaller pubs you might encounter, there is one very large music and dance nightspot, where many people go on weekend nights especially to meet with their friends, have drinks, and unwind from their workday routines. The Club is so expansive, it might have as many as 2,000 patrons when filled to capacity. It is the largest venue for social gatherings anywhere in the Province, with the exception of the fútbol Coliseum, which is located on the extreme northern edge of the Province and quite some distance from The Miracle Mile.

All Provincial Government and municipal agencies and bureaus are also housed within The Miracle Mile. It is the lifeblood and livelihood of the entire Province, a world buzzing with activity and separated from the more tranquil residential zones that surround it.

Since The Miracle Mile was built in the shape of a perfect square, the subdivisions bordered by it are identified geographically by where they are situated in relation to it; Province North, Province South, Province East, and Province West, all forming a large geometric quadrangle that makes up most of the land associated with the populated areas of the Province. The remainder consists mostly of rural farmland, well known for its production of fruit trees, corn, and sugar beet.

The wealthiest people reside in Province West, inhabiting beautiful homes nestled within gated communities. You are not allowed to drive there without a special permit. The idea is to discourage or even prevent the people who live in less affluent neighborhoods from invading the peaceful privacy of the privileged few who can afford the luxuries that Province West provides.

Province South is the area Thomas suggested I should avoid entirely, explaining that it consisted of poorer housing projects and people with tendencies to commit petty crimes. It's even worse than that, he said. In the past month alone there's been four or five muggings and one attempted rape. I wouldn't go there if I were you, Parker.

Province North and Province East are somewhere in between, characteristic of the middle class both in terms of their modest housing, and average but not overly snobbish citizens. The cottage sits in a desirable location near the edge of Province East, less than a ten-minute walk to either the train station or the entrance to The Miracle Mile.

After the Cinema let out, it was still only 10:00 p.m., early yet to head home for the night. Would you like to go to the Club for a drink, Francis? Sure, that sounds like a good idea; I'm thirsty actually from all that salty popcorn we ate during the movie. We headed in the direction of the Club, which was only a few blocks away.

He asked, what about this Club? Won't we be the only gay people there? I said, I don't think so. It will probably be so crowded; who will even notice us?

A line snaked for half a block with people eager to enter the Club. I looked around and saw nothing but straight couples, which made us both a bit uneasy. How about if we just see what it is like inside and have a couple of drinks; if we don't feel comfortable there, we can always leave and get a snack at the Ice Cream Parlor. We finally made our way to the front of the line and were met at the door by a muscular-looking guy checking to see who it was exactly wanting to enter the Club.

Do you have your entrance permits, gentlemen? Entrance permits? No, we just moved to the Province recently and hadn't heard of needing any sort of permit. We just came from the Cinema where no permit was required and were thinking of going to the Ice Cream Parlor later on, assuming they don't ask for one. We are from City Centre and never had to show a permit to enter one of their clubs.

Sorry for this unfortunate inconvenience, but the Office of Alcohol and Substance Control requires permits for drinking establishments in the Province. You will need to apply at their office to get them, either in person or by post.

I see; we were hoping to have just one or two drinks and check out the nightlife here. It is quite good, he said, a big crowd tonight it seems. Francis spoke up, would it be possible for you to make an exception for us this one time while we wait for our permits to be issued? The guy said, I would like to help you out, believe me, but that would violate the edict emanating from the Office of Alcohol and Substance Control. The Club would be subjecting itself to severe fines and penalties and I could lose my job if I let you in.

We understand completely and would not want anything like that to happen. Not for just a drink or two, certainly. But is there some sort of temporary permit that you might be able to give us for tonight only? I wish I could do that, he said, but unfortunately, the Office of Alcohol and Substance Control has a policy specifically prohibiting temporary drinking permits. Perhaps you would like to come back another time; that is once you have both your permits as well as at least one form of official photo identification, for instance, a driving certificate or Province Residency Permit.

Shit, I didn't even know how to drive and hadn't figured out how to obtain a Residency Permit either. How could having a couple of drinks be so fucking complicated? It's alright, Parker; we can have wine at your house. You got any of that Tempranillo from City Centre left? It went really well with that dinner you made. Yeah, I brought the last bottle with me when I moved.

Let's get a snack before we head back home. So we walked the few blocks to the Ice Cream Parlor, where there was no line of people waiting to be served. It turned out to be a Ben and Jerry's modeled to look just like an old-fashioned soda fountain. It was quite an impressive replica except for the fact that they didn't serve either root beer floats or malts.

We'd like two large cones please, one Chunky Monkey and one Cherry Garcia, assuming that we don't have to show any permits. No, only the Club requires a permit now; we used to require a permit in to serve Red Bull, but they did away with that a few years ago. Waffle or sugar cones? One of each, please. For here or to go?

We took the ice cream to go and ate it on the walk home. I don't understand it, Parker; why does everything in the Province require a permit? A permit to drink Red Bull, come on. I said, we don't need a permit for that anymore, remember? He said, thank God for that, but we can't even get a drink here without applying for it first and then waiting in line in some Government office, being told to take a number by some ignorant autocrat behind a desk with an official-looking badge he keeps flashing in our faces.

Well, I said, I guess that's the price we have to pay for living in a free and unrestricted society. Parker, can't you see how you are contradicting yourself? If it is so free and unrestricted, why do we have to ask permission to do everything? At least in City Centre, we can go to a club without some idiotic permit with our photo on it.

It's not that bad, Francis; I think you are exaggerating. Oh really? Why can't we drive through Province West if we feel like it? I said, that's because they don't want people from Province South committing larceny or littering. He didn't seem convinced and said, but yet the people from Province West can drive through Province South littering all they want, is that what you are saying, Parker? No, the people from Province West are afraid to drive in Province South and wouldn't go there to litter. Besides, there is a big fine for littering and I'm sure the people from Province West have better things to do.

Francis had such a negative view of the Province, but it was hard to argue in this case. He is right about how crazy the whole thing with the permits is, but in my mind, there are advantages and disadvantages to any place you might want to live. If obtaining permits was one of the disadvantages, then it was offset by the space and the trees and the peacefulness of the Province that you might not be able to find in the city. Sure, the Timekeeper's brownstone in the city is probably fabulous; good for him. I wonder what he would say if I told him about the experiences we had tonight in The Miracle Mile.

In the meantime, Francis wasn't quite finished making his point. I don't like the people in the Province either. Why not, what's wrong with them? Haven't you noticed, Parker? They are not only rude but also unattractive. A rather distasteful combination, don't you agree? Now if they were one or the other, maybe I wouldn't find them so objectionable. For instance, if they were agreeable but ugly, or maybe crude but handsome, either might be tolerable. But for the most part, they are both ill-mannered and hard to look at, the worst of all worlds.

This hadn't occurred to me until now, but maybe he did have a point. There were many beautiful people in City Centre, and perhaps the people we had encountered so far in the Province were a bit more aloof than those we were accustomed to. They all tended to look alike to me too; featureless, with round, moon-shaped faces. They often had doughy-looking bodies and sullen expressions as they looked right past you.

• • • •

I was outside watering the garden one evening after work when Thomas pulled into the double-wide carport across the way. Without the least bit of encouragement from me, he came right over and started chatting away about his two sons and what he did for a living.

He worked as a supervisor at a large poultry processing plant outside of the Province. He made it sound way too important, like if it wasn't for Thomas we'd all be eating fish sticks every night. Yeah, we chop up about 10,000 of them birds on a good day. Thank God I spend most of my time in the office and don't get chicken piss all over me like the cage managers. Man, those damn creatures sure can scream when they see one of their cousins about to get their head sliced off.

I didn't like him much and he fit Francis' generalized depiction of people in the Province precisely. He has a beer belly and a slightly noticeable body odor. He's not even remotely attractive.

I am okay with an avoidably outgoing person and I can even appreciate their gregarious nature somewhat. They often mean well and can be fun when they get drunk at parties. They can even be likable to a slightly pathetic degree.

Thomas is very much an extravert, but not in a good way. His efforts to appear friendly seem overblown to the point of being obnoxious. He gets up way too close when he talks and he asks lots of personal questions, as if we are actually friends. It's like he wants something more than he could possibly expect from a casual acquaintance. I have no clue what he thinks he will get out of me though, other than some sarcastic come-back, or a quick see you later, I gotta run.

Before I could get the garden hose rolled up and sneak back into the cottage, he cornered me. You know what? We should go for a drink one night after work; did you get your permit for the Club yet? Yes, they came in the mail this morning, one for me and one for my friend Francis. Great, how about tomorrow night then? It's Tuesday and it is Lady's Night at the Club on Tuesday nights. Lots of hot-looking gals will be there buying one drink and getting one free.

I didn't feel much like going with him, but Francis and I can't get together as often during the week now and I didn't have plans for tomorrow. I was curious too about what the Club was like. I hope there are some gay guys there; I don't know, maybe some lesbians like to hang out there too on Lady's Night. The Club might turn out to be a decent alternative when we are not out in City Centre.

Even though there were plenty of Thomas' gals getting two-for-one drinks, the Club was not nearly as busy as when Francis and I ventured there unsuccessfully a couple of weeks back. The same muscular guy we met that night was guarding the door again. I wonder if being a bouncer is his full-time job, my God, I hope not. Not much career path potential standing outside all evening telling people without the proper permits or identification to come back next time.

He was friendly enough though and seemed to recognize Thomas. Nice to see you again; I'm happy to be able to grant you admission, now that you have both a photo ID and Residency Permit.

Wow, this place is enormous, and every bit as nice as the gay nightclubs we go to in City Centre. The main area had a big dance floor surrounded by an impressive sound system that was playing oldies and retro disco music. There were lots of people out there dancing to *Shake Your Booty*, by KC and the Sunshine Band.

I ordered drinks from a cocktail waitress making her rounds and looked more carefully at the couples who had made their way to the dance floor. Would you look at all the fine-looking single gals here tonight, Parker? I checked out the crowd more carefully hoping to find some gay guys, but everyone I saw was clearly straight.

It's easy to tell by the way they dress and by what they are drinking. Okay, I know it's not fair to overly generalize or make hasty assumptions about people, but come on. The gals wore too much make-up, and most of them might have overpaid their hairstylists. The guys mostly wore sneakers that I wouldn't wear on a pickleball court, and they were awful dancers. The disco era was before my time, but other than the glittering mirrored ball reflecting onto the people below, I can't imagine that it had much resemblance to this.

All the guys except me seemed to be drinking beer. Didn't the bartenders in the Province know how to make a Cosmo or a Manhattan? Thomas suggested another round; what'll you have to drink there, Parker? The same friendly cocktail waitress reappeared after we had finished our first round. I was in the mood for a piña colada, but maybe not tonight. I'll have a brewski if you don't mind.

So, Parker, I was just wondering, do you have a girlfriend? No, I'm single; at least according to the people at the Office of Real

Estate Placement, I am. Thomas gave me a funny look. You didn't go there for any help before you bought your place, did you? They have trained monkeys working there. Yeah, I did, and they turned out to be pretty helpful once I got through all the paperwork.

Are you divorced then? There he goes again with all the personal questions; why is he so interested in my marital situation? Maybe I should just tell him I'm gay so he'll quit asking. I debate that for a minute, then figure this might not be the right time. He's going to figure it out sooner or later, like it's kind of obvious. No, I've never been married.

Well, that makes you the only confirmed bachelor in our neighborhood, as far as I know anyway. Every other dude is either married or used to be, that is before their wives told them to get the hell out, or else they decided to pack up and leave themselves. But isn't it, you know, kind of lonely all by yourself in that house?

Not at all, I told him. My friends and I hang out quite a lot, and I keep myself busy at work. I'm trying to manage my way into a promotion to Assistant Secretary at our office. Sure, he said, I'm busy at my job too, but what about the gals? I bet they must be ringing your number constantly on the weekends wanting you to take them out somewhere in The Miracle Mile on a Saturday night.

Must really be something being single at your age, not that I don't love Ms. Thomas and all, but just the thought of all that freedom. You devil, you; the gals must be about pounding your door down. Not too many good-looking bachelors out here in the Province; maybe there are in City Centre, but probably not out here.

The Club was pretty nice, despite being totally straight. Maybe there was more of a mixed crowd on the weekends, or even an LGBTQ night once a month. There was plenty of space and comfortable lounge areas that they clearly tried to make trendy-looking, with soft, colorful lighting and high-definition video screens.

The music they were playing was pretty decent and was piped throughout the Club with an amazing technologically sophisticated sound system. Packed with a couple of thousand people on a weekend night, with some electronica or house music cranked up, this place could be happening.

I order a couple of Sierra Nevadas for us. Lots of single gals here, Parker. Why don't you ask that cute one over there to dance? She's been looking over here checking one of us out. I was almost positive it wasn't Thomas she was checking out.

Nah, I think I'll just sit this one out; I need to get home soon anyway. I have to wake up earlier now that I take the train into the city.

V

I settled into the cottage now, just as the warm spring weather settled into the Western District where we live. You know what? Maybe it might not be a bad thing to get away for a few days. There is a three-day holiday weekend coming up. Hey, Francis, can you take off work next weekend so we can take a trip to the Western Shore for the holiday? Sounds like a good plan, Parker.

Now, I just need to get through this work week and then we'll be off. We booked three nights at one of the gay-friendly guest houses that were popular in town; where we can just leave the car for the entire weekend and walk to the restaurants and happy-hour bars that we love. There are so many good restaurants at the beach, and we've been to nearly all of them.

My favorite place for dinner is a trendy sushi and seafood restaurant called the Scorpion. It has a very cool bar area with two big flat-screen televisions, where we like to share a bottle of cold sake and watch the tennis matches before dinner.

The restaurant has a large screened-in terrace, open for dining during the warm summer months, but it is usually very crowded and you have to have a reservation well in advance to get a table there.

Francis likes spicy food and we enjoy going to a Mexican and Spanish fusion restaurant called Marimbas. It is located just a few blocks from the Scorpion, so we often wind up there if I forget to make a reservation during the peak summer season.

The owner of Marimbas is a heavy-set woman with a noticeable Mexican accent. She knows everyone's name and she never fails to run right over to greet us with warm hugs before showing us to our table. Hola caballeros, welcome. ¡Siéntate por favor! Please, Mr. Parker, sit here. ¿Qué pasa, señor Francis? Francis speaks quasi-fluent Spanish and chats with her, and then orders everything from the menu in Spanish, even though the waiters are usually from somewhere in Eastern Europe and are more fluent in English.

Francis always orders the same thing when we eat at Marimbas; seafood enchiladas. They are stuffed with juicy scallops and shrimp and smothered with a tangy cheesy sauce with fiery-hot jalapeños. I normally order a taco salad with tomato wedges and low-cal dressing. He looks at me like I am from a different planet, but that's okay. Carleton and I were shopping for sexy swim trunks over the winter, and I want to be able to wear mine now without being overly self-conscious.

I love our trips to the Western Shore. In the late evenings, we eat crabs and drink ale out on the patio of a place called the Crab Shack. It is not much more than a shack really, and they substitute newspapers for tablecloths. But they have the best beer selection of any place at the shore.

During the daytime, the beach would be crowded with tourists and locals alike, enjoying the time away from work and hanging out with friends on the soft sandy shore. We could rent beach chairs and a large umbrella and then relax and swim in the cool water while taking advantage of the warm ocean breezes that are frequent now that the colder winter weather is taking a holiday of its own somewhere in the southern hemisphere.

And of course, the gay bars would be packed late into the night, with newly tanned and beautiful men and women...Mr. Parker, may I see you at my desk for a moment?

My mind had drifted completely away from my tedious job as a Government Processor, and to the sound of the waves as they crashed close to where our beach towels lay in the sand. The sound of Ms. Millerton's acerbic voice startled me out of my daydreaming and back to my bureaucratic reality. Yes, Ms. Millerton, what do you need for me to do? I made my way to the platform and up the steps to where she was seated.

A thought occurred to me then. She probably read the application I had submitted last week for the Assistant Secretary position that was posted on the office job board. Could the timing be more perfect? She was about to deliver the good news of my promotion just in time to celebrate at the beach next weekend. I would be able to afford to take Francis out to dinner at one of the better restaurants, one with large windows facing the sea that open onto a shaded deck for outdoor dining.

As you know, Mr. Parker, it seems that we have fallen quite far behind in our cataloging and filing lately, and that means I will need you to work over the holiday in order to become current. I'm sure that you did not have any plans that you cannot postpone, given that you have just recently moved into a new house, and with all the extra work and expense associated with a such move, a holiday away was no doubt beyond your means and out of the question in any event.

I have a long weekend planned at the beach with my partner, Ms. Millerton. Would it be okay if I put in overtime next week to do the extra work? Mr. Parker, the work we do here is quite important, and there are several hundred backlogged receipts and invoices that need to be accounted for. For the sake of your job, not to mention my own, I am sure that you would not like for this situation to remain unattended until next week when it is quite likely that Mr. Sanderson will become aware of it. He has to account for all of the work done by this department, and I doubt that you and your partner's efforts to get an early start on your summer tans will be his primary concern.

Yes, Ms. Millerton. I tried to hide my disappointment. The beach will not go away, Mr. Parker, but the unaccounted-for invoices and receipts certainly need to. I understand, Ms. Millerton.

She said, return to your workstation now. Oh, on Sunday the Timekeeper will not be here; he is taking his wife on a weekend retreat to the Mountain Campgrounds. You will need to make sure to record your time in the log book in his absence and initial it in the appropriate places. Please be sure to record your time accurately and honestly, as any discrepancies would necessitate me having to note them in your Permanent Record.

I was feeling depressed the rest of the day and the last few hours working were painfully slow. Ms. Millerton seemed busy going in and out of Mr. Sanderson's office and luckily wasn't watching me, since I wasn't getting much work done. When she did finally get back with the keys late in the afternoon, I had only a handful of documents that needed to be stamped and filed.

I stopped at the Timekeeper's desk as usual on my way out. I guess you don't have any big plans for the holiday, huh Parker? No, I will be staying here, I told him. That's too bad about all those stupid invoices that got backed up. Maybe if some of your co-workers knew anything about how to manage time, you wouldn't have to stay here to fix Ms. Millerton's screwups and cancel your trip to the Western Shore. I look at him more carefully then and notice the slight grin on his face. She can't manage her time stamp and the keys, let alone the twelve of you.

He is a smart guy with a keen perspective on things, but how did he know I had plans to go to the beach? I didn't mention it to anyone here, except for Ms. Millerton. She was busy with Mr. Sanderson all afternoon and I'm pretty sure hadn't gone over to talk to the Timekeeper at any point. How come he seemed to know so much about me?

• • • •

You're kidding me, right, Parker? No, I'm sorry; I have to work on Sunday, but I will get overtime pay and take you out for a nice evening with dinner and dancing in City Centre instead. How does that sound?

It sounds great, except for the fact that I won't be here this weekend. We have reservations for the bed and breakfast at the beach, remember? I said, do you think I forgot that? But I just told you we can't go. Then he said, maybe you can't go, but do you want me to just sit around all weekend waiting for you to finish fixing all your mistakes at work? Winston and I can use the room ourselves.

Why can't we ask for our deposit back from the hotel and go another weekend instead? Come on, Parker; you know I would do the same thing for you if the situation was reversed. I'd insist that you and Carleton go to the beach and enjoy yourselves if I had to work. You know that, right?

I wanted to think on that for a bit and didn't answer him right away. Maybe you would have, Francis, but you know what? I would not have even considered going without you. I would stay here and go to City Centre with you, rather than to the Western Shore without you.

He had so quickly jumped at the idea of going on the holiday with Winston, which pissed me off. The main reason for going was so we could spend more time together, the same reason it would never have occurred to me to go without him.

So, I was all alone over the holiday weekend, with Francis, Winston, Carleton, and our other friends away at the beach. A sense of gloom settled itself over me now, stuck in the office with just Ms. Millerton, instead of at the shore as I had planned.

It seems that she had to change her holiday plans too. Before everyone else headed out for the long weekend, the Timekeeper told me that her request to Mr. Sanderson for an exception to allow her to give me the keys to the filing cabinets had fallen on deaf ears.

So the weekend visit with her relatives in the Northern District was not happening. Without a one-time suspension of the regulations, and signed off on by Mr. Sanderson, she would need to oversee all of the work I was not going to enjoy doing and be around to stamp all the invoices and receipts that I would need to file.

She is a strange bird and is hard to figure out sometimes. I feel sorry for her though. Her stern presence and abrupt personality might be unfairly misinterpreted by the workers she supervises. She is a tall and lank-looking woman, who has never been married. Everyone seems to enjoy gossiping behind her back, especially about her sex life.

Francis once referred to her as a paranoid crank who needed a bigger vibrator with a twelve-volt motor. I'm not sure how he feels about his own bosses at work, but I know he doesn't like mine. He considers Mr. Sanderson a pervert and a low-life civil servant. You ever notice how he stares at Carleton's ass, Parker? No, I hadn't noticed. What a closet case he is.

Today, Ms. Millerton worked quietly at her desk on its elevated platform, getting a lot of work done with Mr. Sanderson on holiday, and only me to gaze at across the empty rows of absent Processors, where I was busy working at the file cabinets lined up behind them.

With little to distract me, I worked quickly and was almost done with the cataloging and filing by early afternoon. I might still find time to relax and enjoy what was left of the holiday.

I hope Ms. Millerton will be grateful for the effort I made to finish early so that she can also enjoy the later part of the day away from the office. Maybe she can still find time for a shorter family visit to the Northern District. It's less than a two-hour drive from City Centre.

There might be a silver lining to all of this. She's got to notice my hard work, and maybe that will be the decisive factor in her recommending me for the Assistant Secretary promotion.

I'm all done, Ms. Millerton; should I sign out on the Timekeeper's log now? What, finished so soon? It seems that you can work at a more acceptable pace when you apply yourself, Mr. Parker, when you are not distracted by thoughts of your vacations to the Western Shore, or by your friends who visit you here inappropriately.

I dare say that we both could have gone away as we planned if you had not fallen so far behind, with nearly 500 invoices and receipts backlogged as they were.

Francis did have a point, possibly. Maybe just a small vibrator with those little AAA batteries would be sufficient.

Yes, Ms. Millerton, but those invoices and receipts were not all mine. The other Processors fell behind as well. As you can see, I took care of that situation for them so they could enjoy their holiday.

You are quite correct, she said; you did finish their work for them, but you are one of the Senior Processors and you should be setting the best example for them when they are here, not just when they are away. If they observe you putting forth less than your best effort, there is no reason to believe that they will act differently.

Perhaps that is why the work fell so far behind. You must concentrate harder and show more commitment to the job, she said, and in the process, the work ethic you exemplify will be emulated by others, no doubt. In the future, perhaps neither of us will have to spend our holiday here, instead of at the Western Shore in your case, or the Northern District in my case. Now please sign out on the Timekeeper's log and be sure to note the correct time so that I can initial it in the appropriate places.

· · · ·

It was only 1:30 in the afternoon when the train dropped me off at the station in Province East. What a beautiful day it was, much too nice to waste sitting in the office half brain-dead from monotonous paperwork, and Ms. Millerton's musings about my being emulated by others.

Who was she trying to kid? The other Processors are mostly lazy sacks of shit that the Government is stuck with because they have too much seniority to get rid of without cause. It made me laugh to think that even one of them might give a shit about how fast I work or what example I set.

With such perfect weather, I decided to use what was left of the afternoon to further explore The Miracle Mile. I had been there just twice so far and both times at night; once with Francis to the Cinema and the ice cream parlor, and once with Thomas to the Club.

Looking up, I saw the sky was a spectacular cobalt blue that seemed to go on forever, with the bright white billowing of cumulus clouds drifting past; puffy giants, sculpted by the wind to form what looked like enormous cotton balls. Perfect for a long walk through The Miracle Mile, which I knew would be bustling with holiday activity.

I walked directly from the train station to the main Province East Gate, which is one of about ten guarded entrances to The Miracle Mile. They have to check everyone who comes in for security reasons. There, a line had formed with people waiting to get through.

They recently started enforcing a new rule that anyone who wants to enter The Miracle Mile has to show either a Province Residency Permit or a valid Visitors Permit issued by the Office of Provincial Security. They claimed this was necessary because of a recent uptick in thefts and other misdemeanors, presumably perpetrated by residents of Province South.

They got so many damn rules here in the Province, I thought to myself. I also learned that the Residency Permit has to be carried with you at all times and that it must be surrendered for inspection if requested by the police or any Province security person.

I am sometimes forgetful and tend to be a bit of a scatterbrain. Plus, I am not accustomed to all these regulations, since I never had to deal with them when I was living in City Centre. On one unfortunate prior occasion, I was approached by a Transportation Officer while waiting to board the train that would take me to work.

I was not able to produce my Residency Permit, having carelessly left it sitting on the kitchen counter by mistake.

I'm sorry, sir, but I forgot to bring my card with me when I left this morning. Can you let me board the train just this one time so I won't be late for work? I promise to be more careful in the future and keep it with me. I just moved here recently and am not used to the new regulations.

Let me see some other photo identification, he said. Luckily I hadn't forgotten to bring that with me. Technically speaking, I have the authority to deny you access to the train. However, since you say you are a new resident, which I have no reason to believe is not true, I will make an exception just this once. Keep in mind though, that in extending this courtesy to you as a new resident, such an oversight by you may not be acceptable in the future, either by me or by another Transportation Officer who may be on duty. There is a steep fine for failing to carry your Permit, and repeated offenses may be punishable by up to five days of incarceration.

Holy shit, five days in jail? I need to be more careful from now on. I better not tell Francis about this; he'll be all over it and remind me for about the 50th time that I should have stayed in the city. They didn't even have such a thing as a Residency Permit there.

Now I have reached the front of the line at the entrance gate after waiting just a few minutes. I am met by an Officer who displays his badge. May I see your Residency Permit, please? I fumble around in my pockets, thinking for a moment that I forgot to bring it with me again. But after digging around some more, I manage to pull it somewhat dog-eared from my back pocket.

What is the purpose of your visit today, Mr. Parker? I was planning to take a walk and enjoy the beautiful weather while getting to see more of The Miracle Mile. I have only been here twice, both times at night and I didn't get to see very much.

You must have some sort of destination in mind; if you are just wandering aimlessly, you could be stopped for loitering, which is strictly prohibited as you may already know. I said, I would not consider loitering. Taking a stroll and some widow shopping probably, but not loitering. Still, you must have some purpose, some intention as to where you wish to go; otherwise, I cannot allow you to enter. We have experienced recently several incidents of petty crimes, and occasionally more serious infractions as well.

Well, sir, I'm guessing those things were perpetrated by people from Province South, but as you can see from my Residency Permit, I live in Province East, just a short walk from here. It is not for me to determine who committed those crimes or where they came from. That responsibility falls on the Constable's Office, not the Office of Provincial Security, for whom I am currently employed.

I said, so far, I have only been to the Ice Cream Parlor, the Cinema, and the Club. The Club does not open until 6:00 p.m. on holidays, Mr. Parker. Well, I've just had lunch and am not in the mood for ice cream just yet; I think I will go to the Cinema and see what pictures are showing today then.

I will need to stamp the back of your Residency Permit with the date and time; enjoy your visit then, Mr. Parker. Thank you, sir.

As I start walking down the street and away from the entrance gate, I get the strangest sense that the Officer is watching me. I already know the movies that are showing at the Cinema and have zero interest in any of them. I have even less interest in spending the afternoon indoors on a day like this, but it might be a smart move though to stroll in that general direction; better to avoid undue suspicion from the Security Officer, whose eyes I still perceive are following me.

I had not noticed them at night, but now cameras are evident on virtually all of the buildings, and at the East Gate as well. I think everyone is being monitored. Well, that's alright with me; I'm not planning to commit any petty crimes. I continued walking until I reached the Cinema, then just kept on going.

The Miracle Mile is a vastly different place during the daytime hours. Throngs of people of nearly every description strolled through the wide streets, in and out of restaurants and shops; all talking, laughing, and seeming to be enjoying their holiday weekend away from work.

Children of every age were present, accompanied by their families or friends, adding to the bustling atmosphere. Elderly individuals, some using canes for support and others in wheelchairs, moved slowly through the throng. I couldn't recall ever being in a crowd this vast before. The scene was a whirlwind of activity, but it felt chaotic and slightly overwhelming, making me somewhat uncomfortable amid the relentless activity and noise.

It was getting very warm in the late-afternoon sun and I was becoming quite thirsty now from the heat, so when I regained my bearings and saw that I was near to the Ice Cream Parlor, I stopped in to order an extra-large snow cone. All the benches that lined the street I was on were already taken, so I sat down on a curb that was shaded by two large Cypress trees. From that vantage point, it was easy to check out the people who walked past me by the hundreds.

It troubled me some, coming to the inevitable conclusion that Francis may have been right; there are no gay people in the Province. At least none anywhere around here as far as I can tell.

Pretty much everything that happens anywhere in the Province happens in the Miracle Mile. Entertainment, amusements, organizations, and in particular, the Provincial Government Offices can only be found within its confines and guarded by its ten or so gateways. Museums, eateries, concert halls, hospitals, courts of law, and much more, housed exclusively here.

Sure, there are businesses that exist in the four surrounding residential neighborhoods, but they are the exception. They provide just the basic necessities that Province residents need to have close at hand. There are gas stations, grocery stores, and walk-in clinics in Province East, for example. You might see a 7-Eleven, but never a delicatessen. A liquor store, probably. A wine bar, sorry.

Beyond these few essential conveniences, for all other needs and interests, you will have to make your way over to The Miracle Mile. There you must be willing to wait in line probably and deal with somebody from the Office of Provincial Security absolutely. For me, this is a minor annoyance; for Francis, an exasperation.

You'll get used to it, I told him. Just remember to bring your Visitors Permit with you next time. If there is a next time, I thought to myself. He says he won't go to The Miracle Mile again. He'll change his mind. When I tell him what an awesome sound system they have in the Club; he'll change his mind. He'll want to see for himself.

· · · ·

The Miracle Mile is to the Province what the sun is to the solar system; the light and energy source at the center and the foundation of all life contained within it. If a bomb were to be dropped in the center of The Miracle Mile, all of the surrounding areas, including all of its inhabitants, would either drift away or wither completely. It's no wonder that the Province Administration and its law enforcement officials are so determined to guard its safety and peacefulness.

I walk beyond the Cinema and toward the center of The Miracle Mile, where I have not been before. There, I see a large plaza that fascinates me. It is made to look exactly like Saint Peter's Square, though a scaled-down version, I imagine. There is a complete replica of the Basilica, with its Tuscan colonnades and the elliptical square in front of it.

Somebody put a hell of a lot of thought into this and left out very few of the details. At the center of the ellipse is a copy of the Egyptian obelisk that had miraculously been transported from Egypt to Rome during the reign of Emperor Augustus. Why go all the way to Italy when we've got pretty much the same thing right here?

I read somewhere about a big entertainment venue on the other continent, where they build these sorts of detailed historical replicas; I think in a place called Nevada if I'm remembering it right. But I've never been there, or to Rome either. I hope I get to visit them both someday.

I wonder if the Pope would consider giving mass at The Miracle Mile's version of the holy site. I seriously doubt that; shit, he'd probably be put off by how phony this must all appear to someone so intimately familiar with the real thing.

At first glance, I am amazed by what I am seeing. But on closer inspection, everything in the Square is so obviously fake, even to a person like me who doesn't have much knowledge of historical architecture. What appeared initially to be real stone columns, turned out to be some sort of corrugated stucco material when I looked carefully. Inside the church, a close inspection of the etchings on the walls copied from the original building revealed carefully touched-up photographs in this one, and the marble flooring from the Cathedral has now been replaced by terrazzo tile instead.

Still, there were several people kneeling at the altar, deep in prayer apparently. I found that hysterical for some reason. Francis and I occasionally attend a community church in City Centre. It is relatively unadorned and quite small, but at least it is real, its polished oak pews having been in use for more than fifty years by the church's congregants.

Just beyond the Square sits a very large modern-looking building, at least twenty-five stories high. Out front, there is a huge lighted sign that reads:

Miracle Mile Desert Sands Resort and Casino

I found this quite amusing, keeping in mind that we are situated in a semi-tropical region, and the closest desert is at least 5,000 kilometers away. I have never seen a palm tree except in pictures on the Internet. They have them here though.

The entrance to the hotel is framed by two beautiful tall palm trees, the kind you might find in a place like Punta Cana. They sure looked real, but when I touched one of them, I could tell the trunk was made from some sort of treated bamboo, and with the foliage crafted from polythene or similar synthetic plastic.

Francis and Winston love the craps table, so maybe they should come here on their next holiday without me. Or else we could all come and invite Carleton too; get dinner at the Pizza Palace, and then play the slot machines or video poker at the Casino.

I thought about going inside to try my luck at the roulette wheel, but my stomach is turning a little bit now by all of this, so I head for home instead to wait for Francis to get back from the shore.

• • • •

Of course they need to see a Residency or Visitors Permit, Francis; do you think they want to see loitering and petty crimes in The Miracle Mile? He was back now from his getaway at the Western Shore.

Forget it, Parker, we're not going there. I refuse to apply for another stupid permit. Let's go somewhere else instead tonight. There is nowhere else to go, unless you want to have dinner at Jack in the Box. No thanks; we'll get a frozen pizza from the grocery store and a Black Box Chardonnay from the liquor store. Besides, I have to get a Visitors Permit first, remember? I feel like just staying in at your place tonight. I didn't mention that his permit arrived in the mail the other day. I thought, we'll use it next time and just stay in at the cottage tonight.

Tell me, Parker, did you happen to encounter any gay people during your holiday excursion to The Miracle Mile? No, I didn't manage to run into any, actually. That's because they don't exist, just like I told you in the first place. Nothing but straight people here, and I'm already tired of their bad moods and ugly hairdos.

Let's not argue anymore about it, Francis; come on, you just got home. Tell me instead about your trip to the Western Shore. He put his arm around my waist and held me a bit closer while we sat out on the porch. It was very beautiful, Parker. The only thing missing there was you.

It felt so nice sitting there with him now. I noticed he had tanned some from the sun and the sand. You're the beautiful one, Francis.

It is during these moments that it seems clear to me I've been more or less on the right path with him for the past seven years. These are the feelings I deserve to have when we are together. Friction and disagreements will ensnarl any relationship, but they have too strong a grip on ours. We need to find ways to contain and untwist them. Left alone, they might wrap themselves around my spirit and strangle it.

A sense of calm embraces me as I think of the good times we've spent together at the Western Shore. It's such a peaceful place; I wish we could live there. For some reason, we never seem to fight or argue much at the Western Shore. It's as if we find a slice of our own paradise when we are there, without the daily stresses of our regular lives to trample on it.

If you walk south of town past the wooden boardwalk, the beach widens considerably and stretches for nearly two kilometers before you reach the next of the popular resorts, which seem to dot the shoreline at more or less regular intervals. Here, the crowds will gradually thin, with your feet sinking deeper into the soft white sand. The dunes and their sea grasses form a naturally scenic barrier between the sea and the houses and villas that have sprung up over the past few decades.

In the wintertime, the temperatures are often moderate along the coast. On a good day, a long walk with just a sweater or light jacket can be quite pleasant. The sound of the surf pounding the shore at high tide seems a symphony to me. I dream of one day owning one of the villas here, away from the noise and pollution of City Centre, away from the hordes and the heat of The Miracle Mile.

Francis laughs when I mention it. You are such a dreamer, Parker. I had to wonder though; would the two of us ever live together there? Could we be happy enough and content with a simpler existence shared with the seabirds and the dolphins?

Maybe it was a dream, a fantasy probably, but one that I loved to imagine. You never know. If we saved our money and were determined enough, it seemed possible enough for me. It would be years from now of course, but perseverance might pay off and make it a reality one day if we really wanted it.

Ah, Parker, what a dreamer you are. Think how nice it would be, Francis. He was laughing at me again. You are such a dreamer.

VI

One thing I know for certain about dreamers is that eventually, we all have to wake up, whether the dream is a pleasant one we hope to repeat or a hellish one hope to banish. Reality has a nasty way of throttling even our most wondrous dreams. When I am stunned by the buzzing alarm clock early Monday morning, that reality has managed to infect my mood and upend my prior tranquil thoughts of the Western Shore.

The commute into City Centre has proven to be a bit more problematic than I originally anticipated. Beyond the walk to the station and the half-hour ride in a crowded coach, I've got to deal with the sometimes unpleasant, or even disorderly passengers. Or on some occasions, the unhygienic ones as well, who I am guessing may have overslept, or for some other reason neglected to allow the time needed for both bathing and commuting.

I think I commented earlier about the predictable reliability of our transit system. What I forgot to mention is the not quite-so-reliability of their air conditioning systems, especially on very warm days. So while I can be confident of an on-time arrival to the Office, my mood might be less than assured once I arrive there.

I stopped at the Timekeeper's desk at precisely 8:08 and signed in as usual. Hi Parker, I trust that you enjoyed your venture to The Miracle Mile over the holiday.

How the hell did he know about that? I didn't tell anyone except Francis and he never talks to the Timekeeper. There isn't any way he saw me there; he was on holiday at the Mountain Campgrounds with his wife all weekend.

I gave him a puzzled look, but before I could ask about it, he said, did you hear what happened to Ms. Millerton? No, I was working with her over the weekend and when I left in the afternoon she was still at her desk.

She must have been about ready to follow you out, when for some reason, she fell and broke her leg. Nobody is sure what took place, but some people are speculating about how it happened. I don't know, Parker, maybe she just missed a step coming down from the platform. Or maybe something else happened.

What do you mean, something else? He said, you know how people talk. They assume the worst. All I know is that she must have banged her head pretty hard too, because when the janitor found her on the floor, she was quite dazed and the last thing she remembered was talking to you.

We did talk of course, mostly about how much faster I work when I'm not distracted. He asked then, is that all you talked about? What are you getting at, sir?

Did she happen to mention that she had to cancel her trip to the Northern District because of all the backlogged invoices and receipts? She did say that, yeah. She also said I set a good example for the other Processors by working overtime over the holiday.

But she blamed you for fact that she couldn't visit her relatives, didn't she? And you were mad because you couldn't go with your partner and Carleton to the Western Shore, weren't you?

Who told him all that shit? I said, are you suggesting that I had something to do with Ms. Millerton's injury? No, Parker, I'm not suggesting anything. But people love gossip, you know that. And her fall seems rather suspicious, wouldn't you say?

No, people fall all the time if they aren't careful, especially on steps. Especially steps that have no barrier or handrail to grab onto, like the ones from her platform.

Well, Parker, I hope this just blows over. Everyone seems to think that she wasn't too happy with your recent work productivity or that Mr. Sanderson made her work on the holiday because of you. You know how people like to assume certain things, of course, I have no idea what really happened.

It's all about time, Parker. Everything is connected by it and always has been, since the beginning of creation. The timing of you leaving and her falling. The timing of your trip to the Western Shore and mine to the Mountain Campgrounds. Everything is woven together by it.

I'm sorry if I misunderstood you, sir. It just seemed to me that you were implying that I knew something more about Ms. Millerton's accident. No, he said; I just said her fall seemed suspicious. I did not mean to imply more than that. People make their own assumptions.

Why not ask Ms. Millerton what happened? Because she can't remember falling, that's why. Well, I certainly can't remember it, since I wasn't here when she fell.

I felt confused by my conversation with the Timekeeper and kind of irritated by the time I made it over to the coffee dispenser. One of the other Processors, the most useless of the group, was also getting his first cup of the morning. I couldn't help but notice the raised eyebrow and his condescending look.

You need something, Anthony? No, I was just looking for the sugar. Well, you might want to stop looking and start working before Mr. Sanderson sees you not doing anything.

I sat down at my desk and checked my inbox. A small pile of receipts and invoices that were not there when I left yesterday afternoon had mysteriously appeared. I wanted to get busy and have as many reviewed and logged in as possible by lunchtime. Since Ms. Millerton would not be at her desk on her elevated platform for the time being, we were all going to have to wait on Mr. Sanderson or someone else to open the cabinets today. I was nervous about that too after what happened the last time Ms. Millerton was absent from the office.

This week is not off to a glorious start. I dial Carleton's number to tell him what happened. The call went to his voicemail and I decide not to leave any message. I know he's busy with work these days; I'll tell him at lunch.

After only about thirty minutes, I realize that I am more than halfway through the work that had been waiting since I arrived. I'll be done early if nobody drops any more shit on my desk.

I sip my coffee and try to relax a little bit. I look around at the other Processors, perplexed by them. Not one of the eleven is doing any work at all. With Ms. Millerton away, nobody is watching them. That fat-ass Anthony is eating donuts and chatting away with Mandy, one of our Clerical Assistants.

It's no wonder the work fell so far behind with everything backlogged like it was. They didn't seem to even notice or care that I was watching them. What was shaping up to be a crap-filled day for me, was looking like a perfect one for them. Perfect opportunity to screw off as much as possible with the boss away.

I don't think they noticed the Timekeeper either. I could tell he was glancing our way, watching what we were up to. I'm not sure if I should trust him or not. I don't know how he does it, but he always knows everything that goes on in the office. I don't think he is getting his information from Ms. Millerton; I'm pretty sure they hate each other.

I went back to what I was doing and finally finished logging everything in the master log. Now, I would just have to wait on Mr. Sanderson to bring the keys, since it was clear enough that Ms. Millerton would not be bringing them.

A big predicament was now facing our department; mainly, who would be assigned to sit at Ms. Millerton's desk, elevated a meter or more above the rest of us. Government protocol required that we be supervised in this way by somebody, and it seemed probable that Ms. Millerton might be unable to resume her duties for quite some time.

I sent a text message to Carleton. *I better meet you at the deli across the plaza for lunch.* I got in trouble the last time he was seen here in the office with me. He wrote back a few minutes later. *Okay, see you there at noon.*

Mr. Sanderson came over to my desk then, but I didn't see any keys with him. I have quite a few invoices today that are ready to be stamped and filed when you have the time, I told him.

I am not here to discuss when might be a convenient time for you to do your filing, Mr. Parker, but rather to inform you that the Office of Internal Affairs will be sending an investigator this afternoon to interview you concerning Ms. Millerton's fall. Why would they want to interview me, sir? I finished working and went home before her accident. He seemed displeased by my response. I am not in the habit of questioning the motivation of the Office of Internal Affairs, only in complying with their directives.

I don't understand why I am being accused of doing something wrong to Ms. Millerton. Has anyone accused you of harming her, Mr. Parker? Has anyone even hinted that her fall was something other than an untimely mishap? The Timekeeper insinuated that I had something to do with it. Ah, yes, but the Timekeeper was not here at the time, was he? Only you were here, so clearly the Office of Internal Affairs would be derelict by neglecting their responsibility of talking to the people, or in this case, the person, who was here. They would have no reason to interview the Timekeeper, or even me for that matter, since neither of us was here. Nobody will accuse you without justification, I can assure you.

I was not comfortable being interrogated all by myself by some investigator with nobody else present. Will you be with me during the interview, Mr. Sanderson? Unfortunately, I am going to be quite busy this afternoon and not available for the meeting. You should be able to understand, Mr. Parker, that there are many more important issues that I need to attend to, and not expect that someone in my position can simply drop everything at a moment's notice just to be present for a matter quite trivial as this.

• • • •

Can you believe he called an interrogation by the Investigator trivial? It was a warm afternoon and Carlton and I were having our lunch while sitting on the grass in the plaza. I think you may be overacting, Parker; they can't really think that you did anything to cause Ms. Millerton to break her leg. Why are they sending the Investigator from the Office of Internal Affairs to interview me then?

I don't know, Parker. I do know that it is too bad you could not have come along with us to the Western Shore instead of wasting the holiday here filing receipts and invoices. It was so much fun. We played beach volleyball and went to happy hour both nights at the Full Moon. That place was packed with hot-looking guys for the holiday.

Ms. Millerton said all the Processors were behind in their filing and I could set a better example by working harder. I bet she was impressed when I finished almost 500 hundred invoices and receipts by noon so that she could go home early. He said, I guess she did not get to go home early, did she? No, she went to the hospital instead. I hope she gets her memory back and remembers all the extra work I did and the good example I set. Yes, he said, and let's hope she remembers that no one pushed her down the steps either. Or tripped her when she went to get the keys to the cabinets. Or argued with her when she said it was my fault that she had to cancel her holiday plans to visit with her relatives in the Northern District. He said, she blamed that on you? Yeah, that's what she said anyway. That bitch, I wish she would break the other leg. Be careful what you wish for, Carleton; I'm in enough hot water as it is.

• • • •

Mr. Parker, I am with the Office of Internal Affairs and am here to talk with you concerning Ms. Millerton. You understand that this interview is being recorded and that anything you say becomes part of the official inquiry conducted by this Government agency, and could, depending upon the conclusions drawn by this agency, result in future disciplinary action.

I dislike the Investigator immediately. His manner is unnecessarily confrontational and he has bad breath. Okay, I said, but shouldn't Mr. Sanderson be in this meeting with us? I'm afraid not; Mr. Sanderson is a busy man, and though I have no doubt he would be interested in participating in the interview, our policy is that such discussions should be private and completely confidential; you understand, of course. Yes sir, but in that case shouldn't someone from the Office of Human Resources be present? I would like there to be an objective observer, someone impartial who can document the proceedings and attest to them later, if necessary. No, Mr. Parker; that is not our policy either.

Excuse me sir, but is it your policy to make accusations that have no foundation? No one is making any accusations, he said; we just want to interview you. With all due respect, the Timekeeper insinuated that I had something to do with Ms. Millerton's injuries, which are quite serious as I understand them. We are not interested in what the Timekeeper has to say; he was not here when Ms. Millerton was caused to fall.

Caused to fall, sir? Didn't you mean to say accidentally fall on the steps that have no handrail or barrier? Since no one was here, Mr. Parker, we don't know what caused her to fall; unless you were here. I was not here; I left shortly after noon and she was still working at her desk. The Timekeeper's log will reflect that.

So then, you have no idea what could have happened? No, I said; she was fine when I left. Mr. Parker, that's all we need to know at this time. As part of our continuing investigation into this matter, we may want to interview you again at a later time. We will notify you of the need for any further interrogation.

Shit, I might not be finished with this guy yet. I hope the next time he flosses his teeth or gargles with mouthwash or something before wasting even more of my time with his stupid questions.

After I got home later that evening, I called Francis and told him about Ms. Millerton's accident. I did not mention anything about either the interview with the Investigator, or the insinuations made by the Timekeeper.

Carleton was probably right. I tend to overact sometimes and blow things out of proportion. The Timekeeper probably didn't mean anything by what he said. Maybe he was still pissed off at me because he had to stay until almost 7:00 that night and got home late for dinner. I wonder what he meant when he said everything is woven together by time. And how did he always know everyone's business?

Francis was obviously amused by my predicament. That's some office you work in, he said. I bet they will ask you to sit up there at her desk and stare all day at the other Processors who pretend to be working when they are actually screwing around. I doubt it, Francis; I'm not too sure they want me to fill in for a Senior Secretary. I just hope I am still being considered for the Assistant Secretary promotion.

• • • •

I was surprised when Ms. Millerton returned to work just three days later. Her leg was in a full cast and she needed crutches to even hobble around. I felt bad for her and could tell she was struggling and in considerable pain too. An angry-looking bruise had formed on the left side of her forehead where she must have hit it when she fell. If it were me, I would still be home recuperating right now, probably watching *I Dream of Jeannie* reruns on the Satellite.

Fortunately, she was able to perform most of her duties adequately, but could not realistically manage to go up and down the steps, so they decided to set up a smaller desk immediately adjacent to the platform where she normally worked.

Mr. Parker, may I see you for a moment, please? I had not even had time to settle in at my desk after signing in with the Timekeeper, let alone get over to the vending machines or the coffee dispenser.

Yes, Ms. Millerton; how are you feeling now? Quite a bit better than before, thank you for asking, but we are not here to discuss my current health per se, but rather the problem facing us as an indirect result of it. Since I am unable to work from my desk on the platform, Mr. Sanderson has informed me that we need to locate a temporary replacement, someone to work from the platform at least until I can adjust to these crutches and manage to get up and down the steps without falling again. I made the unfortunate suggestion that you might be a good person for the job, at which time he pointed out that it would be a conflict of interest for a Processor to be overseeing the other Processors, like a cock guarding the chicken coop, or something like that.

I think he meant it would be like a fox guarding it, I said. That makes even less sense, Mr. Parker. I agree, Ms. Millerton, but if you don't mind me asking, do you happen to remember how you managed to fall from the platform in the first place?

Yes, I was hurrying as usual and just wasn't paying attention. If there was a handrail or some sort of barrier, it probably would not have happened at all. I see, and did the Investigator from the Department of Internal Affairs happen to learn of this news? I wouldn't know, Mr. Parker; I'm not concerned with Internal Affairs, only our own affairs relating to invoice and receipt processing.

Anyway, since we have no one suitable in our department to oversee the Processors, Mr. Sanderson called his friend in the Office of Sanitation and Debris Removal and they will loan one of their employees to us temporarily. I think you may know him; his name is Mr. Carleton.

I let out a short giggle before I could catch myself. Did I say something funny, Mr. Parker? No, Ms. Millerton. Well, maybe just a little bit funny. Carleton watching the Processors seems a bit like the fox guarding the chickens. I'm glad you are so easily amused, Mr. Parker, now please return to your workstation.

• • • •

My neighbor Thomas makes me nervous and I don't like him. He's one of those guys who gets right up in your face when he talks to you. He knows that his physical presence is intimidating, and he takes a sort of weird pleasure from that fact. He is way too much in my business for somebody I hardly know. He acts like we are best buddies too, which I find totally annoying.

I try to avoid him whenever I can now because he is starting to scare me. I haven't made any friends since I moved here, but I have had casual conversations with several of my neighbors, and so far, nobody has had anything favorable to say about him.

I don't like doing this, or even admitting to it, but I look around the front of the cottage before going outside to work in the garden. I know he's going to corner me and try to make some mindless conversation if he gets the chance.

The other evening, I thought the coast was clear because his car was not in the carport. Wrong. I guess either Ms. Thomas or their elder son was out for a drive. She's got a brother or someone she visits in Province West. He's nineteen, I think Thomas said, and he probably has his Driver's Permit.

So I'm out there on a warm Saturday afternoon weeding the garden, watering the azaleas, and minding my own business when he appears out of nowhere. I agreed to go to the Club with him on Lady's Night that time, and that's all he talked about, the ladies. Or else it was the gals, as he likes to refer to women.

Hey there, Parker, what are you doing? Oh, shit, I can't avoid him now. Let me see; I have the watering can out, a rake, and my gardening gloves on. What could I possibly be doing? Just a little cleaning up in the garden, I tell him. How have you been, Thomas?

I've been well, yes, quite well indeed; been going to the Club pretty regularly now. You have any big plans for tonight at the Club? It's Saturday night and it should be a lot of fun. Why don't you come along with me?

I can't figure this guy out. What would make him think I have nothing better to do on a Saturday night? I'm tempted to ask him about his wife and kids and suggest that maybe he should spend more of his free time with them on the weekends.

Ms. Thomas seems like a nice enough woman; why the hell did she marry this loser? Does she just sit home by herself on Saturday night watching movie reruns on the Satellite, while her husband galavants through the Club gawking at women and making lewd comments about them?

No thanks, Thomas. I'm going to City Centre to visit my friend Francis later on. He's not too big on going out in The Miracle Mile now that another permit is required. City Centre, huh? Wow, I bet they got lots of clubs there. Lots of pretty gals too, I imagine.

By now, a little bell should have gone off inside Thomas' half-empty skull to signal to him that perhaps it wasn't the gals that interested me. And I can't imagine how he didn't take the hint when Francis, Carleton, and Winston came over and the four of us sat out on the porch, having cocktails and acting silly. The three of them were hanging out at the cottage quite often, now that the fútbol matches had resumed.

Here you go, another big advantage to the Province that none of us even thought about until after I moved in. You can pick up the fútbol matches on the Satellite here if you buy a subscription package, but the service isn't available yet in City Centre. This is a big deal to Winston and Francis, who both love to watch the Western District Falcons play.

So our little group sits out on the porch a lot, giggling oftentimes while waiting for the broadcast to start. I'm not going to even suggest that I am objective about our friends, and I don't have any desire to stereotype them either. But come on, Carleton leans a little far to the right on the masculinity scale, and he cackles a bit loudly sometimes. Winston likes to crack us up when he gets a little tipsy and does his Betty Davis impersonations.

I know Thomas sees us out there. So does his older son, Harris. I've noticed him peeking through their living room curtains and walking around their front yard when we're around.

But it is Thomas who always comes over to bother me. You fellows seem to spend a lot of time here together; aren't any of you guys married? I have no clue why he is so curious about our marital status. Do I have to check off one of the four boxes again like I did with the Housing Administrator?

I'm losing my patience with him, but decide to give it one more shot at being courteous. No, we are all single, all four of us. He gives me a curious look then. All of you are bachelors; how does that happen?

What also happens is that Harris decides to walk over then, and just like that, my mood is suddenly transformed. He is a knockout of a nineteen-year-old guy. He bears no resemblance at all to his father, lucky for him. I'd seen him twice before outside washing the car, but couldn't see him all that clearly or what he looked like from that distance. What he looked like is something Leonardo da Vinci might have drawn up. He's wearing a brightly-colored T-shirt that seems a bit tight to me, but I'm not complaining, mind you. He has dark brown hair perfectly complemented by eyes of the same rich color, and framed by a beautiful smile.

He put out his hand to shake mine and said, you must be Parker. I'm Harris. Nice to meet you, I said. I meant that too. He was standing a little close, like his father did. I could not imagine they had much else in common.

Do you like fútbol, Parker? They've started broadcasting the matches on the Satellite now and my brother and I like to watch them. He smelled really good, like he was getting ready to go out for the evening. Yeah Harris, we just got our Satellite hook-up last month. My friends like coming over to watch the games.

Father, would it be okay if I borrow the sedan tonight? Mother says you won't need it since you are going to the Club with Tyler's father and he can pick you up. Oh, another date with Lacey, son? No, not tonight. I was planning to spend the evening with Tyler at his place in Province North. But it's Saturday night, Harris, why not take Lacey to the Cinema instead?

Harris and Tyler on a Saturday night sounds much better to me than a date with Lacey on any night. I am sometimes clueless when it comes to such things, and don't put much faith in people who claim they can always tell who is gay and who isn't just by looking at them. That whole gaydar thing is usually bullshit. But my God, unless I have somehow managed to decode the messages completely wrong, Harris is going to have a lot more fun tonight with Tyler in Province North than he would have if he wound up with Lacey in The Miracle Mile.

* * * *

It was so hysterical seeing Carleton sitting at the huge desk on its elevated platform, like some pompous queen looking down from her throne at her subjects. I wonder how long Mr. Sanderson's buddy in the Office of Sanitation and Debris Removal might be willing to pay him to sit up there doing nothing.

One of our Processors recently retired, and we just replaced her with a guy named Crosby. Ms. Millerton decided that I should be the one to mentor him during the mandatory thirty-day probation period. I was happy to comply because Crosby seemed like a pretty nice guy, and definitely a pretty nice-looking guy as well. I was happy too because it is getting obvious now that Ms. Millerton relies on me more than any of the other Processors. This mentoring business should end up in my Permanent Record, no doubt.

Crosby has zero in common with the other Processors, who as a group are older, inhospitable, and generally useless. The only good thing they do at work is staying away from me. Crosby is about my age and everyone liked him immediately. Even the guys in the office seem to find him charming, his boyish good looks and his enthusiasm make it hard even for them to not take a liking to the new guy. He liked a good joke too. Parker, what the hell is Carleton doing up there? It looks like he could use a tiara and a royal robe.

I was showing Crosby the log and explaining the time stamp and the three-hour limit. I don't know how long he'll be up there; Ms. Millerton is afraid to take any chances on the steps with her crutches. I think she might have to keep working at her new desk until they take the cast off.

Mr. Sanderson interviewed Crosby during the recruiting process, and I knew that he had final veto rights over any prospective employee that was being considered. It was clear to me right away that he had a thing for Crosby too. He was hanging around an awful lot now, making small talk and staring at the poor guy.

Crosby and I became friends almost immediately. Hey, where do you live, Crosby? City Centre, how about you? I have a place in Province East. He said, really? I didn't think there were any of us living way out there.

There is at least one more of us in Province East, and he lives in the house directly across the footpath. It was a warm Sunday afternoon and Harris was raking the garden for Ms. Thomas. His shirt was off, and thin lines of sweat streamed down his tanned body.

I resist the temptation to walk over and chat with him. I'm trying to limit my exposure to Thomas as much as possible, and I see that his sedan is parked in the carport. Unless he walked to the Club and is getting drunk in the middle of the day, he is probably at home.

Harris looked over a few times and waved; hey Parker, hot out today isn't it? It was getting hotter each time I looked over at him. I better get my ass back in the cottage and cool off fast before Thomas comes outside and finds it peculiar that his teenage son is flirting with one of the neighborhood guys.

. . . .

Most people would assume that logging and filing documents all day long is painfully boring, but I actually don't mind it. As long as someone shows up with the keys to the filing cabinets before my deadline, I'm good. I can work at my own pace, and most of the time anyway, nobody bothers me. And now, with Carleton working with us at least temporarily, it is kind of fun.

Francis loves to point out and take swipes at the needling bureaucrats where I work, but I understand better than he does how they function and how best to deal with them.

Mr. Parker, may I see you for a moment at my desk? You notice I just said most of the time; I never said the job was perfect. Yes, Ms. Millerton, what do you need for me to do? I want to discuss Crosby's progress, as I will need to prepare the thirty-day probation report and forward it to Mr. Sanderson in triplicate by the end of the week. He has the final say as to which of the new employees should be retained permanently and subsequently removed from probation.

This would be an easy one for Mr. Sanderson, based on how often I caught the boss staring at Crosby's ass. She said then, my impression is that Crosby is doing an excellent job, has surpassed expectations, and should be promoted from Probationary Processor to Senior Processor. Yes, I said, I think he is doing fine, but did I hear you correctly when you said Senior Processor? Didn't you mean to say just Processor, and maybe get the words out wrong?

She has to know that I am a Senior Processor and have been working here for nearly eight years. I mean come on, there is no way Crosby could be made a Senior Processor after just thirty days, even if Mr. Sanderson did have a constant hard-on at work this past month.

There is nothing wrong with either your hearing or my speaking; I did say Senior. Why, is there something wrong with that, Mr. Parker? No, I said, nothing at all. Thank you, now please return to your workstation and finish with your invoices while I get the keys for Crosby.

I'm sorry, but why would Crosby need the keys? Because Mr. Parker, it will take at least thirty minutes for you to complete all of your filing and I can't stand with these crutches for more than five, or at most ten minutes. So I have asked Crosby to oversee the filing until I am finally able to rid myself of this dreadful cast.

When I stood up and turned to head back to my desk, I noticed Carlton not doing anything other than looking down at us. Ms. Millerton's temporary desk was just below his and adjacent to the platform. I'm sure he heard every word of the conversation I just had with Ms. Millerton.

I heard a slight giggling sound coming from the platform. I'm glad at least someone was getting a laugh out of this. Carleton, shouldn't you be working on some computer project instead of just sitting on your ass up there? No, Mr. Sanderson just asked that I keep an eye on things. Alright, I said, then can you meet Crosby and me for lunch at the deli across the Plaza at 12:30?

· · · ·

I look forward to the weekends and hanging out in City Centre with our friends. Saturday evening, I was getting ready to meet Carleton and Crosby in town. Francis and Winston were already out for happy hour and would catch up with us later at one of the bars we like, then I would just stay over at Francis' apartment and have brunch in town on Sunday.

By this time, the five of us had formed a nice little clique and we would often show up as a group wherever we eventually wound up. We attracted our share of attention, and I will say that we looked pretty good by the time we got all fixed up and ready to go.

We still manage to hang on to a bit of our youthful energy and sex appeal, even if the term youthful can no longer be legitimately used to describe us. The five of us are lucky to have been blessed with better-than-average looks.

It took me almost an hour to get ready. I had to try on half the shirts I own to finally decide which one would go best with the new jeans I just finished pressing. I like to tell myself that I am not all that vain, and don't care about conforming to any stereotype imposed by the models of our culture. That's mostly bullshit, though. I enjoy the attention, who wouldn't?

The mobile rings. Parker, when are you finally going to get here? I'm on my way, Francis. Hurry up; you're going to make us late again. Alright, I'm leaving now.

I step outside into the slightly chilly evening air, just as the sun begins to set itself down for the night. I'm going to wait out front for the rideshare I called to take me to City Centre. I don't feel like walking to the station and dealing with the crowded train tonight.

I see my neighbor's front door open; oh shit, I hope that isn't Tomas again. Hey, Parker; how are you? Not Thomas this time, thankfully. Hi there, Harris.

Wow, I'm not the only one who spent too much time getting ready to go out. He doesn't need much fixing up though. He stands a bit close to me again like his father likes to do, but I'm not complaining. I can smell the woodsy cedar scent of the soap he used; my God, is he ever cute.

Natural selection made the right decision when it endowed Harris with his mother's features. Lucky break for both of us. Thomas is nothing to look at and he probably long ago lost any motivation to do anything about it that might impress the gals. Harris, well we're talking about something else entirely. He has his mother's beautiful dark hair and her stately exterior. I keep wondering why she married Thomas of all people, and whether or not Harris is actually biologically related to him.

Are you going to City Centre tonight, Parker? Yeah, sure; I'm meeting Francis and some of our friends there in a little while. He asked me, do you think it would be alright if I tag along with you guys?

In some alternate universe, I would like nothing better than to have him following me around, getting my drinks, and attracting other handsome guys like a swarm of honey bees. My mind quickly kicks in and reminds me what a bad idea that is.

Harris, aren't you too young to get into the clubs? No, the drinking age is eighteen in City Centre, not like here in the Province. Shit, he had me there; I'd forgotten all about the more liberal laws in the city.

Look, maybe it would be better if you went with Tyler instead; you know what I'm saying? If we see you out sometime, you can introduce us to your friend, but I'm not sure it's a good idea for you to go to a club with us. Does Thomas have any clue?

No way, he'd lock me in the basement if he knew where I was going. Besides, Tyler can't go with me tonight; he has a date with Beverly and his parents don't let him go to City Centre at night either. I say, Beverly, huh? Yeah, his aunt fixed Tyler up with her neighbor's daughter. She's real nice, Parker; you'd like her.

Enter stage left. Right on cue, here comes Thomas to deflate the mood and poke around in my personal life. What's going on, fellas? Going to The Miracle Mile again tonight, Parker? No, not tonight, I'm afraid.

Just then, the Uber pulls up to rescue me. Poor Harris, I thought. What a cutie though.

. . . .

There are three prominent gay bars in City Centre, each with a slick and trendy-sounding name; Club Fantasia, the Centre Quest, and the Phoenician Temple. But we like to refer to them more generically as the High Club, the Low Club, and the Club in the Middle. We go to all three of them for various reasons and with differing expectations.

The High Club has by far the youngest and hottest-looking crowd and gets packed on weekends with handsome twinks, shirtless hunks, and fine-looking bartenders who serve up the drinks so fast they seem like street magicians performing their shell game disappearing tricks. We go there mainly to observe, or more truthfully gawk, and blissfully reminisce about our younger days when we gyrated right up there among the beautifully privileged.

The Low Club tends to attract an older crowd and maintains a more laid-back vibe. Here is a place where you can drink and dance in the main bar area and still be heard by the person you're with if you have something worth saying. You can listen in on the performer in the piano lounge, or be corralled into a sing-along to an Ethel Merman show tune. Here, we can enjoy the attention we're much more likely to receive, and which we're not quite naïve enough to expect at the High Club.

The Centre Quest, or the Club in the Middle, is just what the clever name we gave it would suggest. We like going there because you never know who might turn up, or what might happen. This club has some of everything; elegantly costumed dancers, elderly gentlemen in western cowboy attire, punk-looking kids with jaw-dropping tattoos, and burly men in some frightful-looking leather contraption.

We fit right in at the Centre Quest, with our skinny jeans and brightly-colored T-shirts, with the sleeves cuffed to show off our biceps. Anything goes here; one night there might be a kissing contest, and the next a bar-clearing brawl. It's my favorite place of course, and everybody makes an appearance at some point during the...wait, is that Harris?

All five of us were up there with a couple of hundred others on the huge dance floor when a young guy dancing with Harris tripped on my foot. He probably would have gone all the way down if Winston hadn't reached out and grabbed his arm just in time, preventing the handsome twink from completely embarrassing himself. He and Winston made more than casual eye contact as the guy apologized and smiled simultaneously. Hey, thanks; my name is Tyler, what's yours? Oh shit, I could see where this might be heading.

By this time, I was in serious need of a cocktail. We all stood at the bar, while Carleton ordered the next round. I looked around at everyone while sipping my drink, my brain clouded somewhat by this third Bombay Sapphire and tonic that Carleton just handed to me.

Tyler and Winston seem much too intimate when you consider that they have known each all of about seven or eight minutes. He is the same age as Harris, I imagine, which separates him from Winston and the rest of us by at least half a generation.

Winston is Francis' best buddy and has always been good to me. He's kind of on the private side, and I have no idea what he and Francis talk about when I am not around, but my instincts tell me he wouldn't hesitate to put Francis in his place and remind him of the good thing he has going on with me.

He has a face that could stop you cold, with almost perfect sculpted features. His brown eyes have amber-colored specs at the center and are framed by long dark lashes that give an air of mystery when you stare into them. He attracts a lot of very handsome young guys, including Tyler it seems.

Harris was getting slightly drunk and kept nudging up against Francis and me, which brought no feeling of consternation on my part, except when I tried to imagine the scene that would unfold if Thomas were to somehow stumble intoxicated into the bar not realizing exactly where he was.

Harris, what happened to Beverly? She's here somewhere with her girlfriend; the four of us came together. She's cool about Tyler and me. Wait, I said; didn't you tell me Tyler isn't allowed in City Centre at night? He's not; you won't say anything to Thomas, will you? I'll be grounded for sure and I don't know what Tyler's father will do to him if he finds out.

I had to wonder what exactly Thomas would do, and who he would do it to if he found out. I was nearly certain that the subject of a gay son had yet to materialize in the Thomas household. He had a temper, and it's not like he could use the easy threat of grounding me if he found out that Harris spent his evening dancing and drinking at a gay bar, with me being a few centimeters away, instead of where Thomas felt he should be on a date with Lacey or some other girl in The Miracle Mile.

I won't tell on you Harris; don't worry.

VII

Crosby had become an overnight sensation of sorts at work. He had to be the first one in the history of the office to be promoted to Senior Processor after just thirty days. Now, Mr. Sanderson was spending half of his time performing tasks that previously would have been considered beneath him and relegated to either Ms. Millerton or an Assistant Secretary.

In some ways that was a good thing. Maybe not for Crosby, but at least for me anyway. If Ms. Millerton was tied up for some reason, Mr. Sanderson seemed to be not quite so busy and more than happy to step up and come over with the keys. Going past my three-hour time limit? Problem solved.

He could easily kill half an hour or more watching Crosby do his filing, his explanation being that he was relieving Ms. Millerton of having to stand on her one good leg for too long.

Mr. Sanderson is as big of a closet case as Rock Hudson, though any resemblance between the two ends right there. He is a middle-aged guy you would not even notice in a crowd, or ignore if you did. He is easily twenty pounds or more on the plus side, and he wears his mousy-looking blondish hair way too long in a losing effort to cover up a prominent bald spot. His facial features scream out blandness.

His best friend is the Superintendent and Carleton's boss upstairs in the Office of Sanitation and Debris Removal. We all know that Mr. Sanderson has had a long-standing crush on Carleton, way before Crosby came along, which I figure accounts for why Carleton is now seated at Ms. Millerton's desk on her platform instead of fixing computers upstairs where he belongs.

He is a hard worker and highly respected by his co-workers, who mainly deal with the garbage. He should be completely bored by now, with little to do but keep an eye on the twelve of us. But I've kept an eye out too and caught him staring at Crosby several times. When I asked him what was going on, he just laughed and changed the subject.

But best friends band together when it comes to many things, especially when one of those things involves sex. I kept probing until he finally confessed that he and Crosby had hooked up twice already. I've been meaning to tell you, Parker, but haven't had the chance yet.

Carleton, is this getting serious? He says, I don't know; it could be I guess. I like him a lot; what do you think? Does it really matter what I think? Of course it does, he says. You're my best friend and your opinion means just about everything to me. Okay then, I'll tell you. I think you and Crosby made one of the nicest-looking couples at the Club in the Middle on Saturday night.

Ms. Millerton had just finished initialing my log entries and stamping the ninety-five invoices and receipts I reviewed that morning. Along comes Mr. Sanderson with the keys again, good timing.

Mr. Crosby, are you ready now to do your filing? I have some free time this afternoon and can open the cabinets for you. Wait a second; what is going on here? I have a big stack of work to be filed and don't want to go over my time limit. Crosby has not even finished his log entries yet.

Excuse me, Mr. Sanderson, but can I do my filing now also? I've got quite a few invoices and receipts stamped already.

Mr. Parker, was I addressing you? I am very busy and you should not assume that merely because I have time to unlock the cabinets for one Processor, that all of the filing can be done at once. As you know, our procedures require that no more than two Processors be at the file cabinets at the same time, and you should also know that Anthony has requested already that I unlock the cabinets for him.

Anthony, really? he doesn't do anything except flirt with the Clerical Assistants and eat the donuts they bring to the office.

Yes, sir, but I thought as long as you had some time this afternoon, I might do my filing during that time. It probably won't take me more than twenty minutes or so.

Mr. Parker, I should not need to constantly explain to you the department's filing protocols. I will attend to your matters as my schedule and time permit, but at the present moment, if you don't mind, I need to oversee Crosby's filing. That should be easy enough for you to understand; you are a Senior Processor and have been here for more than seven years. But Crosby has been a Processor for a mere seven weeks.

Did you mean to say Senior Processor? What's that, Parker? I remind him, Crosby was promoted to Senior Processor last week, sir.

Nobody with even marginal eyesight could help but notice how closely Mr. Sanderson watched Crosby do his filing. At one point, he was bent over to reach way into the back of one of the lower cabinet drawers, giving Mr. Sanderson a perfect view of his cute rear end. The lecher was practically standing right on top of poor Crosby.

So Ms. Millerton's untimely fall down the steps turned out just fine for Mr. Sanderson. His frivolous conflict-of-interest excuse was laughable, even to someone as brain-dead as Anthony.

· · · ·

He's in a bad mood again. What is it this time, Francis? Didn't you have fun on Saturday night in City Centre? He said then, I just can't figure out what the fuck Winston thinks he is doing with Tyler; he's just a kid. Yes, he is, but a nice kid. It's borderline child molestation, Parker. Don't worry so much about it, I said. How long can it last? His parents hardly let him out of the house.

It's insane; you know Winston has a high-security clearance at his job at the Office of Special Investigations. If they find out that he's tweaking a minor, he'll be in a hell of a fix. They could decide to get rid of him.

I don't think so, I tell him. Tyler is nineteen and no longer a minor, so technically speaking, I'm not sure they could do anything. He raises an eyebrow and says, oh yeah? And what about Tyler's old man? What do you think about him technically speaking?

I never met the guy, but Thomas is starting to make me nervous as hell. Yeah, Parker; he is so creepy. You better keep away from him. We all descended from apes of course, but in Thomas' case, it seems that he got off the bus at the Neanderthal stop and forgot to get back on.

Thomas and Tyler's father are good friends and hang out together quite often. They must have been chatting with each other about the boys' so-called dates over the weekend and managed to put two and two together and figure out that they had gone out in City Centre.

I was home after work one night about ready for bed, when I was disturbed by someone pounding on the front door. I opened it up a crack after noticing Thomas through the peephole, hoping there was going to be a short explanation for this intrusion. He asked if he could come inside. I decided it might be a better idea if I went out on the porch to see what we wanted.

I don't like unannounced social calls, or someone who thinks that it's perfectly okay to just walk right in on my privacy. I like them even less at 9:30 in the evening and when that someone is a pinhead like Thomas. I stepped into the chilly nighttime air, with just a T-shirt and sweatpants on. What is it now, Thomas?

Did you happen to run across Tyler and Harris while you were out in City Centre on Saturday night? I said, why would you come over here at this time of night asking me something like that? Because Tyler's father is concerned that he is hanging out with the wrong type of people in City Centre, and not on any dates with Beverly in The Miracle Mile like he should be.

This guy is starting to infuriate me. What do you mean by the wrong type of people, Thomas? Oh come on, Parker; you know what I'm talking about. There are all kinds of weirdo people there. You must know that; you used to live there.

I have no idea what you are talking about, I said. Now he seems to be getting infuriated by me. He said, I'm talking about the kind of guys I don't want Harris being around. Child predators or queers, Parker. Who do you think I'm talking about?

I'm spooked by this guy and now I want him off the porch and far away from me. You need to ask Harris where he spends his weekends, not me.

He is a big guy with anger issues. To me, he is the type of person who stands right at the perimeter of life; a couple of steps too far and he might go right over the edge.

Much too close to me now, I see his face turning red with rage. Did you see them or not? You need to leave, Thomas, right now. He said, I know Harris hangs around here with you and your weirdo friends; what do you have to say for yourself?

The only thing I had to say to him then was get the hell off the porch.

• • • •

What did you expect, Parker? You never should have let those kids go out with us in the first place. Here we go again. Francis is blaming me because I have an asshole for a neighbor.

Guess what, Francis? I didn't let them do anything. They just showed up on the dance floor. Or were you too drunk to remember that? What are you blaming me for?

Because you went out a couple of times to The Miracle Mile with that shithead neighbor of yours; that's why. I went with him once, I said.

What did I tell you about the neighbors you would have here in the Province? You should have just kept to yourself and stayed away from that homophobe across the footpath.

I'm pissed off at him, but I'm not going to win this argument. It might have been nice if he even pretended to show some support or compassion after I told him about my unsettling encounter from the night before. Instead of trying to reassure me, he ambushes me instead.

Thanks for being so understanding, Francis. It's your fault, Parker. What did you think was going to happen?

I hung up the phone and then called Carleton to tell him about what happened last night. Wow, that's horrible, Parker. Do you think you should call the Constable's office to report Thomas? No, I'm just hoping things will blow over. I am going to try to keep my distance from Thomas if I can. He said then, what about Harris though? He doesn't seem to want to keep his distance from you.

We talked about my continuing frustrations with Francis then. Have you considered couples therapy, Parker? I know a therapist who specializes in these kinds of issues. His name is Dr. Hendrickson and I can give you his number. That's a good idea, but I don't know if Francis would agree to that. I ask him, how do you know about this therapist? You've never gone for counseling, have you? Not yet anyway, he answered. I met the guy at the Full Moon when we were at the Western Shore over the holiday when you stayed here working. Text me his phone number after we hang up, if you wouldn't mind.

• • • •

I settle myself on the sofa with a glass of Chardonnay, my mind drifting once more to thoughts of the Western Shore. Just a short drive from the gay beach sits the Great Western Marsh Preserve. Every time we venture to the Western Shore, I am drawn there, though I usually have to bribe Francis with something to get him to go with me.

I don't have a Driver's Permit, and though small scooters are everywhere in the resort towns, even they require that you have one. So if the other guys are busy tanning or shopping, the only way for me to get there is by pedaling the twelve kilometers on my beach cruiser. It has fat tires and only one speed, so the ride can be tiring, especially on a hot day. I don't care, I might even walk if I didn't have the cruiser.

The Preserve is tucked away between two small towns and is visited mostly by the locals. The tourists either don't know how beautiful it is or don't even know it exists. Let's be honest here; the guys at the beach are interested in checking out the beautiful bodies and can readily pass on the beautiful migratory seabirds.

The Preserve is several thousand hectares that begin with the salt marshes close to the shore and spread inland to the brackish waterways and wetlands that are fed twice daily compliments of the changing tides. These types of environments are rare ecologically speaking and are threatened even more due to climate change and the agricultural runoff from the nearby hog processing plants.

It is always so peaceful and quiet there and I rarely encounter many people; just the occasional bird watcher or photographer, with their powerful binoculars or their expensive camera equipment. I love the sand dunes with the scrub pines and the salt hay grass that help to protect the marsh from erosion.

It smells so amazing there, with the bayberry, wax myrtle, and holly trees providing shelter and habitat for the nearly endless variety of birds and waterfowl that migrate to the area from the extreme Northern District.

I don't usually mind being alone there, but I get depressed at times when I think about Francis and all the things he doesn't want to share with me. I don't care one bit that our interests differ, or that he has his own life to live outside of our tiny universe. But he is not even willing to make small sacrifices. It baffles me that he fails to recognize how much he has to gain in exchange for giving up something so insignificant.

He can be pretty selfish; everyone will agree to that. But isn't my happiness worth a few mosquito bites and a little mud on his Nikes?

So I sit quietly by myself and listen to the symphony being played by the variety of songbirds who don't seem at all bothered by me invading what really is their home turf. At low tide, I take my shoes off and wade in the shallow murky water, where I might encounter hundreds of Spotted Sandpipers waiting patiently for the unsuspecting sand crabs caught unaware as the tide recedes. What a stark contrast this is to The Miracle Mile, where only the occasional house sparrow or crested pigeon might be encountered.

By now, I am beginning to dislike most of what The Miracle Mile represents, a teeming and sweltering jungle of a make-believe city. The Miracle Mile has many of a real city's problems, but few of its advantages. Its amenities are all plastic and fake to me, the buildings' façades all created in the past couple of decades and never with any of the history or beauty that the original ones they attempt to copy usually have.

The chilly receptions and apathetic attitudes of nearly everyone I come across have caused me to want to stay away completely. Here is the problem though; it is nearly impossible to stay away from The Miracle Mile, since just about everything you need or want to do is contained within its guarded and gated entrances.

Francis has sworn the place off nearly entirely, and now I need to come up with new and creative ideas to entice him to go anywhere beyond Dunkin' Donuts.

C'mon, there is a new Continental restaurant that just opened; it got good reviews in the Province East Gazette. How about we try that tonight? I'd rather just cook at the cottage tonight if you don't mind. I asked him, then how about we go to the haberdashery tomorrow afternoon and see if their fall line is on sale? Maybe we can find new outfits for our next trip to the Western Shore.

We can't go tomorrow, Parker. The fútbol match is on TV tomorrow, and Winston asked if he and Tyler could watch it here since there is still no Satellite broadcast in City Centre. Oh sure, I said, that sounds like fun. We can all watch the match at the cottage and cook something special. Maybe chicken cordon bleu or some peach flambé.

Winston is still hanging around with Tyler, nearly two months after the cute guy quite literally fell for him. This surprises me because Winston is so good-looking and is constantly getting hit on wherever we go. He can have practically anyone he wants. What he wants, apparently, is Tyler.

It was fine with me if they came for the game. The Western District Falcons made it to the semi-finals this season and everyone is expecting an exciting game. If our Falcons can pull off one more win, they will advance to the Championship Match in three more weeks.

I knew Francis would kill for tickets to the finals if the Falcons do manage to advance on Sunday. I've come up with a plan too, although it's a bit of a devious one. Mr. Sanderson has season tickets and my idea is to enlist Crosby to use his charms to work Mr. Sanderson and sweet-talk him into a couple of seats at the Coliseum.

Tyler's youthfulness did not change the fact that we all like him. Thank God Francis finally quit complaining about him and asking me what the fuck I thought Winston was doing. I knew what he was doing and so did everyone else; he was screwing Tyler's brains out every chance he got.

Yeah, I know what you are thinking, he is too young, but it's none of my business. Who am I to judge? They are both adults and I'm staying out of it. When it comes to sex, other people's and not my own necessarily, I steer clear.

• • • •

By noon on Sunday, I had everything ready by the time the knock on the door came. Come in, welcome, how've you been Tyler? Winston gave me a quick fist bump and handed me the 12-pack of Imperial Stout ale they brought. I passed one bottle to each of them and put the others in the refrigerator.

Once everyone was settled and we tuned in to the sports channel on the Satellite, I brought out the mushrooms stuffed with crab meat and the pineapple-glazed duck I cooked earlier this morning. It's the first time I've done any serious cooking since that fateful romantic dinner that wasn't back when I was still living in my tiny apartment.

The peaches at the grocery store looked half-rotted, so I skipped the flambé. Just as well; now I don't have to worry about setting the cottage on fire. Don't forget the Cheese Whiz, Parker. Okay, I think I have everything now.

The pre-game show was on and some loud-mouth commentator with a dearth of objectivity kept spouting off some shit about how the Falcons had little chance of advancing to The Championship Match. He kept talking about the tangibles, or maybe it was the intangibles; I'm not sure which. Francis is a big fútbol fan and keeps yelling at the announcer as if he is listening, or could give a crap about what we think.

Tyler and Winston are on the sofa holding hands, while Francis and I crowd together on the big wingback chair my parents gave me for a house-warming gift months earlier. It feels so comfortable sitting close to him and relaxing together with our friends. I wish we had more times like these.

Tyler waits nervously for the game to start. Our best forward is on his fantasy fútbol team, and if he scores today, Tyler will finish the season in first place. The top prize of £150 would pay for the four of us to go out to the Pizza Palace in The Miracle Mile next weekend. That would entice Francis to suspend his moratorium, and for me to satisfy my craving for pizza, since the only pizza you can find in Province East is in the frozen foods section of the supermarket.

Suddenly, there is a knock on the door. Before I can even get over there to see who it is, Tyler has worked his way ahead of me to answer it. Parker, I hope you don't mind that I invited Harris to watch the game with us.

Francis and I exchanged eyebrow-raising glances, both of us waiting for the other one to answer his question, probably with another question, something like, *you did what*?

It's cool, come on in Harris; how's your mom been? He sat on the sofa next to Tyler, while I glanced nervously through the living room curtains and saw Thomas' car in their carport. Harris must have noticed my uneasiness and said, Thomas went with Tyler's father to watch the match in the video lounge at the Club in The Miracle Mile. They had to get tickets online in advance; the lounge only holds about 200 people and sold out fast.

That is no small relief. I feel a whole lot better not having to stress over the prospect of that prick showing up to harass me again, especially with Harris sitting right there next to Tyler and Winston cuddling on my sofa and drinking beer with the queer neighbor and his weirdo friends. I could just about hear him. *Hey buddy, what the hell is going on here?*

We drank all of Winston's Imperial Stout and a few more by the time the game was over, which our underdog Falcons won despite all of the supposedly expert opinions. They don't know what they are talking about anyway, but Tyler sure does. He is £150 richer than he was just a few hours ago.

· · · ·

I've come down now from the combined adrenaline rush of alcohol and the thrill of the match. So has Francis it seems. You need to tell

Harris he can't just drop in on us. What if his father knew he was here? You're right, I said, but I feel bad for him.

This can't possibly end well, Parker. You need to fix this before something awful happens. You shouldn't have kept plying him with alcohol either.

Why are you making it sound like I did something wrong? Winston's boyfriend invited him here, not me. I don't care, Parker; he shouldn't be here drinking with us practically right under Thomas' nose. Can't you see that?

Think back to when you were his age, Francis. How did your father treat you? Was coming out so easy when you were nineteen? Try to relate to someone other than yourself for a change. Imagine how scary it must be for him having to face his father on top of his own insecurities. Christ, let him enjoy a fútbol game and a couple of beers with the guys. Give the kid a break and help reinforce what he already knows.

What does he know, Parker? They're modern kids, I said; they never miss a beat. Didn't you see how at ease they were at the Club? He and Tyler don't live in a locked closet. He knows there is nothing wrong with him; he's just afraid.

Francis said, I guess you are right; he's got to be afraid of that lunatic father of his. That's for sure, and I can't imagine how we can help with that one. Yeah, it will take more than a Falcons win and some imported ale to fix that problem.

VIII

A not-so-minor emergency greeted me the very next day. But first I needed to sign in at the Timekeeper's desk. So, Parker; how did your little shindig go yesterday afternoon? I trust that you enjoyed watching the game on the Satellite in the Province with your friends. Yes, sir, we had a fun time. Good, good; and I'm sure all that cooking you did was much easier in that nice kitchen you have in your new place. Which did you settle on, the cordon bleu or the glazed duck?

I gave him a puzzled look. Who on earth could have told him all of this? He knew about the move out of City Centre, but I never told him a thing about the cottage or the kitchen. Chicken or duck; what the hell?

He just smiled back; it's all good, Parker. Sign in here if you would please. Before I could ask how he knew so much about my weekend, he signaled toward where the other Processors were getting settled. I'm afraid Ms. Millerton is going to be in a bit of a dither today, Parker. You better hurry.

She was seated at her temporary workstation next to the platform where Carleton was already busy doing nothing. Mr. Parker, may I see you, please? Yes, Ms. Millerton. Right now, Mr. Parker.

This is not what you would consider to be the ideal way to start a new week. I was still hungover from all the beer we drank on Sunday, and had not even had the chance for a quick stop at the coffee dispenser before heading over to her desk. Not here, Mr. Parker; please come with me to the Conference Center immediately.

This can't be good. Why would we have to walk all the way there, especially since Ms. Millerton is still on crutches? As we slowly made our way to the more private office space, all sorts of awful images flooded my still-impaired brain matter. Did I miss another deadline? Was she going to put something else in my Permanent Record? Had

Mr. Sanderson complained about me again? I began to sweat from nervous anxiety and caffeine deprivation.

We have an unusual situation that will require your assistance, Mr. Parker. Okay, that didn't sound too terrible. She continued; it seems as if one of the Clerical Assistants has somehow been remiss over the past weeks and did not adequately or properly distribute the incoming invoices and receipts in a timely fashion. This, as you may know, is a rather serious breach of our department protocols.

I see; how bad is it? Very bad, Mr. Parker. Please listen carefully without interruption so that I may articulate for your benefit exactly how bad, and clarify for you how important it is that this conversation be kept completely confidential. I have initiated the appropriate disciplinary action with respect to the person responsible for this oversight. However, I must emphasize again how critical it is that the other Processors and Clerical Assistants do not become aware of this situation under any circumstance. Is that clear? Yes, I understand completely. You need to appreciate what I am going to tell you, and then zip your mouth tightly shut and act as if nothing is wrong. Can I be assured that you will do so?

Wow, someone must have really screwed up this time. She never confided in me on something quite like this before. If she trusted me this much, how far off could my promotion to Assistant Secretary be?

Of course, Ms. Millerton; my lips are already sealed. Good, now here is the situation. There are more than 2,000 invoices and receipts in my desk that have not been reviewed or stamped. That many, really? Mr. Parker, allow me to finish, and don't interrupt me, please. She said then, many of them have been in our department for more than thirty days; do you understand what that means?

There was a fairly long and unusual silence just then. Well, do you? I'm sorry, Ms. Millerton, but I thought you were speaking rhetorically and I didn't realize you were expecting a response from me. No, to be honest, I don't know what that means. She said, what it means is this; should Mr. Sanderson become aware of our predicament, my job, and possibly others, let's just say for the sake of argument, a Senior Processor's job as well, could be in serious jeopardy.

I see. So what we have to do then, if I understand you correctly, is to make sure that Mr. Sanderson does not find out about it. You did not hear me say that, did you, Mr. Parker? No, I said, I did not. Good, let's keep it that way, shall we?

How ridiculous is all of this? There are twelve Processors, and if we all pitch in for an afternoon or two, we could get a couple of thousand invoices and receipts knocked out without much trouble. But since nobody else can know about it, that leaves just the two of us to do the work. Since one of us has a broken leg, two minus one equals...me.

I gave Ms. Millerton my word that I wouldn't say anything, so now I have to keep this a big secret, like it's the nuclear codes or some shit like that. Who am I going to tell, the Timekeeper? He knows everything already. I bet if I tell Crosby and Carleton, we'd have a good laugh about it over lunch. If I were to let them in on this, I can already imagine the scene; the three of us huddled over our lunches, eyes wide with shock and disbelief before bursting into fits of laughter.

Crosby caught up with me later that afternoon. Hey Parker, how was the weekend? Did you watch the fútbol match on the Satellite? Sure we did, wasn't it great? Can you come with Carleton and me to dinner tomorrow after work? Sorry, Crosby, I'm going to have to pass on going out this week. He asked, how come you can't go with us? I'm sorry, but my lips are sealed.

We laughed and joked for a while while Crosby filled me in on his weekend with Carleton. Ms. Millerton looked the other way and pretended not to notice that we were goofing around. It's the least she could do after I agreed to work overtime each night and again over the weekend in order to get all the delinquent filing straightened out.

I don't care much about having to work on the weekend. I can use the overtime pay, and the Championship Match is still two more Sundays away. Francis and I invited everyone over to watch the game at the cottage since Crosby's flirting with Mr. Sanderson has so far not produced any tickets.

We can go to dinner next week instead, Crosby, and don't forget the Championship Match at my place. Sounds great; I can't wait! I'll make an apple cake to bring if that's okay.

• • • •

By the time I reported for work the following Monday, all 2,000 overdue invoices and receipts had been logged, stamped, and filed exactly where they should have been a month earlier. The whole thing was beyond stupid, but I was glad for Ms. Millerton's sake that she didn't get into any trouble with Mr. Sanderson, who as far as I knew was left unaware of any breaches in department protocols. And today she walked around the office for the first time without the cast, which meant that we all had to say goodbye to Carleton, who could now go back to fixing broken computers upstairs where he belonged.

I never found out which of the six Clerical Assistants caused the screw-up, but it didn't matter to me. I think it might have been Mandy though. She has a big crush on Carleton and baked a couple of dozen cupcakes for the little going-away party she and her friends organized for his last day. Anthony ate most of them, and they were all gone by the time I made it over to the conference room to get a glass of lemonade.

Not only are the cupcakes gone, but Carleton is as well, along with the temporary desk Ms. Millerton no longer needs. She is back sitting at her regular desk and her perch from the platform. Finally, everything is back to normal.

Mr. Parker, may I see you for a moment? Well, maybe not quite normal.

Yes, Ms. Millerton; I hope everything turned out okay with Mr. Sanderson. She spoke in a very low tone of voice, but since the desk next to the platform was gone, I don't think anyone could hear us.

Yes, and that is what I wanted to talk to you about. As you may know, all overtime pay has to be approved by Mr. Sanderson. In anticipation of that problem, and in order to ensure that the strategy we previously agreed to would proceed without serious consequences, I took the liberty of telling him that you volunteered to work on the Special Projects that are ongoing in our office. That way, the fifteen hours of overtime to which you are entitled would not arouse any particular suspicion.

I asked her, what Special Projects? She said, there aren't any, but Mr. Sanderson thinks there are. Why? Mr. Parker, I did not call you up here to discuss the intricate workings of our department, but rather to thank you for keeping your end of the bargain. Am I correct in my belief that you did not mention our little secret to anyone? Of course, I didn't, Ms. Millerton.

To be honest, I did tell Francis about the entire episode when I explained that I had to work over the weekend and could not hang out with him.

How can you work for that dim-witted woman, Parker? She put your job in jeopardy because of her incompetence and expected you to lie and cover it up. No, she didn't ask me to lie, just not to tell anyone the truth. Listen to yourself, he said; what the hell is the difference? You can be so naïve sometimes.

Why don't you look for a real job that doesn't require you to cover for a boss who is so inept she can't even manage to go down three steps without breaking her leg? Don't say anything to Crosby about this, okay Francis? I promised Ms. Millerton that I wouldn't tell anyone.

He can criticize my boss and my job all he wants. All I know is that Ms. Millerton and Mr. Sanderson were impressed enough to give me an extra two days off with pay. So next week, I get a four-day holiday weekend in appreciation for either not saying anything in Ms. Millerton's case, or for being proactive and volunteering to work on Special Projects in Mr. Sanderson's case.

Okay, I admit that I am naïve at times, but who got hurt by keeping our little secret from Mr. Sanderson? The invoices and receipts were just sitting there waiting to be filed; who gives a shit? It's not like someone broke their leg because of it. The entire episode was almost pathetic enough to make me laugh.

Why do you keep smiling, Parker? Nothing Francis; nothing at all. I think he is jealous because I'm getting fifteen hours of overtime in my next paycheck, and a long four-day weekend to look forward to while he has to work.

Part III – The Western Shore

No testimony is sufficient to establish a miracle, unless the testimony be of such a kind, that its falsehood would be more miraculous than the fact which it endeavors to establish.

-David Hume

IX

What are you going to do with your four days off? I haven't decided yet, Carleton; what do you think? I know what I would do, I'd get away from here and head straight for the Western Shore. It's going to be a great weekend and packed with hot guys on the beach too.

I can't go without Frances and he has to work. Really Parker? He had no problem going without you when you had to work. I said, how do you expect me to get there, hitchhike? Where have you been, Parker? There are buses that run every day from The Miracle Mile transit terminal; even I know that. They will let you stash your beach cruiser in the storage compartment where they throw all the suitcases, and the bus will drop you off right in town near the boardwalk.

Maybe I can go. I'll have some extra money from my overtime pay to help offset the hotel costs. And I'd love to visit the Great Western March Preserve again; Francis refused to go with me the last time.

I'm not sure about this, Carleton. I don't see Francis jumping at the idea of me going alone. Then he said, you *are* going, or else. Else what? I'll tell Ms. Millerton I know the reason she made you work overtime.

What the hell are you talking about, Carleton? She had me working on some Special Projects. Come on, Special Projects my ass. I know you spent your weekend filing delinquent invoices. Crosby told me all about it. What? How did he find out? He wouldn't tell me; he said his lips were sealed. Give me a break, I said. The only time Crosby's lips are sealed is when he seals them around your dick.

. . . .

He was not one bit pleased to hear that I would be on a holiday to the Western Shore, sans Francis. Too bad, I need to get away. You'd do the same thing if you were me. Alright fine, go alone, but bring me some salt water taffy back with you.

I kissed him goodbye and hopped onto the bus, the cruiser safely stored below. I can't believe I managed three nights at the Sandcastle Shore Inn, my favorite bed and breakfast anywhere. Every place I called was already sold out. Carleton knows the owner of the Sandcastle and got me in somehow. It's probably because Carleton slept with the guy a couple of times last summer, and he was willing to do a favor for an old trick. Or maybe he sweet-talked him and misled the guy into thinking that their little fling might pick up where it left off the next time Carleton took a vacation. Not much chance of that, sorry.

The first day was sunny and beautiful, so I rented a beach chair and umbrella, spending much of the afternoon sipping sea breezes and swimming at the gay beach. What a great idea this is turning out to be. I needed a break from my unscrupulous bosses and their stupid procedures. I watched as a group of cute boys were running in every direction, laughing and making themselves look silly by attempting to play a game that vaguely resembled volleyball.

Not a cloud could be seen anywhere, and the water glistened from the sun and the white-capped surf. There were plenty of kayaks out today, and I saw a few people kitesurfing as well. I was amazed by how fast they moved while catching the waves and performing impressive jumps and tricks.

Francis and I always wanted a kayak, but there was never anywhere to store one in the city. After I moved, we picked up a used tandem one that we keep in the carport. I would love to paddle it now, but it is much too heavy to manage by myself, and I can only imagine the look on the bus driver's face if I asked him to cram it in with the rest of the baggage.

So my only mode of transportation either by land or sea is the beach cruiser. Tomorrow I am going to ride to the Great Western Marsh Preserve with my binoculars and find out what other species might also be on their holidays this time of year.

It's a long ride on a heavy bike, but that's okay. The roads are flat and the landscape is breathtaking. I take a large water bottle along and stop a few times to rest along the way. At one of the rest areas, there is a narrow creek that runs close to the bike path, with Shoal Grass and Mangroves surrounding it. There, I spotted a large Western Reef Egret, a relatively rare occurrence in this part of the country. They are common in the Southern District which has a warmer and more tropical climate.

It stood still and seemed to be staring at me, and didn't fly away for a minute or more, so I grabbed the binoculars and got a good look at the remarkable bird. It had solid grey plumage and a thick orange beak. But now it was bored with me I guess, or maybe there was nothing around to be had for lunch, so it took off. I just watched in awe as it spread its huge wingspan and headed away toward the shore.

The bike path terminates abruptly adjacent to a large open marsh area. There are a couple of benches here, so I decide to sit down and have the sandwich I brought along. I take out the mobile to call Francis, but there is no signal way out here.

So I stared through the binoculars, hoping to spot a beautiful Blue Heron through the glasses, but what I spotted instead was a beautiful guy around my age walking down the path in my direction. He stopped nearby, looking through a large pair of what I was pretty sure were Skymaster astronomy binoculars. What was he looking to see, migrating snow geese or one of Saturn's moons?

Mind if I share a bench with you? I tried to answer, but nothing but air came out. Yes, this guy could take your breath away alright. I'm confident in just about any social situation and comfortable with myself normally. Uh, sure, sit down, umm, what's ah, I mean hi. Way to make a good first impression there, Parker.

His name is Hunter and he's staying, if you can believe it, at the Sandcastle Shore Inn. I should ask to borrow those field glasses to see if my lucky stars are visible through them. After taking a few sips of water to wash down the portion of my sandwich that somehow attached itself to the inside of my throat, I regain my equilibrium and command of the language to some extent.

He sure knew a lot about birds. He produced a pocket-size field guidebook and pointed to pictures of a few of the species native to the region and likely to be seen in the Preserve. Have you spotted anything interesting so far, Hunter?

Not until just now, he replied, smiling at me and showing off his perfect pearl-white teeth. How should I respond to that? I better think quick, something witty, anything but silence. Want half of my peanut butter sandwich?

We sit close together on the bench looking through our binoculars. Our shoulders rub slightly against each other as we turn to change our viewing angle. It's weird, he seems so familiar, It's like a curious sort of déjà vu or something. He said no; he was sure he would not have forgotten such a handsome guy. I guess not, I had to agree.

Still, there is something about him, something almost recognizable but not quite. I look at him again, more closely. I know I've seen this guy somewhere before. In a prior lifetime maybe? Sitting this close, I could feel his warmth and perceive a scent like a mix of Clover Currant and Old Spice. Why is that smell so unmistakable to me?

Finally, he said he had to leave. He was meeting his friends later at the Full Moon bar for happy hour. Would you like to have dinner with me tonight, Parker?

I hesitated for just a moment, thinking, where was this heading? I was instantly attracted to Hunter and my mind got stuck a bit thinking of the possible consequences here. If you are busy, Parker; we can do it another time.

No, sure, I said; dinner sounds nice. Thanks for asking me. Great, I'll see if I can get reservations at The Scorpion. Do you like sushi?

Despite my obvious trepidations, I agreed to meet Hunter at 6:00 that evening for drinks. I knew that what might happen afterward could put a serious dent, or even a fatal fracture in my seven-year tenure with Francis. With my discrepant thoughts and nagging anxiety shoved to the side for the moment at least, I pedal the long ride back to town to get ready.

• • • •

The Full Moon is the most popular happy-hour bar at the gay beach. It took me so long to decide what to wear that I was half an hour late by the time I finished trying on every piece and every combination of clothing that I had brought with me.

The crowd was shoulder to shoulder with very tanned and very nice-looking men and women. It was so packed you could barely move, and only then by slowly squeezing through the crowd, being careful not to step on anyone or bump them hard enough to spill whatever they were drinking.

A lot of the gay bars are just that, and many tend to segregate the men and women. Some of that is by mutual preference probably, since there are plenty of bars that cater more or less exclusively to lesbians or straight people. In some cases, the separation is more blatant, and I am put off by the attitude of either the bar's management or its clientele which might suggest that anyone in particular did not belong.

I have a particular distaste for when older gay guys are greeted with less than hospitable looks when they frequent some of the places where the younger and more beautiful like to hang out. The comments are sometimes loud enough to be overheard and are offensive to me. *What's that old troll think he's doing? He better not try to touch me.*

I remember Francis' quick comeback when he heard that one. *I don't think you need to worry about that unless you've got some extra-strength RID handy and an appointment with your dermatologist.*

No such age or gender issues are evident tonight. Everyone is here after sunning at the beach and taking advantage of the dwindling daylight to show off their new tans and their new tank tops. I moved through the crowd toward the bar at a snail's pace, nudging people and smiling, excuse me, excuse me, please. It took me several minutes just to maneuver myself the fifteen meters or so from the entrance, to where the bartender skillfully handled the cocktail shaker with just the right amount of finesse to chill and mix the ingredients into a perfectly smooth Manhattan.

I looked around anxiously for Hunter but had no idea where to find him. The handsome bartender appeared with a smile and the double Grey Goose and tonic I desperately needed by now to calm my nerves.

The drink was strong and I began to relax considerably after just a few sips. I scanned the crowd once more; would I know anybody here? Relax, Parker; just go with it and enjoy yourself. I kept repeating things like that over and over to myself.

People were crammed all around me and visibly having a lot of fun, the drinks and the laughs flowing freely from every direction. I'm glad I ordered a clear beverage; if a bit splashed out from an inadvertent elbow, it wouldn't create undue stress hopefully to the person next to me, or make an awful pinkish stain on the white Polo shirt I finally decided on that it might have if I had gone with the cranberry and vodka that I really wanted. I hate when some idiot next to me is twirling around half-tanked with a Sea Breeze instead of a Pinot Grigio, or better yet, staying home.

Hey, handsome! I turn around and there is Hunter, looking even better than I remember from this afternoon, having changed into a pair of red shorts and a tight pale blue T-shirt. His wavy brown hair appears now with blondish streaks in this lighting, maybe bleached a bit from several hours at the Preserve. Wow. He is about the hottest-looking guy in the entire place, and trust me, he has a lot of competition for that accolade.

That sudden flash of familiarity hits me again, but I still can't pinpoint its origin. I've never had an experience quite like this before and it unsettles me somewhat. I know this guy, I'm sure. But from where?

Hi, Hunter, are your friends here yet? What can I get you to drink? I'm thankful that I have recovered my verbal acuity in his presence at least. Get me a rum and coke; no, on second thought better make that a Tanqueray and tonic, he said as he handed me a sawbuck. I pushed his hand away; this is on me.

His two friends have managed to find us, and now we are all cracking up and having too much fun. I'm pretty tipsy by this time and I am not alone in that regard. Hunter has his arm around me, laughing at something I said.

Want to have some white wine? Sure, thanks, Parker. The same bartender is right on it and I hand one of the long-stemmed glasses to Hunter. His friends have left to meet some others for dinner, so it's just the two of us now. He kissed me on the cheek and smiled some more; you are so damn cute, Parker. Shit, what am I going to do now?

What I'm going to do now, I decide, is drink my wine and try not to feel guilty about having this sexy guy halfway wrapped around me. Later, we share a sashimi platter and a bottle of sake, blushing and smiling across the table. Carleton's suggestion for me to get away by myself was a good one, and every time I start to wonder what Francis might be up to, I look into Hunter's amazing brown eyes and convince myself that he is managing just fine without me in City Centre.

• • • •

I wind up spending the next two days and nights savoring the beauty of the Western Shore and the beauty of this guy named Hunter. I know I'm going to feel conflicted by this after our little fling is done and I am back at home. Too late now.

He was sharing a small room with his two friends at the Sandcastle, so he relocated in the evenings to mine. His friends were partnered, and I'm sure they appreciated the unexpected privacy I agreed to provide. They were very nice to me and I decided to use some of the small bonus money I received from Ms. Millerton to treat the four of us to dinner on our last night.

I slept peacefully cuddled with Hunter in the cozy room that Carleton had miraculously arranged.

What should I confess to him when I get back? He and I share everything, but our friendship has never ventured to a place like this. Before I left for the beach, I called the therapist that Carleton referred me to, Dr. Hendrickson. We hadn't met the guy yet, but at least Francis reluctantly agreed to give couples therapy a try. Would the subject of my infidelity come up during our sessions?

We had one more chance to visit the Preserve on our last morning before going home. How about if I take you someplace magical, Parker? That aroused my curiosity and I said yes without even asking what the hell he was talking about. We can leave by 8:00 in the morning and get there at low tide. Wear old shorts and sneakers; we might get wet, but it's worth it.

We get up early for breakfast, then hop in Hunter's Citroen and go north on the Seashore Highway, which runs along the eastern edge of the Preserve. Are you up for a little hiking, Parker? We can park within a couple of kilometers of where I want to take you, but the only way in from there is on foot. Let me guess, Hunter; we are going to be the only ones there; am I right? Probably, he said.

Should I be scared of being alone with you in the wilderness with nobody around to rescue me? No, you will love this place, Parker; it's mysterious, fantastic, and weird all at the same time. Wow, that's the way Carleton used to describe one of his former boyfriends.

The hike was a bit rugged and muddy in spots, but very beautiful. We passed through a forest of sweetgums, tulip poplars, and dwarf cypress trees. Along the way, we saw huge colorful dragonflies and even a spotted bog turtle. We bent down to get a close look at him, and he didn't seem to mind the attention in the least.

He's endangered Parker; we may never see one like him again. You really know a lot about these wetlands, don't you? Yeah, I spent a lot of time here years ago. After high school, my parents sent me away to live with an aunt and uncle in the Southern District, and when I decided to return after finishing college, I took a job not far from here.

We were walking again and he took my hand. Watch out for poison sumac, he said; it can mess up your entire holiday.

All at once it seemed, the forest came to an abrupt end and there was a large open salt marsh right in front of us. In the middle of the water, there was what looked like a small land mass, sort of like an island, covered mainly by what looked like moss. Is that a bog, Hunter? Technically, it is known as a fen, but you have the right idea. Come on, the water is shallow.

We waded slowly beyond the mud flats for a hundred meters or so to the edge of the little island. This formation is very rare, he said; it is one of only about half a dozen on the entire continent. It is actually floating for the most part, but with enough mature shrubs and small trees with deep enough roots to extend to the bottom of the marsh and anchor it in place. A strong typhoon could lift it up and wash it completely into the sea. Give me your hand, Parker; I'll help you up.

It was like being on a huge raft, except this one was mostly covered by dwarf trees, grasses, and small shrubs. As we walked, the spongy damp ground gave under our weight. Hunter ran to the middle where it seemed to sag more, and he started jumping up and down and laughing, like a devilish child on a trampoline. Try it, Parker; it's fun. I did, it was.

It did feel almost magical to me. It seemed that if we had a large enough oar, we might be able to paddle ourselves all the way through the marsh and right out to the open sea. I have been to the Western Shore so many times but never imagined that such a place could exist here.

We walk further to where the foliage becomes very dense, the entire area very dark and nearly silent, except for the sounds of the Warblers and the Red Knots. It is eerie but wonderful; almost supernatural. What exactly is this place, Hunter? He said, it is a place where the soul, the body, and the earth all join together. You mean like heaven? Sort of, except there are lots of mosquitoes and you get to talk about it when you get back home.

• • • •

I might have a lot to talk about when I get back home, but mostly I'm going to keep my mouth shut. Francis was waiting at The Miracle Mile transit station when the bus pulled in. Tell me what you did at the Western Shore; you look so tan!

I didn't go there alone to hook up with someone or to cheat on Francis. I am not a cheater. Up until now, I had never allowed anyone to encroach on our relationship in that way, but I was pretty sure that he had. This is more than a gut feeling; there is probably evidence to support it if I look around. But I never looked. I never wanted to confirm my suspicion or validate my conviction that all guys cheat.

That's not why I wound up in bed for two nights with Hunter. I did because he was amazing and incredibly sexy, not to prove anything or get even with Francis for something he may have done. A couple of years back, I never would have considered being with another guy. I had sworn them off totally and remained committed to just him, but I guess I can no longer stand on that moral ground.

Relationships evolve; they advance or retreat, they are constant or fluid. And ours had sprung a leak. Rather than trying to plug it for the umpteenth time, I just let it flow at the Western Shore. I'm conflicted at times and feel shadows of guilt creeping in, but I'm not going to sit here and tell you I am sorry.

I'm not a liar either. I spent most of my time at the Preserve, I tell him. It was so beautiful; I guess that's where I got the tan. I wish you could have seen it with me. That part is the truth, sort of.

I don't always tell the truth, but that doesn't necessarily mean I'm lying. I didn't tell Hunter that I was in a long-term relationship, but would have if he asked.

Here is the salt water taffy you wanted, Francis. Thanks, Parker; you know I missed you, right? He helped me with my backpack and the cruiser while we walked the ten minutes back home to Province East.

There are a lot of things I am not very good at. But I am good at keeping a secret, and that's what I'm going to do. I trust Carleton more than anyone alive, but I figure he doesn't need to know about my little beach flirtation. I was about to tell him, but then I remembered how the furtive overtime invoice episode nearly became public knowledge and thought better of it. Next thing you know, the Timekeeper will be asking me about it.

He and Crosby cornered me immediately at work when I got back. Tell us already would you; were the guys awesome? About average, I said. I did see an endangered spotted turtle though. The two of them gave me puzzling looks, wondering probably what drug I was on.

I don't do drugs, as long as you narrow the definition to exclude alcohol. I don't look down on people who use them for recreational purposes. I just don't like the way they make me feel. I tried a Quaalude once and felt like I was walking upside down, like a bug on the ceiling.

I'd bet anything that creepy neighbor of mine keeps a stash of something handy. I notice him peeking through the front-room curtains a few times while I am sitting on the porch minding my own business and planning the menu for our Championship Match party coming up on Sunday. What does he want from me?

I want you and your friends to stay away from Harris, do you understand? He worked up the nerve to show his ugly face finally, rather than hide it behind the curtains where I wish it stayed.

I asked you to stay off my property, Thomas. I'm not on your property; I'm on the footpath which doesn't belong to you. I don't want my son being influenced by you. I know what kind of people you are; you are all predators. And I know you took him to one of your faggot clubs in City Centre. If you do it again, you are going to pay. Are you threatening me? I will make you sorry, Parker. And not just me; I have friends who hate your kind too. I've warned you before, this is the last time.

I was shaking nearly uncontrollably when I went back into the cottage. I was about to call Francis to see if he could come over, or at least help talk me through this. Wait, Parker; calm down first. Francis won't know what to do either. He is not very helpful in these situations; he'll say, I told you not to move there.

I need to relax; my heart is still racing. I pour a shot of gin into a highball glass and squeeze some lime juice in. I'm a little calmer now, so I dial Carleton's mobile instead. Crosby picks up.

Hi Parker, is everything alright? He's not here; he went to visit his sister and forgot to take his phone with him. I don't expect him back until late this evening. Do you want me to leave him a message? That's alright, Crosby; I can just talk to him tomorrow.

• • • •

I need to file a complaint against my neighbor. Yes, I can hold. I decided to call the Constable's office instead of calling Francis. Sir, is your neighbor there now? No, I'm alone. Are you in imminent danger or in need of medical assistance? If not, you will need to come to the Constable's office to file a complaint. We are unable to send someone out unless you are in a situation that constitutes an immediate threat, which would appear from your description that you are not in.

The nearest office is located in the municipal complex in the center of The Miracle Mile. I wanted to get something on record as soon as possible, so I decided to ride the beach cruiser rather than walk. I was stopped by the Security Officer at the Province East Gate.

May I ask the purpose of your visit today? Yes, sir, I need to file a report with the Constable's office and was told to appear in person. And might that be a criminal or civil complaint? Criminal, I said.

Well then, I need to stamp the back of your Residency Permit. I also need to inform you that bicycles cannot be ridden in the Miracle Mile. Technically, it is within my authority to not allow you to even bring one in, but I see that you are in some distress. I am not supposed to consider such issues, but it seems obvious to me that you are, which is consistent with what you just said concerning the need for you to appear regarding some criminal matter, the subject of which I am not supposed to inquire about either. I will allow you to take it with you this one time only, and remind you not to ride it once inside the gate. There is a hefty fine for riding a bicycle in The Miracle Mile, and it would almost certainly be confiscated as well.

Phew, why the hell didn't I just walk?

When I arrived at the Constable's office, I was given a form to fill out as usual. I sat and waited a few minutes until they motioned over to me. Come this way, Mr. Parker; the Constable will see you now.

I understand from your complaint that you are alleging first that your neighbor Mr. Tomas harassed you, then later threatened you on two separate occasions on the dates in question.

Yes, sir, he has been giving me trouble for some time, and he threatened me today. How specifically did he threaten you, if I may ask? He said if I didn't stay away from his son he and his friends would make me pay. He asked me then, pay for what, exactly? He is accusing me of corrupting his son, which is ridiculous. He called my friends and me predators and he made several homophobic slurs.

I see, but did he say how you would have to pay specifically? No, he didn't. Did he threaten you with a weapon then? If so, that might constitute egregious assault. No sir, I didn't see a weapon. Did he physically assault you; did he touch or strike you in any way? No, it was just verbal.

I'm afraid, Mr. Parker, that we cannot charge Mr. Thomas with assault merely because he said you would have to pay. Pay could mean almost anything, ranging anywhere from paying with your life, obviously quite serious, to paying with hard feelings, clearly much less so. If he has not physically threatened you in some way, even a simple misdemeanor assault charge would not hold up.

I said then, he is a dangerous guy and I think he intends to harm me at some point. Did you check to see if he has a criminal history? I'm sorry, Mr. Parker, but I am not at liberty to disclose such confidential information. But let me ask you this; has Mr. Thomas been trespassing? We take trespassing very seriously, and if there were evidence of such, we might be able to issue a citation for either simple or egregious trespass, first and second-degree misdemeanors respectively.

Yes, sir, I'm nearly certain he has been sneaking around and looking in the windows. Twice now I have walked by the bedroom window at night and saw someone right beneath it. When I went outside, he was gone.

So you don't know for sure that it was Mr. Thomas? Not for sure, no. So, what you are telling me then is that it could have been a prowler, or maybe even someone from Province South? It looked like Thomas, I said. If you can't positively identify him, I'm afraid our hands are tied. I said, are you telling me you won't do anything? We will if he physically assaults you, or if he is caught trespassing. Aside from that, our hands are tied.

X

Do you want to stay with me in the city, at least until things calm down? No, I think I will be okay, Francis. I'm not going to let him force me out of my own home. He said, then maybe I should come over and stay at your place for a while. Really, would you do that for me? Of course I would, he said, it's the least I can do. I don't want that prick coming over again threatening you. You shouldn't be afraid to fall asleep at night with him right under your window again. I can stay for a week or two and see how things go.

I'll take the train with you in the morning, and we can ride back together in the afternoon, at least when I am not working late. We can even go out to dinner at that new Cosmopolitan restaurant you've been wanting to check out. It's Continental, Francis. We can go there too, just remember to bring my Visitors Permit so I can get past the guard.

People ask me why I stay with him. Who can say why? We're just a pair sort of glued together, I guess. Seven years is a long time to be with someone; you don't break up just like that because you don't share all the same interests, or if you argue sometimes. He tells me he loves me and misses me when we're apart. It may take some time, but we are going to figure things out together.

Since everyone will be coming over on Sunday for the fútbol match, Frances said he will pack up some personal items and enough clothes to last for at least a week and drive over on Sunday morning in Winston's car. Then he can just camp out at the cottage for a while.

First, they have to pick up Carleton and Crosby in City Centre before driving to the Province and the cottage in the Miracle Estates East subdivision. Tyler took the bus from Province North and arrived early to help me get everything set up.

I was seriously in need of some distraction from all of the negative shit that had gone on, so being in the kitchen all morning cooking felt almost therapeutic. Now I had it more or less together after Tyler helped me clean up the mess I made on the stove and countertops. We set the table and waited for everyone to arrive.

This will be a great party, he said. Thanks, Tyler; I hope everyone likes what we made. The menu included seared scallops, chicken tartar, seaweed and mango salad, and of course, Crosby's apple cake. Shit, I forgot to buy the cheese puffs; Francis likes the spicy ones.

Francis isn't going to cook anything, thank God. He's dangerous in the kitchen, but he and Winston brought a full case of Samuel Smith Oatmeal Stout, which they claim is the best ale anywhere on the entire continent. Except possibly Imperial Stout, of course.

Winston nearly had an orgasm when the Falcons scored first before the end of the first half. Our team never looked back after that and managed the game three to one. Once it was over and our euphoria had diminished some, we all hung out drinking more beer and savoring both the Championship victory and Crosby's apple cake. For the moment at least, we were content to just relax in the comforting glow of friendship and the smooth balanced ale. I cuddled with Francis in the wing-back chair, grateful that he wouldn't have to leave when it was time for the others to go home.

A sudden loud pounding on the door startles me out of my peaceful inebriation. Harris is inside with us now. What's wrong, Harris? It's Thomas; he is drunk again and I'm afraid to stay there. Where is your mother, I asked; is she alright? Yes, she took my brother to my uncle's house in Province West. He was agitated clearly and so visibly shaken that I wasn't quite sure what to make of it at first. Francis grabbed a glass off the dining room table and poured a shot of gin before squeezing in a couple of limes wedges. Here, I said; drink some of this and try to calm down. You're safe here with us.

He sat on the rug dismayed, with Tyler trying to console him, while I tried sobering up enough to figure out what to do. My present state of mind was not exactly conducive to crisis management. It was only a matter of time for Thomas to be on the porch again with his angry threats, or God help us, some of his friends.

All the wrong elements were converging now, brewing up something horrific like a Nebraska tornado. Rednecks, alcohol, and queers do not mix well, a volatile and potentially explosive combination.

Harris, what happened to your face? Nothing, Tyler, I just, it's nothing, forget about it. I take a closer look and see a slightly swollen area under his right eye and a bruise that was starting to form. He hit you, didn't he? You need to tell us what happened.

He began, I met this guy about three weeks ago from Province South. We've been sending a lot of emails and text messages. I'm not sure, but I think Thomas must have been poking around on my computer and read them. I keep trying to talk about it and reason with him, but he won't listen. He went ballistic on me yesterday and threatened to throw me out of the house if I saw Brady again.

I saw you getting out of Winston's car earlier and wanted to come over here to watch the match and tell you how great he is and everything. I think he really likes me. Now, I can't even call or text him because Father canceled the mobile contract. The only place we can meet is in The Miracle Mile. Yesterday, we were walking there and ran into Jackson.

I say, who is Jackson? He's my dad, Tyler answered. Harris continued. So after the match was over, Thomas came in drunk and started in on me again. It was so awful; I just had to get out of there.

Did that asshole really hit Harris? He's such a nice kid; it's hard for me to believe in the abstract. But there is the evidence staring right at me. I peered out through the front-room window, but everything seemed quiet across the footpath. Nobody was outside anyway.

Tyler, did Jackson say anything to you about this? No, but I'm sure he has figured everything out by now. I know he's been going through my stuff and I think he saw the picture of Winston and me that I keep in my nightstand.

Francis, what are we going to do? He is standing next to me looking out the window. Maybe Thomas is sleeping it off and will calm down when he is sober. I think you and I should go over there later and talk to him. I wasn't entirely convinced about the wisdom of this appeasement strategy, but I couldn't come up with a better plan.

What do you think, Harris? He just shook his head, looking confused and frightened. Everyone else had blank expressions, and all seven of us just stared into what had become the silent abyss of my living room, void of any brilliant suggestions.

As it turned out, we would not have to go anywhere to deal with the problem; the problem was coming to deal with us. Open up, Parker, right now. Tyler, are you in there too? Thomas and Jackson were on my porch now and sounding much too angry, like a tag-team of drunken homo-haters. Father, go back home and calm down; I will come out in a few minutes. We're not going anywhere, let us in.

Carleton spoke up now. Maybe we should try to reason with them; I mean we have them way outnumbered. You wouldn't know by looking at him, but he is not afraid to stand up for himself or be easily intimidated. But these two were beginning to scare the crap out of me. I don't know, Carleton; he's threatened me already. I think we should call the police. Francis went to the door; it's alright, I'll talk to them.

His plan to open the door just a crack backfired immediately. Thomas is no small dude and he seized the advantage he had now and shoved his way in violently, knocking Francis backward against the wall. Now that he is in my house, his anger shifts straightaway to me, along with the forefinger he keeps shoving toward my face, just inches away.

Jackson is there as well, but I sense that he is mainly following Thomas' lead, and probably would prefer to be home with his family, or at least not in the middle of this uncomfortably escalating situation. It had to be embarrassing for him to see his son hanging all over Winston as well. I sized him up almost immediately; far less belligerent than Thomas, who was livid now.

That damn Deputy Constable knocked on my door yesterday because of you. Half the neighborhood saw him too. I warned you before, and you should have listened. You're going to pay for this, Parker.

I was surprised to hear that actually. The Constable had not given me any indication they were planning to follow up on my complaint, only that their hands were tied. That's right, Thomas, and they told me to call them back if you ever trespass again. They know you were looking in my windows too. You better leave right now or we're calling the police again.

My less-than-formidable threat didn't faze my neighbor, as he got right up in my face and violently grabbed me by the front of my shirt. But right then his attention was diverted away from me, and toward Crosby, who was dialing the emergency phone number. Thomas immediately let go of me and took a swing near Crosby's left ear, sending his mobile flying halfway across the living room hardwood.

You may consider Carleton to be somewhat on the wispy side of the spectrum, but his boyfriend, definitely not. Crosby regained his bearings quickly and went right at Thomas. The two were scuffling for several seconds, each with a wrestling hold on the other. We were all yelling for them to stop, and then Jackson got into it trying his best to separate them. He managed to do that and loosen Thomas' grip, but in hindsight anyway, this might not have been his best move. Because in the process he wound up pinning Thomas' arms behind him a little, which freed up Crosby's completely, and our friend had quite enough of Thomas' bullshit by that time, and he let loose with a solid right square to the middle of Thomas' face.

He staggered back, toward where Jackson and Harris were standing, and the two of them eased Thomas onto the floor, still cursing loudly at Crosby, but otherwise subdued for the moment at least. There was a sickening amount of blood running down the front of his shirt and onto the floor. I stared at his face, which was a mess, like a pizza driven over. His nose was clearly broken and off-centered now.

Tyler found a kitchen towel and he and Harris were holding it to his face. I was relieved by the sense of calm that prevailed now, and shortly thereafter by the arrival of two uniformed officers.

The taller of the two took Jackson and Thomas outside and the other one stayed in the living room, interviewing each of us. Ten minutes later, the officer came back inside and the two of them talked privately in the kitchen. I looked out the window but saw no sign of either Thomas or Jackson. Francis, what the fuck is going on here; why haven't they been arrested? He just shook his head and said, welcome to the Province, I guess.

Mr. Harris, you will need to return to your home if you don't mind. Mr. Tyler, please come with me; I will be responsible for seeing that you arrive safely back home in Province North. Mr. Crosby, put your hands behind your back; you are under arrest. We all stared in stunned disbelief for a moment, before I snapped out of it and spoke up. Officer, how can you be arresting Crosby? We were defending ourselves. Stay back, Mr. Parker, and allow me to do my job if you don't mind. Excuse me sir, but what is the charge? Aggravated Grievous Assault. Now if you don't desist, I will arrest you as well.

Crosby had already been handcuffed and was being led outside by the arm, while Carleton, Francis, Winston, and I followed them. Don't worry, Crosby; we'll be right behind you. We'll get to the bottom of this.

After they drove off, Carleton hugged Winston and me. He was dazed and visibly upset. I was trembling noticeably and Francis was holding me close. Don't worry, Carleton; I promise we will take care of this. Thanks, Francis. I'm so lucky to have you guys for friends.

• • • •

Bail has been set at £15,000, Mr. Parker. The four of us were now at the Constable's office in The Miracle Mile. My God, how could we ever come up with that much money? Crosby could be stuck in here for weeks.

Sir, I don't understand why he is being detained; we were the ones assaulted. Thomas forced his way into my house and attacked me.

I beg to differ, but that is not what the witness testimony would seem to support. I said, you call him a witness? Jackson is Thomas' best friend; you don't expect to get the truth from him, do you? I was not referring to Mr. Jackson, he said, but rather the other witness testimony. From who? From Mr. Harris and Mr. Tyler, that's who.

Both of them stated first off, that you opened the door and allowed them to enter, and secondly that Mr. Crosby was the aggressor in this unfortunate situation, and that their respective fathers were just trying to reason with him. That's crap, Francis said. They were never invited in. They forced their way in and slammed me against the wall while doing it. We need to see your Commander-In-Chief.

I'm afraid he is rather busy at the moment, Mr. Francis. Besides, your statement was taken at the crime scene and duly noted, and you might be better served by refraining from arguing this position so strenuously, since as I have already stated, the testimony does not support what you are alleging against Mr. Thomas. I would tread quite carefully on this point if I were you, or you may be facing perjury charges from this office, or civil charges of intimidation or harassment from Mr. Thomas, or both.

That's a good one, Francis intimidating and harassing Thomas. Nobody is going to believe that lying shithead. The Deputy Constable continued. As for you, Mr. Parker; your prior complaint with this office now seems quite frivolous and you might consider officially withdrawing it, given the weight of the evidence and the reliability of the testimony.

You call that reliable? I call it bullshit. What do you expect Harris and Tyler to say? They are terrified of their fathers. That is the least reliable evidence and you damn well know it. I told you when I was here last time how dangerous Thomas is, and you sat there on your ass doing nothing.

If I were you, Mr. Parker, I would be careful of the way you address a Deputy Constable, and show some respect for this Office. Sir, I will show you all the respect in the world, hell I will even kiss your ass if you want, but only after Crosby is released.

After we returned home, I called and left a message for Ms. Millerton, explaining that I had a family emergency to attend to on Monday morning and would be late for work. Winston drove Carleton back home to City Centre.

It is just the two of us now, cleaning the house together in silence. I put away the food still left out from the party, then wash the rest of the dishes. Francis scrubs the blood from the hardwood floor and puts the furniture back where it belongs. We sit on the sofa together holding hands, speechless. What more could there possibly be left to say?

XI

Please, sit down gentlemen. I've read the criminal indictment and summaries of the statements that you gave to the investigating officers. Winston, Francis, Carleton, and I met at the Solicitor's office on Monday morning at 9:30. Mr. Wellington agreed to take Crosby's case and will be appearing on his behalf this afternoon at the Magistrate's Court of Justice.

The Complaint against Crosby is full of horseshit, he told us. This entire thing stinks of horseshit worse than a Kentucky stable. My assistant had a little time to look into this matter further. It seems that Mr. Thomas is not the most likable of neighbors.

That's for sure, I said. He has been harassing me almost from the day I moved to the Province. Yes, Parker; and we can deal with that matter another day. But I see that the prior Complaint you filed supports what you have said and this will be a great help bolstering Crosby's defense.

Yesterday, the Deputy Constable said I should withdraw my Complaint. Please tell me you didn't agree to that, Parker. Of course I didn't, Mr. Wellington; I told him he could kiss my ass. Frances chuckled, that's not exactly the way I heard it.

Can you get Crosby released sir, or at least get the bail reduced? We don't have anything close to £15,000. That might be a problem in the short run, he said. I am going to try to convince the Magistrate to release Crosby at the preliminary hearing this afternoon. As ridiculous as the entire matter may be, the charge of Aggravated Grievous Assault is a felony. I may have to work on this judge for a while. He's a bit of an asshole and may not be too willing to buy our arguments. Don't worry though, Carleton. I know how scary this is, but we'll get him out of there as quickly as possible.

. . . .

The morning was almost gone by the time I signed in at the Timekeeper's desk. I see that you are late again, Parker. The second time this month if my memory serves me correctly. Sir, I don't think that is any of your business. Maybe you should check to see that your clock is properly wound. My, aren't we sensitive this morning; did the Deputy Constable give you a hard time again? Or did we overdo the celebrating after the fútbol match?

I gave him a perplexed look; what did you mean by that? I know what happened to Crosby, he said. I'm very sorry about that, I mean it. I asked him, how did you find out about it?

Who could he have been talking to? I only told Ms. Millerton that I would be late coming to work. I didn't mention anything about what happened at my house after the game. He said, I know everything that goes on here, Parker.

I wasn't sure I believed him still. Yeah, what else do you know, sir? I know that nasty neighbor of yours must have one hellish hangover today. I know what a prick that Magistrate is too. I hope Mr. Wellington knows what he is doing. Sign in here Parker, if you don't mind. I have a feeling Mr. Sanderson is up to something today and you better get going.

I sit at my desk and see my inbox stacked with new work. My head is throbbing from anxiety and the consequences of yesterday's indulgence. I am so worried about what they are going to do to Crosby. And how did the Timekeeper know practically every detail of what went on yesterday?

May I see you at my desk, Mr. Parker? Yes, good morning, Ms. Millerton. I stood and began walking toward her platform. Not here she said, come with me to Mr. Sanderson's office. Oh no, we never go to his office. What more could possibly go wrong now?

Sit down, Mr. Parker; we have an urgent matter to discuss with you. I searched my memory but came up with no clue about what I could have done this time. Everything was normal when I left last week. I hadn't missed any deadlines or anything like that. Maybe they are mad because I was late again.

Mr. Parker, we have become aware of the situation with Crosby and I am quite distressed by it. I can explain what happened, Mr. Sanderson; he was only defending me. He said then, that will not be necessary as we already know what transpired and are fully cognizant of the seriousness of the pending charges. I spoke personally to the Solicitor this morning, and understand also that the bail amount is quite excessive.

Yes, sir, we haven't figured out how we are going to raise that much money, but we will. Believe me. Please don't hold this against Crosby; he didn't do anything wrong. The guy he hit was threatening me.

He said, Ms. Millerton and I are not here to punish Crosby, we are here to discuss his release. Am I dreaming this? What the hell is going on with these two?

In this office, Mr. Parker; we are all considered to be members of one large family, that is to say, we take care of one another and we respond should any of us get into trouble. Somehow, I couldn't escape the feeling that if it was any other family member other than Crosby in such a fix, that right now I would be waiting for one of them to open the file cabinets instead of waiting to hear what exactly Mr. Sanderson was talking about.

He continued, I have considered this matter carefully with Ms. Millerton, and it is our heartfelt belief that Crosby cannot be allowed to languish in the Province Detention Center for even a moment longer than is absolutely necessary. Who knows what thugs are there from Province South harassing him at this very moment? For that reason, I have advised Mr. Wellington to arrange for his parole this afternoon.

Sir, are you saying that you and Ms. Millerton are paying for his bail? You did not hear me say that, did you, Mr. Parker? No sir, I did not. Good. You don't need to concern yourself with the particulars of the arrangement, only with the importance of keeping this conversation confidential. I understand completely, I said. I'm not sure that you do, Mr. Parker, so please listen carefully.

Despite what we have just discussed concerning the importance of supporting one another should trouble find any of us, the Government itself might not fully appreciate our particular situation, if you get my meaning. Our attempts at compassion might possibly be misconstrued, and if the wrong people were to hear of our altruistic intentions, it could have serious consequences for a person in the position of someone like myself, or else Ms. Millerton's for instance. It is therefore essential that nobody finds out any of this. Are you clear as to my meaning? Yes, sir, I understand, but may I ask a question? Ask your question, Mr. Parker, and then return to your post and be sworn to secrecy, once we have concluded this meeting.

Sir, why are you telling me all of this? Why not just arrange for Crosby's release without me? Because in exchange for the favor we are doing for you and your friends, we will expect one from you in return.

If I wasn't already confused enough by these last ten unpleasant minutes, I sure as hell am now. I can be clueless at times, as Francis likes to point out, but I was starting to question the sanity of one or both of these two. What could they possibly want from me?

Mr. Parker, do you remember that incident a while ago involving an investigation by Internal Affairs? Yes, of course; when Ms. Millerton fell on the stairs. Correct. The stairs with no handrail or barrier. They are making quite a stink about that now. It seems like the Office of Worker Injuries and Restitution has filed some sort of claim for reimbursement from our Office for their medical costs, claiming negligence on our part.

Sir, I'm afraid I don't understand. Listen carefully and I will explain it. I told them that I previously requisitioned funds for constructing a handrail and had authorized payment for the work to be done prior to Ms. Millerton's unfortunate accident.

I see, so what's the problem then? He said, there was no such requisition and no such authorization made, so now we need to make it look like there were. What we need for you to do is initial both this requisition entry in the Master Log, and the subsequent payment request form now, and back-date each item for one week prior to Ms. Millerton's fall. That way, we can successfully undermine the medical reimbursement claim and everyone will be happy.

Everyone, sir? Yes, Mr. Parker. Ms. Millerton will be happy, Mr. Crosby will be happy, both you and Mr. Carleton will be happy, but most importantly, Internal Affairs will be happy. Which means I will be happy; do you get my meaning?

I just shrugged and said, alright I can do that. So even though I still didn't get what they were up to, I initialed and dated the log, along with the payment request form where they told me to. What difference would it make? Ms. Millerton stamped them with a back-dated stamp.

Crosby was out of jail and back to work the very next day, so he and Carleton were clearly happy. Mr. Sanderson could hang around again watching Crosby do his filing, and he seemed to be happy. I knew he didn't pay for Crosby's bail just so he could get a favor from me in return. I had to give him credit for coming up with the idea, but even I knew the primary motivation was his fascination with Crosby's cute ass and some delusional idea that he might get a piece of it one day.

Ms. Millerton is happy too, because now the workmen are busy affixing a handrail to the platform so she doesn't fall again. But I was worried and confused still. It's not as if any of this nonsense matters in the least, but what happens if Internal Affairs discovers their little scheme? An easy scapegoat will need to be found, and who might that be? Not a Senior Secretary or Superintendent, that's for sure.

May I see you for a moment, Mr. Parker? Yes, Ms. Millerton; what do you need from me now? I just want to make sure that we are still on the same page, and that you will keep your end of the bargain now that Mr. Crosby has been relieved of his incarceration. You will never say a word to anyone; can I be confident in making such a statement? Yes, Ms. Millerton; I promise not to tell anyone.

It didn't take long at all for me to break my promise, and I told Francis about the bail money later that evening. But nothing else. I didn't see the need for him to know anything about the little deception I agreed to. He asked, why do you think they agreed to pay all that money? I wonder where £15,000 came from. They said that we are all like a big family and have to help each other if someone gets in trouble. I guess Mr. Sanderson came up with the money. Do you trust them, Parker? Oh hell no, but it doesn't matter now.

It didn't matter. Francis, Winston, and Tyler are all happy too. The only one who is not the least bit happy is Thomas. He is still raging, now with horrific-looking bruises in the middle of his face as well. I see him glaring at us from the carport while the four of us are out on the porch enjoying some more of the Imperial Stout they brought from City Centre. If things were different, in a better place and time maybe, I'd happily wave the jackass over to have a cold one with us.

· · · ·

With at least some of the recent awful events in the rearview mirror, I was hoping that things would start to settle down. Crosby and Carleton seemed almost inseparable now as if sticking to each other might prevent one of them from being dragged away in handcuffs again. The case against Crosby was still pending, but Mr. Wellington remained confident that the whole thing would eventually go away.

I arranged to take the day off so that I could attend the next hearing. Carleton had some stupid computer installation project going on and his boss would not let him go. I wanted to show support for Crosby in any way I could, and Mr. Sanderson readily agreed to grant me the day off with pay.

I was still anxious about how the entire back-dating deception would play out, but so far anyway, Internal Affairs had not questioned anyone's integrity. Of course, establishing Crosby's innocence was paramount, but after that, who knows? If the Office of Workers Injuries and Restitution could be persuaded to drop their discomforting negligence claims, I might walk away looking pretty damn good in the eyes of Mr. Sanderson and Ms. Millerton.

The Investigator from the Office of Internal Affairs assigned to the medical reimbursement claims showed up at the office completely unannounced the day before the hearing. I will need to interview you once again, he told me. The same loud-mouth guy with the bad breath. He talked so loud, half the office could hear him. Why the hell should everyone here know my private business? To make things even worse, when he opens his mouth to speak, he exacerbates the second problem and makes me wonder why he refuses to at least try using mouthwash once in a while.

Mr. Sanderson intervenes now and suggests that the interview should be postponed, claiming that the department is extremely busy right now, and why can't the interrogation be done another time. The Investigator is pretty high up on the bureaucratic ladder and outranks Mr. Sanderson. I'm sorry sir, but it is imperative that any matter pending before the Office of Worker Injuries and Restitution be thoroughly investigated and in a timely manner. Shit, couldn't he tone it down a notch? Do the other Processors and the nosy Timekeeper need to hear any of this?

Mr. Sanderson is no pushover and is after all a Superintendent in a major Government Department. Technically, he might be acting above the scope of his authority, but he wasn't about to be bullied by the Investigator. He glanced over at the platform where Ms.

Millerton remained seated, obviously watching all of this. She picked up on his cue immediately and came over to where I was now starting to sweat nervously.

Mr. Parker, here are an additional thirty new receipts that you have neglected to file, even though they have already been stamped, and your three-hour limit is rapidly approaching. I assume that you understand the importance of completing your assignments on time and that you would like to avoid me having to note any further protocol discrepancies in your Permanent Record.

I couldn't help but notice the slight grin on Mr. Sanderson's face, and I was pretty sure I saw him give her a little wink. These two work in perfect tandem, like a midfielder and a striker. I can't decide which is more impressive, their sneakiness or their reputed sincerity. Mr. Sanderson has been at this a long time and is not about to get busted for back-dating logs and requisitions. That sounded like a pretty clear-cut protocol discrepancy to me.

As you can see, Mr. Parker is so busy today and we cannot allow him to fall any further behind in his work, and besides that, he will be absent from work tomorrow so that he can attend Mr. Crosby's hearing. So clearly today does not present the best opportunity for an interview on what you must agree is a rather small matter regarding something that will ultimately result in relatively insignificant medical costs.

The Investigator didn't seem as impressed as I was. If you don't mind me asking, why would Mr. Parker need to miss work to attend Mr. Crosby's hearing? Nobody can answer a question like that better than Mr. Sanderson. Because sir, we are like an extended family in this office, that's why. When trouble shows its ugly face, we will not allow one of our own to suffer the burden alone; we will offer moral support or any other assistance that may be in our power to confer. I would attend the hearing personally, but I am just too busy to arrange it. So Mr. Parker has generously offered to go in my place and work overtime if need be to complete his work assignments.

I was glad that Mr. Sanderson's years of experience dealing with meddling bureaucrats had come in handy once again. And it was a relief not to have to be subjected to another painful interview with one of them.

I'm sorry to say, Mr. Sanderson, that this will cause me a great deal of inconvenience. Ms. Millerton spoke up then, as if the script had been well rehearsed. Sir, inconvenience is what we humans fear most; all of us want for everything to be easy, all of the time. It will be an inconvenience for me to stay late to oversee Mr. Parker while he works overtime, as well as for the Timekeeper, who cannot go home to his wife and dinner until we are finished. But missing dinner is a small sacrifice to make in exchange for helping Mr. Crosby, who is one of our better employees. I am sure you would agree that such an inconvenience is quite diminutive, all things considered.

I wish Francis could have been around to hear all of this. Then he would understand why I would rather work here instead of in the Office of Sanitation and Debris Removal, where Carleton's boss was too big of a prick to let him take a day off so he could be with Crosby tomorrow.

Francis' ears perked up when I told him about it later. You don't think they are doing it for your benefit, do you, Parker? Of course not, but I don't give a shit about what they do. I've got the day off with pay and I will be with Crosby and Mr. Wellington tomorrow; that's what I care about. They said I could work overtime later if I needed to get caught up.

You're a damn good friend, you know that Parker? I'm going to call out sick tomorrow and go with you if that's okay. That's great, I said. Can you afford to miss work though? He said, I'll figure something out, don't you worry about it. Thanks, Francis. Crosby is going to need all the help he can get.

• • • •

The Magistrate's Court of Justice is housed in a grand-looking building in the middle of The Miracle Mile. Probably built no more than a decade ago, it was constructed to resemble an early turn-of-the-century courthouse, with its impressive hulking columns and cone-topped clock and bell tower. The ceilings in the main hall are at least ten meters high, with an iridescent greenish-blue hue emanating from what appears to be a Tiffany-stained glass skylight. The artisans who might have created the original version of this fake reproduction are long dead. Perhaps the art form itself is still alive somewhere, but I'm sure that if I were to climb a scaffold to inspect the stained glass panels up close, I would discover that they were made out of some type of painted translucent plastic.

The courtroom where we are now seated is more modest, with modern wooden benches for spectator seating, and plain-looking work tables for the Solicitors. I have never been to a hearing before, or witnessed an actual trial; my impressions of what the proceedings might be like formed mainly from movies I had seen in City Centre, and from reruns of an old TV series they air on the Satellite called *Perry Mason.*

A hush fell over the courtroom when the judge entered. May it please the Court, I would like to enter a formal plea on behalf of the defendant. Mr. Wellington stood up from the table where he had been seated next to Crosby. He was a tall, good-looking man, who carried himself with an air of confidence. Beyond his handsome exterior, there was a seriousness and edge to his gaze that spoke both to his professionalism and his sharp legal mind.

It was the Magistrate's turn to speak now. The Court will grant you the opportunity to plead your case, but only with respect to the reasonableness of the specific charges being made. There will be no witnesses called, nor any examination of any sort. I will allow the Prosecutor equal time to respond to oral argument only, no deposition or other testimony will be permitted at this preliminary juncture.

The Prosecutor stood up then. If it pleases the Court, I would like to enter the Constable's official report of the investigation of felonious crimes alleged against Mr. Crosby in the indictment. Granted, the Court will review the report. Mr. Wellington, do you have anything you would like to present at this time? Yes, your Honor; I would like to submit the witness statements taken at the scene from Mr. Parker, Mr. Carleton, Mr. Francis, and Mr. Harris.

The Prosecutor jumped in; Objection, your Honor. The first three statements are from potential trial witnesses, two of whom are present at these proceedings. Their statements have not been duly sworn before this Court. Additionally, Mr. Harris is the son of the Complainant in this case, and cannot be compelled to testify against him. His statement should be considered as nothing more than hearsay at this time. The judge looked our way. Mr. Wellington?

Your Honor, the hearsay rules under section III, subsection a. (1) (4i) of the Criminal Code have not been satisfied by the Prosecution. All four statements are relevant, were given voluntarily, and were signed by the investigating officer. That officer is present in the courtroom today and can testify as to their authenticity. These statements are clearly admissible at this time, and they each support the Defendants's argument that the charge of Aggravated Grievous Assault is completely unwarranted. I move that each of the four statements be entered into evidence, and at the conclusion of this hearing, that your Honor dismiss the case against Mr. Crosby in its entirety. In the alternative, I move that the indictment be amended to include a single charge of Misdemeanor Battery.

A heavy-set Bailiff stood up then; the Court demands that Counsel approach the bench. There was a good deal of whispering back and forth between the Prosecutor and Mr. Wellington, none of which I could make out. After about ten minutes, they both returned to their seats and the Magistrate excused himself to consider each party's arguments. Then he just got up and left the courtroom.

All of this was strange to me and I didn't understand much of what they were talking about or what could be so fucking complicated. Unless this judge was a complete moron, of course he would side with Crosby. No version of the events, other than that idiot Thomas' would have caused him to not at least reduce the charge. Even I knew that Aggravated Grievous Assault meant something way beyond a punch in the face. If Crosby had come at him with a knife or something, or really tried to hurt him, well okay then. This had to be a slam-dunk case for dismissal, or else a slap on the wrist and maybe a fine or something.

The Bailiff spoke up again. Hear ye, hear ye, what saith the Court? All rise in his Honor's presence.

Mr. Wellington, I will rule separately on each of your motions. With respect to the first motion, admission of the four statements, such motion is hereby denied. With respect to the second motion, the charge of Aggravated Grievous Assault is upheld as being reasonable based on the circumstances, and such motion is also hereby denied.

Crosby turned and stared right at me with a painful look on his face. It will be okay, I whispered; Don't worry. I was plenty worried though, believe me.

Mr. Wellington spoke to us briefly in the main hall before heading off on another case. This whole thing stinks of horseshit. That judge eats horseshit with his eggs for breakfast. We'll take care of this, trust me.

The three of us left the courthouse and walked together to The Miracle Mile station, so that Crosby could get on the next train back to City Centre. He was quiet and didn't say much about what went on at the hearing. Francis was still staying at my place and we walked close to each other with his arm around me, back to the cottage in

Province East. Fucking ignorant judge, he said. So saith the asshole, I answered.

. . . .

Now do you see why I wasn't too happy about you moving here and living among these people? They don't like us and since the law prohibits them from keeping us out, they elect half-breed judges to administer to their twisted sense of fairness and their warped values. I said, maybe we just got a bad break with this judge; things might not have gone any better in a Court in City Centre, I mean the laws are the same.

I didn't want to push this too far with Francis. What good would that do now? This was not my best opportunity to point out the advantages of suburban living. I sensed he might be in the mood for another argument since he wasted a vacation day and would have to work extra hours anyway to catch up. We'd had a few fights since he had been staying over in the Province, and I didn't want there to be yet another one now.

Our temporary living arrangement had been tense for me. I appreciated the sacrifice he made by offering to stay at the cottage and help shield me from Thomas' volatility. Despite the good intentions, I have to say he is not the easiest person to live with. I was often stressed out from everything going on at work and was really scared for Crosby's sake. It's time now for Francis to go back home to City Centre. I'm going to tell him tonight.

That unfriendly sensation of sadness begins to creep in again. I am worried too that he could be right, that perhaps we might not find justice to be blind in The Miracle Mile. In that case, my decision to move to the Province, and my judgment in general, could be called into question. Stop it now, I tell myself. Focus on what is ahead and on helping Crosby, instead of trying to go back in time and needlessly question decisions that I can't change now anyway.

People love to create these self-defeating catch-22s; if I had done this instead, if only I had listened to you, whatever. I want to avoid the discussion entirely. I'm getting a little tired of hearing Francis say I told you so.

Is this judge really an ignorant homophobe? Even if the Deputy Constable would not reveal the details of Thomas' criminal record, certainly the judge must have had the benefit of seeing it. I hate to admit such a thing, and it feels like paranoia when I consider it, but objectively it seems that Crosby being gay and Thomas being straight might be in play here.

I know what you are thinking. Come on, Parker; this is a modern democracy we live in, and there are long-standing laws that prohibit discrimination against people regardless of their sexual orientation. Still, I am caused to wonder; I don't know what to think anymore. I'm always telling Carleton, don't worry, everything will be fine. The truth though? I don't know shit.

XII

There is a big country and western rodeo dance on Saturday night at the Club in the Middle. It's the annual party that everyone looks forward to, and the perfect excuse to dress up in cowboy attire and to act ridiculous for a few hours. Yeah, like anyone would ever mistake us for bareback bronc riders or think we're tough enough to rope a steer just because we're wearing the right boots and sporting cool-looking Stetsons that cost half a week's pay. But for one night, we get to play the part and have a blast doing it.

The timing is perfect. We can all take a break and unwind a little bit from these traumatic events we've endured over the past few weeks. C'mon Parker; everyone is meeting up soon in City Centre. Francis was already out of the shower and dressed while I hurried to get ready, ironing the creases in the embroidered plaid shirt with the pearl snaps that I bought just for the occasion. Perfect with my somewhat worn-looking black boot-cut jeans. Francis looked hot in his baby blue denim shirt with the horse-sewn appliqué on the back.

I don't know much about county music and it sometimes puts me to sleep, but now we are out there stomping our feet in unison to the line dance moves that Winston showed us. What a great dancer he is. When he and Tyler showed off their Continental version of the Ten-Step Polka, everyone in the club seemed envious and tried to follow their moves, or else they clapped along from the edges of the dance floor if they couldn't get up the nerve to join in.

Later, I wanted Francis to do a two-step with me, but he said no thanks and pointed out to me how silly the other guys looked doing it. Watching them, I had to admit that he was probably right. However I looked at it, there was something anomalous about two guys in overtly masculine get-ups doing a dance that was so obviously created with both a man and woman in mind. I could not manage to make the pieces fit together, no matter how much I wished they would. Still, Tyler and I did the dance just because it was so much fun, and I didn't want to embarrass Francis anyway. At least we came to an agreement about to the cowboy hat I'd given him, which he initially argued was ludicrous. I remember him saying, what am I going to be doing at the Club, herding cattle?

I love to dance and was having a great time, but the country music seemed to drone on endlessly and was twanging away in my ears. You could only take so much of it. The people who ran the Club in the Middle knew this simple truth. Sure, the cowboy macho thing was fun, but you didn't have to be Freud to understand what the manly costume shtick was all about. A harmless way of masking our inner feminine personas; nothing wrong with that. Let's face it, though, before much longer, there might be more than a few bar patrons just about ready to smash the speakers placed above each corner of the dance floor. So precisely at midnight, the relentless line dancers, who somehow now reminded me of marching Nazi soldiers, were finished. The strobe lights on, the disco ball reborn, and the down-home southern drawl giving way to some real dance music.

And that meant real dancing. We could keep this up until the club closed at 2:00 a.m., fueled by the energy of the music and the surge of alcohol. Fun, right? We can sleep in tomorrow, right? Not a care in the world, right?

Wrong. I guess they didn't care much for country music either, because just after the beat changed, so did our moods. Harris and his new boyfriend Brady were among the beautiful people now.

And oh my you-know-what kind of God, were they ever a nice-looking couple. They didn't bother with any overpriced country and Western gear; they didn't need any such gimmicks to get attention. Brady looked like he had been chiseled by Michelangelo himself, with a powder-blue T-shirt that nobody in this bar at least, would complain about being a size or more too tight. Harris had on white cut-offs and a dark tank top and looked like he had been spending a lot of time hiding from Thomas at the local YMCA gym.

Carleton turned red when he saw them, and Francis seemed pretty pissed off too. I can't believe they had the nerve to show up here, he said. What did they think, that they weren't going to run into us? That was true, nearly every gay guy in City Centre under seventy would probably be out tonight. I looked over at Crosby and he just shrugged. I don't care if he's here, it doesn't matter.

Why should it matter? Tyler is here with Winston and from what I know, he hasn't changed his version of what happened that day either. The two of them are equally complicit, both maintaining a silence that might put Crosby away for a year or more. How much blame could we reasonably place on them though? Would any of us have done things differently if we had been in their untenable situations?

Francis though, was not so easily swayed. He blamed Harris more for not speaking up. Logically, it made little sense, but the merits weren't being argued this time before his Honor the Magistrate. You have to realize that he and Winston are very tight, and for him to go after Tyler would be a sizable misstep. His loyalty to his best friend might tilt his objectivity, not quite as centered as I considered my own to be. And though Francis might come across as more than a bit condescending toward Carleton, I know he struggles as much as any of us when he sees the anguish on Carleton's face. And I also know that he cares enough about Crosby to have asked every single person he knew to lend him some of the bail money before my bosses stepped in. The real reason he blames Harris is because he hates Thomas' guts. Even more than I do.

Now they come over to the bar where we are drinking, with a peace offering maybe, figuring out most likely that we need to come to some sort of resolution. None of this is helping anyone. Tyler and Harris are best friends. We can't just stand around looking at one another, debating who we should blame. Nobody in our group wanted for any of this to happen.

I was a bit intoxicated by now and their physical presence did nothing to dampen my overall sense of well-being. I chatted with Brady after he was introduced to everyone. At nineteen, he wasn't quite a man yet, but you could see the obvious potential. He had a youthful charm and tussled dirty blonde hair. He carried himself with the level of confidence that I would not call arrogant, but rather a sort of comfortable self-assurance.

I take a good look at him now, wondering just how much he knows about Harris' father and Crosby's legal predicament. I get this strange feeling that he might be of some use to those of us on the defense team. I bet he has a ton of influence over what Harris does.

I gave Francis our little sign; stay put and don't stick your nose into this just yet; let me try it my way first. He gave me a little nod in return, so we understood each other. That's what happens I guess when you spend so much time with one person; the brain cells fuse a little bit in some mysterious awe-inspiring way. Let's dance, Brady; Harris, you don't mind, do you?

The dance floor pulsed with noise, the crowd pressing us together so tightly we could hardly move, let alone hear each other. Despite the din, none of my other senses were negatively impacted. Lucky me. The scent of his sweat and cologne blended and he smelled like apple cloves and warm vanilla. Easy to understand now why Harris is so excited about the new guy, even if he is from Province South.

He said something about the country dance and how they had nothing to wear, but I didn't catch much else because of the steady, deep kick drum of the music, which seemed to pound right into me. After a few more minutes, he asked if it would be alright if we went outside where it was quiet enough to talk without screaming at each other.

We stepped into the cool late-night darkness. He doesn't know what to do Parker; his father keeps threatening him. He is so scared right now. I understand, really I do, Brady. Even Crosby understands, sort of. I'm not trying to tell anyone what to do here, but I can tell you how this is going to play out. The lawyer says there is no way the judge will not force him to testify. The Prosecutor will argue some sort of immunity because they are family, but it won't hold. The law is clear and the judge will not have any other choice. Eventually Tyler will have to cave too. He is already starting to weaken; perjury is serious business. He is Harris' best friend but he is not going to lie under oath, and I doubt Jackson will either because he will have to protect Tyler at some point.

Thomas is the one who should be on trial, not Crosby. Mr. Wellington will parade each of us one by one in front of the judge, each with the same story to tell. What can I do, Parker? Let me ask you this, Brady; do you know his father? No, I've never met the man. Here is my advice; stay away from him. And get yourself a cowboy hat next time; you'd look really cute in one.

· · · ·

By the time we said our goodbyes and walked the six blocks to Francis' apartment, it was close to 3:00 a.m. We planned to sleep there because the last train to the Province was long gone and Francis was too tired to drive. Sunday brunch and window shopping in City Centre were on the weekend itinerary. We would go home and cook dinner at the cottage later on.

This gave us the opportunity to hash things out and we agreed that he would stay a few more nights with me in Province East. I was grateful for the effort he made in supporting me, but it was time for him to move back home. I will miss him though; train rides to the city in the morning, with cocktails and dinner in the evening. It was like being married almost. I have always lived alone, and it felt safe and comforting to me, watching the Satellite movie broadcasts while snuggling close on the sofa.

We drove back in his car so that he would have it later in the week to take his things home. We knew there was trouble before we even made it to the carport. Black spray paint defaced the white-painted fence, and I saw right away the ugly gay slur written on the front door. The stucco façade was tagged with graffiti and the front room window was broken out.

I felt sick to my stomach and ready to cry, but I forced myself to keep my shit together. There might be someone inside yet. Francis dialed the emergency number on his mobile and said, stay in the car, I'm going to lock the doors. While waiting for the police to show up, he knocked on the doors of two of our closest neighbors. No, they had not seen anyone or heard anything unusual. It must have happened late at night while they were sleeping.

The same two officers that responded the last time arrived in less than five minutes, their bright lights flashing in alternating bursts of red and blue. Stay inside the car if you don't mind, while we make sure it is safe to enter. Luckily, there was no evidence that anyone had been in the cottage, and there was no other damage or anything out of place.

Now do you understand what we are up against? My neighbor Thomas must have done this. Did you witness anything, Mr. Parker? No, we just got home; we were in City Centre last night. How about you, Mr. Francis? He just shook his head. No, I didn't. It was Thomas though, who else would have done this? His son Harris was with us again last night and Thomas must have found out about it. We keep telling you how dangerous he is. Will you arrest him now? He's been threatening Harris and the poor kid is too scared to say anything.

Arrest him? Based on what? Your friend assaulted him in this very house and you want us to arrest Mr. Thomas? *Allegedly* assaulted, Francis corrected. The Magistrate hasn't ruled yet on

Crosby's guilt or innocence, or doesn't his right to due process mean anything in this stinking Province? You better be careful how you address an Officer of the law in this or any other Province. Am I making myself clear, Mr. Francis? I'll tell you what's clear, Francis said. It's clear that the two of you refuse to do your jobs. If you did, none of this would have happened. Now, you listen here young man.

Wait a minute, please everyone, just listen to me. I turn and see Harris coming through our now hideous-looking front door. It must have been my father who did this. When I saw what happened to Parker's house, I looked in our basement where Thomas keeps his tools. I found this on the workbench. He gives the Officer a half-empty can of black spray paint. The tip of his index finger shows a black smudge where he rubbed it over the nozzle. Look, I said; it's still wet.

Finally, Harris came forward. This whole thing had to be just awful for the kid, but I was so happy now that he found the nerve to speak up. Finally, the frivolous case against Crosby would begin to unravel. Maybe Francis can go back home and I can find some peace.

I'm sorry, son, but I am afraid this amounts to nothing more than circumstantial evidence and may prove to be inconsequential. Mr. Thomas may have been working on some home improvement project or any number of things. It might be purely coincidental that his choice of paint color just so happens to match the paint color on the house. Black paint is quite a common color to use, wouldn't you agree?

I've had about enough of this bullshit by now. Of course, I don't agree, I said. The only thing inconsequential here is your concern for our safety. Aren't you going to at least go over there and question the guy? Certainly, we will question him, he replied. You don't need to tell us how to do our jobs. Well, somebody does; we'll see what the Deputy Constable has to say about this. Come on Parker, let's get out of here so these monkeys can do their jobs. There are plenty of bananas in the kitchen if you get hungry.

Will someone please listen to me? It seems Harris is not quite done spilling his guts yet. I wasn't being completely honest when I gave my statement; I'm sorry. I was so afraid of what Thomas might do if I told you the truth.

I have a lot of respect for Harris now, but I'm thinking, man if it were me I probably would have kept my mouth shut and just trashed the paint can. Even after they arrest Thomas, he will still have to deal with his psycho father.

Mr. Harris, your statements and admissions are matters for the Prosecutor's office and his Honor the Magistrate to consider. Mr. Parker; I'm sorry for your inconvenience today, but there is nothing more for us to do here.

You call this an inconvenience? He's dangerous as hell; didn't you hear what Harris just said? With all due respect, Mr. Parker; I believe that you may be overacting. Inconvenience is what we often fear so much. We want everything to be easy, but unfortunately, that's not always the case. My suggestion is for you to contact the Office of Casualty and Property Adjustments so that they can assist you with this inconvenience and begin making the necessary repairs to your home.

• • • •

Monday morning, I called Mr. Wellington from the office. He said there wasn't much else for us to do at this point except wait for Crosby's trial date to be scheduled, and to try to stay out of Thomas' way while his investigator dug up more evidence to support vandalism charges against him.

Someone on your street must have heard something, he said. I've spoken to the Assistant Prosecutor also; they know they have problems with that nut-case neighbor of yours with the loose screws.

Their case stinks like horseshit and everyone knows it. It stinks worse than a Texas rodeo. The charges will be dropped before this thing ever gets to trial.

What is taking them so long, sir? Unfortunately, Parker, the wheels of justice turn slowly. But don't worry, they are turning...slowly.

<h1 style="text-align:center">Part IV – Province West</h1>

There are two ways to live; you can live as if nothing is a miracle; you can live as if everything is a miracle.
    -Albert Einstein

XIII

Francis claims that the only advantages to living in the Province are more Burger Kings and fewer stop signs. There is at least one more that he forgot to mention, a bowling alley. The one in The Miracle Mile is buzzing with activity on Saturday night. I had no problem convincing him to go bowling this weekend, and Carleton and Crosby jumped at the idea as well. This will be so much fun, they both said.

There is no alley in all of City Centre, and neither Carleton nor I had ever tried to bowl before now. But Crosby and Francis are good at any sport you can think of, and they promised to teach us.

Things at home have calmed down some since the spray painting incident. Francis is back in his apartment and I have taken Mr. Wellington's advice to avoid Thomas as much as I can. The weather is turning cooler, so I don't spend as much time outside the cottage now. The garden will not need much attention for the next couple of months, and even on warmer days, I avoid sitting out on the porch if I notice his car in their carport. I don't appreciate having to knuckle under to that crazy bastard, but for now, I think it's the smartest thing to do.

Tonight though, is going to be a lot of fun. We spent the last few weekends in City Centre, and I am looking forward to going out in The Miracle Mile for something different. The three of them will drive over in Carleton's car, and then Francis can take the train back to the city on Monday morning.

We are getting along somewhat better now, but we still have a lot of work to do. He has been surprisingly supportive as I've struggled to deal with all the shit that has happened. Although he agreed in principle to at least try couples therapy, we haven't made an appointment as of yet. He procrastinates and comes up with excuses whenever I raise the subject. I know he's not convinced that it won't just turn out to be a waste of time. I'm going to keep after him about it, but hey, I can't force him to go.

After they arrive, we decide to walk to the East Gate. We can drink as much as we want, and it's a nice enough evening to be out walking the fifteen minutes or so that it takes to get to the Continental restaurant. We never did make it over there when Francis was staying at the cottage and now I was looking forward to checking it out. Everyone is talking about it.

Good evening gentlemen, may I see your Residency Permits, please? I took mine out and handed it to the Guard, along with the three Visitors Permits I remembered to bring along. May I ask the purpose of your visit this evening? We have reservations at the Continental restaurant, sir. He stamped the back of each permit and said, enjoy yourselves, gentlemen. I believe you will find the cuisine quite exquisite tonight. My wife and I were there recently; I can recommend the lobster if you have a taste for seafood this evening. Thank you, sir. Have a good evening then, gentlemen.

The restaurant is something else. I discover that it was modeled after the famous Napa Valley eatery called The French Laundry, which was originally constructed as a saloon around 1900. Later, it served as a French steam laundry, which is how it got its name. Our version is a near-perfect replica of The French Laundry's architectural style, with its blue door, outdoor garden, and the earthy feel of marble, granite, and rough copper floor tiles. The place is quite spectacular, and I make a mental note to promise myself that if I somehow find my way to Northern California, I'll eat there no matter what.

I took the guard's suggestion and ordered poached Nova Scotia Lobster, along with the Hawaiian hearts of palm salad. Francis had American Pekin duck with something called Northern Spy apple salad. Everyone loved what they ordered and we later learned that the restaurant is considered to be among the top five in the entire

Western District. It set us back a big chunk of cash, but it was worth it.

After finishing our espresso, we head to the bowling alley, which is directly across the street. I laugh when I think about it. Only in a place like The Miracle Mile can you find one place so fancy and sophisticated, and another so blue-collar common, within a stone's throw of each other.

First, we need to get shoes, Francis announced. When I spot the funny-looking red and green shoes we need to wear, I am tempted to call the whole thing off and go drinking at the Club instead. Carleton had no problem finding a pair he liked, but mine felt weird and I kept tripping myself up while trying to walk on the carpet in them.

We somehow wind up where we belong on lane 39 and stash our regular shoes under a chair. Let me go first! Wait, Parker; you need to pick out a ball first. There must have been a hundred or more balls of various colors stored on racks behind the lanes. Carleton said, pick one based on the size of the holes, not the color. That's how I pick my boyfriends. Ha ha, good one Carleton. Francis frowned but I thought it was funny. I eventually settled on a pink one, because the black balls left ugly marks on my thumb and seemed much too heavy. Now that everybody had the proper shoes and balls, all we had to do was figure out what to do with them.

Lanes 38 and 40, the two immediately to our left and right, presented interesting contrasts to me. Perfect examples of who you might expect to see out at night in The Miracle Mile. On our left was a young couple about our age with two school-age boys. They were polite and waited to let those on the adjacent lanes take their turns first, which conformed to the protocol that Crosby told us about earlier. Be careful not to distract the people around you, he said. It's rude to charge up to the line just as they are about to deliver their ball. The parents were drinking beer and chatted with us at the scorers' table while we were getting set up.

You guys all have nice outfits, she commented. Do you shop in The Miracle Mile? Not too often, I answered. We mainly go to City Centre. I used to live in the city, she said, but we rarely take the boys there anymore. Isn't it dangerous at night?

I had to stop for a moment to consider how naïve, or more accurately ironic that question sounded. I'd never been involved in a single serious incident in all the years I lived in the city. But in just a few months in the Province, I'd been verbally harassed, physically threatened, made to witness my friend being assaulted, had my house vandalized, and been ignored by the people who had the responsibility to protect us from such things. No, I said; it's pretty safe normally. But it's very expensive to live there and kind of noisy at night. I sleep better here.

Ah, yes; we live in Province West and never have problems sleeping there! I said then, Province West sounds great, but we've never had the chance to drive through to check it out. We don't have the right Permit, and I don't have a car either. I'd like to visit though. Yes, you should, she said. Maybe we can have you over to the house sometime. We have a swimming pool and the boys love to cook out on the backyard barbecue.

On the lane to our right were four young straight guys. They were drinking and getting obnoxious. They had scary-looking tattoos and even scarier-looking outfits. I doubt they shopped in The Miracle Mile either. The least attractive of the group wore an oversized sweatshirt with the words *Province South High School* written on the front. Here we are, situated between these rather diverse groups of Province residents, lanes 38 through 40 arguably representing the three major socioeconomic classes of people that make up the vast majority in most modern societies.

Finally, it was time to start. Carleton, you go first, I said. I wanted to watch for a little bit and maybe come up with a way to avoid making a complete fool of myself. I didn't need to worry, Carleton took care of that for me instead. I don't know why he decided to ignore Crosby's advice, but he did. You are supposed to approach the foul line slowly, but he chose instead to charge full speed ahead and let the ball fly. I guess he figured the added force would increase his chances of knocking down more pins. Uh, not exactly. The ball headed toward the left gutter, but then, seemingly with a mind of its own, skipped like a stone on a pond and right onto lane 38. There, the younger of the two boys patiently awaited his turn, only to find that he would have to wait even longer now, since Carleton's errant ball had knocked down most of the pins that the kid was just about to aim for.

Oh my lord, I'm sorry; I've never bowled before. The boy had a dumbfounded expression on his face, but his parents just laughed. No problem, the guy said; I've had that happen to me once or twice before. Carleton took his time on the second shot, which mercifully stayed on lane 39 where it belonged, and managed to knock down two pins.

Francis was up next and threw a strike on his first try, the clattering pins erupting with a deep resonating sound that can only be heard when the ball is delivered perfectly in the pocket. How did he do that?

It is my turn now and I want to make this look good. I down more beer to give me some courage before I stand there with my pink ball, staring down at the pins. I start forward, but as I bring the ball back, the smooth-soled shoes begin to slide on the highly polished hardwood alley, causing my balance to be off some, and so when I let the ball go, my left foot slid out from under me and I fell right on my ass. Miraculously, and with no help from me, the ball finds the headpin, and all ten pins go right to the floor along with me.

I stood up to cheers and high-fives from people around us, but not from the guys on lane 40. They were getting more drunk and more verbal as the evening progressed. I ignored them and concentrated on the game, which despite my less-than-glamorous grand entrance, was turning out to be so much fun. I managed two strikes in the first game and finished with what I considered a very respectable score of 135.

The family from Province West is very nice and I like all four of them just fine. The boys seem somewhat curious about us but are happy to wait their turns and offer advice to Carleton on several occasions where his shots conspicuously avoid contact with any of the pins. The older of the two, who told us his name was Gordon, took a shine to Carleton right away. He is a sixteen-year-old sophomore at the Province West Preparatory School for Boys. Bring your arm back more slowly and make sure it is straight before you let the ball go, he suggests. Gordon was right; Carleton hit the headpin on the very next shot and knocked nine pins over. We clap and then watch with a mix of excitement and amazement as he now makes a graceful approach, and follows through with a perfectly placed shot to convert the spare.

Their father, Webster, returns from the concessions with six beers and offers one to each of us. I thank him and sit back feeling relaxed now, sipping my beer and awaiting my next turn. Frances throws yet another strike and we all jump up to congratulate him before I give him a big hug. The guy on lane 40 with the Province South sweatshirt gave us a nasty look and made an odd sort of grunting noise, that reminded me suddenly of a sound I seem to recall coming from the baboon exhibit I saw as a child in the City Centre Zoo.

I ignored him, but Crosby glared back. Were you speaking to us? The guy stood there without answering, but there was a flicker of something dark and unsettling that spread across his face. His gaze held mine with a menacing and unnatural intensity that gave me the creeps. Crosby took a couple of steps toward the four of them, but Francis and I stepped right in front of him. Let's just sit down and finish the game, ignore them.

The loudest and most foul-looking of the group decides to speak up for his friend. Who let you fairies in here anyhow? Oh boy, this might be a big mistake on his part. We've seen already that Crosby is not about to just sit there and listen to this sort of crap. I knew how he might react when hearing his friends being verbally assaulted. Be careful here, Crosby, I said to myself. I guess he wasn't listening.

He said, shut up and sit back down before I make you even uglier than you already are. Wow, might a little anger management be in order here? Wouldn't a simple *mind your own business* or even *we have a right to be here too* have sufficed as an opening move? Still, I was impressed by his lack of fear around these assholes; they were after all pretty rough-looking dudes from Province South. They scared the crap out of me. What concerned me also when I took a look at them, were the two young boys on lane 38 taking all of this in.

I bet their father was equally anxious about that. Webster was standing now, trying to make peace if he could. C'mon guys, let's not start anything here. Let's just go finish our games. I'll give Webster credit for at least trying, but the guy with the sweatshirt must have figured out now how to synchronize his brain with his vocal cords. You want your boys watching these faggots hugging and kissing?

It's a damn good thing Francis and I both get a quick hold on Crosby. He better not get loose or this is going to get very ugly very quickly. Carleton was there now too, trying to calm Crosby down. Sit down, please; you know we don't need any more trouble with the law. Everyone back off. But I know Carleton like I know me. He's not about to let them off that easily. He turned to lane 40 and sneered at them; fuck off, all four of you.

But it was Webster's wife Wilma, who got right in the middle of the fracas and restored order before any blows were thrown, or any handcuffs were locked onto Crosby's wrists. Good thing; I don't think we can rely on Mr. Sanderson or Ms. Millerton a second time to bail us out of another mess.

Wilma had some choice comments for the punk guy. Actually, young man, it is of no concern to either me or my husband what our sons see them doing. You, on the other hand, are setting a pathetic example for them, and you need to watch your language in our presence. I suggest you gather up your things now and remove yourselves before I have the manager call the Constable's office and have them do it for you.

Wow, that was something. They come pretty tough in Province West.

I was kind of stunned when the homophobes from Province South did exactly as they were told and were gone in just a couple of minutes. Right then I remembered something my father used to tell me when I got picked on in school for being gay. *Cowards will nearly always back down if you stand up to them, Parker.* I had trouble with that concept as a child, but maybe he was right.

Carleton is quite shaken now, and he and Crosby sit close while we have more beer with Wilma and Webster. Thank you guys, I said. We've been having a lot of problems with my neighbor lately, and things haven't been so great since I moved from the city. It's okay, Parker; nobody deserves to be spoken to that way. Gordon is very clearly captivated by Carleton by this time, and he sits down right next to him. Way to tell those assholes off. Watch your language, Gordon, I heard Wilma say.

The younger boy, Carson, seemed the least affected by what went on, and he resumed his place a few steps from the foul line. Can I go now, Dad? Let's go, Carson. We laughed and resumed our game.

Another group of young straight guys took over the now vacated lane 40, but they were polite and introduced themselves to us. What a coincidence, all four of them were neighbors of mine in Miracle Estates East. *There are no gay people in the Province.* That can't be true, can it?

While Crosby and Webster took turns on their respective lanes, I asked Carson to come with me to the concession stand to help carry another round of drinks and two large tubs of buttered popcorn. I gave one of the popcorns to the new guys next to us.

Wouldn't you know it, Francis rolled yet another strike just as I was setting the refreshments down. This time I just high-five him as he walks back to the scorers' table. Better save the kiss for later, babe. Gordon looked slightly embarrassed, his cheeks now turning a rosy shade of pink. The best-looking of the guys on lane 40 was about to launch his ball when he must have heard me. My comment likely perked up his ears and distracted him just enough, sending his shot flying straight into the gutter. That got us all laughing again.

While waiting at the front desk to pay, Wilma suggested that we exchange phone numbers and keep in touch. That's a good idea, I thought; I don't know anyone who lives in Province West. She said, we're planning a cookout next Sunday and would enjoy having you join us. Feel free to bring more of your friends if you would like. Thanks for inviting us. Francis suggested that Winston and Tyler might like to come along.

No outdoor grilling is allowed in Province East because a lot of the houses are very close together, and because some moron in my neighborhood sprayed about a quart of starter fluid on his grill before trying to light it with a torch. There went the carport, and there came the ordinance. No more outdoor cooking allowed. None of our friends had the space to have a barbecue in the city, so this would be a treat for us. What can we bring along, Wilma? How about a batch of Parker's Carolina coleslaw and one of Crosby's apple cakes?

Webster, we don't have a permit to drive in Province West, I just remembered. That's alright he said; you don't need one. That's just to keep rowdy people from Province South from causing problems. If you get stopped, just show your Residency Permit from Province East and tell the officer you are visiting us. They will know who we are and let you in.

Francis gave me a funny look; really, no permit needed for us? I bet he's wondering what other meaningless rules and regulations we might sidestep and not get in any trouble for deliberately violating. I thought about it more too. Could I really get five days in the slammer for forgetting my Residency Permit a couple of times? I'm always forgetting something.

Let me ask you something, Webster; do you have to show your Province West Permit to take the train into town? I doubt it, but I can't remember the last time we took the train to City Centre. We almost never go anymore, but if we do we just drive. When Wilma and I were dating, we loved to go to the clubs and shows in the city. Now, with the kids and everything, it's easier to just take them out in The Miracle Mile. Wilma said that she didn't much miss the nightlife in the city anymore. I used to love it there after I graduated from college, but now we like the convenience of just staying in the Province and not having to bother with all the traffic and the crime.

I wondered if suburban living would change me after a few years. I considered the reality of what they were saying. Yes, convenience is what we all hope for, all of the time. Who wants to drive around looking for a parking space or worry about the car being vandalized when you could just enjoy a cocktail instead during intermission at the Province Symphony? Why deal with the inconvenience of City Centre's magnificent Theatre District when we can more easily catch

La Traviata at The Splendor, the somewhat embarrassing Miracle Mile replica of Radio City Music Hall?

In The Miracle Mile, the quaint boutique has morphed into a 7-Eleven, the charming café transformed into a Chick-fil-A, the urban department store remodeled and now a Target, and the old-fashioned soda fountain misshapen into a Tastee-Freez. All this to avoid the inconvenience we fear most. A cheeseburger and fries instead of quiche Lorraine, a Diet Pepsi as opposed to artesian mineral water, and a cherry snow cone rather than an Italian gelato.

What time should we be over for the cookout on Sunday? We can't wait!

• • • •

I knew that damn investigator from Internal Affairs would be back before long, with his accusations and his bad breath. Mr. Sanderson stalled him once already, but he doesn't seem like someone easily dissuaded. He came bellowing over one morning when Crosby and I were busy logging receipts from the previous evening. Mr. Sanderson could hear him all the way from inside his office and came running over.

I'm sorry, sir, but Mr. Parker will not be available to answer any of your questions today. As you can see, we are much too busy right now. I'm sure you can understand that. I am sorry to hear that, Mr. Sanderson, and I sympathize with your predicament, but he has no choice in the matter. You see, an Administrative Proceeding has now been filed and I have in my possession a subpoena requiring Mr. Parker to present himself for interrogation.

What do you mean by that, why would an Administrative Proceeding be required for something as inconsequential as the cost of a few medical bills? I'm afraid it may be more serious than that, Mr. Sanderson.

Shit, I didn't like where this was heading.

What do you mean, more serious? Ms. Millerton is off her platform now, and though Francis likes to call her stupid, I know differently. And I can use her help right about now. I'll tell you exactly what I mean, Ms. Millerton. Why the hell did he have to be so loud? Do all 250 people in our department need to know what I did?

He said, the investigation done by Internal Affairs has also revealed some discrepancies regarding certain requisitions and invoices emanating from this department that pertain indirectly to your accident. Since Mr. Parker initialed some of the documents in question, his testimony will be required, as this subpoena so states, and which is signed by the Assistant Administrative Law Clerk from the Department of Legal Inquiry.

I looked straight at Mr. Sanderson, praying for a miracle. He said, it is our intention to cooperate in every way possible, but since Mr. Parker is represented by counsel in this matter, it would be inappropriate for you to interrogate him at this time. Represented by who? By Mr. Wellington, that's who. The Investigator seems perplexed by this. That makes two of us.

So then, am I correct in assuming that Mr. Wellington's fees are coming out of this department's budget? That is correct, sir. Why would you do that, Mr. Sanderson? Because we are like a family in this department, that's why. When trouble presents its face here, we don't look the other way. Instead, we provide whatever support we can. In this case, Mr. Parker is entitled under Government protocol to have counsel of his choosing present prior to the execution of any subpoena, and prior to answering to any type of inquiry. And just out of curiosity, sir, what are the allegations that you keep referring to?

Well, Mr. Sanderson; let me say this. Some of the dates stamped by Ms. Millerton and initialed by Mr. Parker do not seem consistent. Are you serious, sir? All this nonsense because of some typographical error? I'm sure Ms. Millerton and I can clear up any simple discrepancy without the need for such formal discovery.

The Investigator said, I'm not sure that you can. It looks like some of the dates stamped were on a day when Ms. Millerton was absent from work with a bad viral infection. And one of the items initialed by Mr. Parker was on a day when he was away on holiday, to the Western Shore I believe. Sir, just a simple malfunction of the date stamp and a typographical error, I'm sure.

I'm sorry, Mr. Sanderson, but we will need to wait for Mr. Wellington if he is in fact going to be counsel of Mr Parker's choosing. Is he, Mr. Parker? He is, Mr. Sanderson interrupted. The Investigator looked straight at me. Mr. Parker? I pause now for a moment, waiting for the right answer to emerge from somewhere. Can I get back to you on that one?

• • • •

Great, all of this aggravation is going to screw up my weekend. Now I get to worry about the shitstorm waiting for me on Monday morning, instead of enjoying Wilma and Webster's cookout in Province West. I left a message for Mr. Wellington on Friday afternoon, but he was in trial defending a drunk driver from Province South. His secretary said he would call back first thing on Monday.

I'm stuck in the middle of this lose-lose situation. If I lie to protect Mr. Sanderson and Ms. Millerton, I'll lose my job for sure. If I tell the truth, both of their jobs as well as mine could be in serious jeopardy. Even if we all manage to survive, I will have to endure their wrath for the rest of my life probably. I agreed to their little scheme because I hated the thought of Crosby being locked up. But no matter what happens, I will never mention that aspect of the case and the favor they extracted from me.

Maybe Francis will know what to do. He is a lot smarter than me when it comes to stuff like this. I confessed to the whole story about my dishonesty and how I had initialed the log entries after the fact.

They won't take the fall for this, Parker; you know that, right? Maybe you can just get out with a warning or something and not get fired. You're kind of screwed now; they hold all the cards here. I said then, but don't you think Mr. Wellington will be able to help me? I'm sure he will try, Parker; but look who is paying his fees. He can't just blame everything on Sanderson and then send him his bill.

When do you have to meet with Mr. Wellington? Early next week, I guess. He is going to call me first thing Monday morning. If he wants you to come to his office next week, maybe I can take off work for a couple of hours and go with you. Would you do that for me, Francis? Of course, I would. I'd like to hear how he plans to get you out of this mess.

Don't stress out over this, Parker. Mr. Wellington probably has a lot of experience dealing with this kind of bullshit. Besides, Sanderson and Millerton are going to have to back you up because they know they coerced you into going along with their scheme. Trust me, they know very well that you could make them look bad if you felt like it. Both of them are nothing but con artists with years of experience doing shit like this. They will work out a deal with the Internal Affairs people somehow.

Really, Francis; how do you know? Because the whole Government is run by con artists like them. That's where our tax money goes, to pay for their dirty tricks. Didn't you know that? I nodded yes, but until just now, I did not know that.

XIV

We planned to arrive at 2:00 in the afternoon for the cookout in Province West. I called Webster on Saturday to confirm that we were still on. Bring your swimsuits, he said; it will be warm tomorrow.

I made so much Carolina coleslaw that I had to borrow a large bowl from Ms. Thomas to hold it all. Have fun guys, she said, as the six of us crammed into Francis' sedan and drove off. I didn't see Thomas' car and he was probably drunk at the Club by now. I punched the address into the Tom-Tom on the dash, and it had us right to the house in less than half an hour. Nobody stopped us to see our Residency Permits or ask where we were going.

None of us have ever been to Province West until now. I've seen pictures of the homes in real estate ads, but this is something else entirely. The area is so beautiful, the terrain consisting of rolling hills, streams, and a connected system of trails and walking paths. The subdivision where Wilma and Webster live is called Province Victory Gardens, inspired by a French architect who designed the homes and the landscaping. Each home site is very large, a full hectare or more in some cases, with spacious well-manicured lawns and mature shade trees. Most of the houses are either Neoclassical or French Country designs, all of them magnificent.

Webster and Wilma's house is no exception. As Francis is turning up the long entranceway, I notice a new Porsche 911 Coupe sitting in front of the three-car garage. We park off to the side in a grassy area where at least a dozen cars are already parked. The façade of the house is a mix of stucco and natural stone, with a steep-sloping slate roof and a large American-inspired covered porch with several rocking chairs on it. I stare in amazement, realizing this home could easily have eight or more bedrooms. Wow, look at this place, Winston comments, as he climbs out of the back seat. What does your friend Webster do for a living, sell meth?

A young domestic helper greeted us at the door and took my coleslaw and Crosby's apple cake. Welcome gentlemen, come this way, please. We are escorted through an immense foyer, centered by a grand-looking spiral staircase with intricately carved mahogany curtails and polished wood stair treads. The entrance is open all the way to the top of the second storey, from which a large chandelier with imperial crystal glass and at least a dozen glowing illuminated white tapers is hanging.

The backyard and pool area are off the kitchen, which looks like something out of *Better Homes and Gardens*. A chef is sautéing shrimp and vegetables on an industrial-sized stove that has eight burners, and another helper is removing fresh produce from a built-in refrigerator that you can step right into if you need to reach the deepest shelves. Carleton's eyes are as wide as Kennedy half-dollars, trying to take this all in. Can you believe these people go bowling, Parker? And pretty good at it too, I said. Webster broke 200 in the last game and Wilma had at least four strikes.

Hey guys, come on out, Webster said, as he introduced us to several of his friends. They were chatting about the Producer Price Index or stock futures, or something else that drew a blank look from me. These are our friends, Winston and Tyler, who missed the débâcle on lane 40. That got some laughs, and we told everyone about our recent excursion to The Miracle Mile.

They walked us over to the bar, where a real bartender made Cosmopolitans and Manhattans for us. Wilma spotted us then and ran over to give us each a warm hug. Nice to meet everyone; please, grab a plate and some food!

Gordon and Carson were stationed at an enormous chrome gas grill that I couldn't believe. At least thirty hamburgers were sizzling on its burners, along with lots of pork ribs and chicken. Ms. Thomas' huge bowl appeared on the buffet table and people were helping themselves to some of the coleslaw, along with the seared asparagus, corn on the cob, and the impressive array of appetizers and salads.

Gordon perked up as soon as he saw Carleton and the rest of us. I didn't think there was any way you guys would actually show, cool. Hey there Carson, how about a couple of those cheeseburgers for Francis and me? Try the barbecued chicken too, he suggested. I made it myself. Show off, Mom made it. Shut up, Gordon. They playfully jabbed each other while Carson served us from the grill. Did you really make this chicken, Carson? It smells fantastic. Well, Mom helped me, but Dad let me light the fire.

More guests continued to arrive and now there were at least fifty people out around the pool deck area, all from Province West I think. They were well dressed and seemed quite sophisticated and intelligent, talking about golf tournaments, sailboating, and other subjects we were completely unfamiliar with. At the same time, they were friendly and engaging, not a bit snobbish or presumptuous in any respect, and they seemed interested in our Government jobs and how I was enjoying life in the Province.

It's good for the most part, I said, but City Centre has its advantages. Oh yes, we love the Theater District and shopping there, one woman commented. It's a shame we don't get out there more, her husband added. We used to have season tickets to the opera and saw Pavarotti one year. Have you guys been? Not yet, but we go to the clubs there pretty often, and I've been to see the Falcons play. Wasn't the Championship Match fantastic? Webster has a sky suite at the Coliseum and about ten of us saw the game there.

Winston seemed mesmerized after hearing this. Damn, I'm sure he was thinking, why couldn't we have met these people a few weeks ago? I tried to get end-zone seats, he said, but they were all sold out. We did get to watch the Satellite broadcast though and had a really fun Championship Match party at Parker's place. No one mentioned the near brawl or the police arrest.

What a relaxing and enjoyable afternoon we all had, drinking and swimming in the pool and enjoying what was left of our weekend. Gordon is taking swimming lessons and showed me how to do a butterfly stroke. Crosby's apple cake had long been devoured by the time I lazily made my way to the dessert table, after a second Manhattan and having watched Carson show off his diving techniques to Tyler and Francis.

Carleton joined me at the dessert table, where I was loading up a big plate with fresh tropical fruits to take back to the pool area for everyone to share. I asked him, are you alright? I'm scared, Parker; what are they going to do to him? We're all here with you, Carleton. We're never going to let you face this alone. Mr. Wellington says not to worry. He says the case will never get to trial. I hope he is right, Parker. Me too.

Gordon made zero effort to hide his infatuation with Carleton, but both of the boys were polite and we didn't mind them hanging around. I told Wilma and Webster as much when it was time to leave. Your family is great and we had such a fun time today. So nice meeting everyone, they said, let's get together again soon.

• • • •

When I got to the office the next morning, Mr. Sanderson told me that he arranged for a meeting with Mr. Wellington that afternoon. He will be here at 2:00 to converse with you. In the meantime, Mr. Parker, it is imperative that you not speak to anyone about our situation, especially the Investigator from Internal Affairs.

What is going to happen to me, Mr. Sanderson? You need not worry yourself with these matters, he said. You do your job and allow me to do mine. Your job is to manage your invoices and receipts; my job is to manage problems such as this one.

I was very nervous about my job over the weekend, I said. My partner Francis said not to worry, but I'm afraid I might get fired.

I should not need to repeat myself, nor enlighten you further, but since you seem so distracted and therefore not likely to be very productive, I will seek to put your mind at ease. I have been employed by the Government for more than twenty years, and am therefore quite intimate with its inner workings. I am responsible for a department with nearly 250 individuals, which requires that people listen to what I have to say. Now, I want you to listen to what I am going to say to you.

How many invoices and receipts do you need to process today? Oh, about 200, I think. And how long would that normally take for you to complete? At least half the day, assuming that I don't get interrupted too often. Then you go to your desk now and do your work. Work through your lunch break if necessary. At 1:00, I will bring the keys and have Crosby assist you with the filing. If you have everything finished by the time Mr. Wellington arrives at 2:00, I can promise that you will not get in any trouble.

I start reviewing and logging the invoices as fast as I can so I can have them completed and stamped by Ms. Millerton before 1:00, and filed by the time Mr. Wellington gets here. Hey Parker, that cookout was fun, wasn't it? I can't talk to you now, Crosby; I need to finish all this work as soon as possible. Why? It's not going anywhere and it's only 8:15. C'mon, let's go to the coffee shop across the plaza for some glazed donuts and espresso. I really can't, sorry. I promised Mr. Sanderson I would have everything done by 2:00.

Don't worry about that, Parker. I can easily distract Mr. Sanderson, he laughed. I can take care of any problem you have with him. That's true normally, but I don't think Mr. Sanderson will be flirting with you today. How come? Because Mr. Wellington is coming here to talk to him, that's why. Why would he do that? I promised I wouldn't say anything. You can tell me, Parker. You know I won't tell anyone, my lips are sealed. I've heard that one before and it nearly cost me. Crosby, just make sure you are back from lunch before 1:00, okay? I may need your help.

Later that afternoon, Mr. Wellington came by to chat for a minute with Crosby and me before going into a private conference with Mr. Sanderson. He did not say anything about the subpoena or the Internal Affairs investigation. Crosby helped me get all the filing done on time. He kept asking if this had something to do with the case against him. Maybe they are discussing what will happen if I am not acquitted, and whether or not to appeal. It's not about your case, trust me, I said.

It's past 4:30 in the afternoon and they are still in Mr. Sanderson's office. I wonder what the hell is going on. Nearly everyone has left for the day, and I need to sign out with the Timekeeper so I don't go over my scheduled time and have that land in my Permanent Record.

Sign out here if you don't mind, he said. I hear there might be quite a stir with Mr. Sanderson and that low-budget Solicitor they hired. Wasting half a day sorting out some monkey business you had with Internal Affairs. Sir, maybe you can kind of keep this quiet. I don't want everyone here to know about that. And you shouldn't speak about Mr. Wellington that way; he is a respected Solicitor.

Whatever you say, Parker, but if he were such a great attorney, do you think he would be wasting his time in this office? He'd be arguing a case before the Magistrate's Court of Justice instead of defending drunk drivers from Province South.

For your information, I know for a fact that he will be appearing before his Honor the Magistrate on a very serious matter. Are you kidding me, Parker? You think Crosby popping some redneck in the nose is serious? The guy makes his living pandering to low-level civil servants like Mr. Sanderson.

How did you know about Crosby hitting someone? I know everything that happens here, he said. That's why I'm the Timekeeper. I keep track of a lot more than just the time. Everyone has to pass my way twice each day, whether coming or going, whether they like it or not. They don't get paid until I say they can. They can't leave until I say go. Do you realize the power that gives me? No, I don't, I respond. All I see you doing is cleaning your clock and writing in your log.

You're a pretty sharp guy, he said, but think about it. I know you think my job is mundane and yours is more important. Well, he did have a point there, I did think that sometimes. He continued, but I track everyone and everything here, so I always know what's going on. I said, I'm having a hard time believing that, sir.

No? Would you believe me if I told you that Mr. Sanderson claimed that he requisitioned a banister be built for Ms. Millerton's platform before she fell? You don't know that, sir. Or that certain official documents were stamped supposedly by Ms. Millerton on a day she called out sick? I asked him, did the Investigator from Internal Affairs tell you that? It doesn't matter how I found out; don't you understand? Nothing can get past me.

Nothing, sir; are you sure about that? Tell me then, am I in any sort of trouble? Ha-ha, now we are getting somewhere. Do you really need me to tell you? You are smart enough to answer that question for yourself. Well, you just said you know everything, so prove it.

He gives me a little twisted smile. C'mon, tell me what you know, I said. Alright, I will. I know you have been itching for a promotion to Assistant Secretary. I know that you were driving in Province West without a Permit. I know you like to stay at the Sandcastle Shore Inn at the Western Shore. Is that proof enough, or should I continue? No, that is quite impressive, I have to admit. So, you must know if I am in any trouble or not. Of course, I do, Parker.

Don't worry so much, he tells me. Reason it out logically instead. Mr. Sanderson and Ms. Millerton know what they are doing. The whole thing with the logs and time stamps is absurd, of course nothing is going to happen to you. The Government has more important things to do than trying to run you out of town. They want more Processors, not fewer ones.

Then tell me sir; why are they sending the Investigator around with subpoenas and threats? That's what they do, Parker. That's what our taxes are for, so people have jobs and so the Government can justify its existence. If they didn't send the Investigator around, then Mr. Sanderson and Mr. Wellington might not have anything to do. All three of them might find themselves unemployed and how would that look?

Do you think any of our jobs are really important? They could do away with me just by installing a simple computer application to record the time. All six of our Clerical Assistants could drop dead and you probably wouldn't even notice the difference, except there might not be donuts on Monday morning. In just a few hours, one person could scan every single invoice and receipt that all twelve Processors manage in an entire day, and no one would suffer as a consequence. Except for you, that is, Parker. You would be out of a job and so would the rest of us once everyone realized that most of the work we do could be easily eliminated. Think how horrible that would be. What would I say to my wife if I came home without a job; sorry dear, no more vacations to the Mountain Campgrounds? Oh, look at this clock they gave me to put on the mantel.

You know sir, that's pretty much what my partner Francis told me the other day. He said not to worry because our taxes pay for the Government to hire con artists. The Timekeeper said, your partner is a smart guy and I understand is doing quite well with that management firm where he works. I don't remember ever telling you about his job, sir. I'm the Timekeeper, Parker. Remember that, okay?

· · · ·

Mr. Parker, may I speak with you before you leave for home? Mr. Sanderson and Mr. Wellington were finally finished with their meeting. Mr. Wellington has assisted me in resolving these pesky legal problems and you have nothing to worry about. I said, you mean I won't have to be subjected to another interview? The Investigator will not be contacting you again; he's gone. He agreed that the medical reimbursement claim is without merit and there are no factual inconsistencies with the requisitions or the invoices.

I asked then, you said he was gone; where did he go to? He was promoted to Senior Investigator in the Department of Securities and Fraud. Since he agreed to drop the investigation, I agreed to put in a good word with the Superintendent in his new department. He and I were old college drinking buddies. Besides, the Investigator has a background in banking and finance, and it was felt that he was being underutilized by Internal Affairs. Mr. Wellington looked after the legal implications and everyone signed all the forms, so it is done. You may go home to your dinner now, Mr. Parker.

On my way out, I stopped once more at the Timekeeper's desk. You were right, sir; it looks like I'm getting off without even a warning. Of course, Parker; I know everything that happens here. I told you not to worry. Everything, really? You still don't believe me; well it doesn't matter I guess. He asked then, by the way, did Mr. Sanderson happen to mention the Investigator's promotion to the Securities and Fraud Department? I just stared right at him without saying anything. How could he have found out about that, it just happened? You signed out earlier, Parker; you may leave now. I just gazed at him more. Who told him everything? He said, are you alright now? Yes, I'm just relieved this is over, I said. Good night to you, sir.

· · · ·

Later that evening, I got a call from Webster. Would you and Francis like to join us for dinner next Saturday at the new Spanish restaurant in The Miracle Mile? We haven't been there yet, but hear they have the best paella anywhere.

I never tasted paella and wasn't even sure exactly what it was. Something with Spanish rice, I think. Francis said, that sounds like fun; I hope they serve pinchitos or arròs negre. I'm going to try the paella, babe. That sounds good too, he said.

The restaurant is an ornate Modernisme-style building that I guess people are supposed to believe was designed by Antoni Gaudí himself. But he died way back in 1926, so unless the structure was somehow disassembled and shipped to the Province to be reconstructed, it is an elaborate fake. There is nothing fake about the food though. I doubt it would be surpassed by anything we might order in City Centre, or even in Barcelona for that matter. Everything we ordered tasted great. We shared two bottles of Rioja, which was the best wine I've ever had. Not that I'm an expert when it comes to imported red varietals; I mean, we normally drink ale or cheap box wine imported from Eastern Europe. Tonight, we toasted to our friendship with the imported Spanish wine each time our waiter came to refill our glasses.

After dessert, Webster ordered a round of Alabama Slammers. Wilma is the one to gracefully bring up the delicate subject that I see now has been on their minds. It's Gordon, she says; we are a little concerned about him. He gave us a hard time about staying home tonight to look after Carson. He kept complaining because he wanted to spend the night at his friend Cooper's house. I'm too old to be a babysitter, he kept saying.

He's at that age, Webster said, which we understand. But lately, he's been different. It's like he is hiding something and refuses to talk to us. And then the maid found some magazines in his bedroom when she was cleaning. Magazines, Wilma? Yes, male magazines, I'm afraid.

We know it's normal for him to explore his sexuality, and if he decides he wants to be gay, we would do anything to support him. Webster, he won't decide to be gay; he either is or he isn't. Somebody or something else did the deciding already. Of course, I know that, he said. It's just that we want him to talk to us. We want to help him; we just don't know how.

Francis said, if there is something we can do, we would be happy to give it a try. It's just, well, we don't have much recent experience with boys his age. But now that I think about it, Tyler is just a few years older than Gordon. They seemed to hit it off and enjoy swimming together at the cookout. Maybe he and his friend Harris would like to hang out with Gordon sometime.

Gordon seems quite attached to Carleton and Crosby. They would be good role models for him, don't you think? He'd probably be comfortable enough with them to talk about his feelings. Do you think they might be willing to spend some time with him? Sure, they like Gordon. I'll mention it to both of them at work on Monday. They go to the Roller Derby about once a month. Maybe Gordon would like to tag along with them sometime.

Francis remembered something then. We need to tell you that Crosby is in a little bit of legal trouble. I don't know if that will change the way you feel about him spending time with Gordon. We told them about our dreadful experiences with my neighbor, and the irksome charges that were pending still. Mr. Wellington thinks he will get off, but it's been weeks now and the trial is still scheduled for next month.

Webster said, can I ask how Crosby happened to choose Mr. Wellington to represent him? Francis and I look at each other before I speak up. Mr. Sanderson must have made the arrangements. I see, and would it be presumptive for me to ask if Mr. Sanderson had anything to do with arranging bail? We both answered *no* simultaneously. Webster asked if we thought Crosby would mind if he looked into the matter further. A good friend of mine is a Barrister, and he has some connections at the Magistrate's Court of Justice. Maybe he can help you. By the way, Wilma added, what you told us about Crosby does not change how we feel one bit, and yes, I bet Gordon would love to go with them to the Roller Derby.

This could be our lucky break. We are lucky Webster and his family just happened to be on lane 38 at just the same time we decided to try bowling, just for the hell of it. It's funny how things turn out that way, just by chance. Francis claims there is some deeper purpose behind things that appear to be completely random. I never believed in anything like that, but now I am not about to question it. Wilma and Webster were nice enough from the moment we sat down next to them at the scorers' table in the bowling alley. When we took way too long to take our turns, they were patient. They bought us beer and put the nasty guys from Province South in their place. Now, out of the blue, Webster says he has a friend who may be able to help Cosby.

XV

I'll admit it, I am a worrier by nature. True, I don't have to worry anymore about losing my job, but I am still very worried about Crosby's upcoming trial. I worry too that Francis might find out about the little affair Hunter and I had at the beach. Would he stumble upon the text messages that Hunter and I occasionally exchange? I still think about the fun we had together and wonder if I will ever see him again.

Thinking about Hunter brings back bittersweet memories of Duncan. Oh, he was a beautiful boy whom this then-sixteen-year-old thought he loved more than humanly possible. He was both smart and somewhat of a smart ass. His good-natured bantering and sarcastic wit got him into occasional hot water with our school teachers, but they never stayed mad at him for very long. He cast his charming spell over them just like he did with me. Hunter had that same kind of impulsive mastery, it seemed.

Duncan was one of the best fútbol players in the entire junior class, but he never played on the team. I don't feel like it, he would say. It's too competitive and they don't want a gay guy on the team. You don't need to do it for me, I'd tell him, as we kicked the ball around on the field when nobody was around. It was better for me this way too; we could spend more time together if he didn't have to practice every day after school. We could touch each other and make out behind the scoreboard sometimes without the threat of disapproval from our classmates or rejection from his teammates.

The bullies had an uncanny knack for singling out gay boys, channeling their anger and insecurities into relentless harassment. Duncan was my protector then. We spent almost two years together, with me being convinced that he was everything a boy could possibly dream of, and him struggling to remain afloat with such an unlucky draw for parents.

As we meandered through the maze of secondary school, the taunting and intimidation eased somewhat. Our tormentors hadn't gone away, but with the locks snapped off the closet doors, I didn't notice them so much. I found myself less affected by their actions, realizing they never warranted the attention they received to begin with. If the school administrators were determined to ignore the problem, I resigned myself to doing the same thing.

Of course, their hostility was always following just a step or two behind.

Duncan and Parker,
Sitting in a tree...

We built a different sort of space between us and them; a space with no walls to hide behind, but one we could survive in for another year or two. I was so into him that I hardly noticed it by then. Go ahead and make fun of us. There is nowhere else I'd rather be than kissing Duncan in a tree or wherever.

Why are they so mean to us, Parker? We never did anything to them. I had to laugh at his innocence. I told him, it's because they are nothing like you, okay?

I see London,
I see France...

Who cares what the fuck they see? All I wanted to see was his beautiful smile while we lay together in the comfort of the grassy field behind the fútbol stadium.

Most of the time, people liked to pretend that we were something other than what we obviously were. I wondered though, what did they think we were up to on those sleepovers and camping trips? What they knew but pretended not to was that we were anxiously exploring each other's body and mind, lost in a land of our curiosity and desire. And we were happy to keep doing it for as long as they would keep pretending.

We knew it had to end of course. We were just too young and not equipped to grapple with the intensity of our feelings. Ours was a real-world land of make-believe. But I was happy in that world and would even sing about it.

> *We're living in a land of make-believe*
> *And trying not to let it show*
> *Maybe in that land of make-believe*
> *Heartaches can turn into joy*

So let us make believe we are mature enough to overcome the obstacles right in front of us. Ah, shit, we are just teenagers, not magicians. We can't pull off this illusion. It was easier for me. I was carefree and oblivious much of the time. But Duncan was under enormous pressure. Pressure to get into a pre-med program at the University, pressure to have a girlfriend, pressure to give in to his parents' constant demands.

Worse yet, our adolescence had been taken from us by invisible forces we could not even conceive. We had no support from a social order that was thoroughly ignorant of who we were, and fully contemptuous of our deepest feelings. *You're sick, you're disgusting, you're an abomination.* We were everything they hated, but couldn't explain why. And they felt no compulsion to even try. If you hate us so much, at least come up with a reason or two that might make some logic of your senseless loathing.

Then everything collapsed all around me. The day before Duncan was to set out on his incredible journey to a far-away place called Cornell University, he decided to do himself in. And he nearly succeeded too; the emergency room staff having to work on him for two hours, pumping out the poisonous drugs he ingested, and coaxing him back to the land of make-believe he thought he'd left for good.

I saw him just one time in the hospital. His parents were there too, not as badly shaken or saddened as they were disdainful of me. I knew I would not see him again for a long time, if ever, as I kissed him a tearful goodbye.

They blamed me for what happened to him. Go ahead, if it makes you feel better. It was their fault, not mine or Duncan's, I knew. He was pure and beautiful and blessed with about every God-dammed thing you can imagine, everything except an understanding mother or father.

They had him moved to a psychiatric hospital in another district, where he stayed for a very long time. We wrote to each other on and off for about a year but were never allowed a visit. We lost touch eventually and I don't know what became of him. He might still be in the hospital for all I know, or he might not even be alive. I would hate to find that out now, so I don't try to. I don't want to learn any awful truths about Duncan that might obscure or diminish what are only beautiful memories.

I think about him still, but can't picture him. I wish I had some photos of us together. What would it be like if he walked right up to me now? I might not even recognize him today.

I did find out that his parents were both killed in a terrible car accident a few years back, when whichever one of them was driving missed a sharp curve late at night before ending up twisted around a tree. Too bad for them; they should have paid more attention to where they were going while they still had the chance. And they should have paid more attention to helping Duncan while he still had the chance. They chose instead to steal everything from him and maim whatever was left of his spirit just so they could be spared some embarrassment. Then they stuck him someplace far enough away that I would never see him again, never touch him again, or never say the things to him again that might possibly help him get better.

I wasn't sorry to hear they were dead. Justice is allotted to a select few and is often dispensed unfairly. They got what they deserved, and maybe I got the justice I deserved. Call it revenge instead if you want, but I don't care. They hurt Duncan terribly, and I'm going to hate them for as long as I choose, which is longer than forever.

Hunter reminds me of Duncan in a lot of ways. But now we live in a different world where adult-age discretion and responsibility have washed away the land of make-believe we used to know. They control how we are supposed to feel and behave. Our hijacked adolescence is blurred now, as we try desperately to make up for lost time and compensate for what should have been learned when we were young.

It saddens me to think back on those years. Francis refuses to talk about his childhood, and probably for good reasons. By extension, mine is usually off-limits as well. Why bring up all that crap, Parker? Does it really make you feel better? Yes, it does, I should have said, but I just shrugged instead and said maybe not.

That made me feel alone and depressed. I needed someone to hold me and tell me that Duncan did love me, that he didn't actually intend to leave this world with me left alone in it. I don't know if Francis can ever be that person. Maybe I can get him to talk to Dr. Hendrickson about it. If he'll ever go to therapy.

I felt the urge to dial Hunter's number but decided against it. We'd exchanged a few text messages, but never spoke on the phone. I remember how soothing his voice was late at night; he even sounded like Duncan. I don't know what I would say to him now. I felt a little overwhelmed by my despondency and I was sure he would be able to detect it in my voice. So I went to bed and drifted off to sleep alone, not wanting my voice to betray me and burden Hunter this late at night.

• • • •

The impending trial date did little to ease the hollow ache of my depressing mood. Crosby and I were in the office, and I wanted to bring up the discussion of Mr. Wellington representing him. Of course, Mr. Sanderson was close by staring as usual, and he could easily overhear our conversation. I was eager to give him a heads-up about what Webster had told me earlier. I said, I need to talk to you about something important that I don't want anyone else to know about. Can you meet me at noon on the plaza? Sure, there is something I want to discuss with you also, and I don't want Carleton to hear it.

Before I headed outside at noon, I grabbed a Diet Coke from the vending machine and the peanut butter sandwich from my desk. It was an overcast and windy day and nobody else was around. What is it you wanted to tell me, Parker? No, you first, Crosby. He was beaming now; you're not going to believe this, Carleton and I are getting married! Oh my God, that's fantastic. When? He said, just as soon as all this legal business is over with. Carleton didn't want to tell anyone until after the trial, but I know he is going to ask you to be our best man at the wedding, and I figured you could use a little good news about now.

I am taken by surprise with the news and nearly overcome with happiness. You know he is my best friend, I said, and I'm so excited for both of you. Tears of joy begin to trickle down my cheeks. Don't tell Francis yet, okay? He wants to announce it later to all our friends.

Now, what did you want to tell me? I couldn't give him any bad news today, or something else to worry about either. Oh, it's nothing really, just that I had fun at the cookout and that Gordon might like to go to the Roller Derby sometime. He gave me a funny look; that's what you were afraid Mr. Sanderson might overhear? Yeah, well everyone seems to know all my business these days, especially the Timekeeper.

. . . .

Later that evening, the mobile rang while I was relaxing at home watching an old rerun of a TV show called *Leave It to Beaver*. It comes on the Satellite every weeknight at 9:30 and I love to watch it before the evening news at 10:00. This is one of my favorite episodes. Beaver landed a job as a golf caddy and both his youthful enthusiasm and innocence are equally shattered when he catches the guy he is caddying for cheating on the score to win a bet. I better turn off the TV so Beaver's cute brother Wally doesn't distract me while I'm talking to Webster, who is now on the line.

I've got some information about the judge in Crosby's case, he tells me. He's got a hard-on for both Mr. Sanderson and Mr. Wellington. Really, why? He continues, a few years ago Sanderson was found guilty of perjury in some type of conspiracy case where his friend in the Department of Securities and Fraud had been accused of corruption. It seems the guy was getting kickbacks from other departments in exchange for hiring friends of Sanderson's and at least one other Superintendent. Some college buddy of Sanderson's in the sanitation department.

Mr. Wellington took it up to the Provincial District Supreme Court and managed to get the conviction overturned on a technicality. Our good judge was quite embarrassed and was even censured by the Court for his omissions, so now he hates Wellington's guts. And he loathes Sanderson even more, and I'm sure he has figured out that he is the one backing Crosby's defense. Everyone knows the case is complete bullshit, but Crosby will not get a fair trial because of what happened years ago.

Webster, are you saying that Mr. Wellington is crooked? No, Parker; not at all. He did what he was paid to do, he got his client off. He's a good lawyer from what my friend told me. As for Sanderson, well that's a different story. Did you know that he was recently investigated by your office's Department of Internal Affairs for financial improprieties? Yeah, I heard something about that. He continued. And did you know that he supposedly bribed the Investigator by getting him a sweet promotion, are you ready for this, in the same Department of Securities and Fraud where his cronies work?

Of course, none of this came as a complete surprise to me, but I just waited for him to finish explaining to me what I pretty much already knew. What should we do now, Webster? I can recommend an excellent trial lawyer, he said, but he is expensive. Crosby's case might be better argued by someone other than Mr. Wellington at this point. I wish we could afford to do that, I said. But we don't have much money.

I had another idea for you, Parker, but it's tricky. Life is tricky for us, I said, it always has been. We were knocked around as kids and ignored or treated like perverts after that. My first boyfriend was hounded relentlessly by his parents until he finally tried to kill himself. Francis bowls a strike and we almost have to fight it out with punks from Province South. My neighbor accuses me of corrupting his son, then vandalizes my house and defaces it with homophobic slurs. But Crosby is the one fighting for his freedom. Believe me, we know all about tricky. What's your other idea?

Here it is. This judge has no reason to hurt Crosby. He sees him as a stand-in for Sanderson and that's all he can get right now. He's not fit to serve on the Court and has to know that any conviction will end up before the Appellate Court once again. But he doesn't care. He's out for blood and he'll settle for Crosby's if that's all he can get.

Everything was starting to make more sense to me now, and I trembled with anxiety as I pieced things together and realized where all of this was heading. Are you suggesting what I think you are, Webster? He said then, what else can you find out about Mr. Sanderson? Who would know what other illegal or dishonest things he has done? The more dirt that is dug up on Sanderson and his friends, the less this judge is going to have it in for Crosby. If the Magistrate has another way to get even, he'll dismiss the case in a minute, I bet. Is there anyone in your office who is on top of everything, and what would they want to get from you in exchange for information?

There is only one person. Later at work, I asked Crosby, how well do you know the Timekeeper? Pretty well, he said. Carleton and I ran into him and his wife at the Opera House in City Centre a few weeks ago. We went out for drinks after the show was over and had a fun time. We've been out together twice since then. Why do you ask? I tried to hide the little smile I'm sure was there now; what a lucky break this could be. If anyone has the goods on Mr. Sanderson, it's the Timekeeper. Just curious, I told him. Do you need some help with your filing later?

We're at the file cabinets late in the day, with only Ms. Millerton keeping an eye out from a distance on her platform. She won't be able to hear us if we keep our voices down. I asked him, has the Timekeeper ever talked to you about your case or Mr. Wellington? No, we usually talk about things like Italian opera and the wine regions in southern Australia. Has he ever mentioned the importance of our jobs here? I don't think so; we never talk about work.

By 4:45, all the filing was finished and I stopped at the Timekeeper's desk to sign out. Tell me, sir, how do you know everything that goes on here? Still doubting me, aren't you, Parker? Well, no matter.

No sir, I don't doubt you at all. I admit that I did before, but now I am impressed by how well-connected you are. You told me before that they could do away with your job with just a simple computer clock application. Now I understand why they would never do that. No sir, I don't doubt anything you tell me.

I appreciate you saying that Parker, but why now? Didn't you tell me before to mind my own business? I'm sorry about that, I say. I'm not like that at all normally. I was under a lot of stress when the Investigator from Internal Affairs kept showing up here with his accusations and his bad breath. The Timekeeper laughed at this; you have quite a sense of humor, Parker; I like that. I asked then, do you also like my friend Crosby? Very much, he said, and his partner Carleton as well. I was very pleased to learn they are planning to get married soon. They want to invite my wife and me to their wedding.

How does he know that? They have not made any announcement yet, I'm positive. But he knows everything, just like he keeps saying. I said, do you know how much trouble he is in, sir? Yes, I'm afraid I do know. I know everything that goes on here. I said, but how is that possible? Crosby and Carleton decided to wait before making any wedding announcement. Even our good friends don't know about it yet.

It all has to do with time, he explained. There is no true division between past and future, there is rather a single existence. Einstein once said that the separation between past, present, and future is simply an illusion, although a stubbornly persistent one.

Once you learn to understand time, Parker; you will be able to free your mind for so much else. I see real potential for you to learn a great deal if you choose to. Thank you for saying that, but I've never been very smart. I didn't even attend University after graduation.

Oh, that doesn't matter one bit, he said. All of your capacity for understanding comes from someplace else entirely, not from a diploma certainly. Did you know that Thomas Edison, one of the most brilliant people to walk this earth, had only a few months of formal education? No, I did not know that, I said. And Walt Disney, despite his creative genius, dropped out of school at the age of sixteen? I didn't know that either, but I loved watching *Dumbo* and *Mary Poppins*. Sign out here, if you don't mind, Parker. Yes sir, good night then.

I called Webster later that evening, before *Leave It to Beaver* came on the Satellite. I said, there is someone who knows everything that goes on in the office. He practically knows things before they happen. He asked, who is it? The Timekeeper, I said. I get along with him pretty well, and he seems to really like Crosby and Carleton. I don't think he cares much for either Ms. Millerton or Mr. Sanderson.

• • • •

There is no way Mr. Sanderson isn't aware of what's going on here, or that the judge is out to get him. He has too many years of experience perfecting the art of deception; an executive flimflam artist more or less. Now, along comes Crosby conveniently enough with a grievous assault charge that might take some of the heat off of him. If there really is any heat on him to begin with. He's got friends with influence all over the place; how am I supposed to figure all of this out? How is the Timekeeper going to help Crosby?

I couldn't sleep much at all that night, my mind knotted up with all of these questions. I went over and over it again, trying to think up some possible answers. Maybe the Timekeeper knew everything that was going on, but I wondered if there was someone closer to Mr. Sanderson, someone more intimate with the intricate workings of our office. By the time I finally fell asleep, it seemed like only minutes passed before the alarm clock startled me. I hit the snooze alarm too many times, and now I have to hurry to catch the 7:30 morning train to City Centre.

Mr. Parker, may I see you for a moment, please? Shit, she didn't even give me a chance to hang my jacket up before I found myself with eyes still glazed over from lack of sleep, walking toward her platform. What do you need for me to do, Ms. Millerton? Not here, Mr. Parker; let's go somewhere more private. My mind is racing now, trying to disperse the remnants of its grogginess. What new emergency could have possibly emerged overnight that would necessitate a private meeting with Ms. Millerton this early in the morning? I hadn't even made it to the coffee dispenser yet or had a chance to clear my head or collect my thoughts.

We walked to the conference room and closed the door. She began, Mr. Sanderson has given us a Special Project and I was hoping you might be the right person for the job. Special Project? Yes, but I need you to listen carefully and be fully cognizant of the fact that this project is very serious in nature. It is imperative that no one find out what you are working on. Mr. Sanderson's reputation may be at stake, and someone in your position, not to mention my own, might find themselves in a compromised situation if what I am asking you to do is somehow misconstrued. Do I make myself clear, Mr. Parker? Yes, quite clear, Ms. Millerton.

Let me explain our situation so that you might better understand it completely and begin working on this assignment. You no doubt remember our prior conversations regarding the Investigator from Internal Affairs and their unjustified probing into what in fact turned out to be legitimate invoices and requisitions.

Yes, I said, but I thought that the matter was cleared up and that the Investigator was promoted to another department in exchange for agreeing to drop the inquiry. There was no such exchange, Mr. Parker. He was caused to realize that there was no basis for his allegations to begin with. His promotion was merely coincidental, I can assure you.

Caused to realize, Ms. Millerton? Did you mean to say work out a sweet deal with Mr. Sanderson and Mr. Wellington? She looks irritated now, her face turning a bit red. Where did you hear such a thing? Did the Timekeeper tell you that? No, I answered. I just assumed that's what happened after Mr. Wellington talked to us and said the Investigator was gone.

You should not concern yourself with such issues and I did not call you in here to talk about Mr. Wellington or the Timekeeper. I was confused by all of this now. So I said, If the matter was resolved, then what's the problem? The problem, Mr. Parker, is that this same Investigator is now working for the Department of Securities and Fraud. His previous frivolous allegations of backdated invoices may be dwarfed by what he is investigating now. Instead of wasting the Government's resources trying to uncover a malfunction in our date stamp, he is now looking into rather serious fraud allegations, unfortunately.

I'm afraid I'm confused, Ms. Millerton. Let me explain more fully, but I need your absolute assurance that you will not discuss this with anyone, other than Mr. Sanderson or me. Do I have your word? Of course, Ms. Millerton; my lips are sealed.

I believe you are aware that Mr. Sanderson is good friends with the Superintendent in the Office of Sanitation and Debris Removal. Yes, I am. He's the guy who agreed to let Carleton sit on the platform when you broke your leg. That's correct, she said. There is an unwarranted embezzlement allegation against him pending that is now the source of this new investigation.

I said, that sounds bad, but what does that have to do with us? I just told you, Mr. Parker; he is good friends with Mr. Sanderson. Trouble has shown its ugly face once more, and we cannot just sit back and watch helplessly while a good friend of his is being falsely accused. We need to stand by each other when problems like this occur.

Just who is this woman? And how did she manage to get herself tangled up in some embezzlement charge against a Superintendent in another department? She seems a stern and imposing sort of person, with nothing more important on her plate than supervising us twelve Processors and the endless trivial issues we present. I can see now that she is a lot more important than that. And what if I do get that promotion to Assistant Secretary? Will she expect me to take part in their scams on a regular basis? She's a shrewd and cunning subordinate, I can tell, but is she equally unscrupulous as Mr. Sanderson appears to be?

Now then, it is imperative to Mr. Sanderson that this investigation be dropped, so that everyone can get back to the important business at hand, mainly processing receipts and invoices in our case, and managing the sanitation in their case. As you can imagine, if Mr. Sanderson's counterpart is found guilty of stealing from the Government, that would not present Mr. Sanderson in a very favorable light. I agree, Ms. Millerton. But what can I do?

Mr. Sanderson has learned that there are certain computer files in the Department of Sanitation and Debris Removal's servers that unfairly and inaccurately suggest some wrongdoing on the part of Mr. Sanderson. I see, but Mr. Sanderson is not the one being accused, is he? Mr. Parker, you do not need to know all of the particulars, just that we need your help to get the files deleted because they are irrelevant. The Investigator has lost all manner of objectivity and we do not trust his judgment. Unfortunately, these computer files can only be accessed or deleted by certain employees in the Department of Sanitation and Debris Removal, or by others with the necessary security clearance. Because of the pending investigation, Mr. Sanderson's friend has had his computer access temporarily blocked.

I can't believe this is happening. I am being asked to participate in a scheme to derail what sounds like a serious felony inquiry by a high-ranking department head with the responsibility of protecting the Government's assets. Who knows what they might do to me if I go along with some lurid plan and it gets derailed somehow? And even if I agree and keep my promise and my mouth shut, would that mean anything as far as any assurances Mr. Sanderson might make to protect me?

I'm confused and very nervous now. My head is throbbing and I just want to get out of this damn conference room and over to the coffee dispenser and then back to my desk, so I can start reviewing my receipts from last night. How in the world did Ms. Millerton expect me to gain access to computer files that even Mr. Sanderson did not have clearance to tap into?

It came to me suddenly like a flash of lightning, nearly blinding me with its implications. She is going to ask me to have Carleton get the computer files. He has access to all of their systems and servers. He installs all of their firewalls and cybersecurity controls. There is no way she can ask me for this favor. Carleton could go to jail if he gets caught. And so could I. I've lied enough for them already. I didn't give a shit about some stupid requisition for a handrail. But this is criminal, even I know that.

Ms. Millerton, I can't ask my friend Carleton to look at those files, that would probably be illegal. What on earth are you talking about, Mr. Parker? Why would you dream up such a thing?

Yes, I am a dreamer. Francis likes to remind me of that. I dream of a cleaner world, I dream of pure love, I dream of the Western Shore. But this was no dream that a simple guy like me could make up; this was a nightmare I better wake up from and quick. What then, Ms. Millerton? I will tell you, but what I am about to reveal is very sensitive and extremely personal. Please try to understand what I am about to say. I lean in slightly, making eye contact with her. Go ahead, I'm listening.

Mr. Sanderson and the Investigator have known each other for many years. How shall I put this; they are of a somewhat different persuasion, both of them. I said, you're telling me they are gay? Yes, she says, and I have no doubt that this may come as a shock to you. Not really, I've heard worse things than that. Yes, Mr. Parker, but they were lovers for a period of time. Did you know that? No, that never occurred to me.

Well, after some time, a couple of years or so, Mr. Sanderson decided to end the relationship and get married to Ms. Sanderson. The Investigator was apparently quite heartbroken and very angry with Mr. Sanderson and has never gotten over it completely. That's the reason he keeps pursuing these unjustifiable inquiries that involve Mr. Sanderson, so he can get even. I see, and the plan is, Ms. Millerton?

Mr. Sanderson likes Mr. Crosby and wants the charges against him dismissed. The Magistrate in this case does not particularly care for Mr. Sanderson. The Investigator likes Mr. Carleton as well, oh my, this is so embarrassing to talk about. I see her eyes welling up some and her face flushed with discomfort. I had never seen this side of her before, a rigid and demanding public servant now showing feelings and emotions that I didn't know were in her.

It's alright if you don't want to tell me the rest, I said. No, you need to understand this; our jobs and Mr. Crosby's future may be at stake. Please allow me to continue without further interruption. The Investigator is in tight with his Honor the Magistrate. I said then, I'm not sure what you mean exactly when you say in tight. What I mean exactly, she said, is that he can make the case against Mr. Crosby disappear. Let's leave it at that, shall we? I would prefer to leave some of the sordid details unspoken if that is alright with you. We all have stories we wish to remain unpublished.

He can also get the embezzlement matter resolved without any of us losing our jobs. He is one of the few people who can delete the questionable computer files. Some compromises may have to be made, a deal of some sort arranged, but nobody will be sent to jail. In other words, all of the troubles we have been dealing with these past months can just evaporate, if you can arrange for one little favor.

Oh no, here it comes. If she is not going to ask me to have Carleton snoop into the computer files, then what?

She is shaking a bit now, I notice, and stops to wipe her eyes before continuing. Seeing her this way is almost surreal. She's different than before, a little out of focus. It's as if I am looking at her through a camera lens that needs adjustment. This entire thing is a lot more serious than the other scams she has managed to tangle me up in. She is worried about losing her job or watching her boss being dragged away in handcuffs.

She gained her composure and said, Carleton would have to make some moves on the Investigator, if you get my drift. He would have to seduce him and convince him to agree to arrange for the cases to be dropped in exchange for certain favors.

This, I never expected. So, you want me to ask Carleton to get it on with the Investigator? The guy with the awful breath? Yes, Mr. Parker; it's the best plan we have been able to come up with. It's not too bad of a plan when you think about it. Crosby will be happy because his legal problems will go away. Carleton will be happy because he will no longer have to worry about Crosby going to jail and they can get married like they are planning. You will be happy because you helped your friends. But most of all, Mr. Sanderson will be happy.

What about you, Ms. Millerton; how would you feel? Would all of this make you happy?

She gave me a sad look and said, happiness is like convenience, we all want it, all of the time. I'm sorry to say that unlike you, I am not someone who has ever known true happiness. I did not have a lover to hand me his universe when I was in secondary school. I never shared my life with a partner who would take me to cookouts in Province West, or on trips to the Western Shore. I don't have friends to go with me to the rodeo dance at the Centre Quest. Yes, I will be happy in my own way if you and Carleton will agree to do this.

I was both stunned and moved all at the same time. I never gave much thought to what Ms. Millerton was like outside of work, or what her social circle might look like. But her revelations blindsided me and shook me up big time. She knew everything that was going on here. I never told her a thing about my private life, but she picked it up somewhere. Is she the source of the Timekeeper's information? That didn't seem likely at all; I think they hate each other. Shit, I don't know what to think now.

Let me talk to Carleton and I'll let you know what he says. Thank you, Mr. Parker, but please don't mention our conversation to anyone else. I am very embarrassed by this. I understand; I promise not to say anything.

I stood up to leave, but to my surprise, she wasn't finished. She was leaning forward in a relaxed posture that I don't ever recall seeing before. She is always so stiff and formal. Sit back down for a moment, please. In a softer voice, she said, there is one more thing I want to tell you.

I grew up in a small rural town in the Southern District. Most of our neighbors were religious and we belonged to a church called the Evangelical Continental Partnership. I was always told that gay people were evil and should be put to death. It was assumed that I would believe such awful things. These were my parents' teachings, but I take full responsibility if I have ever done or said anything that was offensive to you in any way.

I thought hard trying to remember even some minor incident that she could be referring to. You never have, Ms. Millerton. That's good, she said. I was afraid I may have done so somewhere along the line, intentionally or otherwise. One's attitudes and beliefs are formed early in life, and mine were wedged between the truth I was told and the truth I desired. These cannot easily be distinguished in the mind of a child. They may be fused into one by strict parenting and harsh preaching.

She stopped for a moment as if to collect herself, then she sat straight up again, her mood serious as usual, her color returned to a normal shade of pale. Now of course we need to do whatever we can to keep Mr. Sanderson happy, if you get my meaning. He is a very busy man, as you well know, and certainly has more important business to attend to than having to defend himself against groundless and retaliatory accusations perpetrated by a scorned lover. Even you, Mr. Parker, should be able to appreciate the seriousness of these assertions and the precarious position we find ourselves in. Please return to your workstation now and remember your promise. No one can know about this conversation.

I stand up again and start to walk out of the conference room. The old Ms. Millerton is back and following me out; the lens on the camera reset to its automatic mode, and the picture much clearer to me now.

XVI

Tell me this, what in the world am I going to say to Carleton? I can't expect him to hit on that nasty Investigator and still keep his lunch down. And since I promised not to say anything about my conversation with Ms. Millerton, he'll assume this wacky plan was all my idea. He'll think I'm a total crackpot. What a dumb fucking plan they came up with. Carleton will be getting married soon and they expect him to screw around with that repellant Investigator so the Government can remain ignorant of the fact that Mr. Sanderson and his college buddy are stealing public funds. *It's not too bad of a plan when you think about it.* I've thought about it and yes, it is.

Carleton and I were having lunch outside alone on the plaza. Crosby was away today at a meeting with Mr. Wellington preparing for his deposition the next day. I've been meaning to ask you something, he says. How did you happen to ask Crosby how well we knew the Timekeeper? Really, can't anyone I know keep even one damn little secret?

I said then, the guy seems to know everything about my life; I was curious if Crosby knew where he gets all his information. You didn't tell me that you have been going out with him and his wife. Yes, and they invited us to dinner at their brownstone in City Centre on Sunday. You should see the rare German mahogany clock they have in their living room. They found it on eBay and it must be worth a fortune.

He said, I need to tell you what else the Timekeeper told me. I can't discuss this with Crosby, but you have good insights about the people at work and I trust your judgment. Will you promise not to say anything to him about this? Of course, Carleton; you know I can keep a secret. I thought to myself, I'm about the only one we know who can.

Anyway, he continued, the Timekeeper isn't positive about this, but is pretty sure that Mr. Sanderson and my boss are being investigated for some type of illegal transactions. I'm not sure what it's about, but he did say that there are some incriminating computer files that have been blocked, and if those files were to disappear, then the Investigator would have nothing to go on and would have to drop the matter. The Timekeeper does not know what is in those files, only that they could hurt Mr. Sanderson and probably destroy my boss.

I see, and you might possibly be the person to accidentally delete the files since you have access to all of your department's computer servers. Exactly, Parker.

Let me ask you something, I said. Do you know the Investigator has the hots for you? He said, Oh, please don't even think that; I'm about to heave my lunch. What made you even say such a thing? And don't tell me you got that from the Timekeeper. No, I said; I just happened to hear it from someone. I promised I wouldn't say anything. You should have kept your promise, Parker. That is pretty disgusting. I'm going to have nightmares now just thinking about it.

So tell me about this brilliant plan of theirs, I said. Even if you agree to delete the files, how will that help Crosby out of his predicament? His trial is just a few weeks away and he is preparing for a nasty deposition as we speak.

I think it could help him, he said. When the Investigator goes looking for the deleted files and there aren't any, he will look bad for pursuing frivolous cases against not one, but two Superintendents. No one takes these sorts of allegations lightly, especially if they involve department heads and have no factual basis.

Mr. Sanderson should be able to work out a deal with him easily at that point. In exchange for Mr. Sanderson not making a stink about an unwarranted and slanderous inquiry, the Investigator will agree to talk to his friend the Magistrate, and get him to dismiss the charges against Crosby. The only reason he hasn't already is because he hates Mr. Sanderson's guts.

How do you know all this, Carleton? The Timekeeper told me, that's how. He also said he would keep an eye out on eBay and let me know if there is an auction for a Seth Thomas antique mantel clock. I'd love to find one for Crosby's birthday next month. I tell him, I have one more question for you. If for any reason the files can't be deleted, or if the Investigator won't agree to a deal, is there a plan B? No, the Timekeeper didn't mention any other plan. Why, what did you have in mind?

Well, I just thought that since the Investigator has a thing for you, shit, never mind, it's a stupid idea. He stared at me for a moment. You can't possibly be thinking that I might agree to make out with him so he will pull some strings down at the Courthouse. Yeah, well the idea did occur to me. I mean to save Crosby, of course. Oh dear God, let's hope plan A works, he said. Or else you and the Timekeeper can come up with plan C! Oh, goodness, the things we are willing to do for the people we love.

Yes, the things we do for love. The things I do for Francis and the sacrifices I make feel so damn lopsided. Just an agreement instead of an argument, just a wink instead of a raised eyebrow, just a little support instead of disapproval. People sometimes ask, are you sure he is the right one for you? I wish I could answer their question with something other than the usual I don't know.

Duncan was the right one for me and look what happened to him. Francis will never take a dive off a bridge or swallow a bottle of Valiums. Neither will he look me in the eye like Duncan did and tell me that I am a beautiful example of God's best work.

Love is such a baffling riddle to me. Was the Investigator so much in love with Mr. Sanderson that he still can't get over being snubbed? Or is it that vengeance proves to be a more powerful force than love? Ms. Millerton is not that much older than me and is actually somewhat attractive in her own peculiar way. Is there someone out there waiting for her to notice and fall in love?

• • • •

Mr. Wellington is in office again two days later. He and Mr. Sanderson are in a private conference like the last time. I am so nervous that I keep making mistakes in the log book, and each time, I have to bother Ms. Millerton so she can initial the corrections.

Slow down, Mr. Parker, or I dare say I may need to note these errors in your Permanent Record. While you are here, I need to ask you a question. Have you talked to Mr. Carleton about our discussion from the other day? I decided not to tell her the truth. Not yet, Ms. Millerton. Good, I don't think we will be needing your assistance after all. It seems that Mr. Wellington has met with the Investigator and an agreement has been reached. The charges against Mr. Crosby are to be dismissed by way of a Final Order issued by his Honor the Magistrate by the end of the week.

I wondered then, how did that happen without Carleton even flirting with the Investigator? She said, you should not concern yourself with the details of the arrangement. Just be grateful that Mr. Crosby will not have to answer further to such ridiculous charges, and that Mr. Sanderson and his friend in the Department of Sanitation and Debris Removal have been completely exonerated of any improprieties or wrongdoing. Suffice it to say that Mr. Wellington and Mr. Sanderson decided to go with plan B. Now return to your workstation and for the sake of my sanity and the integrity of your Permanent Record, please be more careful when making your log entries. Mr. Sanderson has to review the log at the closing day each month, and I'm sure he has more important matters to attend to than trying to justify your errors. Yes, Ms. Millerton; I'll be more careful.

Mr. Wellington came over to talk to us late that afternoon and shook Crosby's hand first. Good luck to you and I'm sorry for all of this inconvenience. And Parker, it's been my pleasure working with you, and give my best to Francis if you would please. Of course I will, and thanks for everything, Mr. Wellington.

The Timekeeper sure knew a lot about people, but I think he underestimated Mr. Wellington. Webster was right about him, though; he proved to be a good enough Solicitor in the end. I'll call him and Wilma later on with the good news.

C'mon Crosby, let's get out of here. Grab Carleton and we can all go to the High Club for happy hour. I'll tell Francis and Winston to meet us there when they get off work.

Carleton caught up with us just as we were about to sign out at the Timekeeper's desk. Congratulations, Crosby. I'm glad all this bullshit is finally over with. Sign out here if you don't mind. And Parker, aren't you glad plan B worked out instead of that crazy plan they came up with? Imagine the Investigator and Carleton together. I said then, what are you talking about, sir? Really, Parker? give me credit for something, would you? Sure, I said. But tell me how.

Carleton and Crosby were distracted with each other as usual and weren't paying any attention to either me or the Timekeeper. Sometimes it felt like he spoke only to me, or that no one else around could even hear him.

He began slowly, speaking clearly and patiently. I keep track of and manage time. Time is the most critical element in the entire universe, and we must learn to understand it better. It explains all kinds of phenomena that defy logical interpretations. We think just because we've invented a clock or a calendar, that time can be easily measured. But our measurements of time are illusory at best because time is relative and depends on the frame of reference used. Time is continuous and infinitely divisible, which means it does not exist like the numbers on a clock. Time may be best defined as the measurement of the increase of universal entropy.

This is not easy for any of us to understand, Parker. Time can make things happen or not, either fast or slow, either today or tomorrow. You've asked me how I know what goes on here. It's because I have learned to manage time. That's why I'm the Timekeeper. Good night then, Parker; sign out here if you don't mind. I just stared at him in amazement. I didn't exactly get what he just said, but I feel like I am beginning to learn more from him.

Come on already, Parker; we'll miss happy hour if you don't quit your bullshitting with the Timekeeper. I look at him more closely. Yes, Parker, go now and enjoy a drink with your friends. You deserve it after everything you've been through. You and I can explore this more later. We just stared at each other for a moment more. There is much for us to learn together, he said. But not today. Today is for celebrating. Thank you, sir; I appreciate that.

Parker, why are you daydreaming again? Quit bugging the Timekeeper. Let's get out of here.

Go now, Parker. Good night, sir.

In less than half an hour, the five of us are enjoying half-priced drinks at Club Fantasia, or the High Club as it is more generically referred to. There is a great happy hour crowd there on Friday with cheap drinks and hot bartenders. At a lot of clubs, the reverse is usually the case.

I invited Tyler to join us, Winston said. He's going to take the bus from Province North and meet us. We had a lot to celebrate, and I had prepared a little toast in my mind anyway to Crosby and Carleton, who were holding on tightly to each other, as if to prevent some other awful event from stepping in and trying to rip them apart.

With things being so crazy lately, I hadn't had the chance to write anything down. While the bartender was getting our order, I saw Tyler walking toward where we sat at the bar, with Harris and Brady not far behind. I was happy to see everyone after so much time had passed. None of us were mad at them anymore, and even Francis decided to forgive them now that Crosby was no longer in trouble. I was glad I would get the chance finally to talk to Harris and find out how things were going at home.

I took a spoon off the bar and clanged it against my margarita glass to get everyone's attention. I wish I had the chance to write something out, but now I would have to wing it, having had only a few minutes to drum something out. I hope I can make this sound good.

Today we celebrate what only time could achieve and what the strength of our friendships has endured. Today, we set aside our worries for tomorrow, knowing the long, dark nightmare is over. I've come to understand how time shapes our lives and highlights what truly matters. Carleton and Crosby, your marriage is one of those important things. I know you planned to announce it yourselves, but everyone already knows, so don't blame me for spilling the beans. Even Ms. Millerton knew! So I make this toast to the both of you, and to the many happy times you will have together, and that each of us will have right along with you.

It didn't come out exactly the way I wanted it to, but I think they got the point. I leaned back in my chair sipping my drink, feeling pretty good about myself. I hadn't told any real lies and probably didn't break any laws. But Carleton sure had, with those deleted files. But I wasn't too worried about it; I'm sure he covered his tracks so no one could find out.

I down my margarita and ask Francis to get me another one. It's Friday and there's no work tomorrow, and I am planning to drink a few more. I hardly ever get too lit up, but tonight feels like a good time to make an exception. I just want to hang out with my friends without worrying about Solicitors or trials, or that asshole Magistrate. I wonder what I might say if I saw that prick walk into the bar. Not likely; he is too much of a closet case to show up here. Keep it in perspective, I tell myself. Justice has prevailed, at least for today.

Carleton keeps smiling like a teenager at the drive-in movies. He and Crosby are certainly happy. Winston and Tyler must be relieved as hell by the Court's dismissal, and I'm sure are quite happy. Harris and Brady are holding hands and don't look at all unhappy. I polish off my second drink and look over at Francis. I often wonder, is he happy?

Carleton pulled me on the dance floor and thanked me for everything. He said, I love him very much. You know that, right? All my ex-boyfriends either screwed around or just disappeared if I looked the other way. The love I gave them had no value at all. Why do you think people act that way? I said then, It's because they are nothing like you, okay? And everyone thinks you and Crosby are perfect together. Really, even Francis? Especially Francis, I said.

He said, you know, everything seems so easy and natural with Crosby. I know the heart can sometimes take you one step too far, to a dangerous place. But there is no such place with Crosby. The other night he looked right into my eyes and said I was an example of what God could do on one of his better days.

I was sitting at the bar when Harris came over to talk. How have you been, Parker? I like what you said about time. Thanks, but someone at work came up with the idea. Tell me, how are things at home? Not good, I'm afraid. I've been staying at Tyler's house for the past two nights. Father is drinking at the Club a lot. I don't know what is going to happen. He refuses to believe I am gay and keeps thinking I am out on dates with Lacey, even though I told him about Brady. And he is still pissed off at you, too.

I said, yeah, he blames me for turning you gay. Nah, you are just an easy target for him. Mother wants us to go to family therapy, but Thomas won't go. She's threatening to leave him now. I don't know what I am going to do.

Part V – The Miracle Mile

Out of difficulties grow miracles.
-Jean de La Bruyère

XVII

The case against Crosby may have gone away, but my neighbor Thomas has not budged. He glared at me from across the footpath when I was outside. He made obscene gestures and weird noises. Even his friend Jackson has decided to stay away from him. He and Ms. Jackson may have problems conceptually with the idea of Tyler and Winston as a couple, but at least they are making an effort to deal with their son's sexuality and their anxieties surrounding it. Rational people do things like that; they learn to accept even unpleasant realities for the sake of a son who is more dear to them than life itself. Tyler told us that Jackson tried reasoning with Thomas. You've got exactly two sons, he told him. You trying to fuck them both up, or just one?

This Mexican standoff made both of us uncomfortable. One day Francis said, I'm going to go over there and try to talk some sense into him. Maybe he'll agree to some sort of truce. I don't know about this, Francis. I don't think he will even listen to you.

But he was determined to at least give it a try, so on Sunday afternoon Francis knocked on their door with a peace offering, while I stayed inside the house and peeked through the curtains. Ms. Thomas opened the door and let him inside. We figured Thomas would be less likely to go ballistic with her there. At first, I thought that strategy may have worked. Francis came back after about ten minutes with no blood visible anywhere.

So, will you tell me what happened? He said, I told him about how my father had hurt my family, and how there are worse things than Harris being gay. I asked, how did he react to that? He said if my family was screwed up it was only because they had a faggot in the house.

Then he said that Harris isn't gay; he is confused. He blamed that confusion on you, Parker. So I told him that Harris is lucky to have you as a neighbor and a friend and that maybe he should think about the family therapy sessions. Then I told him about what our pastor said at church last month. Only humans can choose the difficult path of understanding for things that are difficult to understand. And what did he say to that? He said get out of my house or I'll knock some of your teeth out.

Francis smiled at me; we took our best shot at least. I was happy to see that Thomas had not taken his best shot and that Francis still had all of his teeth.

He was very busy at work for the next few weeks, and we didn't see much of each other. Ms. Thomas had moved out with their younger boy temporarily to stay with her brother in Province West, and Harris was staying at Tyler's house in Province North. Carleton and Crosby were busy making their wedding plans and even busier screwing their brains out in City Centre. That left just Thomas and me in Province East. I was nervous about being home alone much of the time with him so close by. Maybe he's going to start peeking in the windows again.

Francis knew that and called late one night. Do you want me to come to stay at your place again? I said, for how long, until Thomas is committed? No, you are working so much overtime and don't need to add a long commute to the end of each day. Better if you stay in City Centre, probably.

I had things to sort out on my own and needed some separation from Francis anyway. He still kept putting off going to couples therapy, and I was almost ready to give up on that idea. He should have agreed to go for my sake even if he thought it might be a waste of time.

Hunter had been sending text messages, wanting to know when we could get together again. Ms. Millerton was even more frazzled at work since Mr. Sanderson was nearly hauled off to jail. The Timekeeper found it necessary to share some metaphysical philosophy each morning when I arrived and each evening when I left. My emotions were mixed, and my mind was confused. I wanted to be away from everyone and just spend time alone at the Great Western Marsh Preserve, but I had used up my holiday leave and didn't have any extra money to spend on another vacation.

Most of my savings were gone after paying to repair the cottage. The Office of Casualty and Property Adjustments denied my claim, citing a policy provision that required all vandalism claims to be reported to them within forty-eight hours. They concluded that the occurrence took place sometime late on Friday night or early Saturday morning. I did not report the matter until Monday evening when I got home from work.

• • • •

Mr. Parker, may I see you for a moment, please? Yes, Ms. Millerton; what do you need for me to do? I walked up the three steps to her platform, overcome suddenly by a feeling of doom. What else could she and Mr. Sanderson possibly have come up with? All my filing was up to date and it was almost time to go home. I felt exhausted and just wanted to be alone in the cottage with my Walt Whitman poetry book, with the deadbolt on my door double-locked in case Thomas was lurking again outside.

Mr. Parker, I am speaking for both Mr. Sanderson and myself when I tell you that we are extremely grateful for your cooperation and assistance in dealing with our recent unfortunate situation. Mr. Sanderson has suggested that I put something in your Permanent Record documenting your enthusiasm for assisting with Special Projects. I wanted to laugh out loud. Did they really consider lying and scheming to qualify as Special Projects? Thank you very much, I said. He also suggested that because of your diligence and hard work, you should be given the rest of the week off with pay, in addition to this. She handed me a payroll check made out to me for an amount that equaled a full two weeks' salary.

Ms. Millerton, I don't know what to say. You need to say nothing about this to anyone, as you have previously agreed to, which I am assuming that you have not already done. Am I correct?

Technically speaking, she was correct. Carleton pretty much guessed what Plan A was with me mentioning only the fact that the Investigator liked him, and I think Plan B might have been his boss' idea. I did tell Francis everything but made him swear that he would never say a word to anyone about it. Plus, you aren't supposed to keep secrets from your partner, so that doesn't count, does it?

Of course, I did not say anything, Ms. Millerton. You asked me not to. Then she said, no one needs to know about your bonus or why you will be absent for the next three days either. If anyone questions you about it later on, just say you had a mild case of walking pneumonia or a serious case of hay fever, whichever you think they are more likely to believe.

By the time I deposited my check in the 24-hour self-banking machine in our office, it was time to go home. I stopped at the Timekeeper's desk to sign out. Enjoy your long weekend, Parker. It really should be Carleton getting the credit for saving Mr. Sanderson's ass, don't you think? I guess so, but I don't have any way to share time off with him. You could split that fat bonus check with him if you wanted to. I suppose I could, but he would never accept anything like that. Besides, Ms. Millerton says nobody can know about my bonus and if anyone asks why I was away, I should tell them I was sick.

Tell them it was influenza; there is a lot of that going around. I've logged in five cases from our Office already this month. Nobody's going to believe you missed three days because of hay fever, there aren't even any trees or shrubs in bloom. Would you like to hear about the article I read today explaining the relationship between special relativity and time dilation? Maybe another time, sir. I need to hurry to catch the train back to the Province. Okay, good night, Parker; don't forget to sign out here.

I was tired and thirsty by the time the commuter train arrived at the Province East Station and I walked the ten minutes to the cottage. I opened a cold bottle of ale and sat out on the front porch. Before I could even finish drinking it, I saw Thomas walking out of his house and toward mine.

Why'd you send that sissy boyfriend of yours over to my house the other day, Parker? I didn't send him; it was his idea. I told him not to waste his time trying to reason with a knucklehead.

Why should I give a shit about what any of you perverts have to say? Because we're trying to help Ms. Thomas and Harris, that's why. I suppose you don't give a shit about them either. You listen here, Parker. He took a few more steps in the direction of my porch. Don't come any further, Thomas. They take a dim view of trespassers in this Province. They know you damaged my house too.

Thomas' anger didn't have many boundaries. I'll get you for this, Parker; I'm warning you right now. Another empty threat, Thomas? Tell me, what did Francis say to you exactly? He said some crap his gay pastor told him about a path to understanding. You queers better keep away from Harris and follow that path right out of Province East before something else happens to your house.

He turned and walked right back to his own house. I was shaking a little bit but stayed where I was on the porch and drank the rest of my ale. A few minutes later he came out again and gave me the finger before he got in his car and sped off in the direction of the entrance to The Miracle Mile. Of course, I thought. It's Tuesday and another Lady's Night at the Club. The gals can get two-for-one drinks and work my idiot neighbor into picking up their tabs. At least it would be peaceful for the next few hours here.

I have more money than I've seen in quite a while, having spent so much to repair the damage Thomas caused. I have time off too, but the weather has turned cooler now, so I didn't make any plans to go to the Western Shore by myself. Hunter was sending more text messages wanting to meet me there again. *It's like a completely different place with the colors changing and the migrating Raptors and Waterthrush.*

I decide to stay home instead. I've got to work things out with Francis and not be messing around behind his back. Hunter doesn't need to know about any of my baggage. He knows all about Thomas though and how dangerous he is. *Call me right away if you ever need anything. I'm never very far away from you. I never have been.* Where did that come from?

I'll stay in the Province and spend some of my bonus money on Francis instead. I want to buy him some new clothes and take him to dinner when he comes over on Friday night. We don't need to go someplace so fancy as we did with Wilma and Webster. Even the Pizza Palace or the fish and chips place might be fun.

I sleep in on my first day off and am having a leisurely breakfast at the cottage. I still am rattled after last night's renewed threats. I'm glad I didn't panic and start making a ton of unnecessary phone calls. I didn't want to dump more on Francis and make him feel like he had to come babysitting me again. And calling the Constable's office would have just wasted more of my limited monthly mobile minutes.

The second cup of coffee brought me some clarity. I'm done with this bullshit; I have a right to live in peace with the rest of my neighbors. I know what to do now. I dialed Mr. Wellington's number. He is out of the office, Mr. Parker, but I can make an appointment for you at 3:00 this afternoon.

His office is in The Miracle Mile, just a short two blocks from the Hotel and Casino. Let me head over there at 1:00 p.m. and have lunch first and maybe play a few hands of Texas Hold 'Em before our meeting.

The Casino was enormous and very crowded considering that it was the middle of a work day. I went to the counter where they sell chips, and learned that you can't play table games without a Gambling Permit. The slot machines, maybe? Nope.

Another Permit, are you serious? Yes, I'm sorry sir. The lady behind the counter handed me a form to complete. Please submit this form to the Province Gaming Control Commission. Here's an extra one for obtaining Visitors Permits. You should receive them by post within three business days. If you would like, Mr. Parker, you may play Penny Bingo while you are waiting for your Permits to arrive. The Gaming Control Commission makes an exception for Penny Bingo as the proceeds generated are just enough to cover the costs of printing the Bingo cards, and the winners have their names entered into a drawing for free pizza at the Pizza Palace.

Thank you, I love Bingo. I played for an hour until it was time to meet Mr. Wellington. No free pizza though, damn.

I walked over to Mr. Wellington's office after I left the Casino. Come in, Parker. I'm glad to see you again. How can I be of service? I told him everything that happened last night and Thomas' threat to damage my house again. He asked, did you file another complaint with the Constable's office? No sir, last time they said they could not do anything unless he physically assaulted me or was caught trespassing.

Let me explain this, Parker. Under the criminal code, that is correct. Even a simple assault requires some type of direct physical contact. So, we'll file a lawsuit under the Civil Code instead. Our burden is less and even the threat of physical violence or harm is actionable. We don't have to establish specific intent, the threat itself is sufficient to pursue a cause of action.

I'm not sure I understand what you just said, Mr. Wellington. He said, it means we can file a claim against Thomas in Civil Court and seek damages for intentional infliction of emotional distress. And to recover the costs for the damage to your house as well.

Did the Office of Casualty and Property Adjustments pay you to make the repairs? No, they said it was not covered since I did not report it within forty-eight hours. Oh my God, that is such horseshit. That is more horseshit than a horse on Ex-lax. We will add them as a co-defendant with a separate count for bad faith and breach of fiduciary responsibility. I didn't even ask what all that meant.

How much will your fee be, sir? I received a bonus at work, but I don't know if that will be enough. He said then, If you'd like, you can pay based on a contingency fee arrangement, where we can advance litigation costs that are deemed reasonable and necessary to prosecute the matter. Huh?

It means that you pay a set percentage based on how much settlement money we receive. And you won't have to lay out money for our expenses. Oh, I think I understand now, sir. Let me ask you something, Parker; did you ever think of becoming a lawyer? No sir, my parents couldn't afford to send me to University. I got my first job with the Government right out of secondary school. Just as well, he said. Let me handle this for you.

I said, may I ask you for a favor? Of course, what is it? Can you not mention to anyone that you are representing me in a claim against Thomas? Everyone at work seems to know my business, and this is a very private and personal matter. He said, yes, of course. Everything we talk about must be kept in strict confidence. For me to discuss your case with anyone outside of this office would be a serious ethical violation for which I could lose my license to practice law. Thank you, Mr. Wellington.

• • • •

I don't even spot Thomas over the next four days, so my time off work is pleasant and undisturbed by that asshole across the footpath. I enjoyed Thursday and Friday riding the beach cruiser, raking the autumn leaves from the garden, and playing Penny Bingo at the Casino. On Saturday night, I used some of the bonus money to take Carleton and Crosby out for dinner at the Spanish restaurant in The Miracle Mile. We shared the tapas, two bottles of Rioja, and a huge pan of seafood paella.

They both loved the place. There was a live band playing Spanish Techno music while we ate. We laughed a lot and had so much fun not thinking about work-related scandals or worthless neighbors. On Sunday, we spent the afternoon shopping in The Miracle Mile. I took Francis to a couple of the men's shops that Webster suggested. He picked out a pair of Italian leather dress shoes and a sharp-looking Armani sports coat for work. He stayed with me at the cottage until Monday morning when we took the train together into City Centre. Don't forget to bring your Residency Permit, he reminded me, as we headed out the door.

I stopped at the Timekeeper's desk to sign in after kissing Francis goodbye outside the Office of Accounting Payables and Receivables. I trust you enjoyed your long weekend, Parker. Yes, I said, it was very peaceful for a change. And were the paella and Rioja satisfactory? Oh, they sure were. You and your wife should go there sometime. Yes, he said, we have made a reservation for next Saturday. Well, sir; let me recommend the olive and cheese tapas. They paired quite well with our wine. Very nice, Parker.

May I ask how your meeting with Mr. Wellington turned out? I said, that is a very personal matter and Mr. Wellington promised not to discuss it with anyone. Of course not, Parker. That would be a serious breach of confidentiality. I have never spoken to Mr. Wellington about anything. But how then?

He looked at me and said, did you know that our feelings and awareness are closely linked to our perception of time? There is a theory called embodied cognition that attempts to explain how the perception of other people's emotions changes our sense of time. Embodied cognition hinges on an internal process that mimics and stimulates another's emotional state, enabling us to better tune in to and sense what they are feeling. It's fascinating stuff when you learn about it and I can recommend some excellent literature for you.

Thank you, sir, but that sounds pretty complicated. He said, yes it can be, but all learning is complicated. Learning about time and how it affects our perceptions particularly so. Keep in mind though that it is the steady, patient, and uncompromising study of the nature of the physical universe and our place within it that ultimately accounts for much of our knowledge. Study and learn, Parker. The more you do the less often you will need to ask how. Now, sign in here if you would. I would not be a bit surprised to find out that Ms. Millerton might need something from you again today for some absurd purpose.

I tried to keep my head down and work as quietly as possible, hoping that the Timekeeper's embodied cognition regarding Ms. Millerton was off today. She seemed unusually busy and kept going up and down the steps from her platform, and in and out of the door to Mr. Sanderson's office. I hoped they were distracted enough by important business matters to not even notice me.

No such luck. Mr. Parker, may I speak with you for a moment? I noticed the large clock on the wall behind her desk read 4:23, just about time for me to go home. Yes, Ms. Millerton. What do you need from me now? Most of the other Processors snuck out early while she was not looking and nobody else could hear what she was saying.

It seems that a problem has arisen concerning your recent time away from the office. I need you to listen carefully and remind you one more time that conversations of this nature must remain completely confidential.

I'm afraid I don't understand, I said. Are you referring to my three-day bonus holiday that I returned from this morning? Yes, Mr. Parker. It turns out that Mr. Sanderson did not have the necessary authority to grant you leave with pay. Such authority needs to be approved in advance by the Executive Director of the Office of Accounting Payables and Receivables. Mr. Sanderson was questioned this morning concerning your whereabouts last week, and thinking very quickly and perceptively, he told the Executive Director that you were at a three-day training seminar at the Government Training and Education Center in The Miracle Mile.

A training seminar, Ms. Millerton? Yes, a seminar on time management more specifically. In The Miracle Mile? Am I not speaking clearly enough for you Mr. Parker? Or is there some problem with your hearing? No, I can hear you fine, but I was playing Penny Bingo in The Miracle Mile, not attending a time management training seminar. Yes, she said, but the Executive Director does not need to know that. As long as he believes you were at the seminar, then Mr. Sanderson will not have to concern himself with the trivial matter of some procedural violation.

Luckily, Mr. Sanderson was able to obtain a copy of the seminar hand-outs from a friend who is an instructor at the Training Center. Please review the materials carefully this evening, so if someone happens to question you about the seminar, you will at least be conversant as to the topics discussed in your absence.

The materials will be useful to you in any event, she said, as she handed me a large binder with at least 300 pages of documents and training exercises. We have previously discussed deficiencies with respect to your attention to detail and your work efficiency, so additional study in these areas will present you with a much-needed developmental opportunity. If you read all the materials and successfully complete the self-study examination at the back of the binder, I may be able to note this accomplishment in your Permanent Record.

I'm at the Timekeeper's desk now to sign out before heading to the train station, the large binder sticking out from the unzipped top of my backpack. What have you got there, Parker? Oh, just some materials that Ms. Millerton suggested I read so I will be able to pay more attention to details.

He said, that looks just like the binder from the time management seminar that you skipped. Hey, I didn't exactly skip the seminar; I didn't even know about it. Don't bother with that shit, Parker. But sir, Ms. Millerton says I need to manage my time better. He said, do you think studying about poor management controls and multi-tasking will help you? You can't manage time by downloading a desktop calendar and scratching things off a to-do list. There is an entire section in that binder on networking and relationship building. It's total crap; don't waste your time with any of that.

Read what will mean something, like quantum physics for example. It will clarify so much for you. How do you mean, sir? Scientists, starting with Einstein and then later with Heisenberg, Mach, and Schrödinger, developed theoretical principles of quantum physics that turned the concept of time upside down. The past does not, and cannot exist until it is created by the present, and the present does not and cannot exist until it is created by the future. They also discussed an additional principle known as observation. This states that something does not exist until it is observed. In scientific terms, this means when an experiment is performed and the results observed by whatever means, only then does the result come into existence. A specific individual reality therefore cannot exist until it is actually observed by someone or something. Prior to that, it is only a probability.

Understanding these principles will help you with your time management. Forget about goal setting and prioritization and the rest of that bullshit. Do yourself a favor, Parker; sign out here, and after you leave, toss that useless manual into the trash.

But I need to complete the self-examination for Ms. Millerton. Give that stupid examination to me, he said. I'll give it back to you later so Ms. Millerton can put it in your Permanent Record, and so Mr. Sanderson can roll it up tight and shove it up his ass. I laughed out loud. You don't much care for Mr. Sanderson, do you sir? On the contrary, I think he is an excellent Superintendent. Even if he does spend half his day fantasizing about giving Crosby a blow job. And look at this beautiful new clock he requisitioned for me last month.

While all of this discussion was going on, a line of four or five people had formed behind me waiting to sign out. They didn't react at all or even appear to hear any of our conversation or what he just said about Mr. Sanderson. They just looked about obliviously, waiting patiently for the Timekeeper to tell them they could leave. How could they not have heard him talking to me?

I heard what he said clearly enough, but couldn't understand much of it. But if he would answer all fifty questions on the examination, I could just look them over before giving it to Ms. Millerton and not have to spend the entire evening at home studying the materials that the Timekeeper said were a waste of time. That should make me conversant enough in the subject matter if someone decides to ask me about it.

I didn't take his advice and toss out the manual. I might have to refer to it later, or Mr. Sanderson might need to return it to his friend at the Training Center. I was sitting on the porch later that evening, enjoying a glass of imported Riesling while leafing through the manual, when I noticed that Harris had come out of his house and was walking in my direction. Thomas's car was not in the carport, lucky for me.

Hi Parker, what are you reading? Just some training manual on time management from a seminar that I missed. May I borrow it when you are finished? I'm done with it already; sure take it. Why do you want it though? I'm thinking of majoring in business management now that I've started at the Community College. I thought it might be useful to read. Okay, keep it for as long as you want.

I said, I've got so much other stuff to read anyway. I took this book out of the library on the space-time continuum. Our Timekeeper thinks I should read it. He said the subject was first explored by 19th century fiction writers like H.G. Wells. Oh yeah, Parker; I have to read *The Time Machine* for my freshman literature class.

I said, I got another book here about the Second Law of Thermodynamics and how entropy in a closed system increases over time. Harris said then, that sounds too complicated for me. It is, I answered. I don't even understand what they are talking about half the time. He asked, why bother to read it then? I explained, to help me with time management and my relationship skills at work. Want a glass of Riesling?

We were on the porch talking for nearly an hour and opened a second bottle. I was getting pretty comfortable by my third glass, sitting too close and getting too tipsy with Harris. It's not that we did anything wrong, but he likes to sit close and is a touchy-feely kind of guy. The pheromones were encircling the space around me as if they were sprayed from an aerosol can. It was hard to breathe when he leaned against me with the binder pressed between us and asked if I had read the section on productivity and decision-making.

He wanted to talk about Brady. Who wouldn't? I think I love him, Parker. But he lives in Province South and his parents don't have the money to pay for tuition at the Community College. How will I know if he is the right one? I want us to be like you and Francis when we get older.

Older, yes! I have to stop and remind myself of the abyss of an age difference between us. He asked me, when did you know that Francis was really the one?

Even if I were totally sober, I'm not sure I would know how to answer that one. The truth is, I'm still asking myself that question after years of being more or less glued to Francis. Even if he isn't exactly the right one, it might not matter that much now. You reach a point where you accept the other person and recognize that the emotional and physical connections might never be perfectly fused. As long as they don't short-circuit and blow things up, well, okay.

You'll know over time, Harris. When your life seems less meaningful without him, then you will know. In the meantime, just enjoy each other and feel good about what you have going on. Don't feel guilty about Brady, no matter what anyone else thinks. Your feelings are good and natural. Time will fix everything else for you.

Can we go inside now, Parker? Father will be home soon, and I don't want him to find me here with you. That seemed like a good enough plan for me. We sat on the sofa in the living room, finishing off the wine while watching a rerun on the Satellite of a very old TV show called *The Honeymooners*. Harris had never heard of Jackie Gleason before and couldn't stop giggling through the scene where Ralph and Norton wind up handcuffed on the wrong train while heading to the Raccoons Club convention.

. . . .

Ms. Thomas had found her way home from her brother's house, and she found me at home with no problem the very next evening after work. I was reading a book that the Timekeeper loaned me called *The Images of Time: An Essay on Temporal Representation*, by Robin Le Poidevin. I was struggling with a section that discussed how certain aspects of time can be mind-dependent. I can't seem to grasp this, I thought, and then my confused state of mind was interrupted unexpectedly by quite a loud and impatient-sounding knock at the front door.

I didn't feel much like having visitors at the moment, but I let her in. She sat down on the living room sofa, and I just listened. It's about the lawsuit Mr. Wellington filed, she said. I know I have no right to ask you of all people for any favors, but we are going through a difficult time. Thomas is agitated and has been drinking more since your case was filed. He's even angrier with you than he was before and hardly speaks to Harris since he told us about Brady.

We had to hire a lawyer and he is very expensive. We may have to take money from the boys' college fund to pay his bills. The thing has hardly even begun and Mr. Wellington is scheduling depositions left and right and filing more and more papers with the Court every day. Harris' tuition for the winter semester is due next month and I'm worried that we might have to sell the house if this continues much longer.

She was tearful and I felt sorry for her. None of this was her doing. I brought two cans of soda from the refrigerator and a box of Kleenex from the bedroom nightstand.

I'm sorry to hear about all of this, I said. I guess I never thought too much about your house, just all the money I spent fixing mine. It wasn't always this way, she said. Thomas was much different when we were first married. We had fewer problems and were better off financially. We even put an offer on a house in Province West years ago. Thomas had been promoted to Senior Detective in the Office of Special Investigations.

That sure got my attention. Shit, Senior Detective? That meant Thomas would have been allowed to carry a firearm legally anywhere in the Province. Can you imagine anything more screwed up than that?

She continued. But then he was fired from his high-paying Government position and had to take a job at the chicken processing plant. It seems that privilege and pain often go hand in hand. It's just gone downhill from there. After Henry was born, Thomas started drinking more. Then the Club in The Miracle Mile opened three years ago; well, I think you get the idea. He's not such a bad person, and I should know. We've been together for nearly twenty-one years. The two of you may have more in common than you might think.

I like Ms. Thomas, but I had to interrupt her at this point. Blood runs through both of our veins, but that's where the similarities end, I'm afraid. And you saw the awful things he painted on my fence and house, and you heard him threaten to knock Francis' teeth out when all he did was try to make peace. What about that?

She said, I think I can convince him to reimburse you for the damage to your house. If he will do that, will you be willing to drop the lawsuit? I thought about what she was asking for a minute or so. I wasn't out for much else, and I felt bad hearing that she and her children were suffering too. But what about Carleton and Crosby and the pain he caused them? And what about Francis? He still gives me grief about my decision to move to the Province and often uses Thomas as an example of how much smarter he is than me.

He is smarter, everyone knows that. He has a master's degree from the University. I never even applied to the Community College. He is an Assistant Director at his company and eats lunch with members of the Executive Committee. I can't manage a promotion to Assistant Secretary, and eat my lunch on the grass in the Plaza with Carleton. He writes business plans and makes presentations to Vice Presidents. I write log entries and cover for an insecure woman and her conniving boss. He digests and summarizes detailed technical data. I can't understand half of what the Timekeeper patiently explains. He earns a good salary and lives in a fashionable apartment in City Centre. I don't make enough to live in a building with an elevator.

But I don't resent any of that. I want him to be successful and respected. But I want him to respect me as well and appreciate our differences rather than constantly bringing them up. I'd like him to stop belittling my job and reminding me that my bosses are cheaters. I want him to stop reminding me how sharp he is and how dull I am.

Ms. Thomas is wiping her eyes and waiting for me to say something. I'll need just one more thing; Thomas will have to apologize. He will have to admit to vandalizing my house and tell us he is sorry. He will have to apologize to Francis for threatening him and making him uncomfortable when he visits me here. Then I will ask Mr. Wellington to forget the whole thing and we can move on.

I don't think he will agree to do that, Parker; he is very proud. I shouldn't be surprised, I suppose. Proud, really? Do pride and ignorance necessarily go hand in hand? Must they always be set on the table side-by-side, like the bread and butter?

I told her, Francis is very proud too. But not too proud to knock on your door with a hand extended to the man who has insulted and threatened his life partner. Oh, he is proud, believe me. But he will stand there respectfully, keeping his feelings to himself while he gives Thomas every opportunity to make amends for what he has done. Neither of you will see the tears that hide beneath the surface or hear either of us demanding more. We are too proud for that.

She is shaking her head and crying more when I finally get done venting my frustrations, not exactly intentionally on her. None of this is her fault, but she is the one to get more than an earful from me.

I return from the kitchen with her salad bowl that I washed and dried after the cookout. I am reminded then of Wilma and Webster with their friends from Province West, where I now know Ms. Thomas once dreamed of living. If things had been different, in a better time and place perhaps, we might have invited them to come along for the cookout.

Ah, what the hell am I thinking? You're a dreamer, Parker; that's what you are. Francis loves to remind me of that.

XVIII

The Timekeeper handed me the completed self-study examination when I stopped to sign in at work the next day. I intentionally answered a few questions incorrectly, so as not to arouse any suspicion from Ms. Millerton. She may not be ready to believe that you could score 100 percent on the subject of time management. I had to laugh at that. No, I guess not. The other day she said I seemed too scattered at times to properly separate the invoices from the receipts. He said, you will have to sign and date the declaration at the bottom of this form and attest to the fact that you did not receive any help or look up any of the answers in the manual while taking the exam. I thanked him for his help and signed both the form and his log.

By the way, Parker, how is your reading coming along? Oh, pretty well so far. I'm nearly finished with that last book you gave me. I did not want to admit to him that much of what Le Poidevin hypothesized went right over my head. I see, and which of his postulates did you find to be of the most interest?

Here it is, not even 8:00 a.m., my mind still absorbed and distracted by my discussion with Ms. Thomas from last night, and now the Timekeeper is asking me about the links between the metaphysics of time and temporal representation.

I look at him with a mix of admiration and confusion. He is an avid reader with a brilliant mind. He knows about quantum mechanics and can tell you how the speed of light was calculated. He is so perceptive that he can understand things even before time has allowed them to take shape. Yet for some reason, he has taken an inexplicable interest in me and what he believes I am capable of learning. If only there had been just one teacher like him when I was in school, who could say what I might have become? But there had been none. None with his intelligence or his passion for learning.

The answer to his question came to me suddenly. I did not need to grasp everything the author was saying. I could understand just some portion of what I read and still learn from it. Well, sir, the thing I found most interesting is that the book seems to dispense with the more traditional discussions of the philosophy of time. What do you mean by that, Parker? Oh, just that it seemed a fresh perspective to me, and that it focused on psychology, art, and literary theory, not only the science. Very well stated, Parker. You have learned a good deal in a very short time.

May I ask a question now, sir? Yes, of course, he said. Why did you choose the profession of a Timekeeper instead of a university professor? He paused for what seemed a long time before answering. As a professor, I would only encounter a select few, those with both the knowledge and privilege required to gain acceptance to an institution of higher learning. As a Timekeeper, I can meet from a broad spectrum of people, with virtually limitless potential to learn from them. I asked, but what have you learned? I've learned that the simplest of minds may have something exceptional to add; that the brightest of individuals might be found in the most unlikely of places.

The jobs people do here are insignificant, but the people who do those jobs are extraordinary. Each of them has to stop by twice each day whether they want to or not. Yes sir, I remember you saying that gives you a great deal of power. It gives me more than that, Parker; it also gives me great learning opportunity. Each may have some small bit of knowledge to share in that brief moment when they stand before me. It may look as if they are just checking the time, signing the log, or saying good morning. Yes, they do all of those things each day, but I learn from them as well. So you see, Parker, I am not a teacher; I am a student. That's why I'm the Timekeeper.

I grab an expresso from the coffee dispenser before dropping off the self-study examination on Ms. Millerton's desk. I don't see her around anywhere, so I head over to Crosby's desk to catch up with him before starting to work. We joke around and I tell him what the Timekeeper just said. What do you suppose he learns from Ms. Millerton when she logs in? I laugh and nearly spill my coffee when he says, mostly perfecting the art of deception.

Hey, look, we just got the invitations back from the print shop. What do you think? He handed me a beautifully printed card on lavender-colored stationery etched with a silvery laced pattern. I struggled trying to read it; my vision now blurred and my eyes watering.

Because you have shared in our
lives by your friendship and love, we
Carleton and Crosby
invite you to share in the beginning
of our new lives together
as we exchange our marriage vows
on the 15th of September at half past five o'clock
at the home of
Webster and Wilma
25451 Victory Gardens Way
Province West
Reception and dinner to follow

I nod and smile at him, choked up a little. It's beautiful, Crosby. Now my thoughts are interrupted suddenly by the barbed voice coming from Ms. Millerton's desk. I was so absorbed for a few minutes, I hadn't seen her come in.

Mr. Parker, may I see you, please? Yes, Ms. Millerton. Do you need for me to do something? Yes, I need for you to explain why you signed in eleven minutes ago, but have yet to begin your work assignments. Have you even glanced at your in-basket yet? I shook my head sheepishly. Well, you may not be in such a playful and jocular mood with Mr. Crosby once you discover the 133 new invoices and receipts that need your attention. Yes, Ms. Millerton. I'll get a start on them right away.

You are an enigma to me, Mr. Parker. I have your self-study examination right here and see that you scored ninety-four percent after just one or two evenings of what certainly must have been attentive study time. Yet here you are, the very next day wasting time and disturbing Mr. Crosby as well. I intended to make a notation of this achievement in your Permanent Record, but now I find myself conflicted by your lack of effort this morning. Honestly, Mr. Parker, I am at my wit's end with you sometimes.

Big fucking deal. I was almost done with all the work by the time Crosby and I met up with Carleton out on the plaza for lunch. That is so cool, I said. I had no idea that Wilma and Webster were planning to host the reception.

We told them no, but they refused to hear of it. Wilma said, why rent an expensive hall when we have a beautiful garden that is perfect for a wedding? I asked, but what if it rains? They have a clubhouse overlooking the garden that we didn't even see when we visited them. Webster says it can easily accommodate forty-five people.

It's way too much; we don't know them that well. When I told them that, Webster just put his hands over his ears and Wilma shushed me and asked what type of flower arrangements we would like. They are paying for the dinner too and said that will be their gift to us. When I objected to that, they ignored me completely. The only thing they said was to give us a time when you can meet with the caterer. Oh wow, that is so nice of them, I said. Can you believe that, Parker?

It was even harder to believe how quickly the afternoon passed. All of my invoices and receipts were logged in and stamped by 2:30, then filed well in advance of my deadline after Mr. Sanderson came by to supervise and stare and Crosby while he and I took our turns at the filing cabinets. As I was getting ready to leave, I kept having recurring thoughts of Ms. Thomas and how upset she was last night. I wanted to just accept their reimbursement money, but couldn't convince myself that it was the right thing to do. How would that guarantee that Thomas would not cause more problems later on? No, I need an apology and a promise. That's what matters most, much more than the money.

I stop at the Timekeeper's desk on my way out. You look stressed out and I'm guessing things did not go well last night. No sir, they didn't. My neighbor's wife came to my house and I gave her a really hard time. I feel pretty bad about it. Yes, I see that, but try to be patient and not judge her harshly, he said. She is no doubt in a good deal of distress right now. Remember that forgiveness is not a luxury, Parker; it is a necessity.

It is our human ability to forgive that binds us to one another. Wohl and McGrath investigated the influence of the actual duration of time and subjective temporal distance on willingness to forgive someone. Their psychological studies suggest that our perception of time and the ability to forgive may be intricately connected. I have their paper filed somewhere at home and I can bring it for you tomorrow if you would like.

Thank you sir; I would like to read it. It seems that you teach me something new almost every day. But this morning you said you are not a teacher. I'm not, he said. I am a student. I may be telling you things, but I am learning from you. I asked, how though? By watching what you and others do and how you learn, I gain perspective. The greater one's perspective, the more knowledge they can absorb. That is what separates a good student from a bad one. It's not about how fast you read, or if you know how to cram the night before an exam. Real learning requires perspective. The bad student lacks perspective, so how much can they really be expected to learn?

One more thing, Parker; watch out for that neighbor of yours. What's his name again, Thomas? Yes sir; he lives right near me and is hard to avoid. He said, be careful, he has limited perspective and even less compassion. He is full of anger and bitterness that he refuses to let go of. Subjective temporal distance may have little influence on someone like him. He may hold a grudge for a very long time.

I think you may be right, sir. He stared right at me with a serious look all of a sudden. Listen to me, Parker. Steer clear of him. Can you promise me you will be careful? Yes, I'll do my best; I promise. Okay then, sign out here if you would. Thank you again, sir. Good night to you then, Parker.

• • • •

Two weeks before the wedding, Francis and I went to be fitted for our tuxedos. I was excited about being Carleton's best man. I've never even worn a tuxedo before. On Saturday afternoon, Francis and I went to pick up the matching black tuxedos with dark grey vests. Then we went to the hairstylist for the finishing touches. Later that evening, Winston and Tyler were going to meet us at the Pizza Palace, and then we were going to the Casino. My Permit from the Gaming Control people arrived after just three days, and they included four Visitors Permits since I was a Province resident. I called Carleton to see if he needed us to pick up anything. I think everything is all set, he said. I'm so nervous! We're in The Miracle Mile and just got our tuxes, I said. Wait till you see how hot Francis looks in his.

Saturday night, the Pizza Palace was packed, and since I completely forgot about making a reservation, we had to wait at the bar for almost an hour before they found us a table. The restaurant is enormous, bigger than any place I'd ever been to in City Centre. There had to be at least 300 people already seated, every last one of them straight as far as I could tell. I think we may be the only gay people here, Tyler noticed, not all that perceptively. Francis looked at me. What a surprise, huh Parker?

I didn't care; the pizza was great, and they had more than a hundred different beers on the menu, including a few unusual ones nobody had heard of from the other Continent. I was drinking something called Dogfish Head 60 Minute IPA. I can't tell you what any of that means, but it was nice and smooth. After having to show his Driver's Permit to prove he was old enough, Tyler ordered one called Colt 45 Double Malt, which sounded way too masculine for anyone in this group. Here, try it, Parker. It had a slightly sweet and malty flavor and a rather high alcohol content.

After dinner, it's time to head two blocks over to the Casino, which is crowded with noisy and excited players, hoping that this night will be a lucky one. We showed our permits at the window where they sell chips, and the same lady who suggested I play Penny Bingo the first time was working. Hello again, Mr. Parker. May I have two rolls of quarters, please? I couldn't wait to play the slot machines. Winston and Francis wanted to try their luck at the craps table and bought £100 in chips from the nice lady. May I see your ID young man? Tyler looked embarrassed, being asked to prove yet again that he was an adult, but he fished out his identification from his jeans pocket and showed it to her. Thank you; good luck to you boys!

I love the sounds and colors emanating from the slot machines. Unfortunately, they don't seem eager to show such reverence for me, and all of my quarters are gone in less than thirty minutes. So I head over to the craps table where Winston and Francis are playing with a small group of players. I watched them for a few minutes, but the game seemed too complicated for me. I could not figure out what they were doing. Someone yelled out, roll that point, then everyone standing around the table was clapping and cheering for whatever reason.

A cocktail waitress appeared with complimentary drinks.

White wine, sir? Yes, thank you. I took two of the plastic wine glasses from her tray and gave one to Tyler, who I don't think had any idea how craps was supposed to work either. I noticed a young straight couple to my right. The guy was quite handsome and built like a linebacker. He had one of his bulked-up arms around an attractive woman, who introduced herself to us.

Hi, my name is Brittany and this is my fiancé Campbell. They asked for something called Pabst Blue Ribbon when the waitress returned with her tray. We all shook hands when I introduced them to Tyler. Are you guys here alone? No, those are our partners over there, trying not to make fools of themselves, Tyler said, as he pointed toward Winston, who was smiling back at his cute boyfriend. Ah, I see. We didn't know you were gay.

Whenever someone says that I am tempted to ask something like, why would you know? It seems like a rude question maybe, but when you stop to think about it, how can they not know? The short hair, the tight Diesel jeans, the nice cologne, the shrill voice when a seven is rolled. So instead I ask Campbell, is that a problem? No, no, I'm sorry. We have gay friends in City Centre, it's just that we never see any of them in The Miracle Mile, or anywhere in the Province come to think of it. Yeah, I know, I tell them.

Tyler and I both live in the Province, I said. Brittany said, we do too, in Province South. But we're planning to buy a house in Province East after we get married. Tyler says, hey, that's where Parker lives. In Miracle Estates East. What a coincidence, Campbell says. We found a place we like with a nice garden and a white-painted fence in your subdivision. We've been working with someone at the Office of Real Estate Placement to see if we qualify; we might be neighbors soon.

Brittany says, have you ever been to Atlantic City to gamble? No, I've never been out of the country but hope to go there one day. What's it like there? She says, it's exactly the same as here only different. Tyler just gives her a puzzled look, wondering probably how these two managed to get all the way from Province South to New Jersey East.

I happen then to look across the large open space of the Casino and feel a prickly chill of goosebumps tingling on the back of my neck when I see him standing not more than twenty meters from where we are. A sinking feeling and a wave of dread wash over me when I realize that it's Thomas sitting at a Black Jack table. I glance around but don't see Ms. Thomas or Jackson anywhere. He's here by himself, I think. Oh shit, look over there, Tyler.

Campbell notices this and says, what's wrong? Before I can come up with any explanation for this dreadful disruption to what so far has been a perfectly nice evening, the prick looks up from his cards and stares right at me. Francis and Winston are distracted by the excitement at the craps table and are oblivious to what is happening.

The Timekeeper's ominous forewarning hits straight at me, and my initial thought is to collect them both and get the hell out of there. Wait a minute, that shithead isn't going ruin my evening. He can go fuck himself. Hey, you guys want to try our luck at the roulette wheel? Sure, Brittany says, that's a lot easier than poker.

I'll be honest. I don't even like roulette, and I suggested it not because all of us are smart enough to play, but because the two roulette wheels are at the opposite end of the Casino, as far away from Thomas as we can get without being back in the bowling alley.

But even before I can orchestrate a reasonable attempt at an escape, there he is right next to me, with his loathsome expression and his flabby body. He starts right in; Tyler, what are you doing here? Is Harris with you? He's not supposed to be in here; he's not allowed to drink or gamble. No, Thomas; I haven't seen Harris for a couple of days. I don't know where he is.

What the hell do you mean? He is supposed to be staying at your place. Tyler says, not for the last two nights he hasn't. He said he was going home. Well, he hasn't been home and his mother hasn't spoken to him. Do you know where he is, Parker? I answered, how should I know? You told me to stay away from him, remember? The last time I saw him he wanted to borrow some study materials for the management class he's taking.

Winston and Francis are there with us now, neither of them looking particularly pleased by having their game so unpleasantly interrupted. Why are you bothering us again? He ignored Francis, his interest suddenly shifting to Brittany instead. Who's the good-looking gal, Parker? You decide to switch sides and quit being queer?

I can't tell you what kind of dumb shit would make such disparaging comments when a guy the size of Campbell, who he knows nothing about, is no more than a meter or two away. Who the hell is this asshole, Parker? He looks like he's ready to start something with Thomas, but Winston, Francis, and Brittany have already stepped between them.

Look, we haven't seen Harris. Why don't you try calling him instead of hassling us? Because his mobile contract was canceled, that's why. I can't call him. He's supposed to be with you, Tyler. Well, he's not here, so leave us alone. He looks like he is ready to boil over with anger, and he gives me that furious look again. Even Thomas is smart enough to look around and size things up by this time, especially the size of Campbell's biceps. He's reconsidered his options and decides to take off. I hate your guts, Parker, he said as he made his less-than-graceful exit. Yeah, I got that, Thomas. Why don't you go home to your wife and try to help your son instead of bothering us?

Who was that guy? Campbell seems a bit shaken and concerned by my obvious discomfort after Thomas is gone. I said, he's my neighbor. I don't like him at all, Parker. You guys want me to go outside and make sure he doesn't bother you again? No, better to just ignore him, I think. Better to let Mr. Wellington figure out what to do with him.

Everything had changed, but nothing had changed. Crosby was cleared of the Grievous Assault charge, but I was still being harassed by my vengeful neighbor. My moods fluctuated between wanting to get closer to Francis and wanting to be further away from him. It seemed that Tyler and Winston were falling in love, but Harris was falling apart. Nobody had heard anything from him. Where the hell has he been these last three days?

Tyler, do you think he might be with Brady? I don't see how, he said. Brady's parents don't know about them I don't think. And I don't have an address or anything for Brady, so how can we call him? All we know is that he lives in Province South. Don't worry, Winston said. He'll show up. It's weird neither of his parents have heard from him, don't you think? Tyler said, if I don't hear from him by Monday morning, I'll go to the Community College and see if he is there. I know he has an accounting class at 9:00 a.m. Good idea, Tyer.

The next day we were too busy getting ready for the wedding to be thinking much about Harris. I did look out the front window of the cottage a few times while we were getting dressed, but there was no sign of him. I was tempted to knock on their door to see if Ms. Thomas was home, but Thomas' car was parked in the carport. There went that idea.

I can't think about all this crap right now; I need to focus my thoughts instead on Carleton and Crosby. This is about the most important day of their lives, and they are about the most important people in mine.

Are you ready to go, Francis? We don't want to be late. Yes, yes, shit; where did I put my bowtie? I helped him with it. You look great, Francis. Now where did I leave the car keys? Calm down, will you? We're not the ones getting married. He wasn't about to pop that question anytime soon, I'm sure.

We drove again in Province West without a Permit and nothing happened. We pulled up the driveway at 5:00, just as the other guests were starting to arrive. There was a valet who took the keys from Francis and parked the car for him. The weather turned out just about perfect, with hardly a cloud to be seen in the brilliant blue sky. So the ceremony and the dinner will be held in the garden instead of the clubhouse. Wilma and Webster greeted us as we came through the kitchen.

Man, this is some big event they planned. The caterer has the jump on things and there is food spread throughout the kitchen. Two servers are right on it, one with flutes of champagne, the other with a tray of crab-stuffed mushrooms. Everything just looks so perfect.

I step outside, and it's even better than I imagined. About fifty chairs have been arranged for the ceremony behind the pool area, shaded beautifully by two large maple trees. An aisle down the middle is lined with tea candles placed in small glass jars, leading to a white gazebo adorned with ribbons and flowers. A string quartet is seated at the front, playing pieces by Schubert and Haydn. Closer to the house, six large round tables are set with white linen cloths and striking arrangements of amber dahlias and tropical hibiscus. I've never seen anything like this before.

I noticed Crosby and Carleton talking with the clergyman who would be performing the ceremony. We went over and were introduced, exchanging hugs and congratulations. Here are the rings, Parker. You'll hold on to them until Reverend Lewis asks for them, okay?

Gordon and Carson ran over to us, each dressed in sharp-looking dark charcoal-gray tuxedos. Don't you two look fancy, I said. I guess you're not going to show us any diving techniques today, huh Carson? No, Dad said to stay away from the pool so nothing falls in. Parker, can you sneak me some wine later? We'll see, Gordon.

Just then, the Timekeeper came over to us and introduced his wife. So glad to finally meet you, Parker. My husband talks about you all the time at home. I thanked her and reached out to shake the Timekeeper's hand. Hello, Parker. I sense that you were not overly lucky at the Casino last night. Not at all; I spent all my money before we even got a chance at the roulette wheel. Yes, and no doubt you met up with at least one disagreeable patron. I trust that your evening was not made too unpleasant by him.

I noticed the beautiful silver and black Breitling watch he was wearing, sparking in the late afternoon sunlight. He glanced down at it then. Almost time for the big event to start, I believe. These Swiss timepieces keep the time with amazing accuracy. I was wearing my cheap Timex Ironman watch that I'm always forgetting to wind or push the time an hour when we switch to or from daylight savings time.

People were moving toward their seats now, the ceremony about to begin. Everything after that was pretty much a blur for me, as I stood close to Carleton, clutching the rings tightly in my hand. I remember him saying this:

> *I promise to be your best friend and loving partner for the rest of our lives. I will help fill our house with laughter, patience, and understanding. I will make it a place of joy for you and for whoever may live or visit us there. I will grow with you, and grow old with you both. For whatever may come, I will always be there as your partner, through all of the adventures and all the happiness that our future holds.*

Crosby said something I can hardly remember about sharing his universe or sharing something, I forget. Then it was time to exchange the rings. Reverend Harris begins; if I may, Parker. Francis holds my hand while the edges of my vision begin to blur, the tears threatening to erupt at any moment. Damn, I left the handkerchief back at the cottage; I'm always forgetting something. Not much I can do about that now.

> *You have chosen to exchange rings as a sign of the promises you are making today. For thousands of years, the ring has symbolized many kinds of human relationships. Kings wore them to express their imperial authority, while friends exchanged them as expressions of their goodwill. Today, the giving and receiving of rings symbolize your love for one another, which like the circle, knows no end. Crosby and Carleton, you have consented together in lawful wedlock and have pledged your love and commitment to each other, and have declared the same by joining hands and by the giving and receiving of rings. Therefore, by the powers vested in me as a Justice of the Peace for the Provincial Commonwealth, I now pronounce you to be married partners for life.*

The guests are all on their feet now, clapping and smiling as Francis and I follow them down the aisle to the reception area. We greet everyone with hugs and handshakes, while waiters appear with bottles of expensive Cabernet Sauvignon imported from Sonoma Valley. More friends were congratulating the newlyweds when Crosby announced that they would be going to Monte Carlo in a few weeks to celebrate.

They planned to leave right away, but Carleton's boss would not give him the time off until he finished with their department's Windows Borealis upgrade installation. What a prick he is. He doesn't even bother to show up at the wedding, despite Carleton putting his own ass on the line to save his and Mr. Sanderson's.

Mr. Sanderson was out of town and not there either, but Ms. Millerton came by then to chat with us and to offer her best wishes. I remembered then what she told me about growing up in the South, and how her mind was poisoned by the cruel lies preached to her. I almost didn't recognize her. She had her hair done up nicely and she wore a coral blue floor-length chiffon evening dress. She looked pretty hot considering that she was Ms. Millerton.

Mr. Parker, may I speak with you privately for a moment? Francis gave her a puzzled look, and I just shrugged and said, of course, what is it?

We walked a short distance before she stopped. I just wanted to let you know that you were not selected for the Assistant Secretary position. It will be going to another one of the Processors. I tried hard to hide my disappointment, but that wasn't possible for me. She said, I know you had been hoping for it and it was a difficult decision for Mr. Sanderson and me to make. We don't always get what we want out of life, and I dare say that you and I both have been subjected to worse dissatisfactions than this one. I nodded; of course, I understand.

Honestly, it was very hard for me to understand. But as I looked at her expression more closely and listened to how she spoke, I realized suddenly that the decision was not hers to make. And I also knew that she had advocated for my promotion and that it was Mr. Sanderson who vetoed her first choice. She didn't say that, of course, but I could almost read her mind. I had learned from the Timekeeper how to better interpret a person's manner and gestures. I had a great deal of respect for him, and now a little bit more for her as well.

I'm sorry, Mr. Parker; I just thought you should hear it from me first, and not through the gossip chain that inevitably exists when a decision like this is made. I did not feel it appropriate for you to hear it through the grapevine first thing Monday morning should you arrive at the office before I do.

Francis and I were seated at our table for dinner and I was quiet. He leaned over and whispered, what did that bitch for a boss want now? Oh, nothing, I said. Just that Mr. Sanderson said he was sorry he had to be away and could not be here today. Really? She couldn't have said that in front of me? She's a very private person, I said. Quite shy actually.

The Timekeeper and his wife were seated near us, but Ms. Millerton was at another table. Good thing that Crosby and Wilma thought through the seating arrangements carefully; the two of them hate each other I think.

That is a beautiful watch, sir. Thank you, Parker; my wife gave it to me on our twenty-fifth anniversary when we were vacationing in Santorini last year. He turned toward her and they both smiled.

What an interesting couple they are. She is an attractive middle-aged woman with a charming personality. I can see why Carleton and Crosby enjoy spending evenings out with them. She spoke about their travels abroad and their two daughters, who were both married and settled with their own families somewhere in Western Europe. She read extensively and knew about the best wine regions in Chile and Argentina. No doubt the many years spent together had been good ones for both of them.

I said, what are your favorite places to visit? Oh, that's an easy one, she answered. There is nothing quite as peaceful or more enjoyable than our trips to the Mountain Campgrounds. And it's not on some foreign continent with language barriers or odd cultural dissimilarities. Or exhausting time zone changes either, the Timekeeper added.

We fill the time with pleasant conversation while the waiters fill our glasses with more excellent wine. She says to me, my husband tells me that you have been reading that literature he has on time displacement or some such thing. Yes, well, I don't grasp a lot of it, I say. I don't either, Parker. It's so confusing, isn't it? I enjoy reading mostly about medieval history and cultural primordialism. That time warp stuff he keeps trying to sell me makes no sense at all!

The Timekeeper just smiles at her. Don't believe everything she tells you, Parker; she understands more than she lets on. My wife is both an excellent student and teacher as well.

How well-matched they are, it seems remarkable to me. They blend together like mac and cheese. I look over at Francis, who is chatting it up with Wilma's handsome younger brother and not paying attention to me. We are nothing like the Timekeeper and his wife. We blend together like a Big Mac and caviar. He's moving ahead with his career and probably won't be very supportive when he learns I've been passed over for promotion. He won't be able to appreciate how disappointed I am.

The happiness of the occasion is tempered by my depression. I fight off the urge to keep feeling sorry for myself. Finally, he decides to speak to me. Wilma's brother and his girlfriend like bowling too. Want to try it again next weekend? Sure thing, I said. That was so much fun, wasn't it? I'm feeling better already. But let's see if we can avoid getting into a fight next time, okay?

The Timekeeper overheard us. He said, it seems the bowling alley has become quite popular with people from all over the Province. It's all good in the long run; I don't imagine you will have any problem next time with people on the adjacent lanes. I just stared at him in amazement. I'm almost positive Crosby did not mention the bowling alley incident to anyone at work.

I think back just a few short months to when I didn't like the Timekeeper much. I thought he was no more than a meddlesome co-worker with nothing better to do than stick his nose into other people's affairs. He has been sitting at that same desk for the last four years. Why have I not taken much notice of him until recently? Is it my lack of perceptiveness, or just stupidity? Maybe it was our recent troubles that caused me unconsciously to seek him out. And why did he choose me as his primary pupil, and then claim with complete sincerity that he was the one learning from me? I'll never be smart enough or learn enough to deserve his frequent praise. You are a good teacher and student both; he likes to tell me.

He is a mystery to me. I see him smiling at his wife and chatting with the others at the table. He is describing a vacation they took one year to the Canadian Maritime Provinces. He says, it was absolutely beautiful there, but we froze our asses off. We all chuckled when he said that. Then he tells a story about their travels in Peru. He said, I thought I understood the language well enough, but I guess not. We somehow got on the wrong train to Machu Picchu, and by the time we realized it, we were halfway to Bolivia.

Everyone is laughing and enjoying the stories he and his wife share. I don't hear a word about time distortion, or Einstein's theories, or any of the stuff he tells me about. I don't even know where Bolivia is. Why am I the only one who can hear what he says to me?

While the other guests are finishing their dessert and coffee, I find myself alone at the bar, daydreaming as usual, and thinking how happy I am seeing my best friend married. They are so in love. I push away that pang of jealousy as I watch them on the makeshift dance floor crafted from the pool deck area, with the lounge chairs and umbrellas gone off somewhere, and replaced by the DJ and sound system.

The Timekeeper came over then with a half-filled bottle of wine. Try a glass of this Frontera Pinot Noir, he suggested. It's one of my favorites. It was dry and with a slightly earthy flavor that reminded me of figs or chocolate. Thank you, this is very nice.

Don't worry about that stupid promotion at work, it doesn't mean anything. I said, but I really wanted to move up and make more money. And they know I can take on more responsibility. I know that, Parker. But you will not be judged by your income, or whether you supervise the clerks or date stamp the invoices. Those things won't mean a thing to you in the long run.

Instead, focus on what matters most to you; your friends, your studies, your partner Francis. I'm happy to have met him finally. He seems to be quite a nice fellow. We're having some problems, I tell him. Yes, I sense that you are, but conflict is often a good thing ultimately. I said, but how can you say that? You and your wife seem to get along so perfectly. Well, it's been nearly thirty years since we first met; we've had plenty of time to get it right. There may be a close connection between conflict resolution and our perception of time distortion. We can study more of this later if you would like. I have some literature on the subject at home in the basement somewhere. I'll see if I can find it and bring it to work on Monday.

I was enjoying the wine and our conversation. Your wife is very engaging, I said. Does she like bowling by any chance? I'm not sure if she has ever played, he answered. Did you know that the first mention of bowling in writing dates back to 1366 from England's King Edward III? No, I didn't. And that there is archeological evidence unearthed in Egypt of a primitive form of bowling dating back to 3200 BC? No sir, I just assumed it originated much more recently in a place like Milwaukee or Detroit.

It's Monday morning, with the wedding in the review mirror, and Webster and Wilma's garden put back where it belongs by the domestic helpers. And still, nobody has heard a thing from Harris. I called Francis; what are we going to do now?

Let's just wait and see, he said. Winston took off from work and went with Tyler to the Community College this morning. My God, Francis; he's been missing for at least four days now. I know, I know, let me think of something. Shit, I'm late for my meeting. I'll call you when it's over. Maybe I'll hear something from Winston by then. In the meantime, you can call Mr. Wellington and see if he has any thoughts. Good idea, maybe his private investigator can dig up something.

I called the office, but Mr. Wellington was at the Courthouse and I had to leave a message with his secretary. I understand that it is urgent, Mr. Parker. I will ask him to call you as soon as possible. Don't worry, I expect to hear from him within the hour.

Don't worry. Why is it that everyone is always telling me that? How am I not supposed to worry about Harris? I had trouble concentrating on my work and on top of everything else, now I was worried about missing another deadline. Ms. Millerton was not on her platform and had not stamped my invoices yet. Mr. Sanderson was still out of town and would not be starring at Crosby or anyone else today. I was worried about another black mark in my Permanent Record.

Ms. Millerton returned to her platform with an armload of paper. Mr. Parker, may I see you for a moment. Yes, Ms. Millerton. What do you need me to do? Three of our Processors have called out sick today. The Timekeeper tells me that the influenza epidemic has made its unfortunate presence in our department and I have nearly 300 invoices here. Please endeavor to have them logged and ready for me to stamp no later than 3:00 this afternoon so that you can file them before you leave today. Yes, Ms. Millerton. I wondered which of the Processors was getting promoted to Assistant Secretary and why they couldn't help with some of the extra work. I'll get started right away, I said. Let me have those invoices.

The Timekeeper called me over on the way back to my desk. Do you know who got the promotion, Parker? No, Ms. Millerton is waiting until Mr. Sanderson returns from his trip to make the announcement. He said, that dumb shit Anthony, that's who.

Damn it, sir, you can't be serious. He doesn't do any work at all. He sits around all day making eyes at Mandy and eating donuts. He said, yes, and I see you have a big stack of work to do with a short deadline. It sucks actually; I better get started or I will never be done with them by 3:00. Give me those stupid invoices, Parker. Where is your log? I'm going to teach you something about time management that you won't find in their useless manuals. It doesn't matter that Anthony got the promotion; he is ignorant and can't learn anything beyond the level of a twelve-year-old.

I was curious about what the Timekeeper was up to, so I brought over the log after I saw that Ms. Millerton had vacated her platform and would not notice that I hadn't yet started my work. He flipped through the invoices for a moment and then told me to go back to my desk and see if any important phone messages were waiting for me. I had not heard back yet from either Francis or Mr. Wellington.

After only about fifteen minutes, the Timekeeper signaled for me to come to his desk again. All the work is done, he said. Just look busy for the next couple of hours and take them to Ms. Millerton for her to stamp later this afternoon. She will be impressed that you finished all of the work on time. She is actually expecting to have to put something in your Permanent Record again.

He explained how he did three hours of work in just fifteen minutes. They think time management means not wasting time.

Okay, fine then. Don't waste your time on this shit. What do you mean, sir? He said, you just need to dazzle them a little bit. Huh? Give them what they want; make it look complicated when it isn't. Show them a little razzle-dazzle.

Let me ask you something; how often do you find a discrepancy in these invoices? Almost never, I said. And if you find something wrong, does that change anything? No, we just make a notation in the log. He said then, so if you spend five hours or five minutes doing this stuff, does it really matter to anyone? Only to Ms. Millerton and Mr. Sanderson. Exactly, Parker. They don't want problems and they hate discrepancies, so give them what they want.

What do they want, sir? They want convenience, we all do. Just pretend you are reviewing the invoices and sign and date the log. Every now and then, make up an error or discrepancy for Ms. Millerton to keep her happy. Just give them to her well in advance of your deadline so she can't complain too loudly if no one opens the cabinets for you. Make believe you are working; she won't know the difference.

But the filing takes up a lot of time too, sir. He said, just stick them in folders wherever they fit. No one is going to go looking for them again. On the off chance they do need to locate one later and can't find it, just blame it on that useless sack of shit Anthony. He's too stupid to even know it wasn't him who screwed up.

I'm still a bit dubious that the Government's idea of effective time management means make believe you are working. Are you sure about this, sir?

Think about it, Parker. It makes sense in a perverse sort of way. We live in a world of make-believe. Anthony doesn't do a microgram of work, but we make believe he does and then promote him to Assistant Secretary. Crosby is promoted to Senior Processor in just thirty days because Mr. Sanderson likes to make believe that he will get to screw around with him one day. Carleton's boss bribes the

Investigator so he will make believe that no crime was committed. I told you before, the work we do here is meaningless. Just dazzle them some and they won't know what hit them.

I went back to my desk with a somewhat renewed sense of confidence and self-importance. Maybe now I might have more control over what goes on at work, just like the Timekeeper. I'm going to review my invoices and receipts at my own pace and log them in at my convenience. I'm not going to stress out anymore over paperwork that is meaningless anyway. I'll ignore Anthony if he asks me to do anything and pretend I didn't hear him. I'll politely disagree with Ms. Millerton if I feel like it and not cave in to all of her unreasonable demands. I'm going to show them some razzle-dazzle from now on.

My fantasy is interrupted suddenly. Mr. Parker, may I see you for a moment, please? I strode right up to her platform, beaming with my newly found self-assurance. Yes, what do you need now? I need for you to process these additional 100 invoices by 3:00 this afternoon.

Excuse me, Ms. Millerton, but may I ask why you don't assign any of this extra work to Anthony? You may ask of course, but it is none of your business. My job is to assess our department's needs and to delegate the work accordingly. Your job is to do what you are told. Does that answer your question? Yes, it does, I said, but I have another one if you don't mind. While assessing our needs from your platform here, did you happen to notice that Anthony does not even make believe that he is working, but instead has been flirting with Mandy and eating donuts since he arrived?

She looked stunned and taken completely by surprise. I have a question for you now, she said. Do you understand that as a result of your insolence and what might be construed as insubordination, I have no choice now but to record this incident in your Permanent Record? I understand, Ms. Millerton. Let me have the additional invoices and I'll see that all of them are reviewed and logged in by 3:00 this afternoon.

That's better, she said. Now return to your workstation with due haste and begin what will be the arduous task of a thorough review of such a large volume of work, with the added pressure of of your deadline looming. Do I make myself clear? Yes, completely clear, Ms. Millerton.

I returned to my desk and saw that there was a message from Mr. Wellington. I leaned back in my chair and relaxed a little bit, knowing that I could easily pretend to be busy and do the work at my own pace, or not at all even. Added pressure? The only added pressure I could see was the pressure exerted by all the undigested donuts in Anthony's fat belly. I dialed Mr. Wellington's number and his secretary transferred me right away this time. I felt in control of what was happening for once in my life. Don't worry, Parker. My investigator is on it now and I'll let you know as soon as we find out anything.

Sir, with everything going on with Harris, maybe we should drop the case against Thomas. They have so much else to worry about. I will do whatever you feel is best, Parker. I am looking out for your best interests. I do need to advise you that if you decide to voluntarily dismiss your Civil Complaint, his attorney will seek an Order of Insufficient Prosecution.

What does that mean, sir? It means that you won't be able to file a claim against Thomas in the future and the matter will be closed forever. Forever, sir? Forever, Parker, and that is a rather long time.

Time is what I am beginning to understand better now. Ms. Millerton asked Crosby to oversee my filing because she was busy attending meetings in Mr. Sanderson's absence. I spent hardly any time filing and just put things roughly in alphabetical order, or wherever they fit easiest. I was done in less than half an hour.

Gee, Parker, you're getting pretty fast at this. I explained it to him. The Timekeeper has been working with me on improving my time management skills. He started giggling; what the hell are you talking about? Do you really think I'm dumb enough to believe that reading a treatise on Special Relativity helps you file invoices any faster? Well, Crosby, the Timekeeper says that understanding time and our place in the universe helps with nearly all aspects of our lives. He laughed some more. You're full of shit, Parker.

We finished all the extra work well before 4:00 when I stopped by the Timekeeper's desk before heading to the train station. Finished with all those invoices so soon? Yes, sir; you've really helped me manage my time better. He asked, does Mr. Wellington advise you to drop the claim against your miserable neighbor? He says he will do what is in my best interests. He said, maybe you should head home quickly and see if his investigator has found out anything. I said, yes, I suppose so.

Do you have any idea where Harris might have gone to, sir? Ah, well unfortunately I do not. I wish I could be of some help to you, Parker, but I think you will have to reason this out by yourself. Yes, sir; I guess I was hoping you had a convenient suggestion. Yes, convenience, or course. We all want that. I can offer just this to you, Parker. Use what you already know and what you have learned about people's perceptions and their sense of time and space. Focus on the problem directly and do not allow distractions. But how, sir?

Centuries ago, Newton discovered fundamental laws of physics and motion that are indispensable to scientists even today. But much of his work seemed shrouded in riddle by his contemporaries, and many of the era's scholars were unable to decipher his writings. But we do know that he used his knowledge of what Kepler and Copernicus had discovered before him. Make careful observations to gain insight and use what you have already learned to guide you. Can you remember to do that? I'll try my best, sir. Good luck then; sign out here if you would. Good night, sir.

On the train ride home, I thought about the Timekeeper's advice. What knowledge have I already gained that will help me find Harris? I have no clue where he went. What the hell, Newton was a genius. He knew where to look for answers, but I needed someone to explain the obvious. Like how easy it is to shortcut Ms. Millerton and avoid stressing out over something meaningless.

As I walked from The Miracle Mile station, my brain felt flooded with mostly scattered thoughts. If only I could think of some way to find Brady, I bet he can help us. But we don't even have an address for him. What am I supposed to do, ride the cruiser all through Province South asking punk kids if they know where he lives? I can just imagine how that scene would play. *Yo, dude, what's he look like? Hey, man, you know where I can score some weed?*

As I walked down the footpath toward the cottage, I saw Thomas and his wife out front. She said, Parker, no one knows where he went. We called the Constable's Office and reported him missing, but so far they haven't come up with any leads. We need your help.

Thomas is asking for my help, how crazy is that? But Ms. Thomas is tearful, so I don't say what I am thinking, which isn't a bit flattering and won't help anyway.

Instead, the three of us sat on their porch, while I searched my brain for that elusive clue. Thomas kept grumbling about Harris. Wait till I get that kid home; he's going to be grounded for the rest of the decade. It's so strange sitting there listening to him, instead of telling him to fuck off. What was it again that the Timekeeper told me about cognitive dissonance and time distortion? I wish I could understand more of what he tried to teach me.

He left this note, Parker. We don't know what to make of it. It was nearly three pages long. I read it twice, trying to figure out exactly what it meant and if there might be any clues buried somewhere in it. For the first time, I realized just how serious this was.

Like Newton, Harris had written something masked with riddle and ambiguity. Vague references about feelings of hopelessness, and a fuzzy mention of a better life somewhere. A cry for help at least. A veiled suicide threat? I closed my eyes and concentrated as hard as I could, but nothing came to me. When I opened them again, Ms. Thomas' were overflowing with tears. Help us, Parker, please.

Think, Thomas, I said. He must have said something or left some sort of clue. He had the usual stupid look on his face. Well, there were some emails on his laptop to that queer guy Brady. But they didn't help much.

His laptop, of course. Why didn't I think of that before now? I can be so damn slow sometimes. I don't know how the Timekeeper stays so patient with me. Where is his laptop? Please don't tell me he took it with him. No, it's in his bedroom.

My friend Carleton can do anything with a computer, I tell them. I dialed his number and Carleton said he'd get in the car and come right over. How ironic is this? Imagine him agreeing to help the very person who caused so much distress. What did the Timekeeper say about forgiveness and temporal distance? Shit, I can't remember how he explained it.

The four of us are together in Harris' bedroom now. First, I need to get into his computer; it's password-protected. That took all of about five minutes for Carleton to figure out. People use such obvious passwords, he said. Oh, good, it looks like they used the IMAP protocol with this email account. I should be able to trace some of them. He was scanning the hard drive looking for whatever secrets were buried there, mumbling something unintelligible about transmission control protocols and POP accounts. Okay, I found some IP addresses, I might be able to track his approximate location. Wow, I thought; I bet Kepler and Copernicus would be impressed.

This could take some time, do you mind if we take his laptop back to Parker's house? I want to connect it to Parker's iMac and copy all the files. Thomas gave me a dirty look, but Ms. Thomas spoke up. We agreed to let Parker help us, remember? He's not taking the computer out of this house; figure it out from here.

There were a lot of riddles for me to solve, but this asshole was one I never would. Thomas was more agitated now, glaring at me. Hurry up and get the hell out of here, he said. I shouldn't have even let you in here. Carleton looked at me, shaking his head. I wanted badly to be far away from Thomas but resisted the urge to just get up and leave.

Being in his house gave me the creeps, but something was calming about Harris' room. There was a big plush comforter on the bed I was sitting on that reminded me of being back home with my parents. There were posters hung on the wall of some of the Falcons players, and one of Chris Martin and his band Coldplay from when they performed at the Coliseum years earlier.

Give me a few more minutes, Carleton said. I might be able to do it from here. He sent off some emails to his own address, then stuck one of those little USB flash drives into the side of the laptop and waited for the files to copy. He turned to me then, his face a shade of red from anger that was foreign to me. It took a lot to piss off Carleton.

Let's get out of here, he said. We'll find Harris without any help from him. Thomas said, both of you queers get the hell away from me. I was so relieved when we were back in the cottage and away from any further confrontation with my crackpot neighbor. That guy is poisonous, Carleton said. Don't I know, I said.

In my room, things were calmer. He was working at my desk now, staring at what seemed like endless lines of disconnected gibberish. I told him about the ominous note that Harris had left for his parents to read. I'll read it later, he said. Right now I need to think.

While he was thinking, I called Francis. Have you heard back from Winston? Yeah, they couldn't find him on campus and he didn't show up for his classes. He asked, where are you now? At home with Carleton; he's hacked into Harris' computer and we might be able to track his emails. Really? How'd you manage to get his computer? I said, believe it or not, Thomas let Carleton into their house.

After I hung up, Carleton said, this is strange, it looks like he's been sending emails almost simultaneously from City Centre and The Miracle Mile. I looked at the screen and the lines of data he had mysteriously extracted. It wouldn't have made less sense to me than if it was written in Swahili. Look, this might have been sent a few hours ago from someplace near the Low Club. Don't they have a coffee shop out front with free Wi-Fi? Maybe that's where he is. Come on, I said, let's get over there. Wait, here is another email sent from The Miracle Mile, near one of the South Gate entrances, it looks like.

That's a bad area, I said. Thomas told me punk kids from Province South like to hang out there on the weekends. I wonder what he would be doing there. I don't know, Carleton. Maybe he's been at Brady's house. His family lives in Province South. This wasn't much to go on, but at least it gave us somewhere to start looking.

While Carleton continued working, I called Francis again. We decided that he and Winston would search around the gay neighborhood in City Centre. I said, check around all of the clubs; he might be there today with Brady. We'll head over to The Miracle Mile and see if we can find him there. Carleton was closing his laptop, and said, we need to bring this along. We can take my car and park near the South Gate main entrance. Maybe one of the guards there has seen him.

My mobile rang then and it was Mr. Wellington calling back. We found a possible address for Brady, he said. My investigator is on his way to Province South to talk to him or his parents. I explained how we cracked into Harris' computer and were able to track some of his emails. We are about to head to The Miracle Mile now. Good, Parker; call me back if you find out anything else. I can have my investigator meet you there later on if you have any more leads.

I wish we had a better plan, or at least something more insightful from the Timekeeper to go on. I'm feeling apprehensive about what might happen now, but keep telling myself that we can't just sit home waiting for a miracle. In a few more minutes, we're stopped at the Province East Gate. I fish out the two Permits I remembered to bring along, then lie and tell the guard we are on our way to Mr. Wellington's office, figuring that's easier than trying to explain why we need to talk to the Security Officers at the South Gate.

He asked, would that be a personal or professional visit? Professional, I answered. He stamped the back of our Permits with the date and time. Remember, there is no parking allowed on any street in The Miracle Mile. Parking is permitted in designated parking lots only, and there is a hefty fine for leaving your vehicle unattended for more than five minutes.

After we made it past the gate, we turned south onto Miracle Boulevard, in the exact opposite direction from Mr. Wellington's office. We go about two kilometers, then find a near-empty garage just a few blocks from the main South Gate entrance. By the time we got out of the car and started walking, the sun had almost set and it was getting dark out.

Neither of us had been anywhere near here before. I hadn't given any thought about what it would be like this close to the edge of Province South, which was separated from us only by broken-up pavement and a rusted-looking chain link fence.

The narrow streets were choked by shadows and dimly lit with flickering street lamps. A frigid breeze bit at our skin, as it snaked its way through the alleyways. Out of nowhere, a gust of wind came up suddenly, snatching dust and loose trash from the street and whirling it past us.

When I walked over to the fence to get a closer look, I saw only dilapidated tenements and run-down mobile homes, some with ancient-looking TV antennas jutting out from their roofs. I heard a couple of dogs barking in the distance, but everything else seemed eerily quiet for this early in the evening.

You don't suppose Brady lives anywhere near here, do you? I hope not, Parker. I cringed at the thought. Every time I gazed at the neighborhood on the other side, the decrepitude of the place stared right back at me. I looked further into the dim distance and then heard Carleton let out a little shriek as a rat scurried across in front of us, just inches on the other side of the fence. Was the rat equally startled by our presence, or did the creature intuitively understand its place in the order of things and decide it was better off not venturing to cross the border into The Miracle Mile?

Let's keep moving, he said. This place gives me the creeps. I wasn't about to question that idea. For some reason, I felt more settled while walking, rather than just standing there staring into the shabby-looking subdivisions. The streets were dark now, and many of the streetlights were broken out and with shards of glass swept to the curb by traffic or the elements. There were hardly any stores or other business establishments here, and the ones we did come across were all closed. Mainly we saw shuttered storefronts and old grungy-looking warehouses. We passed by a large liquor store that was well-lit, but when we went to check it out, we discovered the windows and doors well protected with a wrought iron gate and heavy-duty padlocks.

We do not encounter a single person until we walk several more blocks and stumble on a pawn shop that appears to be open. The store is located just inside the main gate near the entrance from Province South. From outside the shop, I can see three Security Officers stationed there. All of them have pistols holstered, which

I've never seen at the East Gate. There, the Officers just wear official-looking badges, but no firearms.

We head inside the pawn shop. Behind the front counter, a young, disheveled-looking guy is smoking a cigarette. He has long blondish hair and the start of a coarse goatee. I can't help but stare at the jagged scar near his left ear. But I do manage to resist the urge to point out to him that smoking in public establishments has been illegal for years in the Western District.

He looks us both up and down for a moment before speaking. Youse guys got somethin' you wanna get rid of? How 'bout that watch you got there, dude? Carleton was wearing the sharp Movado that Crosby gave him as a wedding gift. Shit, I thought, maybe we should have left that back at the cottage. Hey dude, whatcha got there, a MacBook? I might be able to give y'all a couple a hundred for it.

No, we aren't here to sell anything, I said. We're looking for someone. We do our best to describe Harris and Brady to the guy, who scratches the stubble of his goatee and stubs out his cigarette right there on the floor.

Yeah, maybe I seen one of the dudes. Come to think of it, a young guy was in here a little while ago. Coulda been one of 'em, I guess. Wanted to know if we had free Wi-Fi; ain't that some funny shit?

When was he here? Oh, probably just an hour or so ago, I reckon. I ask, do you have any idea where he might be? Not sure, he said, but I saw him enter through that gate with another dude. Right there where you see them damn Officers. They don't do nothin' but hassle the folks that do business here. They've been trying to get this place shut down forever. You sure you don't want to pawn nothin'?

We thank the guy and head over to where the Security Officers with the guns are standing. Right away, they wanted us to produce our Residency Permits. Perhaps it may not be such a good idea for you to be hanging around here at night, one of them says. Carleton produced his Driver's Permit, and when I showed him my ID, he gave me a strange look. What's someone from Province East doing here; you looking for trouble? No sir, we're looking for our friend. We gave him our best description of Harris and said he may have come through the gate late this afternoon.

The three of them seemed bothered by our presence and gave us curious looks. You expect us to recognize every drifter who comes through here? He's not a drifter, I said. He is a student at the Community College who may be in trouble. His parents have not heard from him in days, and we are trying to help them.

You might be better served seeking help from the Constable's Office, not here. Missing persons are their specialty, not ours. Carleton piped up then, what is your specialty if you don't mind me asking? Eating donuts and wasting taxpayer's money?

One might be tempted to question Carleton's occasional lack of diplomacy, but certainly not his audacity. Most people would be intimidated by these three guys. I sure as hell am. I see that you live in City Centre, Mr. Carleton. My advice is for you to head back there and stay away from The Miracle Mile. Carleton said, we didn't ask for your advice, we asked for some help. Or does your specialty exclude helping a nineteen-year-old kid? We can stay here if we feel like it.

Let's get out of here, Carleton. These three aren't going to be of any help to us now. I'm going to call Mr. Wellington and see if he's heard anything.

Before I could even get my mobile out or start dialing, the Officer who had been seated inside the guard station booth poked his head out. Do you know Mr. Wellington personally? Yes, he's our lawyer; what's it to you? The three of them looked at each other, then one of them shrugged before speaking up again. I see, well you should have mentioned that fact earlier. Your acquaintance with Mr. Wellington might just possibly change things somewhat.

I'm intrigued now, and the puzzled look Carleton gave me confirmed that both of us were wondering what the hell just happened. What did our knowing Mr. Wellington have to do with whether they had seen Harris this afternoon? I'm just going to call him and see what happens. His secretary answered on the first ring. Yes, ma'am, I can hold for him.

Let's not be hasty, one of them says. Maybe it was Harris that came through earlier. It is quite possible based on your description. Come to think of it, I may have stamped his Province Residency Permit myself. No need to bother Mr. Wellington, maybe we can help you ourselves.

I asked, did Harris say where he was going? No, he just said something about his father and wanted to know where the nearest Constable's Office was located. He seemed rather agitated, now that I recollect it better. Then his old man showed up and he didn't seem all too happy, as I think back on it.

I told the Officers, he might still have a license to carry a concealed weapon. Did you check him for that? No, it isn't our policy to search every Province Resident who wishes to enter The Miracle Mile.

It seemed almost inconceivable that someone like me could be so hounded about bringing a bicycle in, yet someone full of rage like Thomas could just wander around with a loaded gun and no questions asked. I said, are there any bars nearby? He doesn't go very long without a drink. Only one close by, one of the Officers answered. It's called the Southern Exposure. I seem to recall that Mr. Thomas may have been heading in that direction, as a matter of fact. Just walk up the street there for about four blocks to Miracle Drive South, and turn right. You can't miss it.

By any chance, would one of you be willing to go there and talk to Thomas with us? He's a mean drunk and I don't expect a warm welcome when we do find him. No, I'm afraid not; we are under strict orders not to leave the entrance gate area. Maybe you should call the Constable's Office if you need assistance, but they get a lot of calls for problems in Province South and it may take them a while to respond.

Mr. Wellington came on the line just then. Yes, we are at the Province South Gate right now. There are three Officers here, but they have not been very helpful. No, we have not seen Thomas, but we think we know where to find him. Yes, sir; hold on. I looked at the three of them. He wants to speak to the Officer-in-Charge.

The Officer still seated in the guard booth took my mobile. He seemed to be listening intently and I didn't hear him say much, other than an occasional yes sir, or no sir. He gave me my mobile back and said, I am not allowed to leave my post here, but I will contact the Constable's Office personally and ask if they can have an Officer meet you at the Southern Exposure. Be careful though, there tend to be some unsavory characters hanging out there at night. In that case, I said, Thomas will fit right in.

Carleton said, don't worry about us. I'm sure we can handle ourselves in a redneck bar. I wish I was so sure.

When we start to walk up the street where the Officer pointed, we discover that it is in reality a dimly-lit alleyway. To our left, there is a ghetto-looking apartment complex, separated from us by a tall barbed wire fence. We spot several people walking around outside, illuminated slightly by the dim light escaping from some of the apartment windows, and from the red glow of their cigarettes as they inhale on them. I can just make out the large banner hanging near the top of one of the buildings.

Now Renting – The Pine Trails of Province South

I don't notice any pine trails, only littered walkways and overflowing trash dumpsters. Everything about this setting looked ominous to me, and I silently prayed that nobody would notice our disturbance and decide to come after us. Let's get out of here, I whispered, as we walked away as quietly as possible.

It was near total darkness now, on an overcast and gloomy night. So it was hard to see exactly where we were going. I barely avoided falling when I tripped on a piece of rusted rebar sticking out from a broken section of the curb. I stopped and noticed the bottom of my pants were torn and my leg was scraped and bleeding a little. Let's keep going, I said.

The further we went, the darker and gloomier it became. I held on to Carleton's sleeve because it was so hard to see. I wanted to use the flashlight app on my mobile, but after waiting for Mr. Wellington to take my call, I saw that the battery charge was low, and I knew better than to waste what was left of it. There wasn't enough time to charge it before leaving Province East, and Carleton had forgotten his mobile in his haste to get to my house.

I stepped on a piece of broken glass that made an unexpectedly loud crunching sound, then heard the screeching of a startled cat that ran right through our feet. That scared the piss out of me, and now we both moved together in silence, afraid of stirring up even more ghastly creatures, especially the human kind.

We passed several side streets and alleyways, but never came across Miracle Drive South, or any other road where you might expect to find a bar. Had we somehow gone the wrong way or missed the street in the darkness? I don't see how we could have. Let's go a little further, Carleton said.

After a few more minutes of walking aimlessly, we had to concede that we were lost. We might have tried retracing our steps back to the South Gate, but neither of us had any desire to walk past that fence again and whatever or whoever might still be lurking nearby.

We need to use the GPS on your mobile, Parker. To conserve the battery, he set the brightness to the lowest level possible after I handed it over, but the signal was so weak that we couldn't get a fix on exactly where we were. Let me try the laptop, maybe we'll get lucky. No, after fiddling with it for a couple of minutes, Carleton said there was no Wi-Fi signal anywhere nearby that we could tap into.

We decide to walk in a circle, figuring that there was no way to miss the bar if we kept moving toward the center of it. The light was somewhat better now, the moon having begun to rise and enabling us to at least avoid the frequent breaks in the pavement. Maybe we should spread out a little and cover more ground that way, I suggested. The street was wider here and easier to navigate.

I'll be right over here, he said, as I went to the right where the street curved. I walked just one block to the next intersection, but once again the street became very dark. There were clearly no bars to be found here, or anything else other than a couple of boarded-up dwellings that I hoped did not house any drug addicts or over-grown ghetto rats.

I walked further on, but it was so oddly quiet and nearly pitch black. So I turned back to retrace my path and catch up with Carleton. But now it looked different to me for some reason, and the wind had picked up and was making a ghostly howling noise as it moved stealthily through the openings in the buildings. I was beginning to sweat, despite the cold wind.

There is a small warehouse to my right that is littered with trash. It does not look even vaguely familiar to me. I couldn't have passed by here before, I don't think. I call out to Carleton but only hear the echoing of my own voice calling back to me. Where the hell did he go? I hadn't walked more than 100 meters at most.

I stood perfectly still now, then called out to him again in a louder voice. Just silence in return. I was suddenly overcome with a prickly wave of panic. I was alone and had no idea which way to go. If only I could find my way back to the pawn shop. Maybe the guy was still there and could help me. How would I find it by myself? I was practically blinded by the veiling darkness.

I better call Francis, I thought, but the signal was still weak and I kept losing the connection. The low battery warning came on while I tried to calm myself down and figure a way out of this mess.

As I started walking toward a spot where I was sure I had been, I saw him walking toward me in the darkness. Good, at least I'm not lost by myself. But as he approached, I saw that whoever it was had on a light-colored sweatshirt. Carleton was wearing a navy blue wind breaker. What the hell; Carleton, is that you?

Definitely not. This guy was bigger than Carleton, and now he was close enough for me to see a whole lot meaner-looking as well. He staggered some as he came closer, and then a surge of terror swept through me and I felt an unfriendly tingling sensation as the hair stood up on the back of my neck. I wanted to turn and run the other way, but I seemed to be oddly frozen in place. He was carrying what looked like a gun.

When he was no more than about thirty meters away, he swayed beneath a flickering streetlamp which illuminated his face clearly. And clearly, it was Thomas. He was teetering as he came closer, and at one point it looked like he might fall onto the cracked and uneven asphalt. I gasped as our eyes met finally, and he raised the gun slightly in my direction.

That's all it took. I turned to my left and ran as fast as I could into what looked to be an abandoned industrial area. I stumbled a couple of times in the darkness but managed to stay on my feet. I called out loud to Carleton one more time but didn't see him or anyone else. I was pretty sure that Thomas was running after me and I could hear the sound of footsteps slapping the pavement.

I stop under an overpass and crouch down to hide. My heart is pounding, and I need to catch my breath. And I need to figure out where Carleton could have possibly gone. I listen carefully but only hear the not-quite-still silence of the night and some distant chirping insects.

I start to shake uncontrollably now, horrified by the thought that Thomas might find Carleton before I can warn him. I need to calm down, and I need to think. That's what I keep telling myself. I wait in silence as my breathing becomes deeper and more regular. I need to figure out how to solve this problem.

Then something very curious happens. I start clearly remembering random things the Timekeeper had told me. But what do these startling recollections mean and are they somehow connected?

As human thinkers, we use visual-spatial metaphors all the time to solve problems and conceptualize things.

Being able to use your body in problem-solving alters the way you solve problems.

Repetitive visual approach to problem-solving is not necessarily any more effective or less intimidating than mentally trying to solve a complex problem.

How am I supposed to use any of this to help me? He tries so hard to teach me things, but I am too slow to pick up on most of it. I wish I could just squeeze my brain and force an answer to come out.

I concentrate harder and think about Harris again. It is so disheartening and frightening to think of the trouble that might have found him by now. If only the Timekeeper were here to walk me through this.

I can't just sit here hoping for a miracle. I have to think of something. What was it that he said to me this very afternoon?

Make careful observations to gain insight.

Careful observations? I can't see a damn thing. Wait, maybe he didn't mean visual observations necessarily. There must be something else; spatial observations, time perceptions. God help me; I can't remember. What were the hidden secrets he tried to explain?

Use what you have already learned to help guide you.

With my life possibly coming to a premature end, I sat down on the packed gravel street. I was very scared but determined to stay focused. I tried to consider what I had already learned. What experiences, thoughts, or mental images reminded me of this situation? Absolutely none came to mind. I thought about it for a few minutes more. When in my life had I felt this scared, this alone, and this helpless?

Only one time. The day I had to say goodbye to Duncan. He shielded me from fear and pain. Things felt so empty and lonely without him. I wish I could picture him now, but my memories of him are blurred by the passage of time.

I pulled the mobile out of my back pocket. The red low battery indicator was flashing, but surprisingly there was a decent signal now. I dialed Francis' number. Where are you, Parker? Somewhere in The Miracle Mile near Province South. I'm lost, I told him. I can't find Carleton anywhere. I saw Thomas here; he might have done something to Carleton. He's here looking for us, and he has a gun.

He said, just go back home and I'll meet you there. I don't know how to get there, Francis; I'm lost. Help me, please. I heard his voice as the signal faded; Parker, Parker...can you hear me? Where?

The mobile died and along with it, maybe a little part of me did as well. Finally though, I stood up and listened for some clue as to which direction to go. Other than the spectral and unearthly sound of the wind swirling around me, the night seemed disturbingly silent. I felt nearly overwhelmed once again by such intense fear and worry.

Try not to worry so much, Parker; reason things out logically instead.

I knew what I had to do. I had to overcome my fear and find my best friend. Carleton and I would find Harris together and get the hell out of here. And I promised myself that after we did, I would get far away from The Miracle Mile and never come back.

I moved as quietly as possible through the deserted streets, looking for a familiar landmark that would lead me in the direction of the South Gate and the Security Officers stationed there. Maybe they had seen Carleton or Harris by now. Or else I'd find the Southern Exposure; it had to be somewhere nearby.

The street I was on now seemed more familiar to me, so I kept moving without turning off onto any alleyways. Maybe I was near the street where the pawn shop was. I hoped the guy would still be there having another cigarette. *Yo, dude; you back with somethin' else to hock?* I'm sure he would let me use their phone and I could call Francis or Mr. Wellington. I checked the mobile once more, but the battery had completely given up.

If only I hadn't lost Carleton. How stupid of me to wander off alone in a place like this. I surprise myself sometimes by how careless I can be.

Distracted momentarily by the trouble I was in, I almost didn't hear the faint distant sound of gravel crunching from what sounded like approaching footsteps. I hid in the dark entranceway to a boarded-up storefront and waited. Flickering shadows from the abandoned building sent shivers through me, the moonlight casting an eerie glow as it streamed through the passing clouds. The footsteps were louder now, my heart hammering and my forehead breaking out in sweat despite the cool night air. Someone was coming close down the street and would pass right by me. But it was dark in the recessed doorway, and if I stood perfectly still, they might not notice me.

I held my breath and waited. The footsteps slowed and there was a shuffling sound immediately to my left, like sneakers chaffing against the crushed stone unpaved street. I carefully peeked out around the edge of the building without making a sound. I can see him walking directly toward me, but it's hard to make out much detail in the darkness. It's not Carleton, I know that much. I don't think it's Thomas either; this guy is slimmer and his gait is steady, unwavering.

Then, he is suddenly right in front of me, like some shadowy apparition emerging from the darkness. My heart pounds in my chest, and my breath catches in my throat as my terror finally begins to loosen its awful grip. He just stops and looks straight at me, his eyes piercing through the dim light. Parker, what the hell are you doing here? Shouldn't I be the one asking you that, Harris?

XXII

A sense of enormous relief washes over me, and the tension tightly wound around my chest begins to ease. We gave each other a warm hug and then sat on a partially broken wooden bench in front of the shuttered storefront. We just looked at each other for a moment, before I said, maybe you should go first.

He began explaining everything that happened over the past few days. Brady's parents had to go to the Eastern District for his aunt's funeral, and they left Brady to stay with his younger brother. I told Tyler I was going back home, but then I decided to stay at Brady's house instead. It was a good chance for us to spend some time together. You know, Thomas was all over me and kept threatening what he would do if he found out I was with Brady again. I know he was reading my emails too, and I couldn't face him. So I skipped some classes and stayed the last few nights in Province South.

I said, why didn't you tell Tyler or someone else where you would be? I don't have the mobile anymore and couldn't text or call him. I sent him a couple of emails, but they all came back as undeliverable. Yeah, well, I guess that explains the emails Carleton traced to Province North.

I didn't know they were looking for me, or that Thomas had seen you guys at the Casino. I figured they would just assume I was still staying at Tyler's house. If Thomas hadn't run into you and Tyler that night at the Casino, none of this would have happened. Anyway, Thomas somehow got Brady's address and he showed up about an hour ago with a gun, if you can believe it. I was a kid when he got fired from that job in Special Investigations. I didn't even know he still had that damn thing. He was threatening Brady and we were so scared, all of us just got the hell out of there.

I said, where is Brady now? He ran back home to stay with his brother there. He's only eleven years old and was scared out of his mind when he saw the gun. I found the Constable's Office here in The Miracle Mile and they said they would send an Officer to stay with them at their house until they find Thomas. I wanted to go back home and be with my mother, but I was worried Thomas might show up there. I don't even know if he has been arrested yet.

Not yet, I'm afraid. We knew he was here somewhere and then I saw him about twenty minutes ago. He started chasing me, but I got away. We, Parker? Yes, Carleton came here with me, but then I lost him. Oh, shit, he said. Why did you have to come looking for me? I don't know what Thomas will do if he finds you. Yeah, and I think he's drunk now too. The Officers saw him walking toward the bar here, the Southern Exposure.

He was very upset and shaking his head. We sat closer on the bench and I put my arm around him. He wore just a lightweight shirt and was shivering noticeably. So, I took my jacket off and draped it over his shoulders. I immediately felt the sting of a cold wind biting through my own clothes. The temperature must have dropped at least fifteen degrees in the past hour.

He said, I still don't understand why you came looking for me. I said, no one had any clue where you were or why you hadn't tried to contact one of us. Your mother was worried sick. Thomas even handed over your laptop to Carleton so he could track your emails. And they let me read the note you left for them.

He asked then, what about the note? Well, it sounded to me like a suicide threat. What? I'd never do anything like that. What are you talking about, Parker? I said, that part you wrote about being in a better place someday got me thinking. It kind of scared us. That? I meant when Brady and I can be together finally and be happy like you and Francis.

Ah, yes; Francis and me. Right then for some weird reason I think of what Ms. Millerton said about being happy, and that unlike me, she had never experienced it. It strikes me as remarkable that people just assume I am happy. How do they know that?

I once asked the Timekeeper how he defined happiness. He said, happiness is primarily the absence of pain or discomfort. It is dominated by time as is nearly everything. As such, happiness in its purest form is a balance between the positives of affective and cognitive empathy and the negatives of pain or discomfort over an extended period of time.

Despite everything that Francis and I have been through, I know he must be sick from pain and discomfort by now. The truth is, we need to start working together to find that balance the Timekeeper was talking about. And I need to start right now and find a way to get a hold of him.

Come on Harris, let's get out of here. We stood up and started walking, but just as we stepped from the building's shadows and into the street, I felt something heavy strike the back of my neck and head. And a split second later, I heard Harris cry out before the dimly lit world of The Miracle Mile went completely black.

· · · ·

It seems I am constantly fading in and out of consciousness, with strange patterns of light alternating from stark white to a deep black before my eyes. My vision blurred; I couldn't make out anything or feel my body. Voices echo through my brain, distant and distorted, as if spoken from far away. Some words make it through the haze, but their meanings slip away from me. Unfamiliar sounds blend together, heightening my disorientation. I feel suspended in some in-between space, both awake and asleep, trapped in a state where strange dreams merge with reality.

Where am I? No idea. I don't think it can be on the gravel street near Province South. Isn't that where Brady lives? No, that's not right; I'm confused. I'm someplace warm now. I can't still be in

The Miracle Mile I don't think. It was cold and I was shivering; not anymore. I don't feel cold. I don't feel anything.

Parker, wake up. Another bizarre dream? It's me, it's Hunter. I try to open my eyes, but I can't see anyone. Is someone here with me? I've never been far from you, I hear him say. I know that voice; it's Duncan. Even after so many years of being apart, I recognize that soothing voice. Duncan, where are you? No, it's Hunter. Don't you remember me? From the Western Shore. But how did you get here? I asked him. It doesn't matter right now, it will all make sense later on.

I remember him alright. I remember the warmth of his body and his perfect smile. I remember when he told me I was what God could do on one of his better days. I remember when I kissed him goodbye and my world crumbled.

It's him, I'm sure. I've missed you so much, Duncan. You were always there to protect me, and here you are again. I was so afraid something bad happened to you. Why did you have to leave me, Duncan? I'm Hunter, don't you remember? From the Sandcastle Shore Inn. I kept thinking, what is he talking about? Did he change his name for some reason? How did he find me, and where the hell am I?

. . . .

I open my eyes and everything is brightly it. Someone is turning me on my side and humming a soft tune. I feel the warm water and the towel being used to dry my back. What is this?

Mr. Parker, you're awake! Yes, I said. I still have no idea what's going on, but I sense from the sounds around me that there are others in the room. I hear another voice and the whooshing sounds of somebody scurrying around.

I try to focus on my surroundings, but everything is a blur. I lift my hands to my face and rub my eyes. They feel dry and crusty. When I do manage to unstick them, I see a man and a woman on either side of the bed I am in. Two nurses, maybe? Yeah, that makes sense now. I'm lying in a bed, and the antiseptic white walls and the medicinal smells give off a distinctive sterile metallic tang. I'm in a hospital room.

My friend, Duncan, where did he go? I'm sorry, Mr. Parker, but no one has been here to visit you today. Visiting hours don't start for another couple of hours. Stay still, please. The doctor is on his way now to check you out. You may be a little confused for a while.

But he was right here next to me, just a minute ago. The male nurse spoke up then. There was nobody here, he said. It was probably just a bad dream. No, it wasn't a dream; he was real. Stay calm, he said. Try to relax. You've been asleep for a while. Really, for how long? Quite a while.

Part VI – The Western Shore Revisited

To love someone is to see a miracle invisible to others.
  -François Charles Mauriac

XXIII

Thomas was initially charged with felonious assault with a deadly weapon, among other things. A conviction on that count alone would have landed him in prison for at least five years. Was I surprised when he was released after serving just five months? Not really.

The matter was assigned to the same idiot closet case of a judge who handled Crosby's case. At the end of the day, Thomas' lawyer was able to get a sweet enough plea deal. By pleading guilty to a single charge of assault and battery, the agreed-upon sentence was just twelve months. Time off for good behavior reduced it to less than half that amount. Shit, I was at home recuperating for almost that long.

You might be wondering how that could be. The Magistrate's reasoning was simplistic. Or moronic, if you asked me. But nobody asked. It went something like this. Thomas never pulled the trigger, and it turns out, the gun was not even loaded. Not a deadly weapon without bullets.

Came pretty damn close though. I sustained a skull fracture with moderate hemorrhaging inside my brain. They inserted a small tube to reduce the swelling, and just like that, awake and with no loss of memory, and hopefully no permanent consequences, on the seventh day. I rested at home until the seventh week.

Francis moved into the cottage again temporarily and spent every evening and weekend there with me until I was able to go back to work. I'm not going to do any overtime until you are well, he decided. The recovery was slow and painful, but with him there to help me, it was much easier.

We ate at home most days since I usually wasn't well enough to make it to a restaurant. Imagine this; Francis decided that he would do some of the cooking. This sounded like a very bad idea at first, but I helped him in the kitchen when I felt up to it. He said he found cooking to be therapeutic and he created an account on epicuirious.com and a few other foodie websites. We'd pluck recipes off his laptop and work together. On some days it was hard for me to stand for very long, so I'd shout out instructions from the living room sofa. My God, is he ever dangerous in the kitchen. Half a cup of that, Francis, not half a gallon!

There was one little silver lining to all of this. Thomas was given three years probation that included community service, as well as an injunction that under no circumstances would he be allowed to come within 100 meters of me. His house was closer than that, but we hardly ever saw him. He never showed any remorse or apologized for everything he had done, but he never bothered me again either. That's fair enough, I guess.

Mr. Wellington did not agree. He amended the civil complaint against Thomas to include negligent injury and intentional infliction of emotional distress. Serious stuff that could have bankrupted the family. But the case against Thomas was ultimately dismissed by the Court. There was no witness testimony or other evidence sufficient to prove that he was the one who damaged the cottage. As for the injury allegations, the judge felt that those were adequately addressed in the criminal matter and that no further punishment was warranted.

Things did not go quite so well for the Office of Casualty and Property Adjustments. Not only did the Court find that they were liable for the costs to repair the cottage, but I was also awarded an additional £20,000 in damages for their bad faith and breach of fiduciary responsibility. I admit I don't know what the hell that means, but who cares? I've added that to the rest of the money I've saved working for the Government over the years.

A decent down payment on that villa at the Western Shore for when we retire, don't you think, Francis? He gave me a big smile.

You're such a dreamer, you know that, Parker? Sure, I know that, but it's a nice dream. Yes, it sure is, he said.

• • • •

My recuperating was a slow and difficult process. Some days I hardly got out of bed. I slept much of the day and was lethargic for the rest of it. There was some partial paralysis in my right leg, and a physical therapist made house calls three times each week. Over time, it improved to where I hardly notice it anymore. My vision was blurred on and off for much of the first few weeks. It's normal, the neurologist said. It will clear up; don't worry. Me worry; really?

Francis was patient with me, even when I complained incessantly. I said, I just want to get well enough to go back to work. Take your time, Parker. Those bosses of yours can manage their scandals without your help for a little while longer.

I missed seeing Crosby, Carleton, and the Timekeeper every day though. They visited mainly on the weekends with Winston, Tyler, and Harris. Tyler said, the fútbol season will be starting next weekend. Do you think you are up to having us all come over on Saturday to watch the game on the Satellite? Oh, hell yes, I said. You won't have to do anything, and we'll bring the food and clean up after the game. You can just rest here on the sofa and we'll keep the sound off if you are sleeping. I'll make an apple cake, Crosby said.

Mostly, I managed by myself when Francis went into the office in City Centre. Ms. Thomas stopped by at least once a week with a pot of beef stew or something else she cooked for us. I watched old reruns of *Laverne and Shirley* and *I Love Lucy* on the Satellite and read books the Timekeeper sent over when I felt well enough.

Francis seemed more changed than I was by my brush with death. In some ways, he may have suffered as much as I did. Winston and Carleton revealed a lot to me when they came to visit. Winston said, he stayed nearly the entire week at your bedside while you were unconscious. Half the time, he spent the whole night sleeping on a reclining chair. He sat patiently on the edge of your bed every day, not saying anything, just waiting for you to open your eyes. Only when the doctor came in, did he perk up. Has there been any change? He would ask.

Carleton told me, he was so scared he might lose you. He is not the same anymore, I don't think.

He's not the same, changed by death's close call that almost destroyed us. He looks at me and smiles, and his touch lingers longer, filled with a tenderness I'd almost forgotten. We still have our issues, believe me, but we try to confront them head-on instead of pretending they don't exist. We talk about the bumpy road ahead and how we will navigate it together. I'm moved by the transformation I've witnessed, and the promises he whispers late at night as I drift off to sleep. Promises of forever, a future I once thought might never be.

We can't possibly escape the bitter irony of all of this. One drunken split-second decision from someone as useless as Thomas to flip the switch for Francis, revealing what had always been right there in front of him. Winston told me, you scared the shit out of him, Parker. You being asleep like that woke him up, I guess.

I gave up on the couples therapy idea. We don't need to go anymore, Francis said. We're much better together now. You and I can deal with things ourselves.

He's right, we are better. But I had my own issues to resolve, and there was plenty of crap to deal with and dump on Dr. Hendrickson, who treated me for more than a year. Francis and I avoided the subject of what went on during our sessions. He would only ask, is he helping you feel better about yourself? I think so, I answered. Okay then, good, he said.

When I first got home from the hospital, he filled in some of the blanks about what happened on that chilly night in The Miracle

Mile. Thomas saw Harris and me walking together after we got up from that old bench. Enraged, he hit me from behind with the butt end of the pistol. Harris managed to run into the darkness to get help and found his way to the Southern Exposure, where the Officer from the Constable's Office was waiting. Carleton had found his way back to the South Gate where he waited with Mr. Wellington's investigator in case we showed up there.

Francis said, I just have one question. Who is Hunter? You were mumbling something about a guy named Hunter while you were unconscious. I said, he's someone I met up with at the Western Shore the last time I was there. I've known him since secondary school; we used to date way back when. I've told you about him before. His name is Duncan actually. He was my first boyfriend. Remember?

Well, he called me to check on you that night. What do you mean, Francis? Right after your signal went dead and I couldn't reach you, the mobile rang and it was some guy named Hunter asking for you.

I asked, how would he get your number? I have no idea, but he said he hadn't been able to reach you and wondered if your mobile had been disconnected. He seemed to know somehow that you were in trouble. I told him the last thing I heard you say was that you were near Province South somewhere. He said his name was Hunter, though.

He seemed so concerned about you. I don't have anything to worry about, do I? I'd hate to lose you to some old boyfriend from high school. Since when do you worry about anything? I asked him. I'm the worrier, remember? Yes, you are, and a dreamer too.

With Harris back at home and dating Brady out in the open now, and Thomas out of the picture hopefully for good, there is much less for me to worry about. As for my dreams, well those will last for an eternity, I hope.

XXIV

I am startled from a deep sleep suddenly by a loud sound outside the villa. I sit up, looking around and rubbing the sleep from my eyes. I get out of bed and step out the front door and onto the porch. Two adult mockingbirds are up early and singing their piercingly loud song in the red pine we planted in our front yard the year before. It's nearly 7:00 a.m., and I would have been awake before much longer, even if the neighborhood birds hadn't so rudely disrupted my sleep. I can't complain though, I sleep much better here than when I lived in that noisy little flat in City Centre.

I stand on the porch for a couple of minutes, enjoying the crisp morning air. Looks like another beautiful day at the beach, I say out loud and to no one in particular. Hearing a familiar voice, our poodle Max came running from his favorite spot on the back deck to join me. He let me cuddle with him for a minute or two before I brought his water bowl and some Alpo and set them out on the porch.

Francis was already up and gone to the grocery in town. We have a big day planned and he wanted to get an early start. I heard the beeping sound from my Mr. Coffee and smelled the aroma of the South American brew that filled the villa. I flipped the switch and then came back out with my souvenir Falcons Championship mug filled to the brim with steaming coffee and milk.

I sat down and relaxed, then waited for Francis to get back home. My mind drifted back over the years, thinking how many seasons had passed since we watched that fateful game on the Satellite at the cottage, the day Crosby broke that weird fuck Thomas' nose.

Max heard Francis' car from at least two blocks away and charged off the porch to be ready to greet him when he got out of the car. He was still getting the grocery bags from the trunk when Max jumped up excitedly, not willing to wait even a moment longer to be petted.

Max is a good dog, and generally friendly to everyone. But no one dared to get between him and Francis. Yeah, maybe it's true that a dog is a man's best friend, but the reverse is true as far as Max is concerned. He hardly tolerates being separated from Francis for more than a few hours.

Francis joined me on the porch, while Max arranged himself at his feet, looking up with his sad face begging for attention. I set the bags on the kitchen counter, then brought out another mug of coffee for him. We drank them together while talking about our plans for the day.

Today is Francis' 60th birthday, so Winston and Carleton thought it would be nice for us to celebrate the event at the Western Shore. Francis and I were both lucky enough to have retired relatively early, thanks in large part to his lucrative pension. He had done well at work, and his most recent promotion to Executive Director carried along with its impressive title, some equally impressive retirement benefits.

I quit my job at the Office of Accounting Payables and Receivables two years ago, but even as a Senior Processor, I managed to save enough to contribute substantially to the cost of the villa, which we decided to pay cash for. We fell in love with this small, but nearly perfect two-bedroom house less than two kilometers from the gay beach. We've been happy here, even when I consider the Timekeeper's narrow definition of the word.

To celebrate Francis's big day, we decided to have a cookout on the back deck this evening. Our friends will be coming to the Western Shore this afternoon, less than three hours by car from City Centre.

We unloaded the grocery bags in the kitchen. Francis picked up chicken and ribs that he wanted to cook on the built-in grill that came with the house. We laughed when we first saw that grill. It looked very much like the one Wilma and Webster had in their yard, except it was about one-fifth the size.

After retiring, he decided to take some cooking classes at the local Community College. I cracked up when he came up with that idea, I mean there were so many other adult education courses they offered that made more sense. I wondered how the classroom instructors were being tormented by the idea of Francis doing anything with food besides eating it. But he picked up from where the two of us left off making dinners together in the cottage, and though I hate to admit it, he's not at all a bad cook now.

So I didn't offer much resistance when Francis said he would take charge of the outdoor grilling. I preferred to work in the kitchen anyway, where I didn't need to be concerned about blowing the grill up or lighting the villa on fire. I'll be responsible for the roasted herbed eggplant, the Nicoise salad, and the cherries jubilee. He asked, aren't you going to try the cherries flambé again? Nah, I nearly burned the kitchen down the last time. He laughed, put his arm around me, and said, this will be fun tonight. Happy birthday, Francis.

Max barked excitedly when he heard the noise outside. Anyone home?

Crosby and Carleton offered to show up early and help us get set up for the cookout. They are going to stay in our second bedroom, which doubles as a guest room and office for Francis.

In addition to cooking, Francis does quite a bit of writing in his free time now. He did a lot of writing during his long career, but it was always technical stuff and not very creative. Now, he is working out the ending for his first novel. He let me read an early draft and I was impressed. I never knew you had this in you, I said.

The story has an uncanny surreal feel to it, like a Dali painting. It centers around a young guy who wakes up in an unfamiliar place one day, only to discover in his disoriented state that he is one of only a small minority of straight people living there. Nearly everyone is gay and heterosexual intercourse is illegal. Babies are conceived only through artificial means and sexual activity between members of the opposite sex is punishable by public flogging and incarceration. Heterosexual rights groups have formed, but are maligned in the mainstream press. Our lead character is forced to hide his sexual orientation and is constantly harassed by a nasty gay neighbor, who has him all figured out. I can't wait to see how this is going to end.

Come in, come in! We had not seen our friends for a few months and I missed them so much. There are very few bad things about living at the Western Shore, but this one is at the top of my list. Max must have missed them as well, and he jumped up and licked them both eagerly when they kneeled down to pet him. Crosby handed me the apple cake he made and two bottles of pinot noir imported from Napa Valley, while Francis took their bags.

I don't know how he does these things, but Carleton managed somehow to reserve five rooms at the Sandcastle Shore Inn for the next two nights, even though the summer season had already started. His old fling still owned the guesthouse, though he was semi-retired by this time, and hired workers now ran the place. The Sandcastle had become an icon at the beach, boasting more than twenty guest rooms and a full-time cook.

Crosby is still working in our office and is now an Assistant Secretary, the position that forever eluded me. I was happy for him when the well-deserved promotion was announced. But Mr. Sanderson collapsed one day in the office, and later that afternoon we learned had died of a heart attack on his way to the hospital. Ms. Millerton could not be consoled and cried uncontrollably while Crosby and I tried to comfort her until Carleton said he would take her home to Province North in his car.

My best friend was such a whiz when it came to computers. With Mr. Sanderson no longer around to run interference for his old college friend, the Investigator was eventually able to make embezzlement charges stick against Carleton's boss. Voilà, meet the new Superintendent in the Office of Sanitation and Debris Removal.

Winston will be coming with his partner Hayward, whom he met at one of the Phoenician Temple's annual Halloween parties years ago. He and Tyler finally decided to call it quits when Tyler was accepted to medical school at the University of Chicago. Their love had endured way beyond anyone's expectations, plenty strong enough to overcome the generational gap. But the prospect of maintaining a relationship with an ocean wedged between them was understandably insurmountable.

We've kept in touch over the years, despite the fact that Tyler eventually married his partner Dawson. The two of them wound up settling in a small beach community in Lewes, Delaware. Tyler said he wanted to live there because it reminded him so much of the Western Shore, which he missed terribly while living in the frigid mid-western part of the continent. He complained to us that there was not much real fútbol there, but he had come to appreciate the North American version of the game and was now a big fan of a local team called the Baltimore Ravens.

Harris and Brady were already at the beach, having decided to take the entire week for an extended holiday. They managed to work their way through some difficult times with their respective families, but made good on their promise to each other, for better or worse. We're happy, Harris told me; just like you and Francis.

After finishing his courses at the Community College, Harris continued studying at the University and eventually got his master's degree in business management. In what I considered to be an almost unimaginable irony, Thomas was stabbed to death in a bar brawl while he and Ms. Thomas were vacationing in Acapulco. At least to some extent, the grief and pain of his tragic death were softened by the £250,000 life insurance policy that he had taken out. Maybe

Thomas knew better than anyone where his broken road in life would eventually end up.

With a portion of the insurance money, Harris and Brady opened a Mexican restaurant in The Miracle Mile called La Hacienda. It's a fun place and we try to get over there whenever we visit the Province. They make a big deal of it and always wait on us personally when we do. They had a rocky beginning certainly, but they've done right by each other. I'm happy they could get away and spend time at the beach with us.

Wilma and Webster are still in Province West, but spend part of the year in the vacation home they bought on the Amalfi Coast in Southern Italy. Francis and I have been there twice to visit them, the only two times I have been out of the country.

We have to visit Rome, I told Francis. I want to see the original St. Peter's Square and attend mass there. It was quite an inspirational experience for me. The promise I made to myself to never again set foot in The Miracle Mile quickly fell through, but I refused to go back to that fake St. Peter's Basilica.

My original thought was to sell the cottage and move back to City Centre, but Francis talked me out of it. Don't sell your place, he said. It's nice spending time here. But you said there are no gay people in the Province, remember? He said, you're here, aren't you? That's all that matters.

So we balanced our lives between the city and the suburbs, finding the best of both worlds, I believe. It was less than a half-hour drive for him to come to see me in Province East, and he had a covered space in the carport when he got there. Not many people in City Centre could claim that convenience. I didn't mind the commute to work either. The trains were almost always on time, and most of them had been replaced over the last couple of decades with more modern coaches and better air conditioning.

I wasn't the only gay person in the Province, of course. Quite the opposite as things turned out. Miracle Estates East had become a bit of a small enclave for gays and lesbians who appreciated a quieter existence away from the city.

I'm glad Francis convinced me to stay. When Ms. Thomas sold their house and rented a condo to be near her brother in Province West, a retired gay couple moved into the house just across the footpath. Now it was peaceful and quiet at the end of the cul-de-sac, with nobody pounding on my door uninvited late at night, or making threats to hurt us. I'd wave to my neighbors as I walked with Max to the park nearby. Good morning, isn't it a beautiful day?

My straight neighbors didn't seem at all concerned by the fact that the neighborhood had become quite diverse over the years. Brittany and Campbell wound up qualifying for the house they wanted with the white-painted fence, and they moved in just a couple of blocks away after they got married. We stayed friends and enjoyed going to the Casino to play roulette with them.

One night while we were at the Pizza Palace, Brittany asked if I had ever had real New York-style pizza. No, I said, I've never been to New York. What's it like? She said it's exactly the same as the pizza here, only different. Francis gave her a funny look, wondering, I'm sure, how someone like Brittany managed to find herself in a place like New York with a hunk like Campbell.

They had season tickets to the Roller Derby, and Campbell offered them to us occasionally. I had no interest in going, but sometimes Francis would take them and go with Gordon.

The Timekeeper lost his wife to cancer after forty-two years spent together. I remember the day he returned to the office following her funeral. I'm so sorry about your wife, I said. Thank you, Parker. Our time together was extraordinary and unforgettable. Einstein once said that any man who can drive safely while kissing a pretty girl is simply not giving the kiss the attention it deserves. I can only hope that I gave her the attention and the time she deserved. Sign in here, Parker, if you don't mind.

If retirement had proven to have even one disadvantage, it was missing out on the privilege of sharing that little bit of time with him, twice each day. He kept after me to keep reading and learning, but I complained often that I wasn't smart enough and wasn't worthy of the time he gave to me. Nonsense, Parker; you are an excellent student and teacher both.

I never knew if he really believed that. He was probably just being nice to me. No matter what he tried to teach me, I would always be a little bit of a dim-wit. Someone as smart and perceptive as the Timekeeper could not have missed something so obvious. But he never showed any frustration by my lack of ability, or by the blank looks he must have seen on my face when he talked about subjects that bewildered me.

He would say, learning is an ongoing process, it's like aging. We each experience it in our own way, and at our own pace. Don't sell yourself short; you have great capacity for many things, especially for learning and caring for others.

We wanted him to come to the beach with the others, but he declined. He had quite a few more gray hairs these days, and moved around deliberately, sometimes with the help of a walker. But the passage of time had done little to diminish either his wisdom or his insight. I was disappointed but knew that the trip would have been strenuous for him. Crosby and Carleton offered to drive him in their car and get a room at the Sandcastle, so he could stay in the guestroom.

Thank you, Parker, but it might be best if I stay here in City Centre instead. I'll catch up on my reading this weekend if you don't mind. I've fallen way behind these past few months.

Crosby went back out to the car to bring in the gifts the Timekeeper sent along with them. There was a birthday card and a case of Imperial Stout Ale. How could he possibly have known that it was Francis' favorite beer? There wasn't a chance in hell I ever mentioned that to him. Crosby just shrugged when I asked him about it. He said, he keeps track of everything. I guess that's why he was the Timekeeper for all those years.

There was a gift for me as well. A book called *The Fabric of the Cosmos: Space, Time, and the Texture of Reality*, by Brian Greene. We all had a good laugh when I was flipping through the table of contents and noticed one of the chapters was titled *Einstein in Drag*.

The book was a thick 600 pages or so and I knew it would be an effort for me to get through. I was eager to get started on it though so I would be able to discuss it intelligently the next time we visited with the Timekeeper in City Centre. Francis came over and I showed him the inscription that was written on the inside book cover:

For my good friend Parker, whose search for knowledge and resolve for learning have been an inspiration for much of my own.

What a beautiful gift, Parker. Let's call later to thank him. He handed me one of the bottles of ale just as there was more knocking on the front door. Hey, look who it is everyone, Webster and Wilma. Just a couple of minutes later, they were followed by Gordon, Carson, and Carson's wife Melinda, who were driving behind them from Province West.

Gordon had not chosen to be gay, of course, but he was anyway. He graduated with a law degree from the University of Edinburgh and was now working as a Solicitor at Mr. Wellington's firm. I asked him, you been seeing anyone special? He blushed and said, well, I met a nice guy a few weeks ago at the Roller Derby. He's coming over to the house for a cookout next weekend; I'll introduce him to Mom and Dad.

Carson had been on his diving team while in college, and was a two-time Olympic finalist, though he never actually competed in any events. He studied culinary arts at the University and was now the Assistant Head Chef at the Continental restaurant in The Miracle Mile. He settled in Province North with Melinda, who he met at the Olympic trials in Barcelona. They had twin daughters who were away at the Preparatory School for Girls in the Eastern District.

XXV

I was so excited by the time everyone arrived and we were ready for the cookout. We'd never all been in the same place at the same time as far as I could remember. But the thirteen of us managed to squeeze in together at the outdoor table we had on our back deck.

Carson helped Francis with the ribs and gave him some tips on how to best season, and then slow-cook them on the grill. I brought out the rest of the food from the kitchen, and there was plenty of everything to go around. We kept opening bottles and filling our glasses from the half-case of Australian Shiraz that Webster and Wilma brought from Province West.

We were there for two hours or more, toasting our friendships, reminiscing about how our lives had become so nicely intertwined, and sharing stories and laughs. Everyone was drinking their share of wine, and Winston had us all cackling when he did his Sara Palin and Dolly Parton impersonations.

Then came the memories we all shared. But there were so many of them; where to begin? Everyone had funny stories to reflect back on.

Carleton had us laughing hysterically when he described the time he was working from Ms. Millerton's platform when her leg was broken. You looked so pompous up there, I said. We had so much fun in those days. We were hoping she would have to stay with those crutches for a couple of weeks more.

Parker, you were so frantic then, Carleton said. Probably because she made you mentor the new guy and you were nervous. Do you remember that?

I sure do, I said. I remember she put something in my Permanent Record after I made a crack about how funny you looked up there on her platform. Carleton laughed out loud, thinking back to our days in the office together. He said, that was when I saw Crosby for the first time. It's the best memory I'll ever have.

Francis recalled the night at the bowling alley when we met our new friends from Province West. He said, I thought for sure Crosby was going to pop another redneck in the nose.

I don't remember that, Carson said. That was a long, long time ago; you were just a kid, Francis said. But mostly I remember seeing Parker standing up there with that pink ball and tripping over his bowling shoes. You were so cute that night.

But there was something else he wanted to say. He became more serious then, his eyes showing more intensity as his gaze seemed to pierce the nighttime air with deeper contemplation. He said, I wasn't sure I deserved someone like you. When you were so determined to move to the Province, the reason I tried to talk you out of it was because I was afraid we might drift apart and I could lose you.

I glanced over at Carleton then and noticed a little nod. He remembered too.

Francis said, when you talked about living at the Western Shore, I just thought you were being naïve again. I was wrong about that too. Ah, Francis, I said; it was just a dream of mine. What a dreamer you are Parker; just don't ever quit your dreaming about us, okay?

With a subtle shift to lighten the mood, I recalled the perfect anecdote and the time I suggested Carleton should try to seduce the Investigator. Crosby said, what? You mean that loudmouth with the bad breath? How'd you come up with that one, Parker? I didn't come up with it, I admitted. It was Ms. Millerton's idea. That got everyone laughing again.

Harris suggested, tell us something none of us ever knew about you before. Or tell us something you learned over the years, Crosby said.

I said, before we go there, someone needs to fill this wine glass. We passed the bottles around one more time. Then everyone just looked at me and waited. I hesitated for a moment or two before continuing.

I've learned from each of you, I said. I've learned how important it is to understand time. I've learned to appreciate how time has shaped our friendships and brought us all here.

Someone quipped, did you learn all that from reading the books the Timekeeper gave you? Laughter rippled through the group once more. Nah, I replied, I learned it from all of you. From sharing those moments together. Those are the memories that truly matter to me.

· · · ·

The Full Moon was packed as usual the next night for happy hour. But our entire group managed to squeeze in along with everyone else. This weekend, the bar was celebrating its 35th anniversary, and it was decorated with pictures taken there over the past three and a half decades. One entire wall was covered with a couple of hundred creased and fading photographs.

I looked at them, recognizing several people in the pictures. I half expected to see one of Francis or me. We all had drinks now and we toasted to one another. A piano player and cabaret singer performed. The young guys showed off their summer tans. It was just like old times, almost. Exactly the same only different, as Brittany would say.

Luckily, I remembered to make a reservation well in advance at Marimbas, and they had a big table for us upstairs on the outdoor deck. The woman who used to own the place died long ago, but her son was now in charge of things and kept it pretty much the same as it had always been.

Hola, amigos; welcome everyone. Your table is ready here. ¿Qué pasa señor Francis?

Everything had changed, but nothing had changed. Francis ordered seafood enchiladas just like he always did. But for me, no more taco salads with the low-cal dressing. What for? It's not like any of us are going to impress anyone with skimpy swimsuits.

What would you like to order, señor Parker? Let me see, let me see…give me the Muy Grande Burrito smothered with guacamole and cheese, with a side of nacho chips. Oh, and another couple of pitchers of margaritas, please.

The restaurant is loud and crowded like it always is during the summer season. At first, I don't even notice them when they are ushered out onto the deck and seated nearby. I can't believe it; it's Mr. Wellington and Ms. Millerton. Crosby saw them now too; hey, look who's here!

I knew from talking to Gordon that they were dating now, but I had not seen either of them since I stopped working. It's so great to see you, please sit with us, there is plenty of room. We pushed some of the chairs around to make more space for them.

She's getting up there a bit in years, but Ms. Millerton looks pretty good to me. And she looks pretty happy too. She said that they both liked margaritas, so I asked our waiter to bring another pitcher and two more glasses.

She is still the Senior Secretary at the Office of Accounting Payables and Receivables, sitting each day at the desk on her elevated platform, and looking out over the rows of Processors that she supervises.

How do you like working for your new boss? I asked. Well, she said, he is a bit of a schemer and is always creating some new crisis or causing some emergency we have to deal with. Not at all like Mr. Sanderson.

I laughed so hard that some of my margarita nearly came out of my nose.

Did I say something funny, Mr. Parker? Yes, you actually did, I said. She said, you know how much we miss having you in the office.

It's not the same anymore and certainly not as much fun without you there. Am I correct when I say that, Mr. Crosby?

He wasn't about to disagree with the boss. Not the same at all, Ms. Millerton.

Mr. Wellington talked about his upcoming retirement, that is after he wrapped up a big personal injury lawsuit he was defending. He tells us about the longstanding malpractice case against a well-known physician, and the Province Healthcare Services Center.

He says, the damn thing has been around for so long, I probably should just hand it off to Gordon and quit working. The case stinks of horseshit worse than a barn at the Preakness, but the insurance company is nervous and wants to settle. He moved closer to Ms. Millerton and smiled. She said, yes, and we're thinking of moving in together eventually, once I finally decide to give my notice.

Everything had changed, but nothing had changed.

• • • •

It's late Sunday afternoon, time for our friends to head back home. I feel a fleeting twinge of sadness when we have to say goodbye, leaving me misty-eyed as we hug each other and make the usual promises to get together again soon. Promises that I know will be kept, but still, knowing this wave of despondency might stay with me once the door is closed, and Francis and I then left alone.

They each felt something similar, I'm sure. I could sense it in the look on their faces and the tone of their voices. Cognitive empathy is how the Timekeeper once explained it for me.

Let's give him a call and thank him, Francis said, after everyone had driven off. I dialed the Timekeeper's number on my mobile, but there was no answer. Later that evening while we were watching old reruns of *Leave It to Beaver*, I tried once more. Straight to voice mail again, so I just left a message.

He's probably sleeping, Parker. Or maybe he decided to go out to dinner with one of his friends from the Science Club he joined.

The episode showing on the Satellite was a surprisingly progressive one, given the post-war suburban idealism that characterized the show. It presented a somewhat shaded but nuanced view of alcoholism, as seen through the eyes of the young Theodore Cleaver. Ward and June tried to shield him from the harsh reality of an old friend with a drinking problem, but their plan backfired when the friend enlisted the help of an unsuspecting Beaver to sneak him a bottle.

I cuddled with Francis on the sofa and was sound asleep by the time the next episode came on. After such a long and hectic weekend, I was completely worn out.

I got up before dawn the next morning and ran about three kilometers on the beach while Francis slept in. Later, while we were having coffee again on the front porch, the mobile rang.

Hey Carleton, I said. What's happening? I let out a little gasp, then dropped the mobile and slumped to the floor on my knees. Francis knew what had happened just by looking at me, I'm pretty sure. That's what can occur I guess when you spend so much time with someone; the brain cells fuse in some mystifying way.

He picked up the mobile; what is it, Carleton? He knew but needed to hear the news for himself.

It was the Timekeeper. He died in his sleep during the night, and the housekeeper found him in the morning when she arrived to make him breakfast and tidy up the brownstone.

I just sat there on the floor stunned, while Francis put his arm around me and waited for the tears that now ran down my face uncontrollably to stop. After a little while, I managed to get myself together and told him that I needed some time alone. Don't worry about me, Francis; I'll call you later on. I'll be fine.

There was only one place for me to be now. The most peaceful place in the entire world that I might be able to get to. I still didn't know how to drive, so I got on the beach cruiser and headed toward the Great Western Marsh Preserve.

It's kind of a long ride, but I pedaled fast and it wouldn't take too much time. As I rode, random thoughts drifted through my mind. My God, why can't I have just one more chance to talk with him? How will my life be from now on without him as my friend and mentor? How can he really be gone?

Study and learn, Parker. The more you do, the less often you will need to ask how.

As I turned off onto the gravel road that runs into the Preserve, I kept remembering more and more things he used to teach me.

There is no true division between past and future; there is rather a single existence.

Did you know that our feelings and awareness are closely linked to our perception of time?

Remember that forgiveness is not a luxury, Parker; it is a necessity.

I rode along the edge of the Preserve until I came to the small gravel lot where Hunter and I parked his Citroen that beautiful day so long ago. I chained the cruiser to a small White Cedar tree, though there was nobody around to mess with it.

To my right is the trail we had taken that winds its way through the forest of cypress trees and scrub pines, to where it ends abruptly at the salt marsh. To the left, there is another trail that goes across the sand dunes and onto the beach. I went left and walked about one hundred meters past the salt meadow hay, winged sumac, and the other beach grasses that help protect the marsh and mudflats from flooding.

I am sitting now on the wide sandy beach, gazing out over the vast, glistening blue-green ocean in front of me. Dawn has broken over the horizon, casting a warm soft glow. It's low tide, so there are hundreds of Western Sandpipers and Black-Headed Gulls feasting on the unsuspecting baby Bluefish and tiny Sand Crabs.

The sky transitions from a deep indigo and the sun begins to warm the sand, still damp and cool from the receding tide. It is completely deserted here, so serene. Then I remember something else the Timekeeper once said to me.

> *Focus on what matters most in your life; your friends, your studying, your partner Francis.*

Yes, let me call Francis, I decide. But when I try to dial his number, I realize how weak the signal is way out here. The call drops before he can even answer. A few minutes later, I am able to send him a text message. *I'm at the beach, babe; be home soon :)*

I close my eyes and feel the rhythm of the waves pounding the coastline, the sounds of the sea at peace with itself. I am feeling much better now, tranquil even, knowing that the Timekeeper had gone peacefully in his sleep.

When I open my eyes again, I see a guy walking way down the beach, coming in my direction. As he got closer, he looked vaguely familiar. Now he is no more than fifty meters away, and I look more closely. Is that Hunter? He looks just like him.

He stopped for a moment as he passed close to me. He was watching the sea birds through what I am pretty sure were a pair of Skymaster astronomy binoculars. He smiled and said, sure is a nice morning, isn't it? Yes, I answered; it's perfect. He has beautiful brown eyes, just like Duncan.

He gives me a little wave, and then continues his walk. Before long, he is just a tiny speck way down at the far end of the beach. The mobile buzzes then with an incoming text message. *I love you, Parker. See you soon!*

I get myself up and head back down the trail before unchaining the cruiser. I just want to be back at the villa with Francis now. I need him to hold me and tell me it will be okay. I need him to remind me that the Timekeeper lived a long and full life; that it was time for him to go now.

Living at the Western Shore, there would be plenty of time to visit the beach and the Preserve. That was always my dream, and I would live it later after we got back from the funeral.

I rode as fast as I could toward town. The cruiser was heavy and had only one speed, so it was hard to pedal. The warm late-morning summer sun had risen higher by now, and my breathing was heavier as I began to sweat.

Something caught my attention near the dirt shoulder off to the side of the road, where the cattails and Salt Hay grass grow close to the border of the Preserve. I slowed down to take a better look.

Standing in the shallow creek is a Great Blue Heron, the most magnificent bird native to the Western Shore. He is very close to where I have stopped, but he doesn't fly away for some reason. I stay as quiet as possible, as the two of us stare each other down for what seems like a minute or more, each waiting to see what the other has in mind.

Eventually, he must have gotten bored with me and decided to take off. His huge wingspan lifted him slowly at first, but then he picked up speed and turned away, heading out toward the sea. I started pedaling for home again, knowing with absolute certainty that I would never see anything that beautiful or that amazing, ever, in The Miracle Mile.

About the Author

Mark Goldstein was born in Detroit, Michigan, and has lived in the Mid-Atlantic region since 1979. He had a successful career in the insurance industry spanning thirty-four years. He is currently working on his fourth novel and is enjoying retirement with his partner in Rehoboth Beach, Delaware.

www.ingramcontent.com/pod-product-compliance
Lightning Source LLC
Chambersburg PA
CBHW051502150726
47997CB00001B/79